OUTSID

Outside In

Selected Prose

ALASTAIR REID

Introduction by Andrew O'Hagan

First published in Great Britain in 2008
by Polygon, an imprint of Birlinn Ltd
West Newington House
10 Newington Road
Edinburgh eh9 1qs

9 8 7 6 5 4 3 2 1

www.birlinn.co.uk

ISBN   978 1 84697 068 9

British Library Cataloguing-in-Publication Data
A catalogue record for this book is available
on request from the British Library.

Typeset in Great Britain by Antony Gray
Printed and bound by Cromwell Press, Trowbridge, Wiltshire

This time for Ella and Ian

Contents

Introduction   9

I HOME

From the Outside In   19

The Transformations: Notes on Childhood   25

The Seventh Day   32

Hauntings   38

Letter From Edinburgh   60

A Fine Day for the Gathering   83

Digging up Scotland   96

Transition   143

II ABROAD

Notes on Being a Foreigner   147

Other People's Houses   159

Aunt Gibraltar   167

Notes from a Spanish Village   186

Remembering Robert Graves   211

Waiting for Columbus   234

Misadventure   273

Basilisk's Eggs   276

In Memoriam, Amada   308

Fictions   311

Acknowledgements   315

Introduction

Extremely good prose is seldom a mirror of contentment. It is seldom a cloak of reassurance. There are times of course when it can be these things, just as it might be anything good, prose finding it natural to bend and spring upon and accommodate meaning. But, generally speaking, it is not always natural for extremely good prose to want to make you feel better about what you already know. It is more likely to creep up on your uncertainties, making you see, perhaps, that there is more to life and more to literature than one's previous convictions about it.

The writing of Alastair Reid proves that one does not have to share a writer's certainties in order to admire their expressive force, their native elegance, and their truth. Not everyone would feel, as Reid does, that Scotland is subject to a 'disastrous emasculation', but I would defy anyone to exclude it as a possibility entered into the world by a thoughtful writer. Reid is one of the best Scottish writers because he has what he once admired Robert Louis Stevenson for calling 'a strong Scots accent of the mind'. Reid has it, as surely as James Boswell had it and as firmly as Muriel Spark, his old friend from the *New Yorker*. Perhaps because of Stevenson's thrawn and valiant roaming, I have always imagined that a strong Scots accent of the mind must be something attaching itself to what we might choose to call an international outlook. Stevenson and Reid were never more Scottish than when oceans away, yet they always brought a mental weather along with them, a certain turn in their prose and an indwelling habit of self-inquiry. In other words, wherever they travelled, they carried a quantity of good Scots soil in their shoes.

Alastair Reid's childhood, like Proust's, is a gold and azure dream of specificity, a perpetual present, 'a peculiar mix,' Reid writes, 'of earth and air, of the practical and the impossible.' He is a writer who seems always to have been possessed of the psychological specialness required for poetry and first-rate prose – 'the dimension of amazement' – and we reach into his work with the same appetite for strangely recognisable beauties that can make us fall in love with the sentences of F. Scott Fitzgerald. It is surely an appetite that over-responds to the pull of the past, of which each of us has a little bit and some of us a lot. It is 'the thrill of retrieval' we find in Nabokov, as Reid notes in one of the best essays to be found in the present collection, 'Digging Up Scotland'. And in Reid's case, too, it leads somehow to a prose of miracles, wherein a quality of attentiveness meets its couthy neighbour in a facility of grace, the reliable feature of his writing as we find it on every page and in every paragraph of this timely collection. Reid is a writer who can make us visit the world anew, who can make us see shadows of ourselves and our dreams on the shifting sands, or beneath trees we have known all our lives. With him, beauty and loss, like laughter and memory, are made to seem natural, and I believe we read him in order to see what talent can do when it comes to the commandeering of human delight.

Alastair Reid was born in the Galloway town of Whithorn in 1926. His father was a minister and his mother a doctor ('necessary angels', as Wallace Stevens might have said, 'of heaven and earth'). One imagines a childhood spent among encyclopaedias and those famous cows that stood in the fields in a smirr of rain: the Atlantic was always out there, as it was for those of us up the coast in Ayrshire, seeming always to promise some benighted passage for the imagination if not for the soul. In time, the family moved from Whithorn to the Borders town of Selkirk – from cow country to sheep country, from the wee environs of Robert Burns to the much brisker world of James Hogg, the prose genius who nailed Scottish duality in his masterpiece *The Memoirs and Confessions of a Justified Sinner*. If the grown-up Alastair Reid shows a wonderful blend of the flexible and the tough in his harmonic sentences, a tenderness of inquiry plus a rage for precision, then I believe he derives much of it from his experience of transitions. From Whithorn to Selkirk to the wide world – that would be enough for any writer. Here's Reid at his very best, invoking the deep sources of his style in the very instant of its deployment:

> Churchgoing was something I grew used to, letting my mind wander about in an uncontrolled mixture of attentions; but as I took in the bewildering anthology of human faces – I gazed as often as I dared at a man with white hair and a ginger moustache – I was listening in a subliminal way to the cadence of my father's voice, mesmerised by the sudden incandescence of a phrase, fascinated by the convoluted metrics of certain hymns, stirred by the grave measures of the liturgy, aware of language as a kind of spell, and astonished when, freed by a dismissive organ voluntary, the congregation made its way out into the unsanctified air, and all burst out talking at once, as thought to make up for the imposed silence of the church.

Reid joined the Navy late in the Second World War and when this was finished he came home to complete a degree at the University of St Andrews. As the artist grew, so did a propensity that we see in several Scottish writers of the first water – we see it in the seldom-homesick Boswell as much as the often-homesick Stevenson, in the adaptable Compton Mackenzie, in the cosmopolitan Spark: an almost metaphysical urge to leave home in order to install a sense of freedom in one's writing self. Reid speaks of the tawse and of an obligation to obedience in his native land, but that is not necessarily to disparage it. Not all writers, not all people, have the same character, and some who live by their imagination will find it natural to forge their literary identity in the smithy of otherness. In any event, Reid travelled in 1949 to the United States and felt immediately liberated. It is true that some writers live (to use Reid's words) more by fluidity than by roots, and the transfer to America allowed Reid to join the ranks of the world's wandering Scottish imaginers, filled with the freedom of the old songs. Such people are never more consonant with the hungers of home than when launching themselves from dock to dock, as the Orkney exile Edwin Muir had sought to do. In Reid's case, there would be Spain and South America and a warm succession of possible Edens. The writing in this volume shows an open heart for the open sea, but then for villages and houses at the other end, for peace, quiet, and the flavours of eternity, the vast fluidity of life as it is made and lived by other people. (One might do well to remember that David Livingstone is an ancestor of Reid's.) Yet with this author, as with so many artists, the journey tends eventually to lead back to oneself. 'Sooner or later,' writers 'discover that the islands of their existence are, in truth, the tops of their desks.'

Spain and its former worlds proved to be a magical part of Reid's literary formation.

> From my first chance landing there, I was drawn in by a certain human rhythm, a temper that, the longer I lived there, I felt to be an antidote to my frowned-on beginnings, to the earlier wringing of hands. There is a frank humanity to Spaniards that makes them accepting of, perhaps even delighted by, their own paradoxical natures . . . They had achieved human imperviousness.

Among his many vivid and arresting travels, one might judge that the journey from one language to another, from Scots English to Spanish, describes in Alastair Reid's case a remarkable embracing of difference. Not only a turn towards happiness (though that is always implied) but an expansion of selfhood and an opening up of character that came to mark his work as a journalist and a poet and a translator. Transition gave vent to his many selves, to a cascade of persons, which may be understood to be the moment of glory in the life of an interesting writer. (It was Fitzgerald who said there could never be a good biography written of a good writer. 'He is too many people,' he wrote, 'if he's any good.') The greatness of Reid's writing may come from its brilliant depiction, overall, and in many ways, of a man escaping from a single definition of who he is. Piece by piece, and line by line, it shows a writer peopling himself and finding an emphatic home in the wider world. The Spanish word 'escueto' is derived from the Latin 'Scotus', meaning 'a Scot'. In its modern form it can be said of people who travel freely, as Reid notes in one of these essays, 'unencumbered', 'without luggage'.

That is the sort of writer Reid has been, one deeply inscribed with Scottish DNA, allowing that some strings wish constantly to break off and attach themselves to the cultures of elsewhere. In time, Reid's languages formed their own double helix, encoded in the most creative way with both exile and belonging, and that is something to celebrate the way we might celebrate any new and interesting combination of life. Reid is a modernist with an ancient heart, and the growth of his writing, to be witnessed in the pages of these wonderful volumes, tells a story of unstinting commitment to the writing personality. Reid is my kind of Scottish writer, magnetised by the world and its tongues, its seasons and its arguments, as much as by the meaning of hearth and home. Such a writer will see inflections everywhere and will send himself out, as Keats once did, to disappear into things that are more than oneself. Strangely, for a good writer, that may turn out to be the only way back to the child that was father of the man.

Home and abroad are the organising principles in this book – as natural and Scottish an opposition as North and South, or islander and mainlander, or Old Town and New Town, or Catholic and Protestant – allowing us to discover Alastair Reid at his best, in transition, or just in transit. Being away is a condition of existence with some writers, as it was with Hemingway, Bruce Chatwin, Norman Lewis, and Alastair Reid. It involves not only turning absences into strong presences, but in finding the colours of life at a distance from the very obvious. Some writers, indeed, live off a sense of homesickness, and the Germans have more meaning packed into their word *heimweh*, the condition of being homesick for nowhere in particular. Yet to read the pieces collected here, you feel it might have been Reid's skill to evolve homes out of the mystery of belonging: he goes over plain and forest and distant mountain, whilst seeming in every way to be looking for himself. Sometimes, I suppose, one must be willing to become a foreigner if one is serious about finding the person one imagines. Reid's work shows him to have possessed – or been possessed by – a talent for foreignness beyond the ordinary. And it is his readers over five decades who had felt the benefit, for he has given them parts of themselves and the world they didn't know.

How elegantly he has brought us through the centres of nowhere in search of somewhere. How beautifully have his explorations in prose been at one with their punctuation. (In some respects, punctuation is the heart of his aesthetic.) Airports are colons as surely as this: they make a promise about something interesting to come after. 'A café is a stage set for an Absolute Nowhere,' writes Reid, 'a pure parenthesis in the swim of time. . .There in a café, everybody is, by temperament, a foreigner. And to be a foreigner is not, after all, a question of domicile, but of temperament.'

'Notes from a Spanish Village', extracted in this book, captures the characters and eccentricities of the place Reid went to in the 1950s, but it also catches the rhythm and the appetites surrounding a way of life. As readers, we enjoy a sense of who the author is becoming, but also one is brought to see the elemental strangeness involved in the effort to inhabit a new place and a new self. 'To settle down in a village is a conversion of a kind,' Reid writes, 'and although I am practised at it by now it still takes time because one is rooted forever in two worlds and for some people the simplification that village existence requires may be – however desirable – forever impossible.'

Simplification. In all his travels, in all his writing, that always seems for Reid an admirable goal. He has a stomach for essences and he wishes to take us to them, to simplify, in a not uncomplicated way, our feeling for places in the world and the worlds in us. 'To live in the village, even temporarily, is to translate existence into a pure particularity.' In Deyá, Mallorca, during his friendship with Robert Graves, we find the young Reid learning how to live as a writer. He wants to own his own time, as he writes in his fascinating memoir of Graves included here, but also to know somehow by heart the rigours of writing English prose. Graves set him to a little translating and I believe that Reid, already so rooted in the aesthetics of rootlessness, so animated with the complications of Scottish memory, found his writing voice in Graves's editorial shadow. 'A good translator,' he reports Graves as having told him, 'must have *nerve.*'

The harvest festival of that early planting appears in the second of these volumes edited by Marc Lambert, but let me just say, for my own part, that Alastair Reid's translations show an artist perpetually at work and perhaps definitively at home in the space between utterance and meaning, rhythm and reason. For my generation, and the one before mine, his translations of Borges and Neruda, Padillo, Montejo, Infante and others, have changed our understanding of what is meant by the personal and the political. They have changed forever what we think we mean when we speak of fiction and they constitute a brilliant and, yes, magical cartography of Reid's own literary imagination. Reid's very personal-seeming transliteration from Spain to the splendours of Latin America is perhaps the central strand in his writing life, and we see the fruits of it – fresh and juicy and ready to pluck – in the pieces he wrote from the Dominican Republic and elsewhere for the *New Yorker*. They find a very natural home here too. Reid joined the *New Yorker* under the editorship of William Shawn and we can't be sure exactly what he learned from that brilliant editor. It is plain, though, that he must have shared something of Shawn's rage for particularity and for dynamic colour; every one of the pieces he wrote for the magazine conjures a world of rampant specifics, where all observation is humorously guided by the principles of clarity and beautiful surprise. The same can be said of those review-essays, sampled in Volume Two, that first appeared in the *New York Review of Books*. They are the work of a writer who seems gloriously unattached to the pieties of place, and who is therefore ironically best placed, as they say, graciously to hymn the work of writers who seem capable of howking every historical and political piety from the ground, tossing them high and wild to make a carnival in the air.

It is with these pieces that one begins to see in Reid's Latin American excursions a magic realism all of his own: it is the mythic fantasy we find rooted in ancient Scotland, where Adamnan once wrote of St Columba conjuring snakes out of the sea not far from Reid's childhood idyll of Whithorn. In Reid's prose we find it married by choice to the perfumed imaginings of Borges and Gabriel Garcia Marquez. There is a strange, rare charm in all of Alastair Reid's writing: the best is here in the book you are holding. To my mind, it represents a flowering in several literatures, but most assertively, most pleasingly, it shows itself at the close of the day to be among the best prose writing to have emerged from Scotland over the last hundred years.

ANDREW O'HAGAN, July 2008

I
HOME

A man sets himself the task of drawing the world.

As the years pass, he fills the blank page with images of provinces and kingdoms, mountains, bays, ships, islands, fish, houses, instruments, stars, horses, and people. Just before he dies, he discovers that the patient labyrinth of lines traces the image of his own face.

Jorge Luis Borges

Whenever asked for my occupation, I have put down Writer, for writing has occupied me as long as I can remember, and has been my livelihood. As an occupation, writing has some appealing advantages – minimal equipment (pencil, notebook and available tabletop), the freedom to live anywhere, to follow one's curiosity, and, most of all, the luxury of owning one's own time. There are also disadvantages – an enforced solitude, an income over the years that resembles a fever chart, and an overall unpredictability, the state of wondering, of lying in wait.

By now, writing prose has become second nature to me, although I remain eternally grateful for having begun as a poet. Poetry breeds a precision of language, a care for sound and rhythm, qualities that are, I find, every bit as relevant to the writing of prose.

As the pieces in this volume will demonstrate, much of what I have written has to do with place, with the interactions between places and the people who live in them, seen from the outside. I have found too that other languages reflect realities different from my own, realities that become in a sense extended selves. Although I have not changed my nationality, coming back to Scotland at irregular intervals has made me see it and write about it from the outside. Being a foreigner, however, has become second nature to me. The one continuum in my life has been my desk, which I set up wherever I am, and which feels like home to me.

A. R.

From the Outside In

Some years ago, I came across a few references to the Fourth World, a geopolitical coinage that was meant to embrace all those ex-nation states, ethnic and religious minorities, and other sovereignties lost through the twists of history, small races swallowed up at some point by larger, latter-day states. The Fourth World remains, however, a linguistic abstraction: unlike the countries we group together as the Third World, who do have realities in common, those entities that make up the so-called Fourth World are unlikely to pool their grievances or make common cause, for their situations are utterly separate and unique, some of them very ancient indeed, as in the case of the Basques. The demands of such enclaves may very well occupy an international small-claims court for the next century.

In talking about nationalism, however, one fundamental point has to be made especially to those on the outside of such situations. While it is quite possible to understand from the outside the arguments, legal and historical, the entire rationale behind the surges of nationalism, it is impossible to apprehend from the outside the nature and intensity of the feelings involved. I am aware of those feelings, though in a milder form, through my growing up in Scotland, and although I have often enough explained Scotland's case to friends from elsewhere, I know how impossible it is to make them feel how it feels, for it is something close to the bone and fibre of being. Nationalism arises from situations in which a smaller country is taken over by a larger power, which imposes on it a new official identity, a culture, and often a new language, suppressing the native identity and driving it inward to become a secret, private self. So dominated, such peoples are forced to become both bilingual and bicultural. That duality lies at the heart of frustrated nationalism. While many such takeovers have had successful conclusion in human history, some decidedly have not; it is from these that thwarted nationalist feelings arise, from situations of deep discontent, from a resentment of a ruling authority coupled with a deep fear of losing the particular ways and myths of being and believing that have always told a once independent people who they were.

For a very long time, whenever I went back to Scotland, I realise that I put out an extra wary antenna, to pick up any trace of what we used to call the 'Scottish Condition'. The Scottish Condition can show itself fleetingly in the smallest of gestures, a sniff or a sigh, or it can take a voluble spoken form; but it has lurked for a long time in the undercurrents of Scottish life. It wells from ancestral gloom, from the shadows of a severe Calvinism and from a gritty mixture of disappointment and indignation, and it mantles the Scottish spirit like an ancient moss. I grew up under a low cloud of girn and grumble, yet never quite understanding what the injustice was, for it was never identified. It was just something in the air, a kind of national weather, a damp mist of dissatisfaction.

Scotland would qualify as a senior member of the Fourth World. In essence, the Scottish Condition stems from the fact that, since 1707, Scotland has been an ex-nation, a destiny that its people have never quite accepted or even understood, but one that they have so far been unable to alter. 1707 is a date as dire as Doomsday to Scottish ears. But there was no way of knowing then how much the Act of Union was to become an English takeover. Whatever expectations may have been, no 'union', in any deep sense of the word, took place, no national self-image was replaced by another, no 'British' meta-character evolved. Citizens of the United Kingdom rarely refer to themselves as British, except when travelling abroad, for 'Great Britain' exists more in a diplomatic and legislative sense than in a human one. The Union suddenly handed the Scots a dual nationality: officially, they were British, but in their own minds, their own mirrors, they were Scots. No such duality afflicted the English: for them, 'Britain' and 'England' were synonyms from the beginning, an assumption that has always infuriated. In the eyes of the English, Scotland went from being a troublesome neighbor to becoming a remote northern region, a market, an occasional playground, a ghost of its former fierce self. As Douglas Dunn wrote:

> A land of soldiers, mind, and science,
> A nation turned into a province!

To be left with a culture, a history, and a national character, and yet to have no longer any political control over the terms of national existence, amounts to a disastrous emasculation.

It seems to me that at the heart of nationalist discontents lies always a dilemma of language. As often as not, when smaller states or cultures are overrun by larger powers, they are overrun at the same time by a dominant outside language, so that the native language becomes secondary, separate, secret even: to speak it is a subversive act. A language imposed from the outside forces a people to become bilingual in order to survive, and saddles them with a dual nature. That duality is experienced over and over again simply in the act of speaking. When the public use of Catalan was officially banned in Franco's Spain, the language became for the Catalans a secret weapon, a readily available expression of defiance and complicity, a bond felt in the tongue. Now that Catalonia has its own language restored to it, Catalans use it aggressively and ubiquitously.

It is Scotland's curious linguistic situation that feeds its cultural ambiguity, that underlines its discontents and keeps them palpable. While Scotland and England were still independent countries, the language used by the Scots had much the same relation to the English of England that, say, Dutch has to German today. The two languages had, after all, a common source, and were mutually intelligible, at least in their written form, to English and Scots alike. But English was certainly the more dominant of the two, particularly since, from the sixteenth century on, the Scots had used an English version of the Bible, and through it were well familiar with written English, although they pronounced it in their own manner. After the Union, however, one thing became clear which had not been in any way previsioned: English culture, and the English language in particular, had no intention of moving over to accommodate the Scots in any mode or manner. Scotland needed the Union more than England did, and as their merchants went south to better themselves, they were obliged to conduct their business in the English language, a tacit condition they had no choice but to accept. It was English that was taught in Scottish schools – English was the official, public language, and was synonymous with 'correctness'. I remember well, at school in the Scottish Border country, that we would speak in our own local fashion in the playground, but as we entered the classroom, we crossed a linguistic threshold, and spoke English. A Scots word used in class made us laugh aloud: it was an irregularity. Speaking English was, to us, speaking 'proper', which rendered our own local speech improper by implication, secondary, somehow inferior. David Hume, although the staunchest of Scots, would nevertheless send his manuscripts to English friends for them to weed out his Scotticisms, which he did not consider appropriate to serious discourse. Yet I treasure the Scots I still have, for its downrightness and for its blunt vocabulary, for words as wonderfully apt as the verb 'to swither'. I also feel, as is often the case in bilingual situations, that I write English with especial care, feeling it somehow as a foreign language, and having to dominate it as a form of self-defence.

It is no longer accurate to say that Scots today is a separate language, as once it was; rather, it is a linguistic mode, a manner of using English, yet with a rich extra vocabulary of Scots words. In speech, the Scots reject the mannerisms of English English for a blunt directness, a spare and wary address; engrained in the Scottish spirit is a downright egalitarianism, that insists on taking others as they present themselves, whatever they may represent, a natural democracy of feeling. The way the Scots speak among themselves, in their own words, has remained domestic and intimate, for addressing not the world but family and friends. But although all Scots are well schooled in English, even the dwindling Gaelic speakers in parts of the Highlands, it still has the feel for them of a foreign language, something that, although they live comfortably enough in it, does not quite fit them. Among themselves, they modify it so that it does; but to outsiders, they speak English. As Robert Louis Stevenson put it, 'even though his tongue acquire the Southern knack, he will still have a strong Scots accent of the mind'.

Every time I hear a Scot speaking with an Englishman, I am acutely aware of how different are the two modes, the manners of speaking the language. The 'official' English accent is a curious phenomenon. It is left over from Empire, an accent that is clearly designed to command, that implies a whole morality and a view of history, and carries a certain condescension, a superiority, a distancing. It is not a regional accent, though it became the language of a ruling class. It can be acquired, and is, by Scots as well as English, through the agency of institutions like the English public schools. It is in utter contrast to the manner in which the Scots use English – direct, vigorous, unadorned, even blunt. The different speech modes embody all the differences of history, of nature, of human manner, and although on an everyday level they co-exist easily, they still speak across a distance of being. I once heard Mrs Thatcher's voice on the evening news suddenly cut through the clishmaclaver of an Edinburgh pub, abruptly stilling the conversation, and causing a dark flush to spread collectively up the necks of its grim listeners. Such moments are at the inexplicable core of nationalism; and it is at such moments that it occurs to me all over again that the Union, from the beginning, was not really a very good idea.

After Scotland was deprived of its public existence, it really turned into countless secret countries, private Scotlands, from the sentimental to the politically committed. For that reason, Scottish self-government, while generally wished for, is infinitely disputed. But I think now that the Scots have shed in large part their ancestral glooms and their defeatism, if not their contentiousness, and will do very well at taking charge of their own affairs. In spite of nearly three hundred years of ambiguous history, Scotland has persisted as a reality in its own mind, and it certainly has the energy and the imagination to become one in a responsible, political sense.

A. R.

The Transformations:
Notes on Childhood
1966

Childhood, especially for a poet, is irresistible; his pre-occupation with it would be completely incomprehensible to a child. From the vantage point of his aging consciousness, he finds himself, either through the eyes of his own children or through sudden green transformations of memory, dissolving into these states of pure trance (states which he can never forgive children for being unaware of), in which a single day is a clear, prismatic present, when a glass of water, instead of being a complex molecular structure, or a lucid piece of punctuation in a disordered chain of consequences, or an image in which the whole world is somehow reflected, stands on the table as nothing more or less than a glass of water, wondrously, needing no reason or excuse for its existence. I like nothing more than to listen to people talking about their childhood. Bit by bit, they work their way through a morass of judgment and sophist-icated afterthought, psychiatric blah, and scholastic roughage until they reach, if they are lucky, an unencumbered point of pure memory – a day, an instance, a happening, tragic perhaps, comic more likely, but quivering with sheer life, pure and inexplicable, like the glass of water.

What, in fact, do we save from childhood? On the surface, a miscellaneous collection of odds and ends: birth certificates, because they are so permanently necessary to prove that we exist at all; baby shoes, perhaps, because we cannot otherwise conceive of having been no more than eighteen inches tall; fluffy photographs of our bald, naked beginnings; stamps, shells, feathers, skeletons; thumbed books about gnomes, brownies, and heroes; tickets, scraps, lists, dried leaves. These are the relics and the gravestones, and are meant, in their tiny, wizened way, to evoke an aura, to suggest a state of grace; yet how shrivelled they are, as they lie in a curiously smelling drawer, waiting for the day when we are courageous enough to cremate them.

Childhood is by definition a never-never land, a place where we have unaccountably been without knowing it, a nowhere which took up all our time before we realised what time was. Children drift through their sky-blue days without any feeling of being in motion; landmarks like birthdays loom on the faraway, blurred horizon, and move so slowly that it seems they will never arrive. When I was a child, even to wait for the next day was agonising to me; in prospect, the night seemed so long and impassable, until I grew into a faith in the fact that I *would* wake up in a different, new-made day. For children, the future is so remote that it scarcely exists at all; the odd thing about growing up is the way in which the landmarks begin to move, faster and faster, until they are whizzing past like telephone poles. And the principal irony of childhood lies in the fact that we wander through it in an almost complete daze, unselfconscious, open-eyed, until we find ourselves gawking back at it from an age of realisation, as somewhere we have been without noticing, wondering how we managed to pass the unwitting time.

But still, when we come to look at childhood, at the remove of judgment, do we see it at all? Or, instead, do we somehow accommodate it into the life we have later arrived at, trimming it to fit, forgetting its oddness and contradiction? I listen to people telling their childhood, and wonder, not just at the fact that they ever were children, but more, whether the versions of their own childhood they have come to believe in bear any relation to the small, vanished selves they have left behind. Childhood seems to them no more real than old movies, the after-math of a story they were once told but of which they have only the vaguest recollection.

What most people do, I suspect, is save for their later, full-grown days a few places, a few set pieces, a welter of anecdote (which over the telling years grows more and more original) to serve as memory whenever it becomes necessary to explain away the unconscious, missing years. Of the original, in its original form, little remains. It is, after all, better to decide that one had a happy childhood than to admit one had a relatively unconscious one, better to select the choicest places, the most fruitful occasions, and make of them a serviceable tapestry to suit the blandest of biographers. Or it may be just as serviceable to look back on childhood as the point where everything went wrong, to find, under the unruffled surface, monsters and nightmares. No wonder psychoanalysts take so long to get to the bottom, to find the early secret, the original sin – childhood is in fact bottomless, and has its own strange scale.

The principal difference between childhood and the stages of life into which it invisibly dissolves is that as children we occupy a limitless present. The past has scarcely room to exist, since, if it means anything at all, it means only the previous day. Similarly, the future is in abeyance; we are not meant to do anything about it until we reach a suitable size. Correspondingly, the present is enormous, mainly because it is all there is – a garden is as vast as Africa, and can easily become Africa, at the drop of a wish. Walks are dizzying adventures; the days tingle with unknowns, waiting to be made into wonders. Living so utterly in the present, children have an infinite power to transform; they are able to make the world into anything they wish, and they do so, with alacrity. There are no preconceptions, which is why, when a child tells us he is Napoleón, we had better behave with the respect due to a small emperor. Later in life, the transformations are forbidden; they may prove dangerous. By then, we move in a context of expectations and precedents, of past and future, and the present, whenever we manage to catch it and realise it, is a shifting, elusive question mark, not altogether comfortable, an oddness that the scheme of our lives does not quite allow us to indulge. Habit takes over, and days tend to slip into pigeonholes, accounted for because everything has happened before, because we know by then that life is long and has to be intelligently endured. Except that, every now and again, one of these moments occurs, so transcendent in its immediacy, so amazing in its extraordinary ordinariness, that we get a sudden glimpse of what childhood was all about and of how much the present has receded before a cluttered past and an anxious future. In these odd moments, the true memory of childhood dawns. The glass of water is, amazingly, a glass of water.

*

Quite often, there comes a time when we try deliberately to recover childhood, revisiting a place, a house, a garden. Perhaps it would be better not to; almost inevitably it is a puzzlement, if not a downright disappointment. How wizened it is, how shrunken, how small, how unlike the mysterious nowhere we imagined we inhabited! I recall once revisiting a seaside village in Scotland where I lived as a child, a small harbor town I had gone over lovingly in what I thought was my memory, telling it house by house, hearing the high tides thud against the seawall in my sleep. Yet, when I walked around the harbor, I wondered how I could ever have been carried away by it, even in dream, so ordinary, small, and grubby it was, so unglowing, a poor stage for the wonders I remembered as having happened there in my small, broody days. The particular tree I made a profession of climbing had become only one in a series of trees, not, as it was then, the only tree in the world, Ygdrasil. And the people who remembered me now had to take their place in the context of time; they no longer belonged to the towering world of unchanging legend that my child's eyes and ears had appointed them to. They were mortal. 'Don't change unless I tell you to!' cries the child to the world; and the world, instead of replying, goes quietly about its business of changing us, of turning what once was called growing up into growing old.

*

My own childhood, now that I look back on it with the proper distrust, seems to have been not extraordinary, for all childhoods are that, but a peculiar mixture of earth and air, of the practical and the impossible. My father was a minister of the church and moved and breathed with an extraordinary reverence for things, a reverence we absorbed simply by being in the same house with him. He did not speak often; when he did, I used to listen to him with the proper astonishment. My mother, on the other hand, was a doctor of medicine, and ran her doctoring and her household with a ribald, go-ahead, down-to-earth directness. They were, for us children, like the North and South Poles. Heaven knows what

strange equilibrium they achieved, but we children were the fruit
of it, and we spun dizzily from one to the other, from the no-
nonsense bustle of the kitchen and surgery at one end of the house
to the quiet, smoke-laden, book-lined study at the other. In
between was a long corridor, our limbo. Outside was the world.
Even now, I simplify, for it was never so neat; I cannot even
remember whether or not there was a corridor, but there should
have been. Along it, we were always in motion, disobedient this
side of disaster, but busy with the odd variety of our existence.

Nevertheless, for all our participatory joy, we looked up at our
parents as if we were underwater and they in the air, seeing
them from below, larger than life, through the wavering prismatic
surface, yet unable to call from our swaying, crystal-clear world to
theirs. Our elements were separate, different. My mother was too
busy to reach us, my father too shy; and we, for our part, with
wonder bubbling from our mouths, did not know how to speak
the first word. Even across time, nothing has broken that thin,
taut meniscus, that soundless, separating glass. There comes a time
when it is too late to begin talking, even to oneself.

Scotland we hardly noticed; it was no more than weather and
landscape, and we lived, if we lived anywhere at all, between
garden and water, in a mud-stained leaf-smelling round of errands
and holidays, our feet on the ground, our heads firmly in the
clouds. At school, among our friends, we spoke the local dialect
bluntly and boisterously; at home, we clipped it to suit the household. As a minister's family, we had an odd immunity from the
strata of local society. We knew – and played with – everyone
from the snotty-nosed farm children to the starched and proper
county families, who envied us our worldliness. We knew worse
words than they did, and used them judiciously. At the same time,
however, we were foreigners, never quite belonging anywhere;
we had books at home, and things obviously went on as a matter of
course in our house which never would have occurred in the rest
of the town – blood and sermons, blessings and bandages.

I hovered for years between the surgery and the study, trying to
decide whether I was cut out for the pulpit or the operating room;
but I solved my dilemma by plunging into the mysterious country-

side and by playing endless fantastic games over which, at least, I had control. The poles were noise and silence; I ran wild during the day, and in the evening I crept into the deep silence of books, unreachable. All of us kept passing and repassing one another along the length of the corridor, some on their way to burst, hungry and shouting, into the kitchen, others to tiptoe into the study, breath held, shoes in hand.

And yet, none of this is quite what I remember; it is rather the context and setting for my remembering. I recall, some years ago, taking a long voyage under sail across the Atlantic and passing the night watches – which we took alone at the wheel, under the enormous processes of the sky – by applying my memory to a particular place, a particular day, a particular time. With time – and there was plenty – I found I could recover whole periods of my life which I had not thought of since they happened. I remembered the names of those who had been in my school classes; and, with practice, I could take long walks over stretches of lost country, scrutinising farms, trees, landmarks on the way; so that, night after night, perched alone in the middle of the Atlantic, I replayed most of my childhood like an endless movie, not for the sake of finding anything out, but, as the English say, just because it was there. It seemed particularly appropriate, for then I had no context, save for the sea, the dark, and the innumerable repetitive stars; and I sat under them, saying over to myself long lists of names I was not aware I knew – Kirkmaiden, Catyins, Linglie, Yarrowford, Pirnmill, Altgolach, Imacher, Windygates – amazing myself with their sound, seeing each place vividly in my mind's eye. It was then I realised that my childhood was not lost; all that was required to recover it was the dimension of amazement.

*

In the eyes of children, anything can happen, for so little has happened before; for us, at a remove, we know what is likely and what impossible, and so our propensity to astonishment is much less. Moreover, we tend to forget, as Christopher Fry says, that we were born naked into a world of strange sights and sounds, not fully clothed, in a service apartment, with a copy of *The Times* in our hand. This is why some of the afterthought we apply to the world of children – the books they ought to read, the things they should be interested in, the ways in which they should pass their time – is often preposterous and seems to assume that children are our idea, not theirs. Children are interested in anything except, possibly, the things they are expected to be interested in; and we might as well lay our world open to them and let them make off with whatever improbable treasure they discover for themselves.

I suppose the difficulty lies in deciding exactly who children are, in seeing them mistakenly as small replicas of ourselves, or as raw material, or as undersized animals, or as a race of miniature entertainers, or trainees, or even as income-tax deductions. I prefer to regard them – and, indeed, they demand to be regarded – as sudden visitors from an unlikely planet, frail, cogent messengers from a world which we know by name but have lost sight of, little people who are likely not only to amuse and amaze us but to remind us that life is long, and that they, as much as we, have a right to their own version of it. The mistake we mostly make is to encumber children with the versions we retain of our own child-hood, to imagine that what would have been good for us, as we think we were then, will be good for them, as we think they are now. Children are entitled to their otherness, as anyone is; and when we reach them, as we sometimes do, it is generally on a point of sheer delight, to us so astonishing, but to them so natural.

The Seventh Day
1962

Nothing depresses me as much as other people's Sundays, those long, lame, aimless stretches of waste, sad time, like bad habits, or a kind of doom. When I was a child, I used, every now and again, to have a very telling vision (I was prone to visions of a most matter-of-fact sort) of God resting on the seventh day, sprawled across the universe, pleasantly exhausted, playing with a smile, pleased at the way the world had gone, quietly happy. Everything, I suppose, depends on how you construe 'and he rested on the seventh day,' but to read it as an Absence rather than a Presence seems to me a drastic failure in understanding.

The shape of days is settled at a very early point in life, mainly by what we do with them. Mondays begin and Fridays end, Saturdays celebrate, but Sundays – Sundays are suspended in nothingness, left to the devices of whoever wishes to give them shape, neutral zones in time subject to various interpretations, sacred to miscellaneousness. After an eventful week, nothing is supposed to happen on Sunday; it is a day that confronts us with our own fragile mortality, requiring us to content ourselves with the simple business of being alive, a primal matter that appears to consternate most people to the point of distraction. If all this were properly realised, we might conceivably take a great deal more trouble than we do with the week, to give it pith and moment; and we would have to decide what we wanted Sunday to be, or at least to appear, especially to children.

I happen to love Sundays, an accident of circumstance which derives quite clearly from my childhood. Although I grew up in Scotland, where Sunday was the most shuttered, barren, forbidding and proscriptive of all days, I was saved from the general inertia by the fact that my father was a minister, and that Sunday, instead of being a piece of temporal punctuation, was the Great Climax of the week. On Saturday evenings, we were shovelled out of the way to leave my father alone to wrestle with his own private angel. I still remember with awe the silence of the study, the feeling of sheer thinking that emanated from it like a tangible cloud. I still remember the sharp edge of anticipation in which Saturday expired, like a frail younger brother, and Sunday loomed.

★

Sunday in Scotland is the Sabbath, a day you might easily mistake for Doomsday if you were not used to it, a day that barely struggles into wakefulness. Shops, pubs, cinemas, cafés, bandstands, any-where, in fact, where people with social inclinations might encounter one another, are not only shut but sealed – at least, if not literally, they feel as if they should be. Houses are as silent as safes, and silence is as safe as houses; bottles are not only stoppered but locked; and, in the appropriate season, you can hear a leaf thud to the ground. Ecclesiastical ghosts stalk the countryside; the weather is the only noticeable happening.

Even animals absorb the mood of the day, and lie sluggishly in corners, minding their own drowsy business; people pull down the blinds in their heads, and listen hazily to bells tolling, nostrils twitching hopefully for a whiff of dinner. The guilty feel more guilty, the righteous more righteous, and the children, abandoned to their own tiny devices, wonder where life has gone, scrawling their way through homework which at least gives them the faint, quivering hope that Monday may come, that the world has not ended after all.

But not in our house. As soon as Sunday dawned, gray though it usually was, we sprang into life, aware that the week was about to go off like a rocket. We breakfasted in the dining room instead of the kitchen, and always more handsomely than usual; we groomed ourselves, and nipped into the garden for a sniff at the day. My father always turned up for breakfast, looking suitably serious and responsible – through the week he was a parent, but on Sunday he came down in clerical black, an emissary from a remote but marvellous planet, and we watched him with proper awe.

Church came at eleven; and since we were four children, one of us was always allowed to stay behind. We hugged this privilege, traded it, looked forward to it, saved up for it, took it for what it was, a gift of time. In the kitchen, my mother laid down the bones of lunch; in the study, my father assembled his notes, and absorbed the last of the silence. He left well ahead of us; we always said good-bye to him as though we might never see him again, which in a sense was true, for when he appeared in the pulpit, he was transmogrified, not at all the same person who had been buttering toast a brief hour before. We clambered into our best clothes, dealt out a miscellany of Bibles and pennies, and were off at the first clang of the bell, wheeling into our pew like a small, proud army.

I cannot even now decide which I liked best, my off-days at home, or my official, churchgoing days. Church was certainly never dull. I gaped at the incredible hats, the grave faces; I checked and cross-checked who was there, who was not; I grew to love the woodwork, with a microscopic eye; I listened to the bubbling, breathy wheeze of the organ, and fell in love with a succession of sopranos in the choir; and I gazed at my father, not perhaps hearing what he said, but believing it all faithfully in advance, desperate with love and admiration. I scanned the hymns and the paraphrases, and when the service worked itself up to the benediction, I felt it fall on me like some marvellous light, and walked out into the air with a sense of having been changed into something very different from my grubby, workaday, ink-stained, stone-kicking self.

But the off-days − left alone in the house for an incredible hour and a half, with nobody to say yes or no − these were probably the days. I used to listen for the gate clicking behind the church party, and then I was off, running through the rooms, trying on my father's tile hat, playing the grand piano with *both* pedals pressed down, tearing into the attic, riffling through the bookshelves in search of Something I Didn't Know Yet, wondering whether I might try shaving at the age of nine, writing with a real pen, stirring the soup as I had been told, darting into the garden, walking with a limp and a stick, acting out how many crowded, stored-up fantasies, reading letters which weren't mine, gaping at photographs of the First World War, then racing round to be sure everything was

34

back in its place before the gate clicked again, and the door burst open and spilled in the virtuous, churchgoing survivors. I told them what I had done – 'Nothing, really!' – and they reported that Mr Rodgers had asked where I was, that Miss Smart had got the hiccups – endless, ludicrous happenings. And then lunch.

Lunch on Sundays was for us a ritual of sheer joy, a giddy, unbounded celebration. We wriggled out of our suits, put them away, and came down to a meal that always smacked of manna; it simmered on the stove until my father arrived, restored to his human shape, full of smiles, jokes and fulfillment. We sat round the table until the last possible moment, well-fed and flushed with good will, small lords of the week, planning away the sacred afternoon. On wet days, we put on Hamlet, did circuses or jigsaw puzzles, chewed gum illicitly, and paged through encyclopaedias. Most often, we went for walks, all in different directions, climbing neat, comfortable hills, accomplishing military campaigns and lone sagas of heroic adventure. Sundays gave us our heads, and we took them and ran wildly away with them, as if they were balloons.

In the evenings, as we nuzzled closer to the fire, trimming the ends of our homework, the prospect of Monday troubled us not at all, for we knew that it was only the first, drab step on a ladder that always led to Sunday, when our crumpled busy worlds could be counted on to burst open and rainbow down, when we would all be present at what was, for us, a ritual celebration, not so much of God or John Knox or the Presbyterian virtues, but of the simple, exuberant fact that we were a family.

The odd thing about those days is that I don't think we were particularly religious – instead we were a fairly standard mixture of good and bad, wild and warm, lucky and terrified, like all children. God we knew as a friend of *our* father, his Boss in some incalculable way; and though a goodly company of angels and prophets ran through our dreams, they seemed no more real or awesome than Hamlet or the Bad Brownies. What we did absorb, in mystical osmosis, through our pores rather than our ears, was a curious and deep reverence for things, a feeling which hung like an aura over our Sundays, and which has stayed with me, so that I still look on Sunday as a ritual day, a day on which the meals are to be savored more than usual, the air to be breathed more deeply, when the afternoons are to be luxuriated in, the evenings to be meditated away mellowly.

★

This has stayed with me, even through the war, when there were no Sundays, and even although, since I work at home, Sunday is not externally different from the six other, run-of-the-calendar days. To me Sunday stands on a dais slightly raised above the level of the week; and even if the gods of one's childhood are argued into thin air, there are always others to be celebrated in their places, always new rituals to set up against the swirl of time.

Perhaps it was in reaction to the drear and mournful Scottish Sabbath that ours were so exuberant; but now, when I go back to Scotland, and suddenly see how heavily time must have been hanging outside our garden wall, I begin to realise how lucky we were, and how wise was my father. But the Sabbath, even more so now, seems to me to be a disastrous misinterpretation, from the point of view of religion, or of psychology, or anything else, a wet blanket of a day, celebrating nothing, signifying less. On the Sabbath, Scotland pulls the covers over its head, and groans away the useless silence.

In Spain, I have discovered a Sunday after my own heart, which goes wild in the way ours once did, and seems to me a much more expansive, human interpretation of what God would have liked to do with the seventh day, after making something as complex and exacting as the world. Spain saves up for its Sunday, and spends more than it has saved. Everyone dresses up to the nines, goes to early Mass to give thanks in advance, bursts out, smiling widely, and goes about the business of making the day more memorable than last week, which in its time was more memorable than the week before.

Sunday lunches outstrip even the golden meals of my boyhood, and last into the languorous late afternoon. Time for a walk, perhaps, before the bullfight or the soccer match, time for wine before the crowded, ebullient evening, least time of all for the minimum of sleep before Monday begins when the week staggers to its feet and takes aim. The target? Sunday, with God in His hearty, human, all-giving heaven – a day on which there is more wine than glasses, more feet than shoes, and more kisses than lips.

I am half-inclined to measure the countries of the world by what they make of their Sundays; and if I had my way, I would have all the Scots transported to Spain, and swallowed up once and for all in the sheer good humor of one Spanish Sunday, so that they flew home singing, and broke out their bottles, bagpipes, and brightest bonnets, and hung John Knox in the cupboard where he began, and should have remained, as a meagre, moping ghost, in a dun nightgown of his own loose skin.

Days, one ought to know, are not to be wasted; and so Sunday deserves more than crosswords and aimless walks, casual visits, cold meals. It deserves to be, not a No-day, but a Yes-day. Perhaps it is time we shouted down the Lord's Day Observance Society, and took the Sabbath into our own hands, dressing up for it as we might for a fancy-dress ball, toasting it in elixirs, keeping it clear of obligations other than the one we have to the fact that we are (luckily) alive at all.

Hauntings
1983

My memory had always been to me more duffel bag than filing cabinet, but, even so, I have been fairly sure that if I rummaged enough I could come up with what I needed. Lately, though, certain things have caused me to apply my memory deliberately – to a place, a period in my life, to focus on it and recover it alive. One strong reason has been the death of friends, which shocks one through mourning into a ferocity of remembering, starting up a conversation in the memory in order to hear the dead voice talk, see the dead face come alive. The other impulse to put my memory in some kind of order came from a friend of mine with whom I have kept in written touch for thirty-odd years, who showed me a bulge in his ancient address book where he had had to paste in extra pages to contain more than forty permanent addresses for me since 1950, dotted all over Europe, Latin America, the United States. I looked long at them: French street names scrawled vertically in the margins; telephone numbers that rang very distant bells in my head – some of the places grown so faint that I had to focus hard, pluck at frail threads. I have never kept journals, but I have a jumble of old passports, diaries with little more than places and names, and a few cryptic notes meant to be instant sparks to the memory. Of late, I have taken to picking up threads and winding in, room by room, a house in Spain or an apartment in Geneva; then, with growing Nabokovian intensity, the picture above the fireplace, the sound of the front door closing behind. I have pursued my own chronology not so much to record it as to explore it. Remembering a particular house often brings back a predominant mood, a certain weather of the spirit. Sometimes, opening the door of a till-then-forgotten room brought on that involuntary shiver, that awed suspension. These sudden rememberings are gifts to writers, like the taste of the madeleine – for much of writing is simply finding ways of recreating astonishments in words. But as I began to reel in my itinerant past I found that I was much less interested in recording it than in experiencing the sense it gave me of travelling in time, of making tangible a ghostly dimension; for an instance of remembering can, without warning, turn into a present moment, a total possession, a haunting.

Chronology can be a hindrance to remembering well: the assumption that individual lives have a design, a certain pro-gression, persists in everything from obituaries to ear-written biographies of movie stars. A backward look, besides, is usually disposed to give past time a shape, a pattern, a set of explanations. Memory can be an agile and cunning editor; but if we use it instead as an investigative reporter it often turns up conflicting evidence, for we arrive as we age at a set of recountable versions (long and short) of our private time, a set of serviceable maps of the past to replace the yellowed photographs. If I look at my own time chart, it divides cataclysmically into two parts, two contradictory modes of being. The first part, brief but everlasting, embraces the rural permanence I was born into in Scotland, articulated by the seasons, with the easy expectation that harvest followed harvest, that years repeated themselves with minor variations (growing being one of them), a time when I was wholly unaware of an outside world; the second part erupted with the Second World War, which obliterated the predictability of anything and severed all flow, all continuity. When I joined the Royal Navy, in the later years of the war, I was projected abruptly out of Scotland and to sea, on a series of small ships, around the Indian Ocean – endless ports of call that were all astonishments. It was never made clear to us where we were going, except to sea; so I learned to live by sea time, which is as close to a blank present as one can come. I also learned to live portably. We would move, on sudden orders, from ship to shore to ship, and what we could carry we could count on keeping; the rest was in the public domain. My personal possessions were not much more than a notebook or two; and, coming home after the war through the Suez Canal, I watched one of these notebooks slither from my fingers and shimmy its wavering way down in the lime green water. It was my first serious lesson in learning to shrug. When I got free of the service, I went back to Scotland to finish a degree at the University of St Andrews, and then left, as I had long intended, taking as little as possible and making next to no plans.

Although I passed through Scotland irregularly in the next few decades, finding certain epiphanies in the moods of the place, reconnecting with friends and family, I felt firmly severed from it. It was less the past to me than the point of departure; and, besides, I had long disliked the abiding cloud of Calvinism that kept Scotland muffled, wary, resentful. An obligation of obedience was written into its educational system, which, when it came to imparting information, was certainly thorough, to use one of the Scots' favorite words; but during my school days if we made trouble or persistently misconstrued Greek irregular verbs our extended hand was struck a variable number of times with a thick leather strap, tongued at the end, called a tawse. The last time I was in Scotland, I discovered that the tawse was still in use. Put together a sniff of disapproval, a wringing of hands, a shaking of the head that clearly expects the worst, and you have some idea of how dire Scotland can be. All the other countries I have lived in have seemed comparatively joyful. The gloom, I hoped, would stay in Scotland and not follow me about. Certainly on these visits I felt no pull to stay. I had got used to the feeling of belonging nowhere, of being a foreigner by choice, entering a new country, a new language, in pursuit, almost, of anonymity and impermanence. Scotland seemed to have little to do with my present, and grew dimmer and dimmer in my memory.

In 1949, I first came to the United States, and it felt like immediate liberation. I could sense the wariness in me melt, the native caution dwindle. Fluidity, it seemed to me, had replaced roots, and change fuelled not a wringing of hands but a positive excitement. I taught for a few years, and then decided to live by writing – about the most portable of all occupations, and an always available pretext for travelling. I crossed, and crisscrossed, the Atlantic, mostly by sea, on the great ships that pulled out from the West Side piers in a regular booming of horns; and once crossed under sail. I discovered Spain and the Spanish language, which had far-flung geographical consequences for me, taking me as far as the tip of Chile. I had a number of friends with the same wandering disposition, who would turn up in some of the same places I had stumbled on, and with whom I often crossed paths. What we were all looking for were localities that moved to their own time, unmechanised villages, islands, isolated but not utterly, good places to work in, but with available distraction, refuges, our own versions of a temporary Garden of Eden, which had an illusion of permanence about them, however impermanent the stay. Work would quite often determine my movements; I found that a new place, in the energy of beginning, sharpened the attention. Some of these Edens were remote – a house, a garden, a village, perhaps – and, remembering them, I have to reach far, to remember a previous self. More than that, they are not separate in memory from the people I shared them with. They are places entwined with presences. Looking for temporary Edens is a perpetual lure certainly not confined to writers, who sooner or later discover that the islands of their existence are, in truth, the tops of their desks.

★

I went back to Scotland quite often on brief visits, to see my parents as they grew old, into their eighties; but somehow I had never dwelt much on how I had got from there to wherever I was at the time. Then I spent the entire summer of 1980 in Scotland, on an escapade with my son and some friends, digging up a plastic box – a time capsule – that we had buried nine years previously, on the fringes of the golf course at St Andrews. That summer, I spent a lot of time with my sister Kathleen, who had been my great ally in the turbulence of our growing up. Our parents were dead, and we had met only scantily in recent years, but as the deep green summer rained and rained we found ourselves almost involuntarily rummaging in the past as if it were a miscellaneous attic chest, startling ourselves at a remembered name, to a point at which we were mesmerised by remembering. We had photographs and documents that we had saved from clearing up our parents' papers, but we discovered that in the interaction of our memories we had much more. We re-created our parents from the point that we began, not in any systematic way but in flashes, days and seasons in a single vision. The rain watered my memory, and I found my whole abandoned beginning seeping slowly back, even into dreams.

I was born in Whithorn, in the soft southwest of Scotland. It was my beginning; and, reaching back to it, I realise that for me it has remained in a time warp of its own – my personal Eden, in that although it was lost, the aura that comes back with remembering it stems from a time when house, family, garden, village, and friends were all I knew of the world, when everything had the glow of wholeness, when I had no idea of the passing of time except as anticipation. What I have discovered, too, are the contradictions – in many cases, our own mythifications of that time, the recountable, bookshelf version, which we put together to anchor the past in place. Even so, the myth is bound to predominate; we cannot become who we were or lose what we now know.

Whithorn lies close to the tip of one of the southern fingers of the part of Scotland known as Galloway: isolated, seldom visited, closer across the Irish Sea to Northern Ireland than it seems to the rest of Scotland; closer, too, to Ireland in the softness and cadence of its speech. It is rich, low-lying, carefully cultivated dairy country, with a few small fishing ports, and has a douce, mild climate, thanks to the proximity of the Gulf Stream, which has made certain Galloway gardens famous for their exotic transplantings. Whithorn was also a beginning for my parents. My father came from the midlands of Scotland, a member of the large and humorous family of a schoolmaster I never knew. He had interrupted his divinity studies at Glasgow University to serve as a combatant in the First World War, and had been wounded in the Second Battle of the Somme; had married my mother, who had recently graduated as a doctor from Glasgow University; and had returned, with the war behind him, to pick up his existence. In 1921, he was chosen and ordained as Church of Scotland minister in Whithorn. The church stood on the site of Whithorn Priory, the first Christian settlement in Britain, founded on the arrival of St Ninian, in the year 397, and a very early place of pilgrimage. It was my father's first charge, a village of some seven hundred, embracing the surrounding farms. My parents firmly took root there, my father healed over from the war, which nevertheless always troubled his memory, my mother had a house to turn into a household, and in later years they always spoke of these beginnings as a lucky time in their lives, for Galloway contains the kindliest of people in all that flinty country – all in all, a good place to begin in.

In shape, Whithorn looks much like a child's drawing of a village: built on a slope, it has a single main street – the houses on each side of it joined in a single façade, no two of them, however, exactly alike – which widens like a mandolin as it descends to a semblance of a square, where the shops cluster, where the bus pulls in. The street narrows again and runs to the bottom end of the village, where, in our day, the creamery and the railway station stood adjacent to each other. Every morning, the miniature beginnings of a train would start out from Whithorn: a wagonful of full milk churns from the creamery destined for Glasgow; a single passenger coach, occasionally carrying those who had business in the outside world. Whithorn was a place easy to learn by heart. All round it lay the farms and, beyond them, infinitely, the sea.

As minister, my father had the gift of the manse to live in and the manse in Whithorn was an outpost, set apart from the village. From the main street, under an old arch bearing Whithorn's coat of arms, a lane led, first, to the small white church that was my father's charge, surrounded by a well-kept graveyard, where we sometimes practiced our reading from the gravestones. The lane continued left past the church, crested a small rise, and ran down, over the trickle of a stream, to the white gates of the manse. A gravel drive led up to the manse, past a long, walled garden on the right; a semicircle of huge elm and beech trees faced the house from across the drive. Behind the house were stables and out-houses, and all around lay green fields. If you trudged across them, careful in summer to skirt the golden edges of standing oats and barley, you reached the sea – an irresistible pilgrimage.

The manse had the quality of certain Scottish houses – a kind of good sense realised in stone, made to last. There were ample rooms: attic rooms, where we children slept, and played on wet days, as we were born in turn; a study for my father, separated from the stepped-down kitchen by a long flagstone corridor, which led, through sculleries and pantries, to the garden. But it is a peopled place, not an empty house, in my memory. My eldest sister, Margaret, was born two years before my parents came to Whithorn; but there, in the house, my sister Kathleen, I, and my younger sister, Lesley, saw the light in that order, so that we became a tribe, and fell into the rhythms and ways of the place – a wondrous progression that I took in whole, with wide, unjudging eyes.

Whithorn was not at all well-to-do but thrived, rather, on the comfortable working equilibrium of that countryside. Some of its inhabitants went to sea, fishing, but most farmed; the creamery kept the dairy herds profitable; and the place had a kind of self-sufficient cheer that it needed, for it was truly at the end of a long, far line – it and its small seaport village, the Isle of Whithorn, a few miles beyond it, on the coast. There were not many comings and goings, and, so isolated, the people became their own sustenance, and had the warm grace of the countryside. Seven hundred people, if they do not actually know one another, know at least who everyone is. The village had the habit of churchgoing: besides my father, there was a United Free Church minister and a Catholic priest, shepherding even tinier flocks. The three of them became good friends. Like the doctor and the local solicitors, they had essential functions in the community. It was a harmonious place, with no sides, no sharp edges. My birth certificate bears the spidery signature of James J. Colquhoun, the local registrar, who had a head like a shrivelled eagle and wore pince-nez, and who had memorised the local population and its ancestral connections so well that he often greeted people by reciting their family tree to them – or, at least, the lower branches.

The manse, the center of our world, hummed with our own lives. It had the equilibrium that families often arrive at for a time before they break up into individual parts. Our household had its own modes and habits, which were set by the design of our parents' lives. Our parents fascinated us as children – during our growing, in particular – for, separately, they had natures about as opposite as seemed possible to us, yet they were never separate, and were noticeably devoted. My father, soft-spoken, gentle of

44

manner, edging on shy, with a natural kindness and humor never far from his eyes, grew to be much liked in the place. When we walked with him, people would greet him warmly, and we would include ourselves by clutching at him. When we were assembled as a family, at meals, or on fire-circling evenings, he would question us, tease us, tell us stories; at other times he might take us, singly, on visits to farms; but often, poised at his desk reading, or sitting in an armchair with an unfixed gaze, he seemed to have pulled over him a quilt of silence, to be inhabiting an unreachable solitude. We grew used, also, to his different presences. On Sundays, he appeared in the pulpit, wearing his robes and a grave face, and we listened more than anything to the measured cadence of his pulpit voice. After church, except when it was raining, we waited for him in the garden, for he took a shortcut across the fields and dropped over the garden wall, returned from gravity into fatherhood, much to our relief.

My mother revered my father; and, as if to insure his chosen quiet, she forswore the practice of medicine and took over control of the house, the household, and us children, delegating us tasks according to our abilities. As with all houses in the country, there were endless chores, always a need of hands. The Church of Scotland paid its ministers very small stipends indeed, and although the manses were substantial houses, some of the more remote of them had fallen behind in time. We drew all our water from a hand pump – a domestic replica of the village pump – in the scullery off the kitchen. It was the obligation of the last pumper to leave behind three full buckets. The house was heated by coal fires and lit by oil lamps. These I would watch my father assemble on the lamp table, where he filled them, trimmed the wicks, and polished the funnels – a task I apprenticed myself to as soon as I could. We willingly ran on errands to the village like missions – for it was a common practice there to send notes by hand, using the mails only for letters to the world. When my two older sisters were in the village school, I inherited their task of walking across the fields to the creamery with a pitcher, to have it filled with still warm milk, and would wander home slowly by way of my private shrines.

My mother, whose father, younger sister, and brother were all doctors, showed no impulse to practice medicine. I suspect now that, having grown up in a medical household, tied always to one end of a wire of availability, she did not want ours to be so bound. But we got to know the local doctor well, and my mother would stand in for him when he was away, sometimes seeing his patients in the kitchen, which we would unclutter for the occasion. Neither was it uncommon for her to be summoned by an anxious knocking late at night when the doctor was out on call and could not be found. She did not, however, believe in sending out bills for any medical services, and never did. Added to that, my father's stipend was paid in part according to the old Scottish tithing system, whereby farmers who cultivated church land paid a tithe of their crop, or its market value, to help sustain the parish, so we had more than a passing interest in the harvest. As a consequence, our larder, with its long blue slate counter, was regularly replenished with fresh eggs, butter, oats, potatoes, game – the green abundance of that patiently farmed place. My father never carried money, nor did we, unless we were ordered to for something specific. At intervals, he paid all the bills at a stroke, totalling them carefully and going out the next day to the bank to take out the necessary sum. Occasionally, he would let us look at the notes before he paid them over, but I had not grasped the idea of money, and it did not interest us much – except for my sister Margaret, who was already plaguing us with knowing school airs.

My father's single obsession was with cars, and he drove very fast – this always surprised and delighted us – about the country-side, on his pastoral visits, in an ancient Fiat that looked half like a carriage. We had a network of friends on the surrounding farms, some of which were close enough for us, when we reached a certain age, to point ourselves like crows toward them, navigating the fields and stone dikes in between. I loved the days on the farm – the rituals of milking, still by hand; the work that changed according to season and weather – and I used to stay over at one farm, Broughton Mains, for haying in June, and for the golden weeks of harvest in late August: days we passed in the field, helping or playing; days punctuated by the women bringing hampers of food they had spent the morning preparing; the fields orderly at the end of the day, the bound sheaves in their rows of standing clumps; days that felt like rites. After we had left Whithorn, I would go back to Broughton Mains for the peak of the harvest, immemorially, for there that drama of abundance crowned the whole year.

We spent as much as we could of the daylight of our lives then outdoors, the house a headquarters among the fields and climbable trees, or a shelter on days of rain or raw weather. Sometimes we would be recruited in a body to help in the garden – a string of small bearers, baskets of weeds on our heads. My world at that time embraced five villages, a dozen farms, a river, and three beaches, some houses we visited often, a countable number of friends we knew by name. We sailed sometimes on a fishing boat out of the Isle of Whithorn, and we often watched five or six local boats come in with their catches, sometimes with herring for the taking. My father preached there on odd Sunday evenings, in a small white church that protruded into the harbor, waves sometimes leaving their spray on its latticed windows during the service. Galloway mostly has soft winters and early springs, and we learned and looked for signs of growing, we followed the progress of the garden and the sown fields surrounding us, we eavesdropped on the farms, trying to pick up nuggets of country wisdom, and we practiced looking wisely at the sky.

From quite early on, our household grew its own legislative procedures when it came to deciding the shapes of days. Decisions, serious decisions, it was understood, lay with my father; but my mother was his plenipotentiary, and our initial dealings – from trivial to urgent – took place through her. She drove hard bargains, and sometimes we would waylay my father to appeal her rulings, for he was a natural peacemaker, patient in argument, attentive to language, and, we felt, fair. It was action my mother believed in, and if we wanted to talk to her it generally meant joining her in turning a small chaos of some kind into active order. She, too, had different manifestations. We overheard her at times talking to a patient – certain, quiet, reassuring. My father had a fair number of callers, and she had the skill of a diplomat in seeing that they did not consume his time. But when we wanted to talk to her it might involve holding a skein of wool for her to wind into a ball, or picking gooseberries by the basketful while we plied her with questions, which she answered crisply, her hands never still for a moment.

There is one period that I find comes back to me with particular clarity, but I am also aware of having mythified it: I had barely turned four; Margaret and Kathleen, in the turn of the years, were away all day at school; my sister Lesley, still a baby, slept in her pram most of the time outside the front door, which the swallows that nested in the stables every year swooped past all day long. The days then were my own, and I wandered on a long lead from the house, walking the flat-topped garden wall, damming the stream, skirting the bees, poking in the stables, and gravitating, in between quests, to the house. Outside, I was busy peopling my solitude, but when I came in I would find myself in the flagstone corridor, the steps down to the kitchen and my mother's domain at one end, the closed door to my father's study at the other. Some days, turning right, I would seek out my mother in the kitchen as she was baking, stocking the larder ahead of our appetites, and I would sit at a corner of the kitchen table, fascinated by the soft grain of its worn wood, while my mother, who, although she preferred working company, also liked company while she worked. I always took the opportunity to nudge her with questions, for I was extremely unclear about the obvious differences between the conditions of the visitors who came to see my father and those who on occasion would wait their turn to see my mother. When my father was talking with a parishioner in the front room, all that came through the closed door was a murmur of voices, but when my mother saw patients in the kitchen we heard, more than once, discomfiting cries from that end of the corridor. Were there some people who might call to see *both* my father and my mother? My mother avoided metaphysics, but she would give me occasional small seminars on things like the digestive system, or why we yawn – hardly the whole medical education I was keen to extract from her. Sometimes I would go with her on an errand to town, and she would explain to me who people were, what they did, their names – teaching me the village and its ways, for she had chosen to live within its particularities happily and actively, and she was the source of our tribal energies.

On other days, I would turn left along the corridor, open the door to my father's study, quietly, as I had learned to do, and find him at his desk, wreathed in smoke, a pool of concentration. He always took me in – he had his own quiet, and did not need silence – and sat me on a hassock by the stretch of bookshelves that held atlases, books with pictures, and an illustrated history of the First World War. This I would lug out, volume by volume, lying full length and gazing in incomprehension at the sepia photographs of blighted landscapes and the skeletons of buildings. Sometimes, when I had his attention, he would begin to explain the pictures to me, or show me on the map where he had been, where the battle lines met, but never for very long, for the subject frayed him. I remember sitting in that room of words and feeling islanded by not being able to read, for I felt that words were my father's business – his reading, his sermons, his writings, the fact that people came to him for his words. Even now, I am still pacing that corridor.

*

In that encapsulated world, I lived in complete innocence of time, except that school was looming. I could not think of years as doing anything other than repeating themselves, nor did I want them to. But time did intrude, abruptly, into my wide-eyed world: we left Whithorn. My father accepted a call to a larger church, in Selkirk – a town in the Border district, much farther to the east, much larger, with working tweed mills, and set in rolling, forested sheep-farming country, crossed by rivers like the Tweed itself, salmon-famous. Needless to say, I had no voice in the moving, nor did I properly grasp its implications, for I had no idea what moving meant. I had not, after all, moved anywhere before. When we did move, time began for me, and Whithorn became my first loss. After a jolt of dislocation, I found myself in a place I could not recognise, full of strangers, everything to be learned again, and I begged my parents to go back. Bitterly, I mourned for Whithorn, in uncooperative silence, before I began to take a wary look around me. Selkirk was almost ten times as big as the village, and our house had a bigger

garden, lawns, a small wood, more and grander rooms, hills to
look at, even gaslight. It stood not far from the marketplace, which
brimmed with shoppers and gossip; it had a telephone and a con-
stancy of visitors; but I hung back from it, looking bewilderedly
backward through the glass that had suddenly slid between me
and a place that I had belonged to and that had also belonged to
me. Leaving Whithorn was my first experience of acquiring a
past; what I had left behind forever, I think, was the certainty of
belonging – something I have never felt since.

What kept Whithorn alight and gave it an Edenic cast in my
backward vision had to do with the natural world, the agrarian
round, a way of life I had seen and felt as whole. From now on,
these harmonies gave way to the human world, to other sets of
rules and obligations, to a localism we were still strangers to, as we
were to the different lilt in the voices. School began for me, and I
did not find it an arrangement that I took to, except that I realised
that if I were to go through with it I would know how to read at
some point, and the books in my father's library would open and
talk to me. As children, we were before long occupied in putting
together new worlds of our own, making friends, laying down
landmarks. In Scotland, the Border towns, ravaged across centuries
by skirmishing with the English on both sides of the border, had
an aggressive localism to them, something approaching a fortress
mentality. Not to be born in Selkirk, we soon found out, amounted
to an irremediable flaw; in the eyes of the staunchest locals we were
naturally blighted, outsiders by definition – a tag I accepted quite
happily, for I had come to much the same verdict about Selkirk.

Whereas Whithorn, with seven hundred people, had been a
particularity, Selkirk, with around six thousand, remained an
abstraction. Since it was bigger and much less remote – Edinburgh
was not much over an hour away – many more things seemed to
happen, and my parents' lives grew brisker; that made them less
accidentally accessible to us. My father had a larger study, upstairs,
with a window seat from which we could look south to the hazy
blue of the Cheviot Hills, where the border with England lay. I
laid an early claim to that seat as my reading post, and sometimes,
struck book-deaf, I would have to be dragged from it, my eyes

forcibly unfixed from the print. A large kitchen on the ground floor became a kind of operations room, which my mother ran just as energetically as she had run the smaller universe of Whithorn. Our household tasks multiplied, and the burden of a bigger garden spoiled my relations with the soil for a considerable time. With several doctors in the town, my mother gave almost no attention to medicine – at least, until the war loomed. My medical curiosity dried up for the time being; but my father, as if suddenly realising my new literacy, decided to teach me Latin and Greek, for he had been a good classicist. He was patient and enthusiastic at the same time, and I was a diligent pupil, for I felt that these lessons were at last giving me entry into my father's province. When I came to take classics in school, I was well ahead, but I kept the fact secret, because it lightened the burden of the work we were always scrawling away at with inky fingers.

Where Whithorn had been purely a rural community, Selkirk had a different class structure, in part agricultural – a way of life we were in tune with, although after dairy farms I found sheep country dull and somnolent – and in part industrial, for the woollen mills were clustered in the valley along the River Ettrick, at the foot of the town, and sounded their sirens morning and evening. Mill owners, landowners, farm workers, mill workers – the town had an intricate hierarchy. Again, ministers, doctors, lawyers, by dint of their professions, moved easily across those class lines, but the town itself was stiff with them. We found ourselves referred to as the manse children, and a certain expectation of virtue was pinned to us with the phrase. As doctor's children, too, I suppose we were expected to be models of health. My mother was the most downright of doctors, and, I think, suspected the sick mostly of malingering. We certainly could not fool her with imaginary ills; but when she had to doctor one of us with any seriousness we saw her change, as my father did on Sundays, into someone serious and separate from us.

Margaret, my eldest sister, and Lesley, my youngest, formed a kind of parenthesis to our family. It was Kathleen and I, closest in age and temperament, who compared notes, speculated, pooled information; and it was with Kathleen that I shared my perplexities over religion, my father's domain. We were by now used to his transformations from old gardening clothes into the dark formality, clerical collar in place, tile hat in hand, that a wedding or a funeral demanded; but while in Whithorn churchgoing had seemed a cheerful family occasion, in Selkirk the lofty, well-filled church wore a kind of pious self-importance, and church-going took on a solemnity we had not bargained for. Saturday nights, we would get out of the way early, leaving my father settled in his study, hunched into the small hours over the bones of his sermon for the next day. On Sundays, he would appear for breakfast already shaved, dressed, and collared, and would set out for church ahead of us, leaving us to ready ourselves for the summoning of the church bell. The manse pew, where we were obliged to sit, was prominently placed, so my mother, who took appearances much more seriously than any of the rest of us, decreed that, barring emergencies like the Great Plague, three of the four of us would attend church with her every Sunday morning – in a rotation we sometimes used as a trading currency. Churchgoing was something I grew used to, letting my mind wander about in an uncontrolled mixture of attentions; but as I took in the bewildering anthology of human faces – I gazed as often as I dared at a man with white hair and a ginger mustache – I was listening in a subliminal way to the cadence of my father's voice, mesmerised by the sudden incandescence of a phrase, fascinated by the convoluted metrics of certain hymns, stirred by the grave measures of the liturgy, aware of language as a kind of spell, and astonished when, freed by a dismissive organ voluntary, the congregation made its way out into the unsanctified air, and all burst out talking at once, as though to make up for the imposed silence of church.

But to be left at home one Sunday out of four, to be alone, with the run of the house – that was the time we coveted. We were obliged only to keep an eye on whatever was simmering on the stove. We were expected to be chiselling away at homework. But the whole house was ours for a church-length, and we could open otherwise forbidden doors, drawers, and books, and play the piano without fear of being heard, although sometimes I would wander slowly from room to room just to take in the rarity of the silence.

Everything had to be back in place before the gate clicked and the churchgoers tumbled in, smug with virtue but glad to be freed from the weight of it. Sunday lunches were events. More sumptuous than usual, they awaited my father's return, unrobed and predictably cheerful, for he had cleared what seemed to us his week's work – or, at least, its main hurdle – and the rest of the day lay ahead for us like a gift of time, before Monday dawned.

Kathleen and I at one point befriended Tom the Beadle, the church janitor, and, borrowing his keys, we would sometimes go exploring in the empty church: the halls underneath it, which smelled of musty stone; the cushioned vestry, where my father changed; up the back staircase into the church itself, and into the pulpit, where, however, we did not linger. In time, we learned to start the organ and play whatever scraps of music we had at our fingertips, but we were eventually banished by Tom, who feared, I think, that one day we would be tempted to pull the bell rope – his most public and audible formal duty. I feel that what perplexed us then was the sense, where religion was concerned, of having back-stage connections. I realise now that I never felt a religious fervor: for me, the mysteries lay elsewhere. Very clearly, I had worked out the idea that God, in some inexplicable way, was my father's boss, and I saw church services from backstage as weekly programs with minor variations. Besides, my father was much less a religious thinker than an instinctive comforter and clarifier. I knew that he hid his shyness behind an assumed solemnity, and what concerned me most was that his parishioners saw and heard only his grave public self, not the person he changed into when he came back to us, teasing, telling stories, gloom gone. He never laid down laws, nor did we ever discuss religion: questions of doubt or belief did not trouble him, for he was less interested in religious dogma than in its human translation. For him, being a minister implied the same human practicality that was my mother's dimension. We used to suggest to them that they work as a team, but in fact they did just that. It was in his human form that we worshipped our father. His more formal self he left behind in the vestry, with his robes. He forgave us our irreverence – he abhorred piety and did not make us feel any obligation toward virtue. Our family image concerned

53

my mother much more, but our natural anarchy prevailed. Their differences captivated us more and more. My father had infinite patience, my mother very little; and although she was as voluble as he was quiet, she never read, while I had entered a whole universe of reading, and my father would leave books lying about for me to discover. I always read during his sermons, a volume of Oxford *World Classics*, which were luckily bound like Bibles; my father, too shy to let me know that he knew and did not mind, always gave me a new *World Classic* for my birthday. Yet although I had moved into my father's domain of language, I still had a secret fixation on being a doctor – an unmentioned ambition I shelved once the war had begun, for medical students were exempted from military service and I had no wish to be.

Selkirk enclosed us in its rituals, Whithorn receded; and I suppose I began to think of it quite early as my childhood, my lost past, for the connections thinned and the haunting subsided in the frenzy of the present. I now think of that time in Selkirk, when the war loomed, as the beginning of disintegration – a movement from that once-glimpsed wholeness toward a splintering of time, the oncoming of many separations. We would never belong again, in that first sense. In Selkirk, I worked on farms in my vacations, and at a nearby grain mill with a waterwheel – the owner would give me work when I wanted it, and used to put away a part of my wages for me 'just in case', as he would say. I haunted the green and bountiful countryside, but it did not haunt me back. Still, the town grew familiar, wearable, and the vast house enclosed us, although in increasingly separating solitudes, rooms of our own. I can remember those years most easily by the steady progression through school; but we were well aware of the slow edging into war, and then, during the Sunday-morning service, I remember Tom the Beadle suddenly entering the church and painfully climbing the pulpit steps to whisper in my father's ear, and then my father's quiet announcement that war had been declared.

The war disrupted ordinary human time. For anyone over fifty, it forms a huge hinge in time. Nothing, we knew, would be the same again. Our childhood was over at a stroke. The town kept the skeleton of its old life going, but it became the center of a new and shifting one – troops passing through or stationed nearby, local people taking off into uniformed uncertainty, air raid drills, austerities, school periods given over to cultivating an enormous food garden, my mother becoming attendant medical officer at a recruitment center, my father summoned to serve on a variety of committees, blackouts every evening. From that time on, throughout the war, I cannot put my memory in any presentable order, although I can pull back pieces and happenings in abundance. The impediment to memory, I suspect, is that none of that time was chosen time. In the service, we were moved about the world by decisions so anonymously distant from us that they might have been dice throws; and whatever happened – grotesque, exasperating, ludicrous, horrible as it may have been in its happening – soon receded into impermanence, because forgetting made the war much easier to survive than remembering. It scarcely arises now, either in memory or in dream, for I have instinctively enclosed it in a warp outside real time. It makes no more sense in the memory than it did in its nightmare reality.

The war dispirited my father, and he brooded more; but we were all so occupied then that we never stopped to take stock. The war sent us children in different directions and gave years time to pass. We did not project any future, but after that we met as a family only rarely or accidentally. I felt that my past had been wiped off the blackboard, and that only when the war was over could my chosen life begin. Whithorn, our early Eden, our world without end, our calendar of growing, had vanished forever; and when I went home on leave just before going overseas I realised that our family had changed from a whole into separate parts. The war aged my parents, and when it was over my father moved back to the kindlier west, to a village parish, even smaller than Whithorn but tuned to the seasonal round. When I visited my parents there, separate though we now were, in time, in place, in mind, I saw how close they were, and how the corridor that had preoccupied me with its polarities had been more an illusion of mine than anything else. What I inherited firmly from my father was the way he used time. Knowing what he had to do, he gave his days a shape of his own devising, for he was not bound by any timetable except on

Sundays. Sitting at his desk in the evenings, he put his world in order. He owned his own time, and I wanted to do the same somehow. With my mother, I still argued, but we children had always had to bargain for time with her, because she had the kind of restless zeal that fumes at those who do not share it. I found among my father's papers a letter she had written to him when she was in her seventies, from an Edinburgh hospital during a brief stay, a love letter of such tenderness that it made me realise how close they had been, how dependent on each other, across what seemed to us the gulf of their difference.

★

After the war had cooled and subsided and I had separated myself from Scotland, my shifting life began – a long series of transitions. It was too late to return to the garden but not to inhabit temporary gardens. Of the string of houses and countries I inhabited, my memories are clearer – or, at least, clarifiable – since I can recall roughly why I was there, what I was doing, the people who came and went at the time. I still have many friends from those travelling years, and sometimes, scrambling about in the past, a friend and I will come up with something surprising and illuminating to both of us. My son and I, during our travels, spent three years at the end of the sixties living on an old Thames barge converted to a houseboat and moored in a line of others at Chelsea Reach, in London. Not long ago, we sat down and deliberately set about remembering. It was like dredging the Thames, for we recovered a lot of flotsam – sounds and sayings, the sway of the boat rising on the tide, the names and manners of our floating neighbors, incidents, accidents, the cast of characters who crossed our gangplank. We swamped ourselves with memory and returned to the present with a start.

Certain houses, however, retain in my memory a vividness that amounts to haunting – a mill where I once lived in the French Basque country, a street in Barcelona that became a warm locality, a courtyard in Chile that no longer exists, the stony house in the mountains in Spain that served as a retreat for more than twenty years, and that I have absorbed, stone by stone, to the point of being able to assume its silence in my mind. The addresses serve only as starting points: the places are there to wind in, when we have to recall them to clarify the present. But these houses were theatres for such a multiplicity of happenings, of human connections, of moods and modes, that they are mostly touchstones to memory, fixed points for it to start up from, because the houses have, for the most part, outlived our occupation of them. What I find my memory doing is reaching back, by way of place, to repeople past time, to recover lost presences, forgotten emotions. I think I remember more vividly through the ear than through the eye. If I can recover a voice, if I can fix the image and sound of someone talking, the atmospherics of place swim back with the sound, and the lost wavelengths reconnect themselves, across time, across absence, across loss. Voices remain living, and memory, for once, does not tamper with them. I can hear at will the measured phrasing of my father's pulpit voice, as I can the patient encouragement with which he led me through Tacitus, word by word.

I was with my father for the last month of his life, in a thick green summer, in the Border village he had come to rest in. Frail as he was, we would talk in the mornings, and it was to Whithorn that he always strayed, for it had remained his chosen place, the time of his life he liked to wander back to. He had once asked me, a year or two before, to take his ashes there when he died, and I had promised him solemnly that I would. The box of ashes sat in my desk drawer in London for over a year before I could make what is now a complicated journey back to that small, lost place; but I nodded to the box whenever I opened the drawer, and always felt the pull of memory, the trickle of forgotten details. I had negotiated for a small plot in the cemetery, and one Christmas I made the journey north. On a rainy, windswept morning, we buried the small box, attended by the incumbent minister and a small knot of aging parishioners, who remembered him and me. I called on those I still had attachments to, I walked the faint paths across fields more by instinct than anything else, I made a cursory visit to the manse. I did not stay long, for, inside, it had assumed the dimensions of other people – nothing to do with the images I carried. I did, however, verify that the corridor was not in fact endless but quite short, and found that the flagstones had given way to carpet. At twilight, coming back from a circuitous, meditative walk, I saw the manse light up suddenly in the early dusk, and it glowed through so many layers of time for me in that instant that it seemed like a ship that had been moored there forever, further back than I knew. I did not, however, decide to stay in Whithorn, although I felt myself no stranger.

There is a certain irresistibility about returning to past places: the visit may correct the memory or activate it, but it always carries an expectation of surprise. One fall during the sixties, I had to go unexpectedly to Edinburgh, and, seeing a bus that announced 'SELKIRK' as its destination, I climbed aboard it, on a sudden whim, and was soon lumbering south, sparks flying in my memory as the countryside grew at first recognisable and then familiar. As I stepped down into the marketplace, several old films were all rolling at once in my head, and I made my way through a close toward the green back gate, latched on a spring, that I had shouldered open a thousand times. I sprang it open once more, to find not the cavernous house that had been our adolescent battleground, not the towering elm and the monumental beech hedge it had taken me two days to clip into shape, but nothing at all. Open air, bare ground, an idle bulldozer, and a man steadying a theodolite where the yew tree I used to hide myself in had stood. The man told me that within the year a whole housing scheme would take shape where our house once was. I did not go into the past with him. All I found was a surviving sliver of the garden wall, a thin, teetering pillar of stone; but I left without taking even a piece as a touchstone.

> The house that shored my childhood up
> razed to the ground? I stood, amazed,
> gawking at a block of air,
> unremarkable except
> I had hung it once with crazy
> daywish and nightmare.
>
> Expecting to pass a wistful
> indulgent morning, I had sprung the gate.
> Facing me was a wood
> between which and myself

a whole crow-gabled and slated
mythology should have stood.

No room now for the rambling
wry remembering I had planned;
nor could I replant
that plot with a second childhood.
Luck, to have been handed
instead a forgettable element,

and not to have had to meet
regretful ghosts in rooms of glass.
That house by now is fairytale
and I can gloss it over
as easily as passing
clear through a wall.

My parents confessed later that they had not been able to bring themselves to tell any of us about the removal of the house; but the disquiet, I suspect, lay more with them, although Selkirk was a place they had never warmed to, never gone back to. In a country like Scotland, where to endure is all, razing an old house smacks of sacrilege, an insult to the past. Curiously, I was not particularly disturbed by its absence. Physically, it no longer existed, true, and so could not contradict or confirm by its presence the mass of memory it had generated. But I felt that if I were to apply my memory patiently I could rebuild it, restore it, people it, putting together the enormous jigsaw puzzle of detail to arrive at the whole-ness of a household. But, as Borges reminds us often, forgetting is not only desirable but necessary; otherwise memory would over-whelm us. What haunts me most of all, however, is that the house has not gone, nor have our memories been wiped clean of it. All I would have to do is find the thread ends and slowly reel it all in, from dark to light, as when, at the fall of dark, I would go round the selfsame house from room to room carrying a lighted taper. I would turn on the gas and hold the flame close to the mantle until it went *Plop!* and lit up, opening my eyes to a room that no longer exists but is there somewhere, should I ever want it back.

Letter From Edinburgh
1964

On a steely October evening, 1964, I arrived in a sea-smelling town on the east coast of Scotland and made my way to a neat white-washed inn near the harbor called – if I remember right – the Fortune Arms. There was room, said the innkeeper, and he pushed across a heavy leather-bound ledger for me to register in, I wrote my name, then my address, and arrived at a column headed 'Nationality'. There were five entries already on the page, and as my eye passed over them, I hesitated. Opposite the first and second was written 'English'; opposite the third and fourth I read 'British'. But opposite the fifth entry there was written, in a firm hand, 'Scottish'. The landlord was hovering behind me with the key, whistling impatiently between his teeth. At that moment, however, wild horses could not have hurried me to my room, for I felt myself in a profound dilemma. I am a Scot, right enough, born and bred, and in no sense English. At the same time, I am a citizen of the United Kingdom of Great Britain and Northern Ireland. I hesitated and meditated. The whistling grew more shrill. I put down the pen. 'Look,' I said, turning to the landlord. 'If you don't mind, I'd like to think about that column a bit. Would it matter if I waited until tomorrow to fill it in?' He yawned and shook his head, too sleepy to care. I went up to my room, not, as I thought, to sleep but, instead, to turn over in my head the strange hesitation I had felt, and to try and arrive at an explanation. I lay awake most of the night.

When, in 1707, the United Kingdom of Great Britain came into being, the very name 'Britain' implied a new entity and a new state of affairs, which, it was assumed, would be felt and reflected by the inhabitants of the countries involved, who would give up their separate national identities, would stop being Englishmen, Scotsmen, and Welshmen, and would become primarily British. In actuality, quite the reverse happened, mainly owing to the persistence of the English, who kept applying the term 'English' to things that were more correctly 'British'. Almost in self-defense – or, at least, impelled by instincts of self-preservation – the Scots continued to be quite aggressively 'Scots' or 'Scottish', and Britain, instead of becoming a culturally united whole, remained more or less a technical one, existing on the international scene but having little more than a fictional reality. In spite of union, Scotland and England remain as separate and distinct as they always were, and I know very few Scotsmen, Welshmen, or Englishmen who identify themselves otherwise unless they are abroad, where to be British is a diplomatic necessity.

That St Andrew's Night I attended a dinner in Edinburgh given in the baronial halls of the Adelphi Hotel by the Scottish Patriots, a non-political organisation that is particularly intent on the well-being of Scotland and things Scottish. My fellow-diners were a mixed lot, some of them young, raw-boned, and earnest, others red-faced and benevolent in full Highland dress of kilt, velvet jacket, jabot, and skeandhu. Some of the women were wearing tartan sashes across their shoulders, and all of us were presided over by a snow-haired lady called Wendy Wood, about as robust a personage as ever sang 'Scots Wha Hae', Scotland's surreptitious national anthem, and a tireless campaigner for Scottish home rule. On St Andrew's Night, she was at her most benign, as though she were celebrating her own birthday; she gave us dire toasts to drink, and introduced the evening's two speakers with a kind of jocose energy, beaming at what they had to say. It was no wonder. One was a prominent Scottish scientist who steadily deplored the waste and misuse of Scotland's scientific potential; the other was a Scottish Member of Parliament who had made something of a reputation for himself by shouting out for Scotland's sake on the floor of the House of Commons. The tenor of the speeches and of the stray conversation I overheard was pretty much the same: that Scotland was about to come into its own, that the day was not far off when it would be claiming its more than justified independence from England – a name that was never pronounced without indignation.

We paused at one point to think of all the Scots who, in parts of the world as far removed as Tuscaloosa or Tientsin, would be sitting down to eat haggis and drink whisky, as we were doing, and would be listening to many of the same songs that we heard in the ceilidh that followed the dinner. I left on the dying fall of a Gaelic song as unobtrusively as possible. I had to catch the night train to London, and I did not think it exactly appropriate to mention the fact. I also wondered for a second at the station whether it would not be wiser to go armed.

★

The facts about Scotland are fairly simple and straightforward; the country's wavelength, on the other hand, is enormously complex. Everyone more or less knows it by shape – the craggy, sea-horse top of the British Isles, fastened tightly to England on its southern border – and everyone certainly knows it by reputation, because the Scots have thoroughly and noisily infiltrated the rest of the world in numbers out of all proportion to the size of their country, which has a population of just over five million, as opposed to England's forty-three million. For the last three hundred years, there has been a steady flow of Scots out into the world, not simply as the proverbial ships' engineers or missionaries but in every conceivable context, each one with a wistful, misted memory of the small, stony, rain-soaked country that always seems to remain deeply rooted in his bones.

That Scotland is a part of the United Kingdom is an almost inevitable accident; at the same time, the unity of the English and the Scots should never be assumed. It was Sir Walter Scott who pointed out that the Scots and the English had fought three hundred and fourteen major battles against one another before their union; this kind of historical animosity does not disappear overnight. The fact remains that the two countries are altogether distinct in temperament and manner, and their conjunction, although it is by now a working one, has never been resolved to the satisfaction of either. Scotland is bowed under a woeful weight of history, most of it bloodstained and violent.

As children, we learned the wars by heart from our history

books, and muttered under our breath. Any English child who happened by accident to attend our school was in for it; we took out our history on him, and roared ancient war cries across the school play-ground. It never occurred to us once that the past was past. England was still the Auld Enemy, and we were never able to forget it. It is the Englishman's assumption of his own superiority, his apparent unconcern with anything other than himself, that drives the Scotsman wild. Scotland is a naturally democratic country, almost without class, where 'a man's a man for a' that,' and when Scotsmen run up against the intricate English class system, they are momentarily lost and bewildered, for they have little to refer to in their background that is at all parallel.

Of all the grievances nursed by the Scots, none is greater than the fact that the English apparently do not bother to hate back. Still, some of my English friends have owned up to an anti-Scottish disposition. 'What really gets me down,' said one businessman in the City, 'is this incredible myth – created undoubtedly by Scots – of their own reliability, their good sense, their business shrewdness. It used to be said in the City that a Scots accent was worth an extra thousand pounds a year. The Scots sound literally too good to be true, and they are, at that.'

When I returned to Scotland on this occasion – to Edinburgh, in particular – I was prepared to find some of the old grievances still alive, for it is a Scottish tradition to grumble. The climate of the world is now international, and regional differences are beginning to look more and more petty. Yet the principal fact that dawned on me this time was how little effect proximity and cooperation have had on the fundamental differences between the two countries. There is nothing in the Scots at all comparable to the fierce hatred of the Irish for the English; instead, Scotsmen look to the south with an almost comic contempt, an even cheerful dislike. But when I began to think a bit more seriously about Scotland's situation, and to talk to a few old friends and wise men, I found that there was a good deal more to think about than I had imagined, and that Scotland seemed to be heading for a future considerably less grim than the past.

★

Returning to Edinburgh for me is always an occasion for running
across old ghosts, for I was at George Heriot's School there for a
brief period, during which Edinburgh seemed to me the vastest city
in the world, being my first; now, when I return, I find that the
ghosts are little wizened fellows with tartan bonnets and red cheeks,
still eminently cheerful, in a small, windy habitat. For, in truth,
Edinburgh is almost a scale model of a city; it has a population of no
more than four hundred and seventy thousand souls, and appears
to have been laid out by a tidy-minded schoolboy with an eye to
playing soldiers. It is tucked neatly between the rainy green edge
of the Pentland Hills, to the south, and the silvered stretch of the
widening Firth of Forth, to the north. It earns its nickname of
Auld Reekie by being covered by a pall of sooty smoke for most of
the year – smoke that through time has blackened parts of the city
to great effect, since it looks like the stain of age. Edinburgh is
dominated by the great bulk of the Castle, perched on top of
Castle Rock, where it has withstood siege and occupation, near-
destruction and weathering since the seventh century – a kind of
encrustation of Scottish history. Down from the Castle esplanade
to the Palace of Holyrood House, the Queen's official Scottish
residence, run the streets that form the Royal Mile, and along this
famous promenade, under the wings of the Castle, clusters the
Old Town of Edinburgh – tall, small-windowed stone buildings,
typically, with crow-stepped gables; narrow, crooked alleys; pubs
and shops built, it would seem, for dwarfs; cobbled streets polished
to a shine by sheer footwork. Edinburgh has the attributes and
shrines appropriate to a capital city – the impressively volumed
National Library of Scotland; Parliament House, which, in the
absence of a Scottish Parliament, holds the Law Courts (Scots law
is quite distinct from English law); and as many monuments and
history-marked houses as any antiquarian could wish for. The air is
crowded with the noble ghosts of Robert Burns, Sir Walter Scott,
David Hume, John Knox, and Robert Louis Stevenson. And across
the street from Knox's house, I found what surely must be the
most enchanting small museum in the world – a Museum of Child-

hood, which does for toys and all the lineaments of childhood what the Louvre does for painting.

To the north, the Castle Rock falls dizzily and steeply down to a quite different Edinburgh – the New Town, which, for its time, was a quite extraordinary creation. In the early eighteenth century, the population of the city was crowded rowdily into the Old Town, within the precincts of the Castle. To the north lay open fields. Suddenly, as though the capital had decided to realise a new dignity, plans were advanced, and eventually accepted, for a whole new dimension of the city on this open ground – a scheme of elegant proportions. In 1778, work began under the auspices of James Craig and the architect Robert Adam, a member of the famous architectural family. The New Town was conceived not as a system of separate houses but as three parallel broad streets, each with an entirely distinct and gracefully designed façade – George Street as the spine, Queen Street looking to the north and the river, Princes Street as a terrace with a view of the Castle and the Old Town. It takes only a walk today to realise how magnificently successful the scheme was; the New Town gave Edinburgh another side to its character. The Old Town was crowded, intimate, comic, and cramped; the New Town, in contrast, was studied, graceful, aloof, and expansive. The architectural contradictions exist to this day, and Robert Adam is famous as a synonym for elegance. The New Town is part of the reason for the reputation that Edinburgh people have in Scotland of being haughty, aloof, nose-in-the-air; the Old Town, however, gives the lie to the legend. Between them stretches the green expanse of Princes Street Gardens, in the shadow of the Castle – a river of green that ought, ideally, to be full of water, as once it was. Instead, through it run the main railway lines to London, Glasgow, and the north. Anyone with half an eye would wish to turn the tracks into water, for water always gives shape and setting to a city, but Edinburgh, being truthful to its time, substitutes smoke for water, and for me, in memory, always remains the city of trains, of mournful whistles in the windy night, of arrivals and departures.

Princes Street has become a kind of Edinburgh tradition. On Saturday mornings, the idle, the curious, and the visitor make a

point of walking it from end to end; on the mornings of the international Rugby matches between Scotland and the other home
countries, it fills up with exuberant Welshmen, jocular Irishmen,
or phlegmatic Englishmen. Its shops have a fat-of-the-land extravagance about them, and it boasts more shoeshops than I have ever
seen concentrated in such a short distance. Over it towers an incredible Gothic pinnacle of a monument to Sir Walter Scott, and
at its eastern end, on the Calton Hill, there is an improbable
uncompleted replica of the Parthenon, which probably goes
toward justifying Edinburgh's title of the Athens of the North,
even though the title seems fairly preposterous today. When we
came to Edinburgh as children, we always had some museum or
monument in our sights, and they seemed to be inexhaustible; this
time, walking about, I had several *déja-vu* moments, mostly to do
with monuments. Edinburgh is very much of a walking city, all
the more absorbing because of the sudden change of atmosphere
between its Old and New Towns. It holds all kinds of surprises,
the most famous probably being the gun that is fired from the
Castle ramparts every day on the stroke of one o'clock. At the
sound of it, strangers generally jump a foot in the air, while the
local citizenry calmly adjust their watches. When I was a boy at
George Heriot's School, I used to have, from my corner of our
classroom, a clear view of the rampart from which the gun was
fired. Just a fraction of a second before the sound arrived, I used to
see smoke puff out (my initiation into the mysteries of sound and
light waves), and I generally managed to grab my books and be in
the playground that fraction of a second ahead of my classmates.
Nowadays, however, I jump like any stranger.

Such is the topography of Edinburgh. Its proportions are almost
perfect, its history is tangibly present, and it has all the majesty of a
true capital and infinitely more style than the other large Scottish
cities – Aberdeen, Glasgow, and Dundee. The rest of Scotland
tends to regard it as a cold, snooty place; some of the resentment is
that which always accrues to a capital, for it has all the vast head
offices of banks and businesses and no appreciable industry of its
own. It still retains from the eighteenth century – a high point in
Scottish cultural lift – a reputation for elegance and intellectual

superiority; it has acquired a certain international renown through its annual festival of the arts; and it does tend to regard itself as fairly exclusive, keeping outsiders on the outside. Within itself, however, it is intimate, cozy, graceful, and restrained, all at once, and it has a familial warmth. In one or two pubs, one can meet almost all the writers that count in Scotland, and the presence of the university gives a kind of lively tingle to the place. Those who make the pilgrimage to Edinburgh – to the university, to school (for Edinburgh boasts a pride of schools), to the large central offices – take some time to be admitted to the life of the place, and often charge the city with a coldness that it does not have, unless it is chap of the bitter and incessant east wind. The fact is that Scotland contains such a multitude of temperaments in its small bulk that the Scots find it difficult to have a perspective on themselves and their local habitations. Although I have never really lived in Edinburgh in any settled sense, I have never in my life let much time pass without taking the pleasure of returning to it.

★

The division of Scotland that is most commonly made is that between the Highlands and the Lowlands, and this was once as much a linguistic division as anything else. In recent years, however, the Gaelic-speaking population of Scotland has been receding, and the Highlands themselves – bare, mountainous, magnificently wild – have become seriously underpopulated. The Highlanders are Celts, and the Lowlanders are more properly North Britons; the difference in character between the two is enormous. The Highlander is graceful, soft-spoken, proud to arrogant, sly evasive, and irrational to the point of impossibility; the Lowlander is much more downright and blunt, less attentive to grace than to meaning, hardheaded (even thickheaded), and rational to the point of insensitivity. While the Highlands and the Outer Isles of the Hebrides have always seemed to me the most wondrous landscape on earth – purple, brown, gray, stony – they always look as if they might easily do without human life altogether. Their most serious depopulation took place around the beginning of the nineteenth century, at the time of the Clearances, when small crofters were driven cruelly off their holdings to allow large tracts of land to be turned into sheep farms for absentee English landlords. Many Highlanders emigrated at the time, and even now, in spite of the development of vast hydroelectric schemes, the drift away from the region is so steady that it looks oddly possible for it to be abandoned altogether, except by tourists who come to see a part of the world utterly untouched by human hand.

Gaelic-speaking Scotland runs down the west coast, taking in the Outer and Inner Hebrides, that clutter of toy islands, like Skye, Barra, Rum, Eigg, Coll, Tiree, and Mull, that have been nibbled away from the jagged coastline. In the northeast corner, around Aberdeen, lies one of the most curious parts of the country, brimming with song and legend, threaded with the great distilleries of the Spey valley – a region quite alien to Lowlanders. To the south of Edinburgh spreads the part known as the Borders, a rich expanse of sheep, salmon, and tweed country, with a trail of ruined abbeys once pillaged by the English. And directly west of Edinburgh, forty miles away on the River Clyde, sprawls the vast, smoky bulk of Glasgow. In Scotland, there is a marked difference between the east and west coasts, and between their temperaments; east-coasters are known for their silence and reserve, west-coasters for a warm and comic directness. The poles of the temperamental opposition are Edinburgh and Glasgow, between which there exists a fierce rivalry on almost every level of life. Glasgow is the ugly, burly, dirty, raucous, brawling industrial center of Scotland, with a population almost three times that of Edinburgh and a blunt, rude-tongued disgust for the capital, which it regards as aloof, unfriendly, and of little consequence. Edinburgh citizens tend to shudder at the thought of Glasgow and say nothing, and any form of competition between the two cities is uncommonly keen. While I was in Edinburgh, one of the local football clubs, Heart of Mid-lothian, beat Glasgow Rangers – who dominate Scottish football – by three goals to nothing. I went into a pub on Rose Street that evening, and the landlord brought me the sporting paper with tears in his eyes. 'Ah've waited near five year for this, sir,' he said. 'And three goals, an' a' – it's better than winning the war.'

Most of Scotland's heavy industry is concentrated in and around

Glasgow – the giant iron and steel foundries, the docks, the welter of shipyards along the River Clyde – and the belt of central Scotland between Glasgow and Edinburgh is also thick with industry. Scotland's unemployment figures until recently were running at a rate nearly double that of the rest of Britain, and, with something very drastic obviously needing to be done, the Scottish Council, a voluntary organisation that since the war has been applying itself to recovering a kind of intelligent economic health for the country, took it upon itself to try to diversify industry and provide more and varied employment. In Edinburgh, I talked with two or three of the Council's representatives, and found them eminently cheerful about the country's prospects, 'We set about finding new markets abroad – in the United States, particularly – and we tried to encourage firms from outside Scotland to come and settle here,' one of them told me. 'This has gone tremendously well, mainly because we have a lot to offer. We have plenty of space for new factories, and, best of all, we have a fairly sophisticated force of skilled workers looking for new jobs. The result has been not only enormous expansion northward on the part of English firms but investments here by over seventy American corporations – and inquiries from others come in almost every day.'

I found something of the same good cheer when I dropped in at the offices of the Scottish Tourist Board. Over the last five years, Scotland has become a greener pasture for some five million tourists a year – in spite of its climate but certainly because of its landscape, which can change utterly in the space of ten miles, with the colors, not predominantly green but purple, brown, and the blue of distance, often giving it a weird, unearthly look. The Scots, in addition, love strangers more than themselves, and tourists settle easily into the warm, intimate atmosphere of inns and small Highland hotels with stags' heads on the walk and warming pans in the beds. For the Highlands, tourism has been a godsend, since it has provided the possibility of a livelihood to forgotten villages and crofts that specialise in small, snug rooms and huge, home-baked breakfasts, (A Highland breakfast must be one of the most memorable meals on earth; it is not uncommon to conclude it with a large glass of malt whisky.) Fish and game are plentiful, and the Highlands are lairds' playgrounds and sportsmen's havens. Recently, too, a variety of small arts festivals have sprung up in the wake of the Edinburgh International Festival, which sets the city on its ear every August, flowered and flagged and teeming with entertainment. Over the eighteen years of its existence, the festival has gained a substantial reputation, although in Scotland itself there is a good deal of bickering about it. The grumpier of the nationalists complain that it is not Scottish enough, while the champions of the arts accuse Edinburgh of being sluggishly indifferent to culture. It has so far survived a series of onslaughts, and has brought Edinburgh a tinge of internationalism such as it had not previously known since the eighteenth century, Scotland being famously parochial. The country is hardly likely to become a tourist center like Switzerland, but tourism is on the up, and has caused local councils to pay a lot more attention to the grooming of towns and countryside, and to provide the kind of facilities that strangers ask for and that the Scots would never think of for themselves.

★

For the Scots, this conglomeration of facts and prospects leads to one question, which, if it is not exactly burning, does at least burst into flame every now and again: How satisfactory is the present state of the union with England, and how does it affect the efficiency of Scotland's functioning as a small nation? All over Scotland, you come across nationalists of various persuasions – some pure romantics, who dwell wistfully on the brighter times in Scotland's past and go about trumpeting the injustices of history, others romantics who hunger for action of some kind. Recently two young patriots removed the border sign from just outside Berwick, a town whose sovereignty has always been disputed, and replanted it three miles to the south, well into England, and in 1950 there was the famous episode of the theft of the Stone of Destiny, on which Scottish kings were once crowned at Scone, from its resting place in Westminster Abbey, whence it was brought back to Scotland. There have been even more violent incidents. When the present Queen ascended to the throne, she horrified a large body of Scots by taking the title of Elizabeth II, a title historically unjustified, since the previous Elizabeth had ruled England only, and not Scotland. When a letter box bearing her new title suddenly blew up in Edinburgh, the title disappeared discreetly from Scottish mail vans and was replaced by a crown. Squabbles and small incidents have always gone on; Wendy Wood explained to me how the Scottish Patriots stamp English banknotes with the legend 'Home Rule for Scotland' and are ready to agitate over every sign of Scotland's being slighted. Nationalism of the bag-pipe-and-haggis, self-pitying variety can become a bit tiresome, but there are many hardheaded Scots who, without particularly moaning through their bagpipes, see the present administration of Scottish affairs from London as being both clumsy and unsatis-factory. The issue of home rule has cropped up fairly regularly in the past; some twenty-two home-rule bills have been before the House of Commons at one time or another. The difference between the past and the present is that Scotland is on the way to developing a quite independent economic health, which gives the notion of handling its own affairs a much firmer basis in reality.

Briefly, what happens at present is that Scotland is administered from St Andrew House, in Edinburgh, the seat of the Scottish Home Department and the Departments of Agriculture, Health, and Education, the heads of which report to the Secretary of State for Scotland, a Minister of Cabinet rank who occupies the Scottish Office in London, and who, with his undersecretaries, works through the government ministries in Whitehall. In the House of Commons, Scotland is represented by seventy-one M.P.s, and it is over their situation that most of the argument develops, for they are inevitably party men – Conservative, Labour, or Liberal (the Scottish National Party still contests elections in Scotland, and draws a fair percentage of local votes, but not since 1945 has it sent a representative to Westminster) – and vote with their parties on major issues. The difficulty arises when local Scottish affairs are brought up in the House, since the Scottish M.P.s are in such a minority there that their local concerns tend to be pushed aside, and English M.P.s usually desert the House when Scottish questions are on the floor. At the same time, the Scottish Members represent Scotland's interests in such national matters as defense, foreign policy, and government spending – and it is this last that causes most of the grousing, for, considering what Scotland contributes to the national revenue through taxes, the feeling is that the country should receive considerably more than this back in government subsidy, and with industrial prospects so much brighter, this has become a major point of contention between the two countries. What with all this and the continuing administrative confusion, the idea of a separate regional Parliament for Scotland, sitting in Edinburgh and dealing with Scottish affairs, has been gaining a lot of ground of late, not as the whim of a fanatical fringe but as the considered opinion of those who have been reading the omens and looking clearly at the future. The question is not so much one of making Scotland a separate country as of giving Scotland much more responsibility for itself.

*

Behind all this is the peculiarity of the Scottish character, and there is probably more whigmaleerie written about that than about anything else. Scots are supposed to be dour, canny, pawky, coarse, fly, stingy, pedantic, moralistic, and drunken all at once, combining the severity of Calvin with the lasciviousness of Burns. They are characterised as a mixture of the legendary Sawney Bean, the grotesque Galloway rogue who consumed human corpses and lived in a cave, and David Livingstone (an ancestor of mine), who darned his own frock coat neatly in the African jungle. They are, as the saying goes, like dung – no good unless spread – and there is no doubt that Scots do get spread to a quite amazing degree over the face of the earth. There has always been a drift away from the stony barrenness of the home ground out into the expansive world; yet for wandering Scots the homeland never quite disappears. The odd thing is that almost everything said about the Scots is true, but never the whole truth – their character has so many sides to it. Dr Johnson had a wonderfully eloquent dislike of the Scots ('The noblest prospect which a Scotchman ever sees is the high road that leads him to England'), and even today certain of their qualities make English hackles rise. The greatest Scot-hater of all time was a journalist, T. W. H. Crosland, who in 1902 published a masterpiece of vituperation, 'The Unspeakable Scot'. Some of it is worth quoting, if only for the virulence of the prose:

> Your proper child of Caledonia believes in his rickety bones that he is the salt of the earth. He is the bandy-legged lout from Tullietudlescleugh who, after a childhood of intimacy with the cesspool and the crab-louse, and twelve months at 'the college' on moneys wrung from the diet of his family, drops his thread-bare kilt and comes South in a slop suit to instruct the English in the arts of civilisation and in the English language. And because he is Scotch and the Scotch superstition is heavy on our Southern lands, England will forthwith give him a chance, for an English chance is his birthright . . .
>
> When a Scotchman's parents decide that he shall be neither a minister or a journalist, or when a wee laddie who has been dedicated to one or other of these offices kicks over the traces, or turns out something of a failure, there are still splendid openings for him. Far away to the South stretches that land of milk and honey – England – and there is scarcely a square mile of it whereon you do not find either a shop or a bank or a factory, or some other 'hive of industry' created, of course, for the special benefit of Scotchmen . . .
>
> I do not think it is an exaggeration to describe England as a Scot-ridden country . . .
>
> There is no kind of man in the world who makes the drinking of furious spirit a *cultus* and a boast in the way that the Scotchman does . . .
>
> Whether he be a Highlander or a Lowlander or a mongrel, as he mostly is, it is just the same. He is Scotch, and compounded for the most part of savage . . .
>
> The Scotch are in point of fact quite the dullest race of white men in the world, and they 'knock along' simply by virtue of the Scottish superstition, coupled with plod, thrift, a gravid manner, and the ordinary endowments of mediocrity . . .

Crosland's book sold in great quantities, especially in Scotland, where it was greatly enjoyed. What is particularly amusing is his persistent use of the term 'Scotch', in a deliberate attempt to annoy.

To simplify enormously, there are essentially two kinds of Scots – those with a sense of humor and those without. The first accept themselves and their native characteristics without much difficulty, and get on with the business of being alive, be it in Scotland or anywhere else. These are the most successful and agreeable Scots, who never put the matter of being a Scot above the task at hand. Crosland's book must have given them great pleasure, for it took a sledgehammer to their more dour compatriots. The cheerful Scot is a fairly even-tempered citizen of the world – but, oh, his woeful countrymen, with a rocky, heathery chip on their bowed shoulders, girning over their lot! Tartan blood runs sluggishly through their veins, which bleed steadily; bitterness bogs down their oatmeal souls; and a mixture of whisky and sentimentality starts the tears in their bloodshot eyes. Out come the old, quavering songs, the despairing clichés, the wailings, the grumps. 'Here's tae us; wha's like us? Damn few, and they're a' deed!' It is a sorry thing, this inferiority, which breeds a compensatory puffed-up superiority. In it, meanness is all, and it makes of all things Scottish a miserable mockery, whether it is the exile sighing wistfully for 'the lone shieling in the misty islands' – a hut or small cottage, that is, and a place where, were he to see it in fact, he would almost certainly refuse to live – or the native Scot sitting down on January 25th to celebrate Burns' birthday, gorged with whisky and haggis, and grinding out the doom-laden clichés he has chosen to isolate from the works of the National Bard. Burns was a splendid poet, but what sins of mawkish misinterpretation have been committed in his name, for the humourless, bothy Scot loves a cliché not merely of language but of feeling. 'See ye the morn, Sandy, if we're spared.' 'Aye, Wullie, if we're spared.'

Doom. There is no doubt that all Scots grow up with some sense of it, springing in part from the landscape, in part from their education, in part from the Scottish Church, and in part from the heavy weight of history. Scottish history is a chronicle of constant and bloody struggle, if not against the English, then internally; one cannot read it even now without a sense of utter exhaustion. One of the bitterest periods of all was the sixteenth century, the period of the Reformation, which in Scotland took a violently different turn from Henry VIII's cynical throwing off of Rome. In Scotland, John Knox thundered Calvinism across the country, intent on casting out Papist corruption and establishing a truly reformed church, without bishops and administered instead by a presbytery. A whole century of religious confusion and bitter violence followed before the Scots were allowed their own form of Presbyterianism – a grim and stark one, which was won by blood and was maintained by the severest of disciplines. The shadow of Calvin still lies heavy on the land, frowning on pleasure, making a barren waste of Sunday, and insisting that life is something to be endured rather than enjoyed. There is no doubt that Calvinism appealed to the sense of hard logic with which Lowland Scots are endowed; it does not, however, take much regard of their flights of wild joy.

Scottish education has always enjoyed a formidable reputation, and Edinburgh especially is extravagantly endowed with schools, the graduates of which have found their way into many positions of eminence, particularly in England. But, again, Scottish schooling is a curiously stark business. When I was at school, we buckled down to a great, indigestible mass of sheer substance, so that today I find myself knowing things that I never realised I was taking in at the time. For me, Greek irregular verbs are unforgettable, simply because if we had not memorised our quota on any particular day we were given a good dose of the 'tawse', a broad leather strap, by a great brute of a classics master. And later, when I attended the University of St Andrews, it was to find that the curriculum had apparently not been changed much since its founding, in 1411. In silent revolt, we educated ourselves, running riotously around the library shelves; we came out educated, all right, but more in spite of the system than because of it.

So, the highroad to England. It is far from surprising that Crosland, even in his day, found London clogged with Scots. There was a time for all of us when Scotland seemed to shrink to the size of a parish and grow intolerably small, when its self-conscious disregard of the rest of the world was too stifling to endure, when life promised more than Rugby, ranting, and beery parochialism. That this realisation dawns regularly on Scotsmen can certainly be shown by the number of Scots who crop up in every kind of circle in London. No wonder Crosland felt himself put upon by Scots, for they were there, all right, and it is still a matter of glee to the Scots – and possibly of despair to the English – how successful has been their infiltration of the English scene. Sir Harold Macmillan, the former Prime Minister, is a Scot, and his Cabinet was studded with his countrymen; his successor, Sir Alec Douglas-Home, is by way of being a Border farmer. On the other hand, the bitter plea of Englishmen like Crosland for the Scots to stay at home is now being echoed with much more concern by bodies like the Scottish Council. Their hope is that, given some scope and some control, intelligent Scotsmen will stop regarding the highroad to England and points beyond as an inevitable progression.

*

One of the great misunderstandings and confusions about Scotland, both outside and inside, has been that surrounding the language. 'What exactly do you speak in Scotland?' Europeans have often asked me, and it is very hard to give a precise answer. In the first place, Gaelic, though a minority language, has its own literature and continues to have its own separate, healthy life. It is the language of the rest of the country that is so ambiguous, for it involves a kind of bilinguality. After the Norman Conquest, when French and Anglo-Saxon in the south gradually fused to become English, a form of this fusion – the Northern dialect – slowly spread into Scotland, where it was known as 'Scots', while Gaelic receded farther north. By the sixteenth century, both English and the Northern dialect were fairly well established, and had been given definition by literature. But following the Union of the Crowns, in 1603, Scotland was drawn into closer connection with England (also, during the Scottish Reformation an English translation of the Bible had to be adopted in Scotland for want of a version in Scots), and English speech began to be taken up as the language of fashion by those Scots who had connections with the court, in London. Nevertheless, Scots had quite a spell of dominance before English began to creep in alongside it. Even though English began to be used formally in the Church and the schools, the common people maintained their Scots, which, however, broke up all over the country into a multitude of dialects. This is where the curious bilinguality of Scotland begins. In the eighteenth century, Burns and Scott both wrote in a form of Scots – or, more accurately, in a dialect of it – and in English as well. But from the eighteenth century on, 'proper' speech for the Scots has been English, and local or intimate or familial or regional speech has been some form or other of Scots. When we were children in the Borders, for example, we spoke the local dialect with our friends in the town, while at home, since my father was a minister, we spoke 'proper', which meant English, though with a Scots accent. And today speech in Scotland runs a strange gamut, from standard Oxford English, spoken by those Scots who were educated almost entirely in England; through a duality of English and dialect Scots, spoken by those who have acquired standard English with education but still lapse on occasion, like me, into pure dialect; to unadulterated dialect Scots, which is still spoken in some parts of the country. This last, however, its uncommon now, for, with the BBC and such things, all Scots can speak English, though they are likely to spray it liberally with Scots words and turns of phrase, and many times they have a choice of two distinct expressions for the same meaning. I discover that when I return to Scotland my speech changes markedly; in the context of the country, it is natural for me to use Scots expressions and words that out of Scotland I would never think of using, for fear of not being understood. Oddly enough, hardly two educated Scots speak alike, and it would be impossible to place a Scot's class and background by his accent, as is so easily done with the English. A diversity of education and regional background gives each Scotsman a distinct accent, in-finitely more variable than the standard English accent, which will never quite sit easily on Scotland, since too many traces of Scots remain. There is no end to example. Recently, a friend of mine in Edinburgh used the word 'sorning'. I did not know it and asked him what it meant. He scratched his head. 'Well, it's a curious word,' he said. 'It's when someone comes to your house for a meal and just parks there and stays for several weeks. That's "to sorn."

Useful, don't you think?' Similarly, I know a cat in St Andrews that rejoices in the name of Skirlie-weeack, a word in Scots for 'a small person with a shrill voice'. A language in which you can still swither and scunner and talk blether and skyte is not likely to yield up its treasures to the flatness of BBC English.

But for Scottish writers the question of language can be a nightmare. The tradition of pure Scots literature is rich through poets like Dunbar, Henryson, Gavin Douglas, and the Makars, and, further, there is the legacy of the Border Ballads. The problem for Scottish writers has been whether to try to preserve or revive writing in Scots, which would inevitably reduce their range of communication, or to go over entirely to writing in English, a sad transition, since it would mean leaving behind the special qualities of Scots. About 1923, the poet Hugh MacDiarmid set in motion what surely must be one of the most interesting attempts in our time to restore a dying language to vivid life. In the late nineteenth century, writing in Scots had degenerated to a mushy parochialism in the hands of the Kailyard (or Kitchen Garden) School – a kind of sentimental whimsy that came to fruition in the writings of J. M. Barrie. (For Scots writers, whimsy is the great trap; it comes to them naturally and too easily, since it is their spontaneous form of humor.) In addition, there was the elegant belles-lettres tradition of Stevenson, but to MacDiarmid neither seemed to come anywhere near expressing the character of Scottish life. He set out with the grand conception of a Scottish cultural renaissance, the plan of which was to revive writing in Scots, using its syntax and vocabulary for contemporary expression. His own achievement was immense, and his use of Scots in books of lyrics like 'A Drunk Man Looks at the Thistle' began to show other writers the possibilities of using Scots in a fresh manner. In his wake came a whole school of poets who wrote in Lallans, as this old-new Scots came to be called. Unfortunately, Scots was not always the natural language of the Lallans writers and tended to become artificial and forced. At its best, in the hands of MacDiarmid, Sydney Goodsir Smith, and Tom Scott, it revealed the distinctive qualities of Scots speech – an intimate directness, a tenderness, a humor, and an intensely individual kind of expression. It is unlikely now that

Lallans will ripen into a lasting literary language, for inevitably its area of communication is small and it has depended on the existence of figures like MacDiarmid to give it its being. It also has the dangerous effect among lesser writers of making them put an awareness of being Scots over that of being human – the old national problem again. I have listened over the years to endless literary arguments raging in the pubs of Edinburgh – arguments that quite often ended in violence. I cannot think of any other place in the world where writers still fight for their poems' sake. Apart from the Lallans writers, there have been a few who have stuck to English but have tried to reflect their situation by introducing Scots words, expressions, and rhythms, and a certain unmistakable Scots accent. The poets Edwin Muir and Norman MacCaig and the novelist Neil Gunn have done this eminently well. It seems, in the end, the most satisfactory solution. Nevertheless, what Mac-Diarmid did for Scotland was to tweak its ear and show it how provincial and how careless of its own cultural tradition it had become; should the country flower in the near future, his will be the cultural example that it will take force from.

It is particularly interesting that the real artistic strength of Scotland at the moment lies in its painters, who at present dominate British painting. They are luckily spared the paradoxes in the use of language, since the eye makes its own expressions, and they have pinned down the extraordinary visual variety of the country. I talked to one painter in Edinburgh about this, and he told me that no education in color could ever prepare him for the amazement of a sail through the Western Isles. 'We are lucky to have been born here,' he said. 'It's like having a God-given palette.' Whenever I go back, I see the same thing. On one level, Scotland is all blether and argument, a crabby human context, a wild world of odd characters who seem inexhaustibly different from one another, who can enchant and annoy at once. On the other hand, it is a landscape so incredibly moving in its moods, its variety, its astonishment that I know I can never find another to replace it in wonder.

★

The notion of 'characters' looms very large in Scotland. My childhood, I remember, was full of 'characters'. They may have been mad, for all I know, certainly every one I remember seems in retrospect wildly eccentric. I recall Robert John Conning, who sang hymns all day as he paraded the main street of Whithorn with his hymnbook upside down; Charlie McEwen, the gravedigger, who had a child's passion for collecting silver paper and filled his cottage with it; old Willie Erskine, who once a year would walk the hundred and twenty miles to Edinburgh and back, just to remind himself how lucky he was not to have to do it all the time. These were not exceptions, it is just that in Scottish communities there is no norm and a minimum of conformity. The idea of community is elastic enough to accommodate the wildest differences and oddities of behavior, provided they are not to the general harm. A friend of mine who is a practising psychiatrist in Edinburgh remarked to me that had Freud known what Edinburgh was like, he would have moved there at once from Vienna.

This eccentricity is noticeable in one Scottish quality that outstrips all others – the ability to spin an endless, bizarre conversation out of the air, to talk for the pleasure of talking well. One evening, I went to call on Sir Compton Mackenzie, one of the most astonishingly varied men of letters that Scotland has produced and the most curious, kindly, and witty of men, who lived all over the world before settling down in Edinburgh again some ten years ago. A smoky drizzle had come down on the city, making orange pools of the lamps as I walked to his stately house in Drummond Place and made my way through forests of bookshelves to his study, where he greeted me in a jaunty pair of red cord trousers and a tweed jacket. We sat down and began to talk – not so much about anything as about everything, going where the conversation took us. For Sir Compton conversation is an end in itself, and he elevates it to an art – keen, urbane, learned, mischievous, delighted, and wise all at once. He talked about his vast autobiography, which he was deeply involved in, each volume of it covering a period of eight years, up to his present age of eighty-one. 'I don't suppose anyone has ever done this,' he said, chuckling. 'Write an autobiography accounting in detail for every year of his life. I'm doing mine in octaves, for my life seems to have progressed in cycles of eight years at a time. Thing is, I have a photographic memory. I can remember the names, faces, and voices even of maids we had as a child – I can even mimic 'em. And I was lucky enough to know almost everybody in my time – I remember meeting Crosland once, for instance. Frightful fellow. Thing is, I've had a curiously protean existence. I've lived in so many places – Brittany, London, Greece, America, Italy, the Channel Islands, India, England again, Scotland finally, and now France in summer. And I mean *lived*, not just visited. It's been a way of renewing myself constantly.'

'Do you think it comes from being a Scot, this habit of wandering?' I asked, for I had been wondering about that myself.

'Yes, I suppose it does,' he answered. 'We grow up in this small, wizened, parochial place, with England breathing away to the south like a domineering elder brother, and we want to fly as far as we can, to try out the world. Besides, I've always believed the Scots to be extra adaptable. They are sufficiently independent and self-contained to be able to put their roots down anywhere.'

From here the conversation took off in a whirl that, even if I could recall it, would still give no idea of the alacrity and richness of Sir Compton's sleight of mind as he sat in the lamplight, with his small, neat beard and his hooded, amused eyes. We talked about the differences between Jansenist and Mediterranean Catholicism, about his time in Capri in the heyday of Norman Douglas, about his books, about the architecture of Robert Adam, about Siamese cats. Eventually, we came back to the subject of Scotland.

'Thing is,' he said, 'I've never gone back to any of these places I've lived in, but I can almost remember each separate day in them, with that vividness which comes from being a cosmopolite, or a foreigner, or whatever we are to call it. Ever since I came back to Scotland, I have been able to appreciate it with a fresh eye. And it's a good place to come home to. The Scots, I think, have either a sense of natural superiority or a fearful inferiority complex, like those hordes of football fans who pour into London with their rosettes and rattles, being obnoxiously and aggressively Scots. No wonder everybody detests them. It's a splendid thing to *be* a Scot, to inherit this curiosity and thirst for the rest of the world. But it's a curse to be over-conscious of oneself as such, with all that hair-tearing and breast-beating. Heavens, I've always liked and been interested in the English, and found them amusing, if a bit limited. They make a frightful mess of everything, of course, but then so might we, had we the chance.'

He came to the door to see me off into the deepening Edinburgh gloom. I told him I was shortly going to South America.

'Oh, then, will you please write me in detail about Quito, in Ecuador?' he said. 'I've always heard that it has the perfect climate, and I don't like to think my travels are finished yet. In any case, we're bound to meet in Edinburgh again. It's a city that's made for coming back to.'

We said goodbye, and I went out into the windy, whimsical night.

★

Oh and by the way – about that column in the hotel register. I never did fill it in. I left early the next morning, before the landlord was about. I may, however, send him a note, for the record. Because now I know what I should have written there.

A Fine Day for the Gathering
1970

One summer in Scotland I found that the Strathpeffer Annual Gathering was to take place in a few days, coinciding with both my plans and my aspirations, for Strathpeffer is a hamlet in the vicinity of Inverness and I would be able to drop in on some of my Highland friends there. A couple of days before the Strathpeffer Gathering, I drove north, more or less up the spine of Scotland. What is staggering about that miniature country is the extent to which it can change, utterly, sometimes within as little as twenty miles. The low, grass-covered, sheep-sprinkled hills of the Border country give way to the smoky pall hanging over Edinburgh, which always seems too leisurely to be a proper city. North of it comes the Firth of Forth, spanned by the elegant arc of its new road bridge, alongside which the old Forth Bridge, well known to readers of children's encyclopedias, still stands like a sturdily devised spiderweb. Then across the hideous industrial belt of central Scotland, through the drab, slag-heaped wastes of places like Skinflatts (a name that ever since my childhood I have felt to be a synonym for desolation), and, finally, breaking free of breweries and coal mines, one comes into the opulent Perthshire hills. (Birnam Wood, I was glad to see, had grown luxuriantly back.) Signs of the times began to intrude – new inns and guest-houses, ubiquitous placards promising Bed and Breakfast, and a seemingly endless string of house trailers joggling behind cars, either going to or coming from the great unpopulated north. Here and there was a hiker, a cyclist, a clutch of tinkers, and, to my astonishment, the road was a real motorway – no longer the bumpy, rutted ribbon of my earlier journeys. So I swept easily into Inverness-shire, and civilisation quite suddenly fell away behind me.

Whole valleys stretched to the horizon, bare of houses, nibbling at the edges of a loch. Hawks circled. Rain would spatter down for five gray minutes, and then the sun would appear through a small chink in the sky, turning the roadsides a luminous green. In the distance loomed the Grampian Mountains and, beyond them, mysterious and cloud-headed, the great peaks of the Cairngorms. The landscape seemed alternately to open and shut, the road to squeeze through steep-sided mountain passes and then almost to lose itself across the enormous expanse of a broad, flat valley, the mountains to loom and recede, the sky to keep building up and disintegrating in alternate rain and sunshine. Once the Cairngorms had receded behind me, I pulled into Aviemore and had my first sight of the possible fate of the Highlands, for it had been transformed from a small, sleepy village into a spick-and-span, Swiss-looking ski resort, with a smart modern shopping block, chalets and parking lots, and a kind of Aviemore Hilton. The postmistress told me that it was never empty, and she looked flushed with her unexpected prosperity. One window of her shop bulged with tents, crampons, skis, and sleeping bags, and, outside, half a dozen Swedes were unloading rucksacks from a station wagon. Well, at least there was room for them, I thought as I set off north again, eventually crossing the drear moors of Inverness-shire (among them Culloden Moor itself, neatly identified by a new signpost, but still bleak and bitter to the memory). Inverness, at the head of Loch Ness, is the acknowledged capital of the Highlands, and that evening it was fairly seething with people and traffic – a bustling contradiction to the empty moors I had left behind. I caught the little ferry over the Beauly Firth – a parody of a boat which nevertheless carried me steadily across to Kessock, churning crabwise against the tidewater. Kessock is on the Black Isle, which is not an island at all but a peninsula of vast and rich farmland with a view almost all the way across Scotland to the west coast. ('If it werna' for the hills, we could just near enough see tae America,' volunteered the ferryman, without, however, showing much interest in the prospect.) I was staying with Neil Gunn, the novelist, and I found him waiting at his gate to greet me. 'The sky is not to be trusted,' he said, waving a hand at the piling clouds. 'We'll have a fine day for the Gathering, you'll see. Whatever the signs, that day always turns out well. Now come away in and we'll have ourselves a dram.'

We spent the evening talking, and for me it was like tuning in on a wavelength I had forgotten – a subtle, whimsical, gentle talk that hinted rather than stated, and an accent as beautifully cadenced as any you might hear. (Inverness speech is always cited as the purest English spoken in the whole country, but it is really the background of the Gaelic that gives it its tuneful softness.) Eventually, we got around to talking about Highland Games, and Neil began to bring back some of the occasions from his youth, when the local Games were the high day in the year, looked yearningly forward to and wistfully back on. 'We used to be weeks at running before the Games,' he said. 'We'd run to school and back, or we'd practice long jumps until it got dark, for all the small Games had one section of local events for the folk in the neighborhood, and open events for itinerant athletes and pipers. You see, there'd be a bit of cash going in prize money, and these fellows would make their way all around the Highlands in summer, from one Gathering to the next one, picking up what they could and doing pretty well for themselves. So they kept a section of events local, for it was more important to us to beat the lads we knew, especially if they were bigger than we were. That way, you see, you'd be able to bask all year in any glory that came your way. Oh, yes, and then there'd be all the goings on, the dance at night – we always got to stay up late for it – and the tales we'd collect to tell all week after, for the night of the Games was a rollicking one, all right. It'll have changed a bit, but not all that much, as you'll see.' We took a walk along the shore, where the curlews wheeled plaintively over the seaweed, and although it was eleven at night, the sky still had traces of high daylight, and the trees were only beginning to go from dark green to black. In late June in the Highlands, there is hardly any dark but, instead, a perpetual twilight that, when I was a child, stubbornly opposed me to sleep.

The morning sky looked ominous to me, but Neil laughed at me. 'Man, we have as great a variety of weather in a day here as the rest of the world has in a year. Besides, this is Kessock, and you're going to Strathpeffer, and there's a valley of difference. I've had rain falling on my house and not even on the wood beside it – *personal* rain, you might call it. And, while, I watch rain drift across from Inverness and miss us by a few hundred yards. But the Games will be fine. You'll see.' Neil himself begged off from the Gathering. 'I must have seen many more Gatherings than my seventy-odd years. and I can see them all in my head without stirring. You go along. I have a bit to do in the garden, and I've to find the moles that are at my lawn. Give my respects to the Convenor; he'll think I'm writing a book or something.'

So I set off across the Black Isle, the loam almost black, the oats and barley already ripe. I drove first into Strathpeffer itself, which I discovered to have been a popular spa for some two centuries – in fact, up until the First World War. It had a spa look to it – a kind of thermal elegance that is very far from being my cup of tea. A mile or two out of Strathpeffer, I came to the grounds of Castle Leod, the Seat of the Earl of Cromartie, who not only was the presiding laird but had also lent what must have been his paddock as the *situs* for the Strathpeffer Games. The hovering smell of crushed grass had me in a faint of memory. Equally, the raw-cut, temporary wooden fences, the cardboard signs, the lapel ribbons of the officials all smacked of a thousand sports days and Highland shows, fairs, and fêtes that I had blundered through as a boy.

I trudged toward the fenced-off oval of the competition ground and found it already ringed with a truckle of caravans, unfolding themselves one by one to reveal such legends as 'Gipsy Wilson, Oldest Living Gipsy in Scotland, Formerly of Epping Forest – Palms and Crystals', then an unbelievable (and un-Highland) 'Tanya the Tattooed Lady'. 'Hamburgers' suddenly appeared – a word that seemed linguistically out of place here. In the ring, things were beginning to happen, and I took a place close to the perimeter.

Although it was barely noon, the Gathering was in progress, but in a desultory way, for the Open Competitions did not begin until later and only the local events were being run off. As yet, the crowd was sparse, the attention laconic, eyes as much on the clouds as on the oval of the paddock. Small, gnarled, pine-capped hills enclosed us, and the weather was still anybody's guess. On a fir-bedecked dais in the middle of the field, a solitary piper was playing a lament almost to himself, parading around in a graceful slow march. Off under the trees, another set of pipes would whine into sound, then another, and another, as the waiting contestants suppled their fingers or ran over some complicated grace notes. From the officials' small, green-painted pavilion, the loudspeaker crackled, coughed, then told us, 'The piper you are hearing is Mr Duncan McFadyen, of Glasgow, and the tune he is playing is the "Lament for Donald of Laggan."' Poor Donald of Laggan. The lament had a strangely eerie effect on the piper, who seemed oddly lost in it, and on the two judges who sat on a bench listening to him, hunched over their crooks, deep in an ancient reverie. At one end of the field, the relay race for boys under twelve was being readied, and someone had been sent to find two missing boys, who were discovered having a last ice cream before the race. Down the center, where the heavy events took place, two kilted local farmers were whirling the light hammer – a lump of iron on the end of a wooden pole – loosening up for the event. The starter's gun set the boys off, and the first two puffed past, one running in his socks, the other barefoot. A little fellow with twinkling legs took over the baton and opened a wide gap between him and his fellow-runner, who was a head or two taller, inspiring us to a ragged cheer. The sun came out suddenly, the lament dwindled away, and the piper stepped down, mopping his jowls.

I went into the pavilion to have a word with Mr MacLintock, the Convenor of the Gathering. 'Glad you were able to come,' he said genially, shaking my hand. 'We're expecting a good turnout, and the weather's going to be just right. You know, we still all look forward to the Games, even though they don't vary all that much from one year to the next. It's a cheery affair. You see people you haven't set eyes on since the same day last year, and you get some rare fun. Where would you be from, now?'

I told him I was born in Wigtownshire.

'Is that so, now?' he said, in the soft Highland tone. 'Well, I was there for my holidays last year, and it's a bonny part of the country. Well, you've come a long way, now you find yourself in Strathpeffer. Come back in a wee while and take a dram with us.'

On the table at his elbow stood a pride of silver cups, which were to dwindle away steadily in the course of the afternoon. The Earl of Cromartie, Chieftain of the Games, leaned on his crook and received the respects of some of the locals. I felt that, coming from the south, I should have produced some sort of passport.

By now, the enclosure was filling up as cars bumped in over the turf to the edges of the ring and unloaded families, picnics, athletes, clutches of girl dancers in weird tartans apparently of their own devising, and whole kilted families, well buckled and sporraned for the occasion. Horse boxes trundled in, and more caravans unfolded along the perimeter, selling candy floss and tartan bonnets; a pair of bookies took up their positions for the horse races that were to follow. Another piper circled the dais in a slow, somnambulist's walk, skirling over the heads of seven or eight cyclists who were pushing and panting through the one-mile open handicap. Two spreading marquees were busy dispensing lunches and sandwiches; a third was a bar, already well filled and boisterous, with pipers wetting their whistles, and a pair of reminiscing shepherds adding to the ruddiness of their complexions. 'That will do, now, John,' the barman admonished one of them. 'You are talking through the drink.'

'Indeed, and why not?' the other replied. 'It's the truth I am telling you.'

The sun suddenly spattered the inside of the tent with the shadows of leaves. True to prediction, it was bathing the whole valley, greening the field and lending a sudden gaiety to the afternoon. From over our shoulders, along the track leading into the paddock from the road, came the first sounds, swelling as we listened, of a pipe band, and instinctively we all turned to the entrance to watch it approach. On the marchers came, kilts swinging, red tunics and red cheeks puffed out, immaculate white spats all in step, a forest of busbies, bonnets, bagpipes, and battering drumsticks, and a con-certed sound – they were playing 'Scotland the Brave' – that tightened the scalp and made the blood tingle. The pipes may well make people shudder, but, in truth, they have more to do with the pulse and the heartbeat, the landscape, nostalgia, an ancient exuberance in the blood, an antique grief, than with music.

Pompous as parrots, the band blew and battered its way past us, wheeled into the arena, stormed once around the oval of the field, the pipe major resplendent at its head, and came to a gasping halt outside the refreshment tents. Unslinging kettle-drums, letting the air out of the pipes, shedding their bonnets, the bandsmen turned suddenly into human beings, to our astonishment, and, finding ourselves back on the ground, we gave our attention again to the Games.

The kilted girls were waiting in a chattering group for the Sword Dance competition to begin, taking one another privately over a few steps. The loudspeaker crackled: 'We are calling now for competitors for the high jump, for which the Fraser Cup will be awarded. It is interesting that the judge will be Mr Fraser, who gifted the Cup, and who himself won the high jump rather more years ago than he cares to remember.' By now in the center of the field, the heavy events were getting going, and eight or nine giants in singlet and kilt, such as we had been accustomed to seeing all our lives on packages of porridge oats, were stretching themselves in readiness for a series of trials of strength – throwing the heavy ball and the hammer, tossing the caber, wrestling, a culminating tug-of-war. The pipes whined into life and caught hold of a tune, and the first quartet of Sword Dancers began to untwirl the dance, which was punctuated by an occasional falling high jumper and the thud of a weight on the grass. Four small boys came around the edges of the crowd carrying a sheet, into which we all rained coins. 'What's it for?' asked a suspicious soul behind me. 'It's for a good cause, sir,' one of them piped, and they were off, lurching under the weight of their booty. The sun was strong now, and the kilted giants wiped their red, perspiring faces, puffed, and reached for the hammer.

We were half an hour from the horse races that were to cap the afternoon, and, unable to contain my curiosity any longer, I ducked into the tent of Gipsy Wilson, Oldest Living Gipsy in Scotland. The inside was gloomy and smelled of mothballs, and I had to blink a bit before I could make out the figure of Gipsy Wilson herself – wrinkled as a raisin and wearing what appeared to be a tartan turban – crouched over a green-baize table. She waved me to a stool opposite her. 'Now, kind sir,' she began, in an accent elusively marked by travel, 'you have not come here by chance. Destiny has brought you before me. There is the simple palm reading at five shillings, but you may want to have the secrets of the crystal revealed to you as well. The ordinary crystal will cost you ten shillings extra, and the American crystal one guinea.' Unwilling to distract her from my future by probing this bizarre distinction, I settled for the standard (presumably Scottish) crystal, and, placing it on my palm, she began to peer and mutter. She proved to be a mistress of subtlety, especially where syntax was concerned. 'Would I be mistaken, sir,' she began, 'if I were to suggest that you were no stranger to adversity?' – thereby allowing herself to field a yes or a no from me with equal agility. After that, we got down to it. She did not, fortunately, tell me I would soon cross water, for she must have been aware that there was a fair chance of my crossing soon from the Black Isle to Inverness by the Kessock ferry. I admired her for that, and a bit later, when we had dispensed with a couple of dark ladies, a long journey, and some financial troubles that ended luckily in an unexpected blaze of riches, I began to feel quite good. Noticing this, she let me off with a few last gnomic utterances. ('People will always be seeking you out, sir, and what you are doing, you will do yet more.') Assured, finally, of a long and mellow old age, I asked her about her travelling life. 'I'm a Romany, sir, and no tinker, as you can see. My old mother was crowned Queen in Epsom before you was born, and I've been travelling all my life – no houses, no places, just the road. Summers, I always comes back up north to go around the Gatherings, as my mother did in her good time. They treats us rough in the south, sir, nowadays, but here in the north is where kindness comes from, be sure. Now then, sir, go lucky, and, as like as not, you'll remember me again one day. Now here's my hand on that wish.'

Stepping from the tent into the bright sunshine brought me back to earth. The sky had gone suddenly blue and brilliant, and the farmers in the bar tent had carried their nips of whisky into the sun. In the paddock, the crowd was thick around the rail, and no wonder, for the games seemed to be reaching a climax of activity all at once. Out of the woods on my left burst seven horses, their manes streaming, thudding past us hell for leather, their riders half eager and half terrified, as though undecided whether to whip them on or rein them in. The divots flew as they thudded away out of sight, and the wail of the pipes floated over to us again. A crop of girls over fifteen were joggling out the Sailor's Hornpipe, eyes down, lost in the intricacies of their own footwork. The heavyweights were now stretching themselves prior to tossing the caber, the event that always seems to epitomise Highland Games.

Nobody has been able to throw much light on, or to agree even approximately, where the caber competition came from, beyond acknowledging that it antedates the Highland Gatherings themselves. The caber is nothing more than a thick, slightly tapering log, some sixteen feet long and weighing about a hundred pounds. The log is raised to the perpendicular (at Strathpeffer this required the combined efforts of three panting officials and a boy), and the competitor bends down, locks his hands underneath it, hunches his shoulders, and lifts the caber waist-high, propping it against his shoulder to keep it perpendicular. When he is properly balanced, he staggers forward to gain momentum, and then, throwing his hands upward and outward, he attempts to send the log end over end, with the object of having it fall away from him in a straight line. The first difficulty is to time the throw so that the caber does in fact land on its other end and fall forward; the second is to give it the right impetus so that it does not fall off to one side. Watching a throw is a slow suspense – the raising of the caber, the balancing, the stagger forward, the heave, the thud, and the anguished moment when the caber seems to hang before falling forward, or sidewise, or backward, with a turf-shaking impact. Prodigious and legendary caber-throwers from the past are still spoken of in hushed voices – the great Sandy McIntosh, who at the age of seventy-one was still able to toss perfectly a caber weighing well over two hundred pounds, and George Clark, who in recent memory treated the largest and heaviest cabers in all the Highlands with easy contempt, sending them thudding perfectly and cleanly again and again. Strathpeffer had no such giants available, however. As often as not, the caber landed on its end, hung in space for a moment, and then thundered back toward the thrower. The crowd groaned. 'They're brutes, yon cabers,' said a little, bonneted fellow beside me. But at last, under increasing clouds, two throws in succession tumbled end over end, and the giant responsible beamed and waved.

Curiously enough, during the afternoon I went through a kind of metaphorical transference in my memory to the time, three or four years ago, when I lived in the French Basque country and there attended an afternoon of Jeux Basques. The Basques have the same ancient wisdom, the same 'old ways', the same pride, the same historical uniqueness as the Highlanders, and they have clung even more tenaciously to their localism, to the point of resisting any attempt to regard them as Frenchmen or Spaniards. The Jeux Basques, which I attended in Mauléon, the old capital of the Basque province of Soule, resembled the Highland Games in that the events were peculiar to the region and unlike any other sporting events. I recall an incredible relay race in which the contestants had to run while carrying a live, squealing pig by ears and tail. There were also heavy events, the most dramatic being one in which pairs of contestants first sawed through a huge log and then climbed on top of the two halves and chopped them neatly through with huge axes. The Jeux Basques were a triangular competition among the three French Basque provinces of Soule, Labourd, and Basse-Navarre, and they had a partisan edge to them that the Highland Games lacked, but the attendance was similarly local, the costumes were characteristically regional, and the good humor and the setting – Mauleon lies in a valley ringed by the foothills of the Pyrenees – were strangely analogous to the day in Strathpeffer.

*

As the clouds met and joined ominously together, the events at the tail end of the afternoon were jostled along in haste. Two tug-of-war teams were pawing the ground like bulls about to charge, and five diminutive ponies were being nudged into position for the last race of the day. A rumble sounded somewhere in the sky and the teams leaned back to take the strain on the rope. 'Hup! Hup! Hup!' they went, heaving and bursting with effort, while the ponies, instead of following the course, took off in all directions, ignoring their young riders. One piebald ended up in the car park, with a small blond girl sobbing despairingly in the saddle. The tug-of-war rope began to yaw in one direction, and the eight burly men on the wrong end of it toppled over heavily, like so many human cabers. A few large spatters of rain fell, and, looking anxiously up, we missed the second successful tug. The band donned drums, bonnets, and bagpipes, and began to form for its final round. The teams took the strain for the last tug of the afternoon. The ponies were rounded up by a burly woman who looked as though she might have tossed a caber or two in her day, and then, just as the drums rolled and the pipes wailed, down came the rain – no ordinary rain but solid gray walls of wetness curtaining off the hills, clearing the field of officials, competitors, judges, ponies, and spectators at a stroke. In vain did the Earl of Cromartie seize the microphone to thank everyone for coming and wish them all well, for there was hardly anyone left to hear him. I watched the pipe band retreat in rollicking disorder to their tent, from the inside of which, nobly enough, they tuned up and played us to shelter. From under the canopy of the refreshment tent I took a last, long look at the field, which had the appearance of an abandoned picnic. The judges and guests had gathered boisterously in the pavilion and seemed to be careless of the weather. Gipsy Wilson had folded her tent and magically crept away, unnoticed by me, perhaps forewarned of the rain by her crystal. A few bedraggled souls were stowing away their wares, but by that time not much mattered, not even wetness, for the Games had been observed, the sun had shone by tradition, and not a face showed anything but satisfaction.

I struggled to my car and drove off toward the Black Isle. Hardly five miles from Strathpeffer, the roads were bone dry, the sky was open, the sun was staining the hedges. I thought again of Gipsy Wilson, for the changing Highland weather must have been second nature to her. When I got back to Kessock, it was as fine an evening as you could ever have wanted, with hardly a ripple on the mirroring firth, and the midges hanging in clouds under the still trees. I found Neil laying mole traps along the edges of his lawn. 'Now, what did I tell you?' he said, smiling, when I told him of the rain. 'Their timing was a wee bit off, that's all. Now come along in and we'll have a dram.'

★

That evening, a few people dropped in on their way back from the Gathering, and the talk out-did itself, even for the Highlands. Some of the tales were uncommonly tall, and Neil caught my eye at one point. 'The trouble with us in the north,' he said, 'is that we get carried away by our own imaginations – carried away until we ourselves believe the things we're telling. Robert there, for instance. If you asked him point-blank whether any of these things really happened, he'd be astonished at you for intruding even a mention of reality. And he'd insist that if these things hadn't actually happened, they certainly *should* have. And they might even happen yet. But remember, we're telling *ourselves* these stories, as much as anyone. A fact never kept us awake at all – what might be is as much a part of our setting as what is. You might say we're prone to making a willing extension of belief. That's more like it. People are forever asking me if things in my books really happened – of course they happened, dammit, or they wouldn't be there. But *really* happened, *really* – now, that's a word I wouldn't be wasting much time over.'

An American painter who was present that evening told me afterward about his reaction to Highland conversation. 'What kills me is the crazy way they have of *reassuring* you about everything,' he said. 'You'll ask them if some place is a long walk away, and they'll say, "Och, it's just a wee step," and it'll turn out to be ten miles. They somehow just want you to feel good – I guess it's really that they're telling themselves that everything's all right. And, come to think of it, it is.'

Not a few of the stories that flowed that evening were about Highland Gatherings, and there was one in particular which I carried away, and which I still tell myself with a measure of delight. It is a true story, although it seems churlish to mention the fact. It concerns one of the Highland lairds, well known in the north of Scotland, who, inordinately proud of his lands, his ancestry, his position, and, indeed, the whole tapestry of Highland life, tends to overplay his role to the point of self-parody, taking himself most seriously. The peak of his year is a private Highland Gathering that he stages for his tenants, within the confines of a small, isolated glen on his estates. To it he invites an assortment of important guests, who watch the proceedings from a raised dais overlooking the field. The laird himself, acting the part of a story-book clan chieftain, and kilted from head to toe, directs the proceedings pompously from the dais by means of a microphone. On one of these occasions, his guests included, by some mischance, a rather haughty young Englishman who knew nothing of the Highlands and who watched the afternoon unwind through amused and disbelieving eyes. While the dancing was taking place, the young man turned to his companion and remarked, in a penetrating and delighted voice, on the conspicuous anatomy of one of the female dancers. Unfortunately for him, the microphone, which was close by him, had been left switched on, so that his remark boomed over the valley, convulsing contestants and spectators alike. The effect on the laird was terrible to behold. He purpled visibly, from his bonnet to his bony knees, and then, stamping three times with his shepherd's crook, he glared witheringly at the young man, pointed a trembling finger at the stony horizon, and roared out, in a voice that reverberated round the rocks, 'LEAVE THE GLEN!' Facts falter beyond this point, but I carried away a vision of the young Englishman, uncomfortable in his well-cut tweeds, clambering bewilderedly Englandward over the southerly rim of the valley and turning his back on the Highlands for ever.

Digging up Scotland
1981

I have a friend in Scotland, a painter, who still lives in the fishing town he was born in, grew up in, went to school in, was married in, raised his children in, works in, and clearly intends to die in. I look on him with uncomprehending awe, for although I had much the same origins that he had, born and sprouting in rural Scotland, close to the sea, living more by the agrarian round than by outside time, I had in my head from an early age the firm notion of leaving, long before I knew why or how. Even less did I realise then that I would come to restless rest in a whole slew of places, countries, and languages – the shifting opposite of my rooted friend. Walking with him through his parish, I am aware that the buildings and trees are as familiar to him as his own fingernails; that the people he throws a passing word to he has known, in all their changings, over a span of some fifty years; that he has surrounding him his own history and the history of the place, in memory and image, in language and stone; that his past is ever present to him, whereas my own is lost, shed. He has made his peace with place in a way that to me is, if not unimaginable, at least by now beyond me.

I spent a part of the summer of 1980 digging up Scotland and to some extent coming to terms with it, for although I have gone back to it at odd intervals since I first left it, I have looked on it more as past than as present. My childhood is enclosed, encapsulated in it somewhere, but the threads that connect me to it have long been ravelled. When I return, however, I realise that the place exists spinally in my life, as a kind of yardstick against which I measure myself through time – a setting against which I can assess more clearly the changes that have taken place in me, and in it. When I go back, I am always trying on the country to see if it still fits, or fits better than it did. In one sense, the place is as comfortable to me as old clothes; in another, it is a suit that did not fit me easily from the beginning.

Still, the landscapes of childhood are irreplaceable, since they have been the backdrops for so many epiphanies, so many realisations. I am acutely aware, in Scotland, of how certain moods of the day will put me suddenly on a sharp edge of attention. They have occurred before, and I experience a time warp, past and present in one, with an intense physicality. That double vision is enough to draw anyone back anywhere, for it is what gives us, acutely, the experience of living *through* time, rather than simply living *in* time. People's faces change when they begin to say, 'I once went back to . . . ' Something is happening to them, some rich realisation, the thrill of retrieval that pervades Nabokov's writing, past and present in one. Places provide these realisations more readily than people do: places have longer lives, for one thing, and they weather in less unpredictable ways. Places are the incarnations of a modus vivendi and the repositories of memory, and so always remain accessible to their own children; but they make very different demands on their inhabitants. In Scotland, the sense of place is strong; when I had left that attachment behind me, I had a loose curiosity about new places, and I still spark up at the notion of going somewhere I have never been to before.

Nevertheless (a favorite Scottish qualification), places embody a consensus of attitudes; and while I lived in a cheerful harmony with the places I grew up in, as places, I did not feel one with them. The natural world and the human world separated early for me. I felt them to be somehow in contradiction, and still do. The Scottish landscape – misty, muted, in constant flux and shift – intrudes its presence in the form of endlessly changing weather; the Scottish character, eroded by a bitter history and a stony morality, and perhaps in reaction to the changing turbulence of weather, subscribes to illusions of permanence, of durability, asking for a kind of submission, an obedience. I felt, from the beginning, exhilarated by the first, fettered by the second. Tramps used to stop at our house, men of the road, begging a cup of tea or an old shirt, and in my mind I was always ready to leave with them, because between Scotland and myself I saw trouble ahead.

When I go back to Scotland, I gravitate mostly to the East Neuk of Fife, that richly farmed promontory jutting into the North Sea to the northeast of Edinburgh, specifically to the town of St Andrews, a well-worn place that has persisted in my memory from the time I first went there, a very young student at a very ancient university. I have come and gone at intervals over some thirty years, and St Andrews has changed less in that time than any other place I can think of. It is a singular place, with an aura all its own. For a start, it has a setting unfailingly beautiful to behold in any weather – the curve of St Andrews Bay sweeping in from the estuary of the River Eden across the washed expanse of the West Sands, backed by the windy green of the golf courses, to the town itself, spired, castled, and cathedraled, punctuated by irregular bells, cloistered and grave, with gray stone roofed in slate or red tile, kempt ruins and a tidy harbor, the town backed by green and gold fields with their stands of ancient trees. If it has the air of a museum, that is no wonder, for it sits placidly on top of a horrendous past. From the twelfth century on, it was in effect the ecclesiastical capital of Scotland, but the Reformation spelled its downfall: its vast cathedral was sacked, and by the seventeen-hundreds the place had gone into a sad decline. Its history looms rather grimly, not just in the carefully tended ruins of castle and cathedral but in the well-walked streets; inset in the cobblestones at the entrance to St Salvator's College quadrangle are the initials 'P.H.', for Patrick Hamilton, who was burned as a martyr on that spot in 1528; students acquire the superstition of never treading on the initials. With such a weighty past so tangibly present, the townspeople assume the air and manner of custodians, making themselves as comfortable and inconspicuous as they can among the ruins, and turning up their noses at the transients – the students, the golfers, the summer visitors. Yet, as in all such situations, it is the transients who sustain the place, who flock into it, year in, year out, to the present-day shrines of the university and the golf courses.

The date of the founding of the University of St Andrews is given, variously, as 1411 or 1412: the ambiguity arises from the fact that in fifteenth-century Scotland the year began on March 25, and the group of scholars who founded the institution received their charter in February of that dubious year. Such matters are the stuff of serious controversy in St Andrews. As students, we felt admitted to a venerable presence, even if the curriculum appeared to have undergone only minimal alteration since 1411. A kind of wise mist enveloped the place, and it seemed that we could not help absorbing it, unwittingly. The professors lectured into space, in an academic trance; we took notes, or borrowed them; the year's work culminated in a series of written examinations on set texts, which a couple of weeks of intense immersion, combined with native cunning and a swift pen, could take care of. What that serious, gravid atmosphere did was to make the present shine, in contradistinction to the past. Tacitly and instinctively, we relished the place more than the dead did or could, and we felt something like an obligation to fly in the face of the doleful past. The green woods and the sea surrounded us, the library, and an ocean of time. When I left St Andrews to go into the Navy in the Second World War, the place, over my shoulder, took on a never-never aura – not simply the never-neverness of college years but as contrast to the troubled state of the times. It appeared to me, in that regard, somewhat unreal.

In its human dimension, St Andrews embodied the Scotland I chose to leave behind me. The spirit of Calvin, far from dead, stalked the countryside, ever present in a pinched wariness, a wringing of the hands. We were taught to expect the worst – miserable sinners, we could not expect more. A rueful doom ruffles the Scottish spirit. It takes various spoken forms. That summer, a man in Edinburgh said to me, 'See you tomorrow, if we're spared,' bringing me to a horrified standstill. 'Could be worse' is a regular verbal accolade; and that impassioned cry from the Scottish spirit 'It's no' right!' declares drastically that nothing is right, nothing will ever be right – a cry of doom. Once at an international rugby match between Scotland and England in which the Scots, expected to win comfortably, doggedly snatched defeat from the jaws of victory, a friend of mine noticed two fans unroll a carefully prepared, hand-stitched banner bearing the legend 'WE WUZ ROBBED'. The wariness is deep-rooted. I prize the encounter I once had with a local woman on the edge of St Andrews, on a heady spring day. I exclaimed my pleasure in the day, at which she darkened and muttered, 'We'll pay for it, we'll pay for it' – a poem in itself.

> It was a day peculiar to this piece of the planet,
> when larks rose on long thin strings of singing
> and the air shifted with the shimmer of actual angels.
> Greenness entered the body. The grasses
> shivered with presences, and sunlight
> stayed like a halo on hair and heather and hills.
> Walking into town, I saw, in a radiant raincoat,
> the woman from the fish-shop. 'What a day it is!'
> cried I, like a sunstruck madman.
> And what did she have to say for it?
> Her brow grew bleak, her ancestors raged in their graves
> as she spoke with their ancient misery:
> 'We'll pay for it, we'll pay for it, we'll pay for it!'

And my father, who gleefully collected nuggets of utterance, often told of an old parishioner of his who, in the course of a meeting, rose to his feet and declared, 'Oh, no, Mr Reid. We've *tried* change, and we know it doesn't work.' I noticed on a bus I caught in St Andrews on my last visit, a sign that read 'PLEASE LOWER YOUR HEAD' – a piece of practical advice that had, for me, immediate Calvinist overtones.

Some of that girn and grumble lingers on in the Scots. The choice is to succumb to it or to struggle energetically against it. Or, of course, to leave it behind – the woe and the drear weather – and begin again in kinder climates. What Calvin ingrained in the Scottish spirit was an enduring dualism. 'The Strange Case of Dr Jekyll and Mr Hyde' is the quintessential Scottish novel. The mysterious elixir of transformation is simply whisky, which quite often turns soft-spoken Scots into ranting madmen. Mr Hyde lurks in these silent depths. Virtue had to be achieved at the expense of the flesh and the physical world, in which we were always being judged and found wanting – the world, it seemed, had a vast, invisible scoreboard that gave no marks for virtue but buzzed mercilessly at miscreants. It buzzed for me. It buzzed for me and for Kathleen, one of my sisters, so regularly that we became renegades, outwitting the system when we could. In St Andrews, that dreich outlook regularly took the form of an audible sniff of disapproval.

I was born in rural Scotland, in Galloway, in the warm south-west, a gentle, kindly beginning, for we were bound by the rhythms of the soil, always outdoors, helping at neighboring farms, haunting small harbors, looking after animals, or romping in the oat and barley fields that lay between our house and the sea. My father was a country minister, my mother a doctor. Summers, we shifted to the island of Arran: fish, mountains, and green fields. My father's parish had upward of seven hundred souls, in the village and on the surrounding farms, and, as often as not, my parents' stipends would come in the form of oats, potatoes, eggs, and game. When my father, from the pulpit, read of 'a land flowing with milk and honey', I was overcome by the beauty of the image, and had no doubt at all that he was talking about where we lived, for one of my chores was to fetch from the rich-smelling creamery across the fields a pitcher of milk still warm from the evening milking; the honey my father drew, with our wary help, from the hive at the end of the garden. When we eventually left Galloway for the flintier east, a glass closed over that time, that landscape. We had left the garden behind, and how it glowed, over our shoulders, how it shined!

The peopled world, as I grew into it from then on, seemed to me to take the form of an intricate network of rules designed to curb any spontaneous outbreak of joy or pleasure. The black cloud of Calvin that still hung over the Scottish spirit warned us from the beginning that our very existence was somehow unfortunate, gratuitous; that to be conspicuous through anything other than self-effacing virtue amounted to anarchy. A God-fearing people – but the emphasis lay on the fearing. When I first took my son to Scotland, he asked me after only a few days, 'Papa, why are the people always saying they are sorry? What are they sorry about?' About their very existences, for they are forever cleaning and tidying, as though to remove all trace of their presence, as though bent on attaining anonymity. Nothing short of submission was expected. It seemed to me that the human world ran on a kind of moral economics, entirely preoccupied with judging and keeping score, while in the natural world I saw harmonies everywhere, I saw flux and change, but I saw no sharp duality. The two worlds were out of key.

A college friend of mine who later practiced as a psychiatrist in Edinburgh was fond of saying that if Freud had known anything about Scotland he would have left Vienna like an arrow and taken on the whole population as a collective patient, to treat the national neurosis, the compulsive-obsessive rigidity that permeates its population. Yet as I look back on my childhood's cast of characters I am always amazed at what wild eccentricities the society accommodated, given its stern center – what aberrant madnesses it managed to domesticate. It did so by marking out certain wilder souls as 'characters', thereby banishing them to glass bubbles of their own, and rendering them harmless. When I bring some of them to mind now – Pim the Poacher, who tracked down empty bottles all over the countryside and filled his cottage with them, all but one small room; Sober John, who read aloud from old newspapers in the marketplace – I realise that the people of the town unwittingly kept these poor souls safe by wrapping them in kindness. (A sort of impartial kindness prevails in Scotland, keeping stronger emotions in check – the kindness that takes the form of an immediate cup of tea for the distressed.) But the turning of certain individuals into 'characters' was also used to take care of dissident prophets and critics – anybody who threatened the unanimous surface of things. Similarly, at the University of St Andrews, dissenting students, if heard at all, were listened to with a tolerant, kindly half smile. ('Thank you. And now shall we return to the text?') Such a society must inevitably generate renegades, and Scotland has always done so, in droves – those renegades who turn up all over the world, not just as ship's engineers but in almost every outpost of civilisation, where the cardinal Scottish virtue of self-sufficiency stands them in good stead.

There is also, I think, a geographical explanation for the steady exodus of the Scots over the years from their wizened little country. Scotland is an outpost – the end of the line. It is fastened to England, true, but not by any affection. The union – first of the

Scottish and English crowns, in 1603, and then of Parliaments, in 1707 – created an entity, Great Britain, that has never really taken, in any deep sense. To the native fury of the Scots, the English refer to everything as English rather than British, and the fact that London, the capital, lies to the south is a constant source of irritation. The Scots' resentment of the English is aggravated by the fact that the English appear not to resent them back but treat Scotland as a remote region, whereas it remains, culturally, a separate country. But the sense of being on the receiving end, of living in a country that does not have much of a hand in its own destiny, causes a lot of Scottish eyes to narrow and turn to the horizon, and sends a lot of Scots in unlikely directions, the homeland a far green, rainy blur in their memory.

I had no such coherent notions, however, when I made up my mind to leave, for I must have been no more than seven at the time. Nor was it a decision as much as a bright possibility I kept in my head. We had been visited by a remote uncle, Willie Darling, who had gone to live in Christmas Island as a consulting engineer, and who spent his week with us illuminating that place with end-less stories, pulling creased photographs from his wallet, reciting the names of exotic fruits as we struggled through our salt porridge. What dawned on me then, piercingly, was that ways of living, ways of thinking were *human* constructs, that they could, and did, vary wildly, that the imperatives the Scots had accepted were by no means absolute imperatives (except for them), that the outside world must contain a vast anthology of ways of being, like alternative solutions to a fundamental problem. As that realisation took root in me, I was already distancing myself from Scotland – at least, from its more forbidding aspects. I had no idea at all about where I wanted to go, or how, or anything like that – only that I would. And I did.

St Andrews turned out to be my point of departure. I left it after a brief first year to go into the Navy, and by the time I got back, after the end of the Second World War, I had seen the Mediterranean, the Red Sea, the Indian Ocean, and enough ports of call, enough human variety, to make St Andrews seem small and querulous. Yet the allure still hung over it, and I felt it still –

felt the place to be, especially in the wake of the war years, something of an oasis. I have come and gone countless times since, returning, perhaps, because its citizens can be relied on to maintain it in as much the same order as is humanly possible. (In every town in Scotland, you will find houses occupied by near-invisible people whose sole function seems to be to maintain the house and garden in immaculate condition, as unobtrusively as they can. In New Galloway once, I watched a woman scrubbing the public sidewalk in front of her house with soap and water on two occasions during the day. She may have done it oftener, but I did not feel like extending my vigil.) The presence of the university and the golfing shrines has allowed St Andrews to preserve a kind of feudal structure: the university, being residential, houses and feeds its students, administers and staffs itself, and so provides a pyramid of work for the town, as does golf, whose faithful pilgrims keep hotels, caddies, and sellers of repainted golf balls in business. Others retire there, to its Peter Pan-like permanence, bringing their savings with them. As a result, the place has a bookish, well-to-do air, a kind of leisured aloofness this side of smug. I liked to imagine the wide cobbled center of Market Street set with tables with red-checked tablecloths, between the Star Hotel and the Cross Keys, crisscrossed with singing waiters – Italians or, better, Brazilians, carrying laden trays, sambaing, animating the place, rescuing it from its prim residents, forever hurrying home close to the old stone walls, eyes down, like nuns.

> I do not think of the academy
> in the whirl of days. It does not change. I do.
> The place hangs in my past like an engraving.
> I went back once to lay a wreath on it,
> and met discarded selves I scarcely knew.
>
> It has a lingering aura, leather bindings,
> a smell of varnish and formaldehyde,
> a certain dusty holiness in the cloisters.
> We used to race our horses on the sand
> away from it, manes flying, breathing hard.

Trailing to the library of an afternoon,
we saw the ivy crawling underneath
the labyrinthine bars on the window ledges.
I remember the thin librarian's look of hate
as we left book holes in her shelves, like missing teeth.

On evenings doomed by bells, we felt the sea
creep up, we heard the temperamental gulls
wheeling in clouds about the kneeworn chapel.
They keened on the knifing wind like student souls.
Yet we would dent the stones with our own footfalls.

Students still populate the place, bright starlings,
their notebooks filled with scribbled parrot-answers
to questions they unravel every evening
in lamplit pools of spreading argument.
They slash the air with theory, like fencers.

Where is the small, damp-browed professor now?
Students have pushed him out to sea in a boat
of lecture-notes. Look, he bursts into flame!
How glorious a going for one whose words
had never struck a spark on the whale-road.

And you will find retainers at their posts,
wearing their suits of age, brass buttons, flannel,
patrolling lawns they crop with careful scissors.
They still will be in silver-haired attendance
to draw lines through our entries in the annals.

It is illusion, the academy.
In truth, the ideal talking-place to die.
Only the landscape keeps a sense of growing.
The towers are floating on a shifting sea.
You did not tell the truth there, nor did I.

Think of the process – moments becoming poems
which stiffen into books in the library,
and later, lectures, books about the books,

footnotes and dates, a stone obituary.
Do you wonder that I shun the academy?

It anticipates my dying, turns to stone
too quickly for my taste. It is a language
nobody speaks, refined to ritual:
the precise writing on the blackboard wall,
the drone of requiem
in the lecture hall.

I do not think much of the academy
in the drift of days. It does not change. I do.
This poem will occupy the library
but I will not. I have not done with doing.
I did not know the truth there, nor did you.

When the war and the University of St Andrews were behind
me, I did begin to live what looks in retrospect like a very
itinerant existence. But there is a certain obfuscatory confusion in
the vocabulary: people used to ask me why I travelled so much,
and I used to say emphatically that I did not in fact travel any
more than was essential – what I did was live in a number of
different places, a number of different countries, a number of
different languages. Writing is about the most portable profession
there is, yet sometimes it seemed to me that I was bent on proving
this to be so by turning my curiosity into a kind of imperative to
go off and write about places that had whetted my interest. I grew
used to being a foreigner, but I chose to see it as a positive
condition, as opposed to that of the tourist and the exile, who are
connected by an elastic thread to somewhere else, who talk of
'going home' – a thing I never did. Disclaiming my roots, I
elected instead not rootlessness, since that implies a lack, a degree
of unanchored attention, but a deliberate, chosen strangeness. I
felt the whole notion of roots to be something of a distorting
metaphor, applicable only in certain rural contexts, like the village
I began in. What I was replacing a sense of roots with, I felt, was
a deliberate adaptability. I became enmeshed in the places I lived
in. The absorbing present seemed to me all there was, and I

acquired a kind of windshield wiper attached to my attention, clearing each day of its antecedents.

It was at this point, in the early fifties, that I stumbled on Spain – not by design, since I knew not a word of the language, or by any particular impulse the other side of sheer curiosity. From my first chance landing there, I was drawn in by a certain human rhythm, a temper that, the longer I lived there, I felt to be an antidote to my frowned-on beginnings, to the earlier wringing of hands. There is a frank humanity to Spaniards that makes them accepting of, perhaps even delighted by, their own paradoxical natures. Gravity gives way to gaiety, fatefulness is leavened by a vivid sense of the present. The people in the village we lived in in Spain had a way of standing on their own ground, unperturbed, unafraid, 'listening to themselves living', as Gerald Brenan put it. They all seemed to me to be Don Quixote and Sancho Panza in one. They enjoyed occupying their own skins. They had achieved human imperviousness. V. S. Pritchett once wrote of 'the Spanish gift for discovering every day how much less of everything, material, intellectual, and spiritual, one can live on' – a quality that appealed to me. And as I moved into the language more and more, I felt altered by it. To enter another language is to assume much more than a vocabulary and a manner; it is to assume a whole implied way of being. In English, if I get angry I tend to become tall, thin, tight-lipped; in Spanish, I spray anger around the room in word showers. Spanish, as a language, demands much more projection than English does. Hands and body become parts of speech. And then, of course, I began to read, discovering a whole abundance of literature that had been nothing more than a vague rumor in my mind. Spanish is quite an easy language to enter on the kitchen, or shopping, level. Beyond that, it grows as complex and subtle, in shading and tone, as any language does in its upper reaches. When I first met Spanish writers, I felt infinitely foolish at being able to utter no more than rudimentary observations, and I burrowed into the books they gave me, occasionally translating a poem, out of nothing more than zest. Translating was something that came to intrude more and more into my life, not so much out of intention as out of reading enthusiasm. But I felt in those first years in Spain that I was growing another self, separate and differently articulate. That experience was liberating, just as my first arrival in the United States had been – liberating in its openness and fluidity, as it is to all British people except those who cling excruciatingly to their meticulous, class-ridden origins.

I would go back to Scotland now and then, mostly in passing. It had receded in my attention, and I gave no thought to returning other than to reattach, in a fairly spectral sense, my irregular thread to the web of family. The point of going *back*, as I still said then, seemed an ever-diminishing one. People from my father's village, staunch citizens of St Andrews, members of my family, even, would fix me with a wary eye and say, 'You've been Away.' I could feel the capital *A* of 'Away' as a dismissal, a deliberate uninterest, and I conditioned myself to listen to the running account of local woes that followed. I would hardly have thought of referring to those occasions as joyous homecomings, although they had their revelations, mostly in the wet, soft, weather-stained landscape. They were nods in the direction of my origins, not much more. Scotland had become one of a number of countries with which I was comfortably familiar. I came across a poem by the Mexican poet José Emilio Pacheco, while I was translating a book of his, that so coincided with a poem I might myself have written that while I was translating it I felt I was writing the original. Here is my version:

> I do not love my country. Its abstract splendor
> is beyond my grasp
> But (although it sounds bad) I would give my life
> for ten places in it, for certain people,
> seaports, pinewoods, castles,
> a run-down city, gray, grotesque,
> various figures from its history,
> mountains
> (and three or four rivers).

It was not long ago that my friend John Coleman pointed out to me the Spanish word *escueto*, deriving from the Latin *scotus*, a Scot. In present Spanish usage, it means 'spare', 'undecorated', 'stark';

but when we eventually looked it up in Corominas' etymological dictionary we found that Corominas had an extensive commentary on it, remarking at one point: 'the word seems to have been applied to men who travelled freely, impelled by the practice of going on pilgrimages, very common among the Scots'; and he gives the meanings of 'free', 'uncomplicated', 'unencumbered', and 'without luggage'. The pilgrims obviously travelled light, probably with a small sack of oatmeal for sustenance.

The word absorbed me, for it is clearly a *Spanish* notion, or translation, of the Scottish character – a view from outside, which chooses to interpret Scottish frugality as a freedom rather than a restraint. It was just the word for the transition I was then making. In Scotland, I had felt cumbered; in Spain, I was learning to be *escueto*, unencumbered.

★

In July of 1980, I returned to Scotland with a more specific purpose than I had had on innumerable previous visits: namely, to meet certain friends and dig up a small plastic box – a time capsule – we had buried there some nine years before.

★

By an accident of circumstance, I brought up my son, Jasper, by myself from roughly his fourth birthday on. Our existence together continued itinerant – houses, countries, schools strung on it like beads on a chain. We invented a way of life that could not have a design to it, for we had no points of reference. At certain times, pretexts for moving somewhere else arrived, and we grew to accept these as omens. Spanish was Jasper's first language. Born in Madrid on August 9, 1959, he missed by about seven babies being the two-millionth inhabitant of Madrid, whose population now exceeds three and a half million. We rented an old house in Palma de Mallorca from Anthony Kerrigan, the translator – a house in which Gertrude Stein had spent a winter, we all later discovered, a steep, cool old house with a persimmon tree, close to *a parvulario*, where Jasper first went to school, in a blue smock, as Spanish children all did then. Waiting for him at the end of the day, I would hear fluting Spanish voices telling alphabets and numbers, an awe of first school in their voices. We moved for a year to New York, where I would walk Jasper to school in Greenwich Village and gain a new sense of the city through his eyes. But my father had been seriously ill, and though he had recovered, I had the feeling of wanting to be within range of him, so we sailed to London, and eventually came to rest in a houseboat on the Thames, moored with a colony of other boats along Chelsea Reach. There we floated for the next three years. Jasper walked to a Chelsea school along the Embankment, and would report sightings from the murky Thames – once a dead pig, floating trotters up. We took the train to Scotland sometimes – that northward transition in which the towns gradually shed decoration and grow starker, stonier, the landscape less peopled. The boat felt to us like a good compromise – we could in theory cast off, though our boat, an eighty-foot Thames barge, would, once out of its mud bed, have gone wallowing down in mid-river.

Flist, we called the boat – a Scottish word that means a flash of lightning, of wit, a spark. Many friends came to visit, some of them out of sheer watery curiosity. The boat rose and fell on the tide twice a day, and, with visitors, we would wait for the moment when it shivered afloat, for they would stop, look into their drinks, look around as though they had been nudged by something inexplicable. I was translating some of the work of Pablo Neruda at the time, and when he came to London he took our boat in with a crow of delight and ensconced himself there. He held his birthday party on the boat, a materialising of Chileans, and we had to fish from the river a Ukrainian poet, turned to mudman on our stern. Neruda surprised me on that occasion by insisting that the company return at noon the following day, without fail – not exactly a normal English social procedure. As they straggled in, he handed each one a diplomatic glass of Chilean wine, and the party began all over again. At one point, Neruda took me aside. 'Alastair, you must understand, in your country people telephone, probably, to apologise for something they said or did; but we Chileans, we have learned to forgive ourselves everything, everything.' I felt he was giving me cultural absolution.

The existence of the houseboat fleet was always being threatened by some authority: in the eyes of houseowners and solid citizens, there was something raffish, gypsylike, about our floating community, and we held occasional impassioned meetings, vociferously bent on repelling boarders. Yet on weekday mornings from certain hatches would emerge some of our number, bowler-hatted and umbrellaed, bound for the City. Jasper and I became enmeshed in the life of the river, however, and lived as though with our backs to London.

★

I often wondered about our shifting, our moving, and would sometimes bring it up with Jasper, obliquely, at odd moments. I worried about its effect on him, but the signs were that he travelled well. He felt no particular fear about changing places, and instead had become adept at taking on languages and mannerisms. Moving had sharpened his memory, and he would astonish me at times by his recall. He could evoke sounds, atmospheres, houses in precise detail. If I had told him we were going to Bangkok for a while, he would have immediately looked it up in the atlas, without alarm. I had to remember that in one sense he looked on places like London and Scotland and New York as foreign and strange, familiar though they were to me; but strangeness did not carry the aura of alarm to him — more the sense of another language, another way of being. I would concern myself with *his* feeling of rootlessness, only to realise that for him roots had little meaning. Not belonging to any one place, to any one context, he was in a sense afloat, and felt free to explore, to choose, to fit in or not — a freedom that in the long run made for a cool view. He did — and, I think, does — have a more intense sense of himself in Spain than in any other country. I had bought a small mountain retreat there in the early sixties, and although we did not go back to it with any calculable regularity, I saw how he lightened up whenever we did go. It was the only continuing past he had, and the villagers never failed to tell him how much he had grown, providing in general the trappings of childhood that our travelling life otherwise denied him. The house in Spain, however ghostly and remote it seemed to us from afar, served as the only fixed point in our existence. It was there that we took what we wanted to save – a kind of filing cabinet containing the keepsakes from other lives.

Our wandering life did impose certain restrictions: we could not, for example, have pets, because we moved in and out of the United Kingdom with such unpredictable regularity that the obligatory quarantine would have made them seem like children at boarding school. We had a more Hispanic attitude toward animals, looking on them as semidomestic creatures, whereas many of the English clearly prefer them to their fellows.

*

Inevitably – although there was nothing really inevitable about it – we moved. An invitation winged in to the houseboat one day from Antioch College, in Yellow Springs, Ohio (hard to find in the atlas), to teach for a year, and I accepted. We sold Flist, with many regrets and backward looks, and eventually shifted ourselves to a landscape new to both of us. The year was 1969, and the campus teemed and seethed; Kent State lay only two hundred miles away. Heralds came back from Woodstock with dirty, shining faces; no argument that year was less than elemental. At Antioch, we formed friendships that have lasted both vividly and ubiquitously; it was a year of fire, of passionate rethinking. Jasper trudged to a Yellow Springs school, and grew another American self, tempered by occasional nostalgic conversations and leavened by *The Whole Earth Catalog*, the handbook of the times. We had little idea of where we were going to go next, except to Scotland to visit my father, who was going to be eighty. So when the year ended we flew to Paris on a charter plane full of Antioch students chattering like missionaries, and wended our way north. To my relief, Jasper looked on Scotland as something of a comic opera, and I got glimpses of it through his eyes. He found its formality odd and stilted; he endured conversations that might have been scripted in stone. In a certain sense, he acknowledged it as my point of origin, but he made it clear that it was not his by suddenly speaking to me in Spanish in an overstuffed drawing room, out of pure mischief.

That summer of 1970, after spending some days with my father in the douce green Border hills, we took a spontaneous trip to St Andrews. I cannot quite remember how or when the thought occurred to us, but then, all at once, on whim, we decided to spend the year there. I had some long, slow work to do, and St Andrews boasted, besides its antiquated university, a venerable Georgian-fronted school called Madras College. On Market Street, I went into a solicitor's office peopled by gnomes and crones, and found that a house I had long known by sight was for rent – a house called Pilmour Cottage, not a cottage at all but an expansive country house, standing all by itself, about a mile from the center of town, in a conspicuous clump of elm, oak, and sycamore trees, screened by an umbrella of resident crows, and facing the sea, some five hundred yards across the golf courses. It looked across at the estuary of the River Eden, on the other side of which lay Leuchars Aerodrome, where I had first taken flying lessons, with the University Air Squadron, during the war, and which had later gone from being a Royal Air Force fighter station to the strategic importance of an advanced NATO interceptor base, manned by Phantoms and Lightnings, and consequently, I imagined, a prime nuclear target – an irony sharpened by those benign surroundings. I rented the house without a second's hesitation, and in no time we were lugging our worldly goods across a sand path that threaded through green golfing sward to take possession of Pilmour Cottage for the next year – about as vast an expanse of future as we allowed ourselves in those travelling years.

Of all the houses we rented, borrowed, occupied, Pilmour Cottage remains, in both Jasper's memory and mine, the warmest, the most ample. It had six bedrooms, a cavernous dining room with a long oak table fit for banquets, and a huge, encompassing kitchen, with a great stove like an altar, where we gathered to keep warm, and where we practiced the breadmaking skills we had acquired at Antioch. The kitchen window looked northeast to sea across the golf courses, and had a window seat where we spent a lot of time gazing. Day in, day out, in all weathers (and Scotland can assemble a greater variety of weathers in a single day than any other country I can think of), there trudged across our kitchen vision an unending plod of golfers, heads bent against the wind or frozen in the concentrated attitudes of the game. Jasper, bicycling back from school, would often turn up with a golf ball or two he had found on the path. We looked across at the square stone bulk of the Royal and Ancient Clubhouse, Camelot to all golfers, and we flew kites on the Old Course, their Mecca. It seemed somehow sacrilegious to live on the fringes of a turf whose sacred blades of grass were often clipped and mailed across the world as holy relics and not play golf ourselves; but we never got beyond acquiring a putter, which we would sometimes wield on the empty greens toward sunset, and an old wood, with which we would occasionally drive the lost balls we had accumulated into the whin bushes, to be found over again. The golfers were part of the landscape, like moving tree stumps; but one spring morning we looked out amazed to see the whole course dotted with tartan-bonneted Japanese, who had made their exhausting pilgrimage to play there for one day, and who insisted on photographing us as typical natives.

I looked from my workroom across the expanses of grass, sand, sea, and sky, quite often at the expense of my work, so mesmerising was that landscape. Wind-bare, sand-edged, with clumps of whin and marram punctuating the expanses of rough fescue grass, the landscape had clearly brought the game of golf into being. The Old Course at St Andrews has been both cradle and model; other golf courses can be seen as variations on its fundamental setting. The St Andrews golf courses, four of them in all, are grafted onto the town by way of clubhouses, golf shops, hotels, and wide-windowed bars – an enclosed world through which we passed on bicycles, still clinging to our immunity.

We settled into Pilmour Cottage as though we had lived there forever and would never move. All year long, a succession of friends came to stay, arriving sleepily off the morning train from London and opening their eyes wide when they saw where they were. We explored the countryside, we beachcombed, we sometimes even swam in the chilling North Sea. We wandered into the town and idled in bookstores, the stony town now brightened by the scarlet gowns of the students. Jasper took to saying 'Aye!' and soon had the protective coloration of a working Fife accent. One afternoon, we opened the door to a young man named Jeffrey Lerner, an Antioch student whom we had not known in Yellow Springs but who was spending his junior year (improbably, to us) in St Andrews, reading Scottish history. We all had many friends and turns of mind in common, and Jeff ended up renting a room from us, since we had rooms to spare, even with visitors. The arrangement worked wonderfully well from the start, for I was able to make some necessary trips, leaving Jasper in Jeff's care. Jasper was eleven at the time, Jeff twenty-one and the right cast for a hero, and I felt considerably relieved to have Jeff as an attendant spirit. I went to Spain at the end of the year, briefly, to settle up some matters in the village and to see how the house was weathering. I shivered in the stone house there, bare feet on the tile floor. Scotland was warmer by far, in a winter so balmy that we never once saw snow and throughout which we continued to fly the kites we kept building – elaborate kites, which stood in the hall like ghost figures and which we flew to enormous heights, sometimes even using them to tow our bicycles. Jasper and his school friends took over the outdoors and the trees, tracked through the dunes, and mimicked the crows till they rose in tattered black clouds.

Coincidentally, 1971 was the year Britain changed from its clumsy ancestral coinage to the decimal system. The *Scotsman*, our daily source of Scottish illumination, bristled with angry letters, and on the day of transition Market Street was dotted with dazed locals gazing at handfuls of glistening new change, holding up unfamiliar coins, shaking their heads, sure that the terrible innovation would not last. We hoarded the ponderous old pennies in a jar in the hall, and we had the feeling that the foundations were being shaken for once – that the past was, even in this everyday, metallic form, yielding to the present.

That year, August of 1970 until June of 1971, was the first I had spent in Scotland since I left it, and I found myself taking stock of it – as it, I imagined, was taking stock of me. The Hispanic world irredeemably alters one's notion of time, since it reacts instinctively, existentially, against the imposition of order from outside,

particularly the order of the clock, and substitutes human time.
Things take as long as they need to, and happen when they must.
That had seeped into me sufficiently to make me intensely aware
of the orderliness of St Andrews. Something was always chiming.
Punctually at five-thirty in the evening, the streets emptied; shop
locks clicked shut almost simultaneously up and down the street. It
felt like a place that had taken care to deprive itself of surprises. Jeff,
newly translated from the Antioch of the sixties, could not believe
the receptive obedience of his fellow students. As we settled into
St Andrews, the outside world grew hazy and remote. St Andrews
had domesticated it, making things predictable, untroubled. Yet I
felt that, once again, sitting in the middle of the landscape translating Spanish texts, I was more estranged than ever from the
formalities of the place. The presence of Jasper and Jeff, bringing
back separate, hilarious stories from school and university, set me
sometimes to trying to explain Scotland to them, and in so doing I
came to see how little I identified with it at any point. It was the
year that 'Monty Python' made its first appearance on British television, and in their eyes St Andrews felt like an endless rerun of the
programs.

In April, the Argentine writer Jorge Luis Borges came to visit,
on his way to receive an honorary degree from Oxford University.
Borges was much affected by being in Scotland, although his
blindness denied him the sight of it. He would take walks with
Jasper or Jeff, talking intently, and recite Scottish ballads to us
round the kitchen table. During the week that Borges spent with
us, the official census-taker arrived at our household. The British
are most scrupulous about the census, and the census-taker sat
himself down at the long dining-room table, calling us in one by
one to record not only our existences but a dossier of ancestral
detail. Borges; Maria Kodama, his Japanese-Argentine travelling
companion; Jasper; Jeff – I have forgotten who else, but I was the
only member of the household born in Scotland. As I showed the
official out, he turned to me, scratching his head, and said, 'I think,
Mr Reid, I'll just put you all down under "Floating Population."'
He had a point.

My sister Kathleen lived in Cupar, some eight miles inland from us, and in the course of that year Jasper discovered relatives who until then had been only names to him. Kathleen had five children, who formed a rambunctious household – a family that in human energy far exceeded the sum of its parts, for it put out enough to light a small town. Jasper was astonished by his cousins. He gaped at the whole bewildering whirl of family connection. Our own family structure felt tame in comparison – ludicrously simple. The fact of his having been born in Spain made the others peer at him as though he might be an extraterrestrial. The astonishment was mutual, for my sister's children were voluble and full of questions. By now, however, Jasper had grown expert at being a Martian. His three nationalities – Spanish, British, and American – had made him a foreigner in every school class he sat in, and he wore his oddness quite jauntily. He was, I think, ahead of me.

An early spring brought greenness and soft air, carpets of daffodils surrounding the house, larks, hanging invisibly over the golf course, disappeared into song. The days lengthened, and the golfers played late into the long twilight. We discussed building a tetrahedral kite, modelled on one with which Alexander Graham Bell had once lifted a man, and Jasper looked alarmed. He played cricket for the first time in his life, with a certain disbelief. I came one morning upon a gray heron standing in the driveway like an omen, and we gazed at each other for a full ten minutes. Swallows and swifts appeared, strafing the house all day.

It was on one of those spring evenings that we decided, on the spur of the moment, to bury the time capsule. I cannot remember who raised the notion or why – it may easily have come from a book one of us had been reading, or simply from whim – but once we had the idea in our heads we scuttled about, gathering up elements of the place we felt to be worthy of encapsulation. We found an opaque plastic box with a tight-fitting lid in the kitchen cupboard, and we poured into it first the jarful of obsolete pennies and then the contents of a box in which we had kept all manner of foreign coins left over from various travels. We got together some photographs and letters, the local paper (the St Andrews *Citizen*, which we read assiduously every week), other miscellaneous documents, representative talismans that we turned up at short notice.

We realised that we had to prepare a note to accompany the scrambled contents, and it was at that stage that Jeff pointed out that burying the box would be fairly absurd unless we expressed an intention to dig it up somewhere along the line. So, casting about for an arbitrary date sufficiently far off in time, we came up with Jasper's twenty-first birthday, August 9, 1980 – an occasion so unimaginably far away as to render us helpless with laughter, for then he came up to the height of the stove, and the thought of him tall and grave, with a deep voice, convulsed us all. We packed in the contents, signed our declaration of intent, made some notes on the day and on what we had just had for dinner, then sealed the lid on with epoxy glue. The twilight was deepening into owl-light when we went out bearing the box, a couple of spades, and a lantern lit for the occasion. It had begun to rain lightly as we crossed the front lawn and climbed over the wall into a clump of scrub and rough grass edging the golf course. We decided on that spot because it was public ground, and we wanted the place to be accessible when the time came. A small elm tree stood about twenty feet from the wall, so we chose it as our marker, measuring out an appropriate distance from it, which we all committed to memory, and set to digging. The box was duly buried and the soil restored – with unholy haste and an absence of ritual, because the rain was thickening and the lantern went out in a hiss. We hurried in to get dry, leaving the box behind us in the ground like a knot tied in the past to remind us of something.

Not long after that, a letter came inviting me to Mexico in the fall. It coincided with a vague plan I'd had of spending some time in Latin America, which Jasper had never seen, but with which I was becoming more and more involved, so, after Jasper and I talked about it, after he took a book on Mexico out of the school library and fixed Mexico for himself on his private map, I accepted. I had never raised the question of staying in Scotland, nor had he. Jeff was winding up his year, studying for final exams, making plans – first, to ship out on a French fishing boat, which he did from Lorient, in Brittany, and then to make his way back to Antioch, by way of our house in Spain. The end of spring was crowned by school sports day, the departure of students; my own work was almost finished. When Jeff left, the suspension in which we had lived all year was broken, and we found ourselves back in time. Our lease on Pilmour Cottage would soon be up, and I made plans to go to Spain on the way to Mexico, and once more assembled our worldly goods, dividing what to abandon from what to keep.

There were rituals of passage, leave-takings, last walks, backward looks. We had arrived in and gone from places so often, and seen so many people leave, that we were familiar with all the facets of departing. When the moment came, we took a long look over our shoulders at Pilmour Cottage from the Cupar Road, with a certain quick pang – the house across that low-lying landscape already half hidden in its own elms and pines, the crows hovering. Pilmour Cottage began to dwindle away in an odd kind of smoke. We had already forgotten the box in the ground.

★

For Jasper and me, the summer in Spain quickly became the present – a preoccupying present, because we were putting a new roof on the house there, sleeping, out of necessity, in the ilex forest, and catching up on village matters, changing languages again. Pilmour Cottage had gone into the archives. Certain appendages of it – a wooden spoon, a few golf balls, an etching of St Andrews someone had given us in farewell – joined the array of keepsakes in the Spanish house. Jasper sometimes mentioned Pilmour, already handling the memory like a momento, a token. We caught a boat from Barcelona to Venezuela in early fall and made our way to Mexico. Jasper attended an international school in Cuernavaca, learning, it seemed to me, not much more than the Mexican national anthem, but that indelibly. We spent some time in Mexico City with the exiled Spanish writer Max Aub, an old mentor of mine – and an inspiring presence, because he was forever inventing imaginary writers, writing their works, and then entering into controversy with them. Late in the year, we took a freighter from Tampico to Buenos Aires, stopping, apparently at the captain's whim, along the South American coast. It was almost Christmas by the time we reached Buenos Aires – the beginning of summer there, which meant that all schools were closed. So during our time there and, later, in Chile – the hopeful Chile of Allende, before things began to fray away – Jasper went schoolless, but he was never at loose ends, for the Chile of those days made St Andrews (or would have, if we had ever thought of it) more like an invention of ours, a place we had once dreamed up, a place where nothing happened, as different from Chile as was imaginable.

After that long wander, we came to rest in London. It seemed to me imperative that, with such patchwork schooling, Jasper should finish up within one school system, with a semblance of order to it. So he went to school in Highgate and came to terms with England. Apart from irregular sallies to Spain, we stayed put for four years.

Jeff, meanwhile, had finished up at Antioch, had married Nora Newcombe, a redheaded and warm-witted Canadian girl, who had visited us at Pilmour, and who was doing a Ph.D. in psychology at Harvard. We did not see them for a long while, but we wrote when it seemed unforgivable not to. Then the work Jeff was doing – a Ph.D. thesis on the shifting attitudes toward bereavement in the course and aftermath of the First World War – brought them to London one summer, and we fell excitedly to filling in the missing time. With Nora and Jeff an ease of connection had existed from the very beginning, where we never tired of talking and noticing. The connection they had with Jasper was particularly important in my eyes, and I knew that it was in theirs: they paced his growing, their persistence as recurring friends a matter of great import to him, since he always had so many things to tell them, to ask them, when we met up. We had occasional, surreal, smokily distant conversations about Scotland; but we did not talk about the box.

I went to Scotland off and on from London. My parents grew frailer; my mother died, as emphatically as she had lived; and my father moved between the houses of two of my sisters, where I would go to visit him. On one of these visits, while he was living with Kathleen, I drove over to Pilmour Cottage, took a mooning walk around the house and climbed over the wall to the vicinity of the elm tree. The ground had a thick undergrowth, but I could still feel, at the appropriate distance from the tree as I calculated it, a recognisable hollow, a comforting sag in the ground.

★

From 1970, five years passed without my coming to the United States – an unimaginable hiatus, for I had been in that country almost every year, or some part of it, since I first came at the end of the forties. I'm not sure now why that hiatus developed, except that we were more European-minded at the time, and that in London friends from New York were always passing through, giving us the illusion of being in touch. I was working, also, through another long scrabble of translation, and I was caught up in the flurry of disaster that followed the coup in Chile – Chileans arriving in London, anxieties of not knowing – and in the obvious withering away of Franco in Spain. In the summer of 1975, however, some pretext arose for my going to the United States, and I decided to take Jasper, since he had not seen any of his American relatives in a long time, let alone the landmarks he remembered. New York felt sunny after London – not literally but humanly. I warmed myself with friends I had not seen in too long. Londoners are scrupulous about one another's privacy, and New York seemed loose and luxurious after the primness of the London years. We did, however, spend those London years in Victoria, a neighborhood that had become the headquarters of Spaniards who had left Spain in those lean times to find work elsewhere in Europe, so I 'shopped in Spanish at the street market, kept up with the Spanish football scores, and would translate the odd will or document into English for Dona Angelina, who ran a Spanish boardinghouse close to where we lived, and who knew our Spanish village well.

The United States this time had as visibly liberating an effect on Jasper as it had had on me at first gasp. I could see him taking forgotten selves out of the closet and shaking the dust from them. From this vantage point, London seemed suddenly such a polite place – if anything, overcivilised. When I returned to it, in midsummer, it was with a surge of that extra energy I have always absorbed while visiting New York (though not necessarily while living in it). But I returned for a specific purpose; namely, to take my father back to the house he had lived in in the Borders, in order to give my sisters something of a break. Poor old man, he was already tired of his long existence, although he had bright moments. He rested at least half of each thick, green summer day,

and again I found myself sitting, alone, in that shifting landscape,
writing, wondering, while my father moved closer to dying, too
tired, eventually, to say another word. He died as that summer
mellowed into September, the way it does in Scotland.

> At summer's succulent end,
> the house is green-stained.
> I reach for my father's hand
>
> and study his ancient nails.
> Feeble-bodied, yet at intervals
> a sweetness appears and prevails.
>
> The heavy-scented night
> seems to get at his throat.
> It is as if the dark coughed.
>
> In the other rooms of the house,
> the furniture stands mumchance
> Age has graved his face.
>
> Cradling his wagged-out chin,
> I shave him, feeling bone
> stretching the waxed skin.
>
> By his bed, the newspaper lies furled.
> He has grown too old
> to unfold the world,
>
> which has dwindled to the size of a sheet.
> His room has a stillness to it
> I do not call it waiting, but I wait,
>
> anxious in the dark, to see if
> the butterfly of his breath
> has fluttered clear of death.
>
> There is so much might be said,
> dear old man, before I find you dead;
> but we have become too separate

now in human time
to unravel all the interim
as your memory goes numb.

But there is no need for you to tell –
no words, no wise counsel,
no talk of dying well.

We have become mostly hands
and voices in your understanding.
The whole household is pending.

I am not ready
to be without your frail and wasted body,
your miscellaneous mind-way,

the faltering vein of your life.
Each evening, I am loath
to leave you to your death.

Nor will I dwell on
the endless, cumulative question
I ask, being your son.

But on any one
of these nights soon,
for you, the dark will not crack with dawn,

and then I will begin
with you that hesitant conversation
going on and on and on.

Jasper finished school in London in 1977, and so we shuttered up
the Victoria flat (which I had rented from Lesley, another sister of
mine) and came to the United States again, I on my way to Costa
Rica, Jasper to find himself a job for a year before going to college.
I had been with him, mostly, for close to fourteen years, and there
were moments at first when I would suddenly feel that it was time
I got home, only to remember that there was no particular reason,
no urgency. We were both relieved to separate, I think, for we
needed our own lives, and Jasper seemed quite adept at running

his. Time passed, comings and goings. Nora was appointed assistant professor of Psychology at Penn State, and she and Jeff moved there, Jeff still lugging his thesis with him. I went to Brazil, to England. When I got back to New York, Jasper announced to me that he had been accepted at Yale. We could think of nothing to do immediately but laugh our heads off.

On New Year's Day of 1980, the day before I left for Puerto Rico, we had a party at my apartment in Greenwich Village, for Jeff and Nora were in New York, Jasper had a job in the city over Christmas, and other friends were stopping by from various places. Sometime during the day, Jasper, Nora, Jeff, and I found ourselves sitting round the table practicing writing '1980' on the white table-top. It dawned on us all at the same moment, as though someone had tugged at the knot, that ahead, in summer, lay the box in the ground. We did our share of comic head-shaking and hand-wringing, in the Scottish manner, and then we drew ourselves up, Jasper taller now than we could ever have imagined, and took solemn vows to present ourselves in Scotland in August.

★

In mid-July, I prepared to leave New York, first for London, where I had to see friends, and then for Scotland, because I had not really been back since my father died. I had some work to do in Edin-burgh, and I wanted to be sure of having a place to house the others if they turned up. There was a measure of doubt. I could not get hold of Nora and Jeff, who were somewhere in Philadelphia, and all I could do was leave them a message that I was going. Jasper was driving a taxicab in New York, and was rueful, in the way of students, about time and money. We considered for a moment postponing the disinterment until we were all more moneyed and more leisured, and horrified ourselves by the thought. So I left. I passed through London, took the train north once again, and landed in late July at Kathleen's house in Cupar, in the mainstream of a rained-out summer that was causing even the natives to grumble in disgust.

Kathleen and I have always shared an easy dimension. We forgave each other from an early age. She has a marked generosity of spirit, and is never still. To my astonishment, I found myself surrounded this time by great-nieces: my sister's two eldest daughters, Sheelagh and Gillian, had already had seven daughters between them, and there was a little army of knee-high girls whose names I had to learn. Sheelagh and Gillian had both married solicitors, both of whom worked in Cupar, for rival firms; Kathleen's husband, Charlie, was the bank manager. It all felt very dynastic to me, although at times it took on aspects of a Scottish soap opera.

In Scotland, the buying and selling of houses is generally managed through solicitors, and Sheelagh's husband, George McQuitty, handled such matters with considerable dash. In the course of doing so, he had acquired for himself and his family an imposing pile called Seggie House, built before 1900 for the factor of the paper mill at Guardbridge, four miles from St Andrews along the Cupar Road. The sprawling house had a separate apartment, which I rented from George and Sheelagh. I had known the house under previous owners, but not as it now was, an anthill of activity. It had ample grounds and stands of trees, it had lawns, it had a huge, walled vegetable garden with a grape-bearing greenhouse, and it even had a tower, with a view of the Eden estuary and the surrounding countryside.

George, stocky, soft-spoken, has a quiet, burning energy, and at Seggie he was turning it to account. From a window, I would see him drive in at the end of a day, in a business suit and tie, and not five minutes later a chain saw or a mower would start up: George, in blue jeans, transformed into farmer. They kept pigs, chickens, geese, and three goats. George felled trees, turned hay, fed animals, rescued children. Everything we ate seemed to come from Seggie; what we left went back to the pigs. Sheelagh, in almost direct contrast to George, has such a vivid electricity to her that she seems to move and talk twice as fast as anyone else, and then falls back into the repose of a smile. The girls descended in size from Jane, who, rusty-haired and serious, knew everything about 'Dallas'; through Kate, moonier and more reticent; and Sara, four, with a piercingly unabashed curiosity; to Kirsty, five months old, who sat on the kitchen table and seemed to be fed by everybody. I never knew who was in the house – or, indeed, where anyone was – except at mealtimes, when they all magically materialised, as the food did. Sheelagh shot off somewhere to teach a class, to take a class, to exchange a child. The growl of the mower signalled that George was back. For me, in that humming establishment, writing felt like an indolent pastime.

I dawdled in Edinburgh – still alluring to me, a walking city. It did look dour, though, after New York. I went in to St Andrews, called on some friends, bumped into others. They all asked me what I was doing in Scotland. I told the story once, but not again, inventing some other pretext. It suddenly seemed a rather weird story. August arrived. July, according to some accounts, had been the wettest in three hundred years. I had to tell the story of the box to the children, who thought it terrific, except that they doubted Jasper's existence, for they had never seen him to remember.

There is such a deep green to Scotland in midsummer; even in the drizzle, the greenness emerges, and much came back to me as I breathed that summer in. The countryside swelled with growing, and I sometimes drove through the small, neat villages of Fife: Balmullo, Ceres, Crail, Windygates – names my tongue knew well. Talking to George and Sheelagh, I found them cheerfully liberated from the glooms that still hung in my memory, although they were well aware of them. They also appeared relatively unperturbed about matters of money – a change from the frayed days I remembered, when it would have been unthinkable to buy anything without having the actual coin in hand, and when I once asked my father to show me a pound note and he had to go look for one, since he never carried money with him. But then Scotland had badly needed not a generation gap but a generation gulf, and Sheelagh and George certainly had as acute a sense of the world as anybody, brushing aside insularities by ignoring them. They lived a thoughtful rural life – one that was always being translated into activity. On some days, Seggie House seemed as strenuous to me as New York.

I spent Thursday, August 7, in Edinburgh, recording a broadcast for the BBC. I took a train back to Leuchars Junction, the nearest station to Seggie House, and when I got to the house Sheelagh met me in the hall. 'Your friends are in the kitchen,' she said over her shoulder on her way to feed the chickens. I went through, and there were Jeff and Nora, with children all over them. They had rented a small car and driven up from London. By judicious phone calls, they had traced me to Seggie, but their call had been answered by Mrs Trail, who helped Sheelagh keep the household back from chaos, and her directions had proved unintelligible. They had had to intuit their way. That same evening, a cable came from Jasper saying he was taking the night plane to London and would call the next morning. We sat in the kitchen and talked, the girls wandering down from sleep on some wild pretext ('I just wanted to ask Alastair something, honestly!'), not wanting to miss anything. Sheelagh filed Jeff and Nora away in some part of the house I don't think I had even seen. There was a thunderstorm that night, and in my sleep I heard the goats bleat.

Jasper called the next morning around breakfast time. He was in London with a friend of his from Yale. They were taking the train up, and, with a change in Edinburgh, would reach Leuchars Junction about eight that evening. Jeff and Nora, both goggle-eyed at being back in Fife, went off to explore St Andrews, sus-pending their disbelief. The girls were already enthusiastic about an obvious chance to stay up late. But we kept studiously clear of Pilmour Cottage, as I had done since I arrived. It was for the next day. We drove down at sunset to Leuchars Junction to meet the train, which ground in, salutarily late, and let out Jasper and his friend Allen Damon. We got them into the Mini Jeff and Nora had rented, with some difficulty, for Allen turned out to be six feet five, and intricate human folding was required. We all ended up in the kitchen, eleven of us now, like an assembled freak show, for the sight of Sara standing beside Allen was comical. Jasper had a beard and looked tired. It occurs to me that I have not described Jasper – perhaps because there are for me so many of him, each separate self associated with a particular place, each distinct in my memory. By now, he is about the same height I am, just over six feet; physically, we do not look at all alike, except possibly around the eyes, but we have a wavelength and a language in common, which we fall into very easily. Sheelagh produced food as she always did – less, apparently, by cooking than by willing it into being. We sorted each other out, telling our separate stories, everyone surprised for a time at the presence of everyone else, everyone

talking, a stew of accents. At some point, we made an agenda for
the following day: we would wake early, dig up the box, bring it
back to Seggie, and then make lunch, to which we had invited all
the stray members of the voluminous family that seemed to be
sprouting with the summer. George had already laid out a selection
of spades, shovels, hoes, and picks, and the weather forecast
promised a fair day, as they say in Fife.

*

Next morning, we began to materialise in the kitchen about seven
– Jasper and Allen last, jet-lagged. Over breakfast, we ordered the
day. The five of us would go, taking Jane along with us. George
might drop in later if we were not back. We folded ourselves into
the Mini and set out for Pilmour Cottage.

There was a new way into Pilmour, past a practice green; a
parking area had taken shape where our old imposing gateway
had been. But as we shouldered our spades, trudged round the
perimeter of bushes, and caught sight of the house, it all swam
back, in a trance of time. The house was white and well kept, the
grass juicy around it, the trees enveloping, the day, I am glad to
say, dry, with a suggestion of sun. Golfers were already out; it was
a Saturday morning. I had looked in on Mr Stewart, the present
owner of Pilmour Cottage, at his store in St Andrews, to tell him
sketchily what we would be doing, and he had been quite jovial
about our return, promising us extra spades if we needed them.
We stood by the wall for a while looking at the house, shifting it
back and forth in our heads – all except Allen, who had never seen
it before. A sometime golfer in Hawaii, where he came from, he
gazed across the Old Course with a player's awe. The morning was
warming, and we were in no hurry, except for young Jane, who
could not wait to be astonished. So we turned away from the house
and found the elm tree, now grown into an adult elm.

It was at this point that a hesitation set in. Jasper, given the
privilege, paced off a certain distance from the tree perpendicular
to the wall, dug in his heel, and reached for a spade. 'No!' Jeff was
waving his arms wildly. 'You've forgotten. It was three arm spans
from the tree.' And he started measuring off the spans. But whose

arm spans, I asked him. Jasper's? He had been a lot smaller then. Besides, I told them both, I had been back to the site once, and what we had to feel for with our feet was a depression, a sag – as I began to do, in the thick tangle of undergrowth. We agreed, however, to start digging at Jasper's spot and then, if we did not find the box at once, to dig in the places that Jeff and I had picked out as more likely. Well, we did not find the box at once. We dug in a desultory way for about an hour, expecting with every spade thrust to feel a clunk of a kind, a plastic clunk. We found a teacup, unbroken, and a bent spoon. We talked about memory, leaning on our spades. Jeff and Jasper began to recreate the burying of the box, and even on that they began to diverge. Jasper didn't think that it had been raining that night, and hence surmised that the box must be buried deeper, about four feet down. I was sure of the rain, for I remembered the lantern going out. When we could not remember, we grew adamant. Nora and Allen went off to find some coffee, perhaps in the hope that, left to concentrate, we might clarify our collective memory. We did not. Jane pointed out where she would have buried a box, and she might well have been right, because although the presence of the house began to remind all three of us of innumerable details of the past, it did not tell us where to dig. A trance set in again for a moment. We dug more. I had broken ground where I thought the box was, although I admitted to feeling promising sags all over the place. My spade clanged against something – a buried can. Nora and Allen came back, and Nora told us about 'state-dependent memory', which she elaborated on at some length. It beat digging. Although the presence of Pilmour Cottage was activating our general recall, she explained, we would have to recover the precise mood and emotion surrounding the event to narrow down our memory. But these were nine years behind us now. (She recently sent me an article from the February issue of *American Psychologist* that told me a great deal about state-dependent memory. It is something I have experienced a lot, changing countries. When I go back to some-where I have previously lived, I put my arms into the sleeves of the place at once, and find that I take on not just its timetable and its eating habits; I also experience moods heavy with dormant memory.) We laid out what we dug up, however, as methodically as archeologists, and we soon had a fair array of objects – more spoons, broken crockery, medicine bottles gummy with mysterious resins, a child's tin toy from nurseries ago.

Then George turned up, having already been to his office and subsequently sawed up a felled tree. (Jeff had earlier suggested altering a road sign near Seggie from 'MEN WORKING' to 'GEORGE WORKING'.) George sized up the scene: we had already dug deepish holes at three points of a triangle of which each side was some eighteen feet long – so widely can memory wander. He asked us a few brief questions, then proceeded to excavate a trench, clearing off the undergrowth with a few cuts of his spade, and digging cleanly down, the walls of his trench exquisitely perpendicular and sharp compared with our molelike burrowings. He made us all tired, but we dug, scraping our way, as it were, toward one another. We leaned on our spades whenever it was decently possible, and looked at one another. It was time to be at Seggie for lunch. Spades shouldered, we stumbled back to the car. My instep hurt.

The children, far from crestfallen, were glad to have their anticipation extenuated. Kathleen arrived, with Charlie, bluff, looking not older but more so, as Jasper said, and Gillian, Fiona, another niece, Roy, her husband – here the canvas gets a bit crowded. But we ate well – salmon that Charlie had caught and smoked, a ham we had dealt for with a neighboring farmer, green abundance from the garden, raspberries that Kathleen had picked that morning. I sat on the step with Jeff a few moments. 'Has it occurred to you that this could have a lot of different endings?' he asked me. It had. The girls had put out on the front lawn a table with a white cloth, to receive the box. We looked at each other, gathered our spades, and got ready to clamber back into the car.

It was at this point that George had a brain wave. A doctor friend of his occasionally repaired electronic equipment, and had, he remembered, tinkered with a metal detector for a fellow who lived on the far side of Cupar. He was on the phone in a flash, and in no time we were speeding to pick up the machine – which had been acquired by its owner, George told me in the car, after his wife threw her wedding ring into a field during an argument.

They had not, however, found the ring – an ill omen, I felt. Nor did the machine itself look capable of pinpointing our lost box. We stopped at Seggie to pick up children, for Kate and Sara would not be left out, and neither would anyone else, for that matter, except Charlie, who was already sensibly asleep under a newspaper. We arrived at the site this time like an army, aghast at the chaos we had already created in vain. Jeff and Nora had somehow disappeared, strayed. But we began to dig again while Jane combed the promised ground with the metal detector. After a few excited sorties, we abandoned it, having found that it could not detect even a pile of change we planted no more than six inches down.

George, fortified by lunch, dug off in a new direction. The children pestered us with questions, and we began to feel a little foolish, particularly when a man who was visiting Pilmour Cottage wandered over to the wall. He could not contain his curiosity any longer, he told me, and when I explained what we were doing he looked at me somewhat sorrowfully and wished me luck. The sun was out, the day had turned glorious, Jasper had turned twenty-one, and we had dug up a patch of ground about the size, it seemed to me, of a small midtown office. And where were Jeff and Nora? George, leaning on his spade, looked a bit worn. It was the thought of unproductive labor that was bothering him, I think. It was bothering me. The children had extended our collection of relics considerably, by bringing in odd golf balls and empty bottles from the undergrowth. I hoped they were not losing faith. The clink of golf clubs and the thud of golf balls punctuated the whole day steadily, as golfers, unperturbed by our gypsy encampment, cheerfully hacked their way home. As Kathleen was preparing to remove some children, at a sign of lengthening shadows, Nora and Jeff burst out of the undergrowth, carrying what looked to me like a ray gun with a set of stereo headphones attached. It was a metal detector that looked as if it might have a chance. Jeff wasted no time in beginning to comb the ground with it. Even George cheered up. Nora explained. They had driven into St Andrews and gone to hardware stores in the hope of renting a metal detector. An ironmonger in Market Street did not have one for rent or for sale – fortunately, for it would have cost about as much as a used car – but he remembered selling one last Christmas to a woman who lived on the far edge of town and whose daughter worked in Hendersons, the booksellers. They had tracked down the girl, got from her her mother's address, driven there, explained (I know not in what form) to the *duena* of the metal detector – Mrs Brian, of Schoolbraids Road – and come away with it and more good wishes. At that point, Jeff whooped and jumped up and down, jabbing his finger at the ground. We dug deeper, for Jeff was still gesticulating. Another old can, but this one quite far down, giving us at least a glimmer of faith in the machine. As if to vary our luck, we all took turns, we all jumped up and down, we found seven more rusted cans. Kathleen sagely decided to go back with the baby, but the other children were still glowing, so they stayed. George's face had lengthened like the shadows. Around that time, Jeff and I began passing the metal detector (Adastra, it was called) back and forth between the end of the trench George had dug when he first appeared and the elm tree – closer to the tree. No question, there was an unmistakable hum, a steady hum, a hum that seemed to cover the area of the box as we imagined it. We whistled over Jasper with his spade. He dug, again; again, a bump – and we were on the box. We all stopped. Jasper scraped away the last dirt with his hands, and there it was, less than two feet down, not much more than two feet from the tree. It was slightly split, clearly from the blow of a spade – probably George's first spade cast, we speculated later. We lifted it out carefully and laid it to one side. It was six-fifteen, a golden evening; even the golfers, however, were thinking of going in.

Hilariously, we pitched in to restore a semblance of order to the ground we had combed – with our fingers, it felt. We had to persuade Sara to save only the best of our recovered artifacts. The rest we reburied, leaving the ground as level as we could, to go back to undergrowth. We wound our way to the cars like Millet peasants – tools shouldered, children carried – bound for Seggie. It was going on twilight by the time we got there. We decided to wash off before we got to the box, for none of us were regular diggers and we had managed to cover ourselves with native earth. My instep hurt almost enough for me to limp, but not quite.

When we had assembled ourselves, we moved the box into the dining room and clustered around the table. I had grown curious about the contents, because I had only a vague memory of them. We began to remove them, one at a time. First, however, on top, lay the card we had added at the last minute, before we sealed the box. We read the text aloud. It was full of ironies. 'This chest,' it said starkly, 'containing treasure in coin and various souvenirs of the present moment in St Andrews in May 1971, is buried here by Jasper Reid, Jeff Lerner, and Alastair Reid, in a spot known to these three persons.' George smiled wanly. 'It is their intention to return on the ninth day of August, 1980, to meet and disinter the chest in one another's company, and to celebrate their survival with appropriate ceremony. Sunday, May 30, 1971, a hazy day with sea mist, rooks, curry, and kites.' And under that were the signatures, mine recognisably the same, Jeff's looking somewhat simplified, Jasper's in large, errant schoolboy handwriting.

We looked at one another. There we all were. We had survived even the digging.

The contents of the box, I am sorry to say, amount to a rather frail memorial of a fleeting time, but we took them out, one by one, dusted them off, and scanned them. Sheelagh spread a blanket on the kitchen floor, and we poured out the coins, the children running their fingers like misers through the mound of huge pennies, at last convinced that we had put in the day to some point. There were three small plastic biplanes that Jasper had reluctantly sacrificed from his toy hoard at the time; there was a photograph of Jeff, Borges, and Jasper taken at the front door of Pilmour, Borges talking, Jeff bending to listen, a miniature Jasper mugging at the camera; there was a postcard of the Old Course with an arrow pointing out Pilmour Cottage, a piece of white quartz, a leather pouch of Jeff's that had not stood the test of time as well as the rest of the contents, a copy of the St Andrews *Citizen* dated Saturday, May 22, 1971, which we later read aloud. It might have been the current issue: the same civic preoccupations, the same cluster of local detail. There was a pen, which still wrote; there was an envelope from the Chilean Embassy in Paris addressed to me at Pilmour Cottage in Neruda's familiar green handwriting, a history-examination paper of Jeff's, a copy of the St Andrews *Newsflash* – a small newspaper that Jasper and two of his schoolmates put out, and that ran for, I think, three issues.

There were separate photographs, too, of the three of us, taken roughly at that time. As we passed them round, I grew keenly aware of how differently we must be thinking, Jasper, Jeff, and I, about the piece of time that had passed between our impulsive shovelling of nine years ago and our laborious digging up of that day. For Jasper, it had been transformation – from oven height, happy and puzzled, in the way of children, to full height, a vote, and an independent being. Jeff had gone through the long tunnel of a Ph.D., and had probably changed least, in that he had an early serenity and his curiosity continued as alive as ever. Friendships we formed in the sixties, around that Antioch year, have remained very firm and clear to me, perhaps because, in that vivid time, the talk we had seemed always drastic, it gave off the same exhilaration that the war years did to the British, it became a defining time, and Jeff and Nora kept that directness alive: they foraged for wild plants, they read aloud to each other over the dishes, they took in the world crisply and intelligently, they thought of us exactly as we thought of them – as eternal players in a game of our own devising, fastened together by the habit of making every meeting into a celebration of that very happening, that moment. And my nine years? I had written a number of things, gone through the swirling glooms of translating, but what I think was most important to me was that after vacillating for so many years across the Atlantic, a transatlantic creature, I had shifted and had anchored myself in the Western Hemisphere. New York City is a good place to be when one has not quite decided just where to live – although I think that I have chosen looking for such a place over finding it. Apart from that, I had, as usual, changed every day.

So much for the contents of the capsule – not exactly a thrilling anthology of an epoch. But the fact that these inconsequential elements had lain underground – 'all that time', Kate gasped, for it was longer than her life – certainly excited the children. In fact, at different times we all knelt round the blanket in the kitchen and fingered the coins – 'the real treasure,' as Sara said. The old pennies, some of them bearing the rubbed-down head of Edward VII or Queen Victoria in profile, seemed to animate us all. We rose on our knees, crowing from time to time. Fiona swooned over a twelve-sided three penny bit from pre-decimal days. Sara was searching out the biggest and brightest – dinars, half crowns, and a single Swiss five-franc piece (which she pounced on like a buccaneer). I mooned over pesetas and duros with the obdurate profile of feeble Grand-father Franco, whose death we had waited for so long. I left them to their scrabbling and wandered back to the dining room. In truth, nothing looked any the worse for nine years in the earth except Jeff's pouch, which had yielded to green mold. But it was the card I picked up and fingered – the card on which we had signed our names to an impossibly distant intention, opening a long parenthesis in time that the exertions of the day had just closed.

The children were radiant with the occasion, as though for once life had lived up to their expectations. The rest of us were tired enough to fall asleep in the soup. We ate up the delicious remains of lunch, to save it from the pigs, to take in sustenance. We had all kept out a few coins, for sentimental rather than monetary reasons (although I admit to pocketing a sound American quarter, which had not aged beyond the point of negotiability). George seemed to me particularly broody – lugubrious, egg-bound, like the hens. We took a walk outside, he and I, in a night on which enough stars were out to confirm that they still existed.

'What's up?' I asked him.

We paced in the dark, ignoring the goats, the pigs, the chickens, the geese, the hilarity from the kitchen.

'The truth is ...' I braced myself, for George, when he talks, is nothing if not blunt, emphatic. 'The truth is, I thought at the beginning that today was just one of your wild inventions, that kind of playing with realities you quite often do. But, I have to tell you, it has affected me a lot. I went off and sat on a log and had a long think. I even wept at one moment. I began to think about Sheelagh, about the girls, about Seggie. I tell you, my life flashed before me, probably even more than yours did.'

I was surprised, but not. George had looked all day like the practical digger, but I had seen that something was going on in the recesses of his being.

'I've decided something,' he said. 'And I don't think I'll tell the others until tomorrow. But that box of yours moved me a lot. I looked at Rona, the dog, and thought, Well, she certainly won't be here ten years from now. Then I looked at Sheelagh, myself, the children, Seggie, you, everything – heavens, it all seemed so frail and vulnerable that I decided, Tomorrow we're going to bury a capsule of our own. Ten years from now, Janie will be eighteen, Sheelagh and I will be forty, we move at such a rate that we're bound to be somewhere else – I don't mean physically, I mean in how we see things. So I'm going to tell them all tomorrow at breakfast to get things ready for a capsule, and we'll bury it just before sunset. Ten years seems a good time. Sheelagh and I have a twentieth wedding anniversary then, and I know we'll still be married, still misfiring but married, and I just don't want this sense of continuing time to end, I just want there to be another knot waiting in the string for all of us.'

I felt warmly toward George at that moment, but even so, I had had my share of time capsules for one day. I suggested we put in things from our capsule. Apart from the card (and what remained of Jeff's leather pouch), everything in it might as well go on in time, as far as I was concerned.

We went in. The children had claimed Allen as a private possession, and he rose to their demands. Allen had surprised us all, arriving as the only stranger at the feast and yet entering in with exuberance and good humor. He patiently pointed out Hawaii to them in the atlas and taught them to pronounce it correctly; he was for them too good to be true, better than 'Dallas' (a rerun of which Jane had missed, unperturbed). He became their hero, far more fascinating to them than any of the rest of us – their parents, especially. 'Wee Allen', they called him, to their own squeaky delight. We all had our fair share of blisters and aches, and I went off to bed. Jasper came in at some point and sat on the end of my bed, and we talked, drowsily, about the amazement of the day, of arriving after such shifting, such wandering. It was a point of arrival we would remember, a good moment to go to sleep on.

We all turned up in the kitchen the next morning in a fairly desultory order – at least until George came in and told the children what he had in mind. Immediately, they were seized with a kind of capsule fever and went off in all directions to gather treasures worthy of the occasion, piling them in the dining room. Summer had come out for the day – a warm, hazy heat, an enveloping greenness. Jasper looked quite dazed, grinning and shaking his head. Sheelagh shot off somewhere in the car. We interviewed the children with a small tape recorder, asking them what they thought they would be doing ten years from now. Kate said she wanted a baby. Sara, tired of being small, said she wanted to be as tall as Allen. We all added our own adages. George, who had not been about all morning, turned up with a fat sealed envelope and a brooding expression. I cannot imagine what he had written – but then perhaps I can.

The details of the day are blurred; about six, we gathered in the dining room again, and, through a rather painful process of elimination (it had to be made clear to Sara that if she buried her favorite small blanket she would, of course, not have it around), we eventually filled three vast plastic boxes, wrote out the appropriate documents, signed them, sealed everything up. The experience of the previous day had left its mark: we wrapped the boxes in aluminum foil for the metal detectors of the future, and picked out a spot equidistant from three trees – a holly, a chestnut, and a sycamore. George dug a deep, immaculate hole, and we all trooped out, planted the gleaming boxes in the bottom, took stock for a moment, and then shovelled back the dirt, taking turns to tamp the surface level. As the sun was going down, we lit a bonfire over in the grove where the goats lived, and sat about on tree stumps drinking hot chocolate, gazing into the fire, while the goats nuzzled our knees and nibbled at our shoelaces. One by one, the children began to droop and were carried off to bed. Jane looked rapt. I asked her what she was thinking about. 'Nothing very much,' she said. 'But I like best of all being here listening to what people say.' The fire began to die, and the dark came down.

★

That's just about it. Such a small event, and yet the ripples from it ran across the pools of our attention, stopped us, affected us. The next day, Jeff, Nora, Allen, Jasper, and I, after returning the metal detector to a delighted Mrs Brian, took off for a five-day drive through the places of my past – to the Border country, drizzling and dotted with sheep, past the gloomy depths of St Mary's Loch, all the way to gentle Galloway, grass-green, smelling of warm damp, to that village of milk and honey, to the house I was born in – stopping to see friends on the way. We told the story of the box in the ground once, maybe twice, and then we stopped, because it was complete in our minds and it was actually quite complicated to tell, as I have discovered. I have found that the telling resembles picking at a loose thread in a piece of whole cloth – seemingly simple to disentangle but winding in eventually a great intricacy of warp and woof, threads that lead in unimagined directions. I did not realise that in digging up that fairly in-consequential box, that whim of ours, I would be digging up a great deal more. Significantly, while we were digging that day away it was the roots that gave us the most trouble. But we covered them over again, and they will clearly endure. I think, in fact, that I am done with the metaphor of roots. I prefer that of a web, a web of people and places, threads of curiosity, wires of impulse, a net-work of the people who have cropped up in our lives, and will always crop up – 'the webbed scheme', as Borges calls it.

There are many threads I did not unravel, many things I skipped over, inevitably, because I had not intended at all to wind in the fabric of the past – a precarious dimension, I think, for even in going over essential pieces of it I realise how much we all edit what has happened to us, how much we all make acceptable, recountable versions of past events. Mulling them over, as I have had to do, I find that sometimes the version and the grainy reality become separated: not contradictory but separated.

I have not spoken of many things. I have not mentioned money, for example. Living by writing, I had an income over the years like a fever chart, but there was always work to do, there was always translating, which I did as a kind of warm-up to the day's work; there was always enough to keep us going. If we needed money, I worked hard; if not, I idled. I have not mentioned various women, who moved in and out of our lives, who were woven into our existence, shifting, affecting. I have not mentioned solitude, which was an inevitable accompaniment to those years. I used to meet the English writer J. G. Ballard from time to time in London. He had raised his children by himself after the death of his wife, and he once said to me, 'Remember, if you are a single father, it's lucky you're a writer, because you can stay home all the time, you have the time for it.' He always cheered me up. Nor did I feel so very solitary. Jasper was the best of company. But there was an essential solitude, the *soledad* of Gárcia Márquez, or of Melissa in Lawrence Durrell's *Mountolive*: '*Monsieur, je suis devenue la solitude même.*' And I saved, on the bulletin board we set up wherever we came to rest, a clipping from an interview that Truman Capote once gave: 'Writers just tend to learn more than other people how to be alone. They learn to be dependent on themselves . . . it just has to be that; there's no way of getting around it.' The self-sufficiency was certainly something I had saved from my Scottish past – that and the fact of still having next to no possessions. Although Jasper alleviated that essential solitude, I fear that some of it has settled on him, by unavoidable osmosis.

I say 'we' too often when I am talking about Jasper, but I have no intention of implying any unanimity of mind. We functioned as a unit, but for me the whole business of raising children meant teaching them to fly, separately and independently, getting them ready for leaving. I have been much preoccupied by fatherhood, for I felt most close to my own quiet father, and Jasper I have known as well as I know anyone. One moment lives vividly in my remembering. We had travelled up to Scotland during our house-boat days, on a visit, and we descended from the London train in the wan light of early morning, on the platform at St Boswells, where my father was waiting. The train chuffed off, and, standing in the rising steam, there were the three of us: Jasper, small and eager, my father, pleased and open-eyed, and I, standing between them, father and son at once. That moment dissipated with the steam, and Jasper and I have exchanged the state of being father and son for that of inhabiting our separate solitudes.

And Scotland? It no longer seems a contradiction to me, nor am I inclined to rant about Calvin the way I once did. I have, besides, a stake in its future. On August 7, 1990, I have to be there, Jeff and Nora will certainly be there, Jasper will turn up from who knows where, Allen has promised his presence, Sheelagh will arrive, breathless but in time, George will have the spades ready, and Jane, turned eighteen, Kate, in a totally different shape, little sparky Sara, and Kirsty, who by then will be older than Jane is now – they will be there. Scotland has reformed itself, in my mind, into the particularities of last summer, a time capsule in itself.

I call Sheelagh on the phone, tell her I am finishing writing the story of the summer. I have in front of me the card we all signed – Jeff, Jasper, and I – and a leaf from the elm tree that sheltered the box, already dried and cracking. A few odds and ends of the story are still lying about, untold. I ask her about the children, the goats, the household. She fires all the news to me.

'When are you coming back?' she asks me suddenly.

'One of these days,' I say to her. I might have added, 'If we're spared.' I do now, but in the nuclear, not the Calvinist sense.

★

The evening I finished writing all this down, at the remove of New York City, resisting the temptation to pick at still another thread, and ready to leave Scotland alone, at least until 1990, I stopped off on the way home for a drink with two old friends, Linda and Aaron Asher.

'What have you been up to?' Aaron asked me, in a misguided moment.

I told him, in the briefest, most encapsulated form.

'But didn't you see today's *Times?*' he said, going to fetch it and ripping out the relevant page. Here is the story in its entirety, page B2, April 24 issue:

'It may be the ultimate skyscraper both esthetically and because of its superb construction, but the Empire State Building has not completely withstood the ravages of time.

A time capsule placed in the building's cornerstone on Sept 9,

1930, by Alfred E. Smith, then former Governor, was removed yesterday in preparation for the building's 50th anniversary celebration next week. The copper box that contained the time capsule was full of water, and most of the contents had been destroyed.

The seams of the box, which evidently had not been properly sealed, had split, according to a spokesman for the building. The pre-cast concrete slab under which the box had rested had not been cemented into place. As a result, all the papers, which included a copy of the *New York Times* of Sept. 9, 1930, pictures relating to the building and paper currency from $1 up to $100 – had disintegrated.'

In Scotland, enduring is a much graver matter.

Afterword 2002

When I finished writing this chronicle, I felt as if some dark creature had lifted from my shoulders and flapped its ungainly way over the horizon. For us burying the capsule was a sudden, spontaneous act, a whim. We had no notion then of how much the ripples from it would go on widening with time.

Capsules generate one another, we have found; for it becomes unthinkable to unearth one capsule without burying another boxful of the living present, to become in ten years time a nutshell of the past. They serve for us as waystations in the continuum, especially for the children, for whom time seems only endless. And, inevitably, capsules bring on a meditative cast of mind.

We have continued, at ten year intervals, to reassemble in St Andrews, that time capsule of a town, on each occasion catching up, remembering, looking forward, in capsule form. They have been joyous occasions. In 2000, we reassembled in Fife - Jeff and Nora this time with their children, Talia and Andrew, and Jasper and Deborah bringing with them their small son, Ian Alastair, just over a month old.

There have also been shadows and changes, shocks and astonishments, private and public.

On May 14th, 1984, Sheelagh McQuinty died, after struggling valiantly against an indefatigable cancer.

On July 1st, 1985, Charlie Drummond died, cheerfully in mid-sentence.

Toward the end of the eighties, Pilmour Cottage was acquired by the St Andrews Links Association, and has become a waystation for golfers.

On July 1st, 1999, the Scottish Parliament convened in Edinburgh, for the first time since 1707.

To the capsule we buried in August, 2000, I added no more than a poem and a note of well-wishing. I felt that I needed no further reminders of the passing of time.

Transition

I woke up the other morning, early, in a country house in Fife, on the east coast of Scotland, amid neatly plowed expanses of oatmeal-colored farmland and an almost audible underground hum of growing. I walked out early on the lawn, encircled by great oaks and a majestic sequoia. The early sun was silvering the thick dew, and there was not a soul in sight or earshot. Scotland moved in the slow, green seep of spring, with pockets of warm air among the colder, and the trees a filigree of light green — not full-leaved, as they would be later. I ate herrings fried in oat-meal for breakfast, and then, to catch the plane to New York, drove clear across Scotland to Prestwick, on the west coast, along the well-kempt motorways that have made it a smaller country than it was — two hours coast to coast. The central plain looked as well groomed as a garden, but then the Scots, almost to a man, are garden-minded: strict orderers of the soil. Toward the west, which was once grimed over by heavy industry, grass had put a soft green head of hair on the slag heaps. From Prestwick we took off in the middle of the day, over a shimmer of sea — first on a short hop to Shannon, where we lounged among the cashmeres, looking out on the green of Ireland, positively luminous under a slate-dark, rain-promising sky. Up we went again, droning backward through the time zones, on what felt like a long, cushioned subway ride, lasting almost a book length, until, in the late afternoon, we came down in the predictable anthill of Kennedy. I arrowed — or, rather, burrowed — my way into Manhattan, and, walking to my office first, to open the mail, was struck every few yards by the variety of human shapes and faces on the street. The people I had said goodbye to in Fife had all been cast roughly in the same mold: kind, fresh-faced, big-boned, but taciturn and undemonstrative, their terse, stone-scripted conversation stark against the abundance of the landscape. The various human exuberances of Forty-second Street would have been out of their range. Looking uptown from my office window, I must have been encompassing with my eyes well over a million people, and yet to offset them I could count on, if I craned my neck, only a small scatter of trees in the International Paper Plaza, between Forty-fifth and Forty-sixth Streets – mere micro-dots of green. The proportions made me uneasy. I unloaded the cumbersome British coins from my pocket, put my passport away in a drawer, and made a couple of phone calls, feeling the douce atmosphere of Fife dwindle down to a name. I felt singularly displaced, for I felt I had slipped off one existence and slipped on another as easily as changing clothes, or switching the coins in my pocket. I felt I had been deprived of the appropriate awe, for my transition had been made sleek, the surprise combed out of it. I wanted to resist taking it as a matter of course, so I observed my moment of awe, and meditated for a moment on a globe I keep at hand which, however, reduces Scotland to the size of a herring's eye – before going out to Fifth Avenue. To compound my confusion, my ears pricked up at once to the uncertain sound of bagpipes, but I could not see where it originated, for the dark had at last come down.

II

ABROAD

Our view of reality is conditioned by our position in space and time — not by our personalities as we like to think. Thus every interpretation of reality is based upon a unique position. Two paces east or west and the whole picture is changed.

Lawrence Durrell: *The Alexandria Quartet*

When I came back to Scotland after wartime service at sea in the East, I had seen enough of the outside world to want to see much more, and I moved, first to New York, where I began to publish poems, and then to Spain in the early 1950s. I knew little about the country and scarcely a word of the language, but I felt there an immediate affinity, a sharpened sense of the present, an opening up. Besides, the experience of being isolated by both language and ignorance drove me to immerse myself, not just in the Spanish language but in all things Spanish. More than anything, I listened.

It was then that I began to write prose. I was learning Spain from the outside in, and I wrote in these years a series of chronicles for the New Yorker *that reflected that experience. Some of these pieces are reprinted here. I found that the state of being an outsider, a foreigner, kept a sharp edge on my curiosity. It also meant contemplating the world from differing vantage points, in all its contradictions. Wherever I am, the ghosts of other places and other lives are always hovering close.*

A. R.

Notes on Being a Foreigner

I come suddenly into a foreign city, just as the lamps take light along the water, with some notes in my head. Arriving – the mood and excitement, at least, are always the same. I try out the language with the taxi driver, to see if it is still there; and later, I walk to a restaurant that is lurking round a corner in my memory. Nothing, of course, has changed; but cities flow on, like water, and, like water, they close behind any departure. We come back to confirm them, even though they do not particularly care. Or perhaps we come back to confirm ourselves?

★

By the time I have finished dinner, I find I have to make an effort to remember the place I left – how it felt, at least. Matches and toothpaste are the only continuities; once they are used up, the previous existence from which they came has withered and died. I walk along the snowy quais in the lamplit dark, breathing a tangle of strangeness and familiarity. Places are a little like old clothes. Wearing them brings nostalgia snowing down. There is both shock and recognition.

★

How easy it is to fall at once into the habits of a place, most noticeably the eating habits – to dine very late in Spain, to eat heartily in England, to change the whole conception of breakfast, to order certain kinds of drink instinctively. Another country is a new self, I am tempted to say – until I notice all the signs of the old self showing through.

★

Later, I telephone two or three friends, and am instantly drawn into a web of appointments, talk, question-and-answer, the no-wheres of friendship, which supersede language, time, place. And somewhere, one of my friends is saying to someone I do not know yet: 'So-and-so is coming for a drink. He is a foreigner.'

★

Natives feel oddly toward foreigners. They may be hostile, aggressive, overfriendly, distant, or possessive; but at least they have the (to them) advantage of being in possession, so that between foreigners and themselves there is a moat with a drawbridge to which they keep the keys. Typical native gambits: 'Why, we almost consider you one of us!' Or 'What do you think of *our* (railways, king, public lavatories)?' Or 'Are you familiar with our expression …?' They have the assurance of Being In Possession.

★

And the foreigner? It depends on whether he is a foreigner by Necessity, Accident, or Choice. One thing, however, is sure: unless he regards being a foreigner as a positive state, he is doomed. If he has already chosen not to belong, then all the native gambits are bound to fail. But if he aspires to being a native, then he is forever at the mercy of the natives, down to the last inflection of the voice.

★

An expatriate shifts uncomfortably, because he still retains, at the back of his mind, the awareness that he has a true country, more real to him than any other he happens to have selected. Thus, he is only at ease with other expatriates. They justify one another, as they wait about in the sun for the arrival of mail or money. Eventually, they are driven to talk of plumbing, the ultimate sign of the superiority of their own civilisation. Whatever they do or write or say has its ultimate meaning for them Back Home. 'Yes, but you have to make it in Boston,' I once heard from a fanatical expatriate. What's more, he said it in Spanish.

★

Exiles, as opposed to expatriates, either wither away, or else flourish from being transplanted, depending on whether they keep alive any hope of returning to what they left, or abandon it completely as forever inaccessible. The hope of returning to the past, even at its faintest, makes for a vague unease, a dissatisfaction with the present. The Spanish exiles I knew were, for the most part, unhappy; Spain, after all, continued to exist, as they were always wistfully aware. The émigrés who left Russia after the Revolution took up, from necessity, another, healthier life, without thinking, and assumed new languages. America has been the most fruitful soil for exiles of all nationalities. America has no time for foreigners as such, being too preoccupied with its own tumultuous present, and being aggressively monoglot. If you are there, you are expected to contribute; you cannot just hang about, as you can in the more wistful cities of Europe. In America, you can join, or leave.

★

Tourists are to foreigners as occasional tipplers are to alcoholics – they take strangeness and alienation in small, exciting doses, and besides, they are well fortified against loneliness. Moreover, the places they visit expect and welcome them, put themselves out for their diversion. Boredom is the only hazard – it takes a healthy curiosity to keep tourists from rushing home in tears, from sighing with relief at the reappearance of familiarity. The principal difference between tourists and foreigners is that tourists have a home to go to, and a date of departure. I wonder how many of them would confess to have found the pinnacle of pleasure from a trip in the moment of returning home?

★

How appropriate tourists are, in certain places, at certain seasons! They set off spas, harbours, and watering places as pigeons set off cathedrals; they exude an appetite for pleasure and diversion. And often, they bring the best out of the places they visit; women who know they are going to be seen take more trouble with their appearance. The only thing that besets them is that they have to invent reasons for visiting the places they visit, or else suffer from

149

their own pointlessness. And the sun, they discover, is not quite sufficient reason for being anywhere.

★

A foreigner has a curious perspective on the country he alights in. His foreignness more or less absolves him from being attached to any particular class – his accent puts the natives at rest. It is easier for him to avoid local attitudes and prejudices. He looks at the whole, first, as a game, and then, should he be serious, as an entire human situation. If he cares about it, he develops a calm and attentive eye, a taste for local food, and a passionate dispassion.

★

'Ah, but, being a foreigner, you cannot possibly know what it is like for us. You cannot suffer.' But unless one wants to submerge, to become more English than the English, more German than the Germans, one does know what it is like; and one does suffer. The expatriate settles in a country for peripheral reasons; his involvement is with back home. The foreigner's involvement is with where he is. He has no other home. There is no secret landscape claiming him, no roots tugging at him. He is, if you like, properly lost, and so in a position to rediscover the world, from the outside in.

★

Belonging. I am not sure what it means, for I think I always resisted it (I still have a crawling terror of being caught in a community singsong). As for families, they are serviceable social units for a certain time only. With luck, the relationships within them will turn into quite ordinary human ones; otherwise they will wither away. If I belonged to anything, it was to the small, but then enormous, landscapes of my childhood, to houses, trees, gardens, walks – only then was my absorption so utter that I felt no separation between myself and an outside world. Childhood landscapes are an entire containment of mystery – we spend a good part of our lives trying to find them again, trying to lose ourselves in the sense in which children are lost. We come away with no more than occasional glimpses, whiffs, suggestions, and

150

yet these are enough, often, to transform suddenly the whole current of our lives. A smell recalls a whole vanished state of being; the sound of a word reaches far back, beyond memory. The beginning of poetry for me was the dazzling realisation of all that seemed to be magically compressed into the word 'weather'.

*

The sense of oddness, of surprise, of amazement. Occupying places, contexts, languages, we grow used to them. Habit sets in, and they cease to astonish us. In a foreign country, this does not happen, for nothing is exactly recognisable; it has not been with us from our beginnings. The architecture is odd, the shops unexpected; the faces provoke curiosity rather than recognition. And the money – the only real money is the money one knows as a child, for one feels strongly about what it should be worth. Other currencies are play money, coupons; as such, one uses them in a more human, less excruciating way. In a foreign country, the pattern of days is less predictable – each one has its character, and is easier to remember. So, too, the weather; and so, too, the shape and feel of newspapers, the sound of bells, the taste of beer and bread. It is all rather like waking up and not knowing who or where one is. If, instead of simple recognition, one can go through a proper *realisation*, then quite ordinary things take on an edge; one keeps discovering oneself miraculously alive. So, the strangeness of a place propels one into life. The foreigner cannot afford to take anything for granted.

*

In a time like this, it becomes more and more difficult to be lost. It is astonishing into what stark, deserted crevices of the world Coca-Cola signs have found their way. But because we have all begun to look, dress, and smell alike, it is still too easy to assume that we are.

*

Language. To alight in a country without knowing a word of the language is a worthwhile lesson. One is reduced, whatever identity or distinction one has achieved elsewhere, to the level of a near-idiot, trying to conjure up a bed in sign language. Instead of eavesdropping drowsily, one is forced to look at the eyes, the gestures, the intent behind the words. One is forced back to a watchful silence.

*

Learning a foreign language is a process of slowly divesting oneself of scaffolding. In the end, something stands up by itself and, if it is lucky, walks away. We lean out desperately to hear how we sound but, alas, we will never know. Not to be able to put oneself into words is the most searing of frustrations; behind the pittering phrases, a huge figure is gesticulating violently. We are suddenly reduced to what we are able to say. And even when we have mastered a language sufficiently well, it keeps trapping us, refusing to allow us to finish a train of thought by deserting us suddenly, making fun of us by coming out wrong. The language we grow up with is our servant; we are always a step ahead of it. A new language, however, already exists; we have to grasp hold of it by the tail, and are never wholly sure where it will take us.

*

How clumsy on the tongue, these acquired idioms,
after the innuendos of our own. How far
we are from foreigners, what faith
we rest in one sentence, hoping a smile will follow
on the appropriate face, always wallowing
between what we long to say and what we can,
trusting the phrase is suitable to the occasion,
the accent passable, the smile real,
always asking the traveller's fearful question—
what is being lost in translation?

Something, to be sure. And yet, to hear
the stumbling of foreign friends, how little we care
for the wreckage of word or tense. How endearing they are,
and how our speech reaches out, like a helping hand,
or limps in sympathy. Easy to understand,
through the tangle of language, the heart behind

groping toward us, to make the translation of
syntax into love.

★

To speak two or three languages is to have two or three totally
different selves, like odd suits of clothing. Some fit more easily
than others – it is rare to find an American or an Englishman who
will speak three languages equally well. As W. H. Auden remarks,
'Like all lovers, we are prejudiced; one may love French, or Italian,
or Spanish, but one cannot love all three equally.' Even so, I am
still aware of having, in Spanish (the language I happen to love), a
personality entirely different from my English-speaking one – nor
is it simply me-in-translation. I realise this most acutely when I
listen to a Spanish friend speaking English. He changes before my
ears, and I think, How can I possibly sound to him? 'If you knew
me in English,' I say – but of course, it is impossible. Language, if
we care about using it well rather than efficiently, forever separates
us. I have often listened to simultaneous translation between two
languages I know well. The meaning? Oh yes, the meaning is
there; but it is just *not the same experience*.

★

Moving between several languages, however, only dramatises what
happens all the time within our own language: whatever our accent,
we do not speak in the same voice to a baby, to a clergyman, to an
old friend, to a foreigner. The feeling, the wavelengths, act on our
voices and change them. Joyce once remarked, in passing: 'Isn't
it contradictory to make two men speak Chinese and Japanese
respectively in a pub in Phoenix Park, Dublin? Nevertheless, that is
a logical and objective method of expressing a deep conflict, an
irreducible antagonism.' If voices are anything to go by, then the
idea of having a fixed, firm self is wildly illusory. We expect those
with whom we are in sympathy to listen to what is behind our
voice; it is horrifying to have someone listen to nothing more than
what we say.

★

What, really, does it mean to speak in one's own voice? Is there such a voice? Possibly, but I doubt whether it would ever coincide with any of the voices or accents we use, either in public or in private. Nor is it the odd, anonymous voice we hear reading poems to us as we sit silently and attentively in front of them. It is something between a movement of the mind and a way with words, a current, an undertow, slightly beneath the surface of our saying. Nobody's voice, but one's own.

★

For a writer, it is an invaluable holiday to speak, in the course of the day, a language other than the one he writes in. When he comes to use his own language, it seems washed and clean. Kraus remarks: 'My language is the universal whore whom I have to make into a virgin.' For the foreigner, however, his own language remains steadily virginal.

★

Children who are bilingual have no difficulty distinguishing between their languages – they associate them with people, and switch quite simply, according to who speaks what. The main problem for people who are genuinely bi- or trilingual occurs when they come to write in any one of their languages; they are too used to language as a mechanism by then. Unless they have felt language as mystery (as children do when they repeat a word like 'boomerang' endlessly, out of delight), they will never be able to convey a like mystery, and stay stranded in silence.

★

Ideally, we may arrive at a point of civilisation where everybody speaks his own language, and understands everybody else's. Unfortunately, although this can occasionally happen, it feels unnatural. A nuance, a figure of speech, can only provoke another in the same language. The most untidy conversations are those in which too many people know too many languages; they inevitably get out of control. The English are rigorously unsympathetic to foreigners, being excessively proud of their own language. I will never forget a

154

small, lavender-clad Englishwoman standing over her frail collection of luggage at Barcelona airport, waving her scrawny umbrella in the faces of a voluble host of Spanish officials, and snorting, 'I don't speak your beastly language!'

*

Why should we take such an odd pleasure in being taken for a different nationality from our own? Perhaps because we have succeeded in getting away with an impersonation, in shedding our distinguishing marks. Why should that matter? Anonymity is peculiarly appealing to a foreigner; he is always trying to live in a nowhere, in the complex of his present. To be fastened suddenly to his past may displace him. Languages are defiant connections to different worlds; as such, they become pressingly important. Still, there is an age after which one can no longer learn new languages, after which the self cannot be extended without danger. New languages can be disappearances, rather than appearances.

*

To marry across a difference of language is no more dire than to marry across a difference of temperament; but it can certainly add to the complexities. Explanations are rendered impossible. 'Ah, but you don't understand' can become very literal.

*

The lineaments of travel. To travel far and often tends to make us experts in anonymity – but never quite, for we always carry too much, prepare for too many eventualities. One bag could have been left behind. We are too afraid of unknowns to ignore them.

*

Airports are the great nowheres of this world; we have made them so. Just as plane trips, be they across oceans or countries, leave nothing to remember but a drone of passing time, so the points of arrival and departure are made to look as alike, as indistinct as possible. Airport restaurants should serve nothing but manna, not tasty but sustaining. The only thing plane trips do for the soul is make it think twice about what it can take with it. Fundamentally, they deceive us by allowing us to travel without a sense of movement.

★

Sea voyages are meat and drink to foreigners, a mixture of delight and despair, a kind of prelude to dying. The prevailing atmosphere is not exactly one of boredom, but of a limbo almost indistinguishable from it. Every ship has its ministering angels, its characters, its messengers of doom – a row of nuns painted to a bench, a woman with performing dogs, a man who can do tricks with toothpicks. Aboard ship, people are removed from either the contexts they have left or the ones they are going to assume; and this affects them in various ways. For some, it is a relief; for others, a deprivation. Some are impelled to tell the story of their lives, because all at once they have no life and must create the illusion of what they have left and what is to come. Others wander endlessly along the polished corridors, through the Bamboo Room, the Aquarium Room, listening to the tock of Ping-Pong, lost. During a sea voyage, a small, artificial community is created, with the intimacy of desperation. One leaves a ship with a flurry of burning addresses, which, five minutes after landing, have already turned to ashes. I once heard of a man who spent an entire Atlantic crossing in the bar, playing chess with himself. It made me unaccountably sad.

★

Trains are for meditation, for playing out long thought-processes, over and over; we trust them, perhaps because they have no choice but to go where they are going. Nowadays, however, they smack of a dying gentility. To travel by car makes journeys less mysterious, too much a matter of the will. One might as easily sit on a sofa and imagine a passing landscape. I doubt whether any truly absorbing conversation ever took place in a car; they are good only for word games and long, tedious narratives. We have come to regard cars too much as appendages of our bodies and will probably pay for it in the end by losing the use of our legs. We owe to them the cluttering of the landscape, the breakup of villages and towns.

156

★

Frontiers fascinate us, for, crossing them, we expect to be metamorphosed – and no longer are. Even though the language changes, the landscape does not.

★

Nostalgia: leafing through an old passport on a winter evening, trying to remember what we did from stamp to stamp. M. can remember vividly meals we ate in odd places years ago, beds we slept in, conversations we had. I cannot – my memory is sharper for states of mind, atmospheres, and weather. It is sad to part with a passport – one has been through so much in its company.

★

It is not exactly loneliness that afflicts the foreigner, but more that his oddness and experience keep part of him forever separate from every encounter, every gathering, every conversation. Unless he can bear this and see it as something fruitful, however, then he becomes simply lost, an exile without even a country of origin.

★

Que signifie ce réveil soudain – dans cette chambre obscure – avec les bruits d'une ville tout d'un coup étrangère? Et tout m'est étranger, tout, sans un être à moi, sans un lieu où refermer cette plaie. Que fais-je, à quoi riment ces gestes, ces sourires? Je ne suis pas d'ici – pas d'ailleurs non plus. Et le monde n'est plus qu'un paysage inconnu où mon coeur ne trouve plus d'appuis. Etranger, qui peut savoir ce que ce mot veut dire.

(Camus, in his *Notebooks*)

★

Cafés in Europe. The no-man's-lands where people come to take refuge from time and from their outside selves, where waiters blink at anything and understand everything, where people watch one another silently, across all boundaries and frontiers, from behind newspapers with indecipherable headlines. A café is a stage set for an Absolute Nowhere, a pure parenthesis in the swim of time. It provides somewhere for the body to be while the mind wanders; and it also provides an infinity of small dramas, a strange polyglot intermingling of wishes and wavelengths. There, everybody is, by temperament, a foreigner. And to be a foreigner is not, after all, a question of domicile, but of temperament.

★

We have weathered so many journeys, and so many forms of love. Would it have been the same, we ask one another, had we stayed still, in the mill with the water running under us? There is no way of knowing.

★

What haunts a foreigner is the thought of always having to move on, of finding, in the places where he comes to rest, the ghosts he thought were left behind; or else of losing the sharp edge, the wry, surprised eye that keeps him extraconscious of things. Even at his most assured, he tends to keep a bag packed, in case. The feeling of being lost, however, is never so terrifying when it is compared with the feeling of being found and dried. It is the state of falling in love with a woman one does not quite know yet; and will never quite know.

Foreigners are, if you like, curable romantics. The illusion they retain, perhaps left over from their mysterious childhood epiphanies, is that there might somewhere be a place – and a self – instantly recognisable, into which they will be able to sink with a single, timeless, contented sigh. In the curious region *between* that illusion and the faint terror of being utterly nowhere and anonymous, foreigners live. From there, if they are lucky, they smuggle back occasional undaunted notes, like messages in a bottle, or glimmers from the other side of the mirror.

Other People's Houses

Having been, for many years, an itinerant, living in an alarming number of countries and places, I am no stranger to other people's houses. I am aware of a certain disreputable cast to this admission; I can almost feel my wizened little ancestors shaking their heads and wringing their hands, for in Scotland, people tend to go from the stark stone house where they first see the light to another such fortress, where they sink roots and prepare dutifully for death, their possessions encrusted around them like barnacles. Anyone who did not seem to be following the stone script was looked on as somewhat raffish, rather like the tinkers and traveling people who sometimes passed through the village where I grew up. I would watch them leave, on foot, over the horizon, pulling their worldly belongings behind them in a handcart; and one of my earliest fantasies was to run away with them, for I felt oppressed by permanence and rootedness, and my childhood eyes strayed always to the same horizon, which promised other ways of being, a life less stony and predictable.

My errant nature was confirmed by a long time I spent at sea during the Second World War, on a series of small, cramped ships, wandering all over the Indian Ocean. Then I learned that the greatest advantage was to have as little as possible, for anything extra usually got lost or stolen, and we frequently had to shoulder our worldly goods, from ship to ship. The habit stuck – today I have next to no possessions, and I have closed the door on more houses and apartments than I can remember, leaving behind what I did not immediately need. If I had a family crest, it should read *omnia mea mecum porto* (all that is mine I carry with me); but it would get left behind.

Innocent in themselves, houses can be given quite different auras, depending on the dispositions of their occupants – they can be seen as monuments to permanence, or as temporary shelters. In Scotland, you find abundant examples of the first on the fringes of small towns, standing in well-groomed gardens, their brasses gleaming, their blinds half-drawn like lowered eyelids, domestic museums served by near-invisible slaves. When I first came to the United States, I felt it to be immediately liberating, in its fluidity, its readiness to change. Few people lived in the place they were born, moving held no terrors, and renting was the norm. Yet people inhabited their temporary shelters as though they might live there forever; and paradoxically, I felt at home. When I began to spend a part of each year in Spain, my other adopted country, I rented a series of sturdy peasant houses devoid of decoration, with white-washed walls and tile floors, and no furnishings beyond the essentials of beds, tables, cross, and chairs. It was a time when a number of unanchored people came to rest in Spain – painters for the light, writers for the silence – setting up working outposts in the sun, whose constant presence does simplify existence. Within these anonymous white walls, one re-created one's own world – essential books and pictures, whatever other transforming elements lay to hand.

In Spain, I grew very aware of houses as presences – perhaps the residual aura of those who had lived lifetimes in them, perhaps a peculiarity of the space they enclosed. I recall visiting a house in Mallorca in the company of Robert Graves, and hearing him, after only a few minutes in the house, making peremptory excuses to leave. 'Didn't you feel the bad luck in that house?' he said to me once we were out of earshot. With time, I came to feel what he meant, not in terms of good or bad luck, but of feeling welcome or unwelcome in the houses themselves, apart from the inhabitants.

Of all writers, Vladimir Nabokov read the interiors of other people's houses much as psychics read palms or tarot cards: with a wicked accuracy, he would decipher absent owners from the contents of rooms, from shelves, pictures, and paraphernalia. When he lectured at Cornell University, it was his practice, instead of having a house of his own, to rent the houses of others absent on sabbatical; and behind him already was a wandering life of exile in

England, Germany, and France, in rented premises. Summers he spent in pursuit of butterflies, in motels across the United States; and when, with recognition, he came to rest, it was in a hotel apartment in Montreux, Switzerland. These various houses and interiors inhabit his books as vividly as living characters – he is always making precise connections between people and the places they choose to live in, between objects and their owners. His *Look at the Harlequins!* is a positive hymn to other people's houses.

I know just what he means. The act of inhabiting and humanising a house, of changing it from impersonal space to private landscape, is an extremely complex one, a series of careful and cumulative choices; and, in living in other people's houses, one lives among their decisions, some inspired, others hardly thought through. I make for the bookshelves with a crow of expectation, for the books, however miscellaneous or specialised they may be, always yield up at least a handful I have never read, or even heard of, and travelling has deprived me of the possibility of keeping a library, beyond a shelf of essential or immediate reading. Kitchens are a less calculable adventure. Some of them are like shrines, where cooking has been raised to a level of high art, and invite culinary adventure; others, incomprehensibly, are as bare as hospital labs in plague-prone countries, their refrigerators bearing no more than a few viruses flourishing in jars, two or three bottles of what can only be assumed to be an antidote.

At one point in our lives, my son and I lived in London, on a houseboat we actually owned, though temporarily, moored at Cheyne Walk, in Chelsea. We had three special friends, families that lived in other parts of London; and we came to an arrangement with them to exchange houses from time to time, for appropriate weekends. We had a loose agreement – we left behind clean sheets and towels, a 'reasonable amount' of food and drink, and, for the curious, some correspondence that could be read. We all relished these unlikely vacations, since we left one another elaborately written guidebooks, and we could take in another part of London – markets, greengrocers, pubs, restaurants. I often wonder why people never think of doing that oftener, except at the wrong times.

In our travels, my son and I occupied rented houses and apartments from Barcelona to Buenos Aires. He can remember every one of them in detail, down to its sounds – the creak and shudder of the houseboat as it rose off the Thames mud on the incoming tide, a house in Chile with a center patio cooled by the cooing of doves, a cottage in Scotland in a wood of its own, guarded by a cranky tribe of crows, and the small mountain house in Spain that was our headquarters. Moving was like putting on different lives, different clothes, and we changed easily, falling in with the ways of each country, eating late in Spain, wearing raincoats in Scotland, carrying little from one place to another except the few objects that had become talismans, observing the different domestic rites – of garden and kitchen, mail and garbage.

Since the fifties, I have lived off and on in many different parts of New York, but very intermittently, since I came and went from Spain and from Scotland, never settling decisively in any one of the three. This fall, I returned from a summer spent in Scotland with no apartment – I had given one up before I left, and was expecting another in the spring; but a friend of mine, a dancer, was to be away for a month, and offered me her place in the East Village. I moved in, and took stock.

The apartment itself immediately felt lucky to me, the kind of apartment you want to stay *in* in, with high windows looking out over St Mark's churchyard, and light filtered in through leaves to a white, high-ceilinged room, with about a third of the books new to me, and a long Indian file of records. I fell in happily with the place, explored the neighborhood, and found its Meccas – a Ukrainian butcher shop, pawnshops fat with the appliances of yesteryear, small Indian restaurants that looked as though they might fold themselves up after dinner and silently steal away. I made half-hearted attempts to find a more lasting sublet – buying the *Village Voice* early on Wednesdays, marking up *The Times* real-estate section on Sunday and then losing it – but that place made me immune to urgency, although St Mark's chimed the hours in my ear.

One evening, I was having dinner with a friend of mine, a camera-woman, who lives in a loft in SoHo. She moves fast and often, and always seems to be attached to the ends of five or six active wires, so when we have dinner, we have a lot of ground to cover. Over dessert, she suddenly sat up straight. 'By the way, I have to shoot in Arizona most of October. Do you know anyone who would stay in my loft and look after my cats?' We made a deal there and then; and, in a flash, I could see the shape of fall changing. Looking out reflectively on the churchyard the following morning, I realised that I was ideally equipped to be an itinerant. I have an office at the *New Yorker* magazine, where I keep books and papers, get my mail, and do my writing, when the time is upon me. What furniture remained to me now graced my son's apartment, and I was portable, to the tune of two small bags. I was in touch with other itinerants, some of whom would likely be going somewhere; and I was myself leaving for South America after Christmas, until the spring. So I dropped the *Voice*, and went back to reading Michel Tournier's *Friday and Robinson: Life on Esperanza Island*, my latest bookshelf discovery.

I had never lived in SoHo, and my translation there in October opened it up to me. I had to have a small course of initiation, in the hand elevator, in the fistful of keys, in the cats, and then I saw my friend off in a welter of camera gear – a less portable profession, hers, compared to writing. But then, I have always given thanks that I did not play the harp. The cats. Alvin, the boss-cat was called, a massive, broad-shouldered animal who looked as if he might lift weights in secret. Sadie, his sidekick, was smaller and dumber, but she simpered and purred, which Alvin never did.

Every morning, I fed them first thing, grinding up liver, cleaning their dishes; and when I came back in the evening, they would collar me and drive me toward their empty bowls. The first Saturday, Alvin got through plastic, paper, and close to a pound of sole when I wasn't looking, about an hour after his ample breakfast. But cats are unpunishable by nature, and we came to terms, which meant that I fed them just enough to keep them from breaking into those nerve-rending cries of simulated starvation. Cats in SoHo have the best life going, I concluded, in a loft that must have seemed like an Olympic complex to them, with me to do the shopping. Sometimes I wished they would go out jogging. But I found I could take a brisk walk without leaving the loft, and there was cable television, which kept me up the first couple of nights.

Out in the street I learned to stroll all over again, and I connected up SoHo with the rest of Manhattan. I even took to working there, learning how Alvin and Sadie spent their day.

By then, I had come to count on what John Osborne once called 'the blessed alchemy of word of mouth', that most human of networks, and it put me in touch with a poet-friend, who was to be away giving readings for a spell in November. Could I stay and look after their plants? Unlike Alvin and Sadie, the plants fed slowly, in a slow seep; and I grew attached to one small fern that required drowning every day, and that rewarded me with new green. Their apartment was in the West Village, the part of New York I have lived in most. The stores were familiar, the kitchen a pleasure to cook in, the books unsurpassable, almost all of them good to read or reread. You can count on poets. Eerily enough, I had stayed in the same apartment once before, on a quick visit from Spain in the sixties, when other friends occupied it. Now it was dressed altogether differently; but every so often, I caught a whiff of its old self and experienced a time-warp, with the kind of involuntary start that often becomes a poem in the end.

As my days there were beginning to be countable, another friend called me, a woman who writes often on Latin America. She was going to Honduras quite soon, and she had two questions: Did I know anyone in Tegucigalpa? Did I know anyone who wanted to rent her apartment for December, while she was gone? Yes to both questions; and, a couple of weeks later, I gave her two addresses in exchange for her keys.

There was, however, a spell in November, between cats, plants, and travels, and also between apartments, when I was saved from the streets by being able to find a room on the Upper East Side. I was finishing a piece on writing at the time, working a long day; but even so I never became a familiar of the Upper East Side, never have. It is hardly itinerants' territory. People don't stroll much there – they seem more purposive, and you have to know where the stores are. You don't stumble on them. It was getting difficult, too, with the subways – I had to think, really *think*, where I was living, Uptown or Downtown, not to go hurtling on the subway in a wrong though familiar direction.

My last resting place lay on the Upper West Side, also a new territory to me, since I have always thought of Forty-fifth Street as the Northern Frontier. It was, however, a revelation. There were oases of movie theaters, comforting even though I never went inside, plenty of odd stores to stumble on, and the neighbourhood, to my delight, was Spanish-speaking, even rich in Dominicans, the pleasantest people in Christendom. Moreover, a number of people I had always thought of as out of range turned out to live around the corner. I had had a hasty airport call from my Honduras-bound landlady that morning. 'Just pile the papers so you can walk around,' she told me tersely. Indeed, her apartment looked as though the negotiations over the Panama Canal had just been hastily concluded in it.

I cleared a camping space first, and then I put the place in order. I have a stern morality about occupying other people's houses: I feel they have to be left in better shape than I find them, and this may mean fixing faucets or supplying anything missing, from light bulbs to balloons. What her apartment needed was restoring to its original order, now only skeletally visible. Anyone who tries to keep up with Central America these days acquires a weekly layer of new information, and her layers went back a few months. When I had the papers rounded up and corralled, the books and records in their shelves and sleeves, the cups and glasses steeping, the place began to emerge and welcome me, and I found, under the sofa, an Anne Tyler novel I had not read. One thing did puzzle me: as I cleaned, I came everywhere on scatters of pennies, on the floor, on chairs, on desk and table, by the bed. I could not account for their ubiquity, but I gathered them in a jar, about enough to buy a good dinner. Christmas was coming to the Upper West Side, with great good cheer; but so was the cold weather, so I went one morning, and booked my air ticket.

Before I left the city, I retraced my wanderings of the fall, going home again and again. If you have lived in somebody's house, after all, you have acquired a lot in common with them, a lot to talk about, from the eccentricities of their pipes to the behavior of their furniture. The tree house by St Mark's looked properly seasonal, with a fire burning. I find I can still occupy it in my head, with

165

pleasure. I went by the West Village, sat talking for hours in the kitchen, and then walked down to SoHo, where I called on Alvin and Sadie, who looked keenly to see if I had brought fish before withdrawing to rest up. I dropped off a winter coat with my son, and made for the airport and the warm weather with my two bags, leaving behind not one city but several, I felt, shedding a cluster of distinct lives. I just had time to call my friend, newly back from Tegucigalpa. Her time had been good, yes, she had talked at length with my friends, the apartment was great, thanks for fixing the closet door, I had turned up things she thought she'd lost, she felt maybe she had caught a bug in Honduras. I asked her about the pennies. 'Oh, yes, thanks for picking them up,' she laughed. 'It's just that I throw the *I Ching* a lot. Have a good trip.'

Aunt Gibraltar
1961

Gibraltar, as all schoolboys and insurance men know, is not so much a place as a thing – a positive monument to durability. Oaths are readily sworn, and vows taken, on the assumption of its continuing existence. I saw Gibraltar often enough, during the war and after, without ever paying much attention to it beyond realising that if anything would keep, it would be the Rock, but more recently I began to brood on the implausible fact of a British Crown Colony's existing on Spanish soil, for if ever two temperaments were unlikely to blend they are the English and the Spanish. So I decided to fly down one Sunday from Madrid, along with a smattering of American tourists who were catching a ship, three rawboned British businessmen, and a solitary, black-eyed Gibraltarian. At the Madrid airport, the Spanish police stamped our passports with a fixed official scowl, which did not surprise me – the resentment felt by Spain over Gibraltar is curiously sharp, considering it has been a British possession for over two hundred and fifty years. I have noticed that while the more sophisticated Spaniards dismiss 'the Gibraltar question' airily as one of little importance, they always add, as a rueful afterthought, 'Of course, it really *is* ours, you know!'

Gibraltar is whimsically small (it could be set down in Central Park, with some spilling over at the edges), but its situation and its blunt burliness lend it a pugnacious emphasis – it forms a kind of thumb on the eastern tip of the Bay of Algeciras, and misses being an island by dint of a narrow isthmus joining it to Spain. As English schoolboys can tell you, it was one of the Pillars of Hercules, and a gatepost of the entrance to the Mediterranean; from it you can easily see the looming African coast, a mere twenty miles to the south, and the neat white Spanish town of Algeciras, across the bay

167

to the west. Its air of spunky self-confidence comes in part from its being an autonomous British Crown Colony – the smallest one in the Commonwealth – with its own colonial government, its own stamps and police force, its own little frontier. To look at, the Rock is quite monumental, towering sheer up from the flat table of the airport to a height of almost fourteen hundred feet, pitted silver-gray, with occasional green wooded shelves. Its presence imposes a dwarfish proportion on the town of Gibraltar, which sprawls up its western side (the eastern side is only sparsely populated), and one finds oneself regularly glancing up at its brooding, changing bulk. It is so emphatically there, and time has endowed it with a great-grandfatherly aura.

A bus set me down in the middle of the town, and I asked the driver if the hotel was far. 'Not at all,' he replied. 'I'm afraid nothing is far here.' He was quite right. One finds oneself walking back and forth along Main Street several times a day, in the hope that it may actually be longer than it is, and I noticed also that after two or three days I began to be conscious of having seen a great many of the people before. With so little flat ground at the foot of the Rock, the town has had to clamber over itself to exist at all; the houses perch on one another's shoulders, and in the steeper streets you look from your basement window into your neighbour's attic. Fundamentally, the town has a Spanish look, with faded pink-and-brown walls, but on top of this has been imposed a brisk, shipshape British tidiness – a thoroughly un-Spanish spickness of fresh paint, lampposts, notices, and polished brass. Also, I had arrived on a Sunday, but it was far from being the lazy, garrulous Spanish Sunday I was used to; instead, the town was shut up in tight disapproval, with not a shop open and the streets haunted by idling sailors gazing aimlessly at windowfuls of silent cameras and watches – British sailors, to be sure, doomed to such shuttered Sundays ashore. As I came down at dusk from a long, climbing walk, a solid English hymn was manfully emanating from the Cathedral, but around another corner or two a cha-cha-cha was having its way in a grubby dance hall. In Gibraltar, you necessarily grow used to juxtapositions of this kind. The place is so many things at once – a fortress, a seaport, an international market, a British colonial capital, a place where people live, a fragment of Spain – and the representatives of these separate functions jostle one another comically and continuously. Stiff-faced service officers, gawking tourists with wallets and cameras cocked, Spanish workmen shuffling in from La Línea de la Concepción – the Spanish town at the top of the isthmus – for day labour, shopkeepers smiling expansively in their doorways, and retired English squires with tweedy dogs all mingle in buzzing coexistence. As far as the town goes, it is first a fortress. The massive gray walls and the names of the streets – Castle Ramp, Engineer Lane, Line Wall Road, Casemates Square, Bomb House Lane, King's Bastion, South Barrack Road – all smack of siege; an occasional sentry with fixed bayonet glares into space, and faraway bugle calls float up from the harbour. One morning, I ran into the changing of the Governor's Guard, a small pomposity in itself, with an apoplectic sergeant major wrenching words of command from his apparently exhausted lungs; simultaneously, a stunted Spaniard, with beret and yellow cigarette end, teetered across the square behind a wheelbarrow of fish, calling '*Pescado*' in a quavering tenor. I felt I had stumbled into the rehearsal of some strange multilingual musical. If I had waited about long enough, the English-looking policeman on the corner might have burst into flamenco, as he did on other occasions.

Eventually, it dawned on me that this apparent English-Spanish ambiguity was quite normal and that Gibraltarians are not only comfortably bilingual but quite distinct in character from both British and Spaniards. The British, for the most part, are attached either to the garrison or to the administration for a particular tour of duty, and seem to speak little Spanish; Spaniards come across the frontier – eleven thousand of them every day – to work in the dockyard or in hotels and restaurants, returning to Spain each evening. The Gibraltarians are the only ones who truly *live* in Gibraltar, and they form just over two thirds of the population of twenty-six thousand. They are, both technically and passionately, British subjects, but at the same time, as they point out, Gibraltar is not Britain. 'We are sometimes referred to as being embarrassingly British,' one of them told me over a drink at his house, 'but we are so out of respect, and also because it has been entirely in our interest to claim our British nationality – we have absorbed so much, and we have acquired our whole civic organisation from the British, even to the extent of imposing income tax on ourselves. But at the same time, as far as our feelings for Britain go, it's like having a foster mother. We are, at bottom, more concerned with our distinctiveness than we are with being British. We tend to make fun of any Gibraltarian who becomes in our eyes too English, but at the same time you will scarcely find one of us who is not thankful for his British passport.'

'But do you not feel strong attachments to Spain – temperamentally, I mean?' I asked him.

'Oh, tremendously,' he said. 'We are very much at home in Spain; in fact, I would say that we count entirely on Spain for our pleasure. Every time I can get away in summer, I drive to the *ferias* – I have a great passion for the bulls, and at the bull-fight I react like a Spaniard. But remember, we Gibraltarians are also realistic. When we take a look at Spain economically and politically, we thank our stars for Gibraltar. We love going to Spain, but when we return, we feel that we are returning to freedom. There is not one of us who would choose to become a Spaniard now – we'd rather be Chinese. We are both British and Spanish, but we are neither. We eat both *potaje* and eggs-and-bacon; we listen to flamenco and to military bands. You notice that we speak both languages equally badly – in fact, we scarcely realise which one we are speaking. My father was a Gibraltarian, but my mother was Spanish, and, as a child, when I wanted to annoy her, I used to speak English.'

At that point, the telephone rang and he picked it up. '*Hola, qué tal?* . . . *Sí, pasa por aquí* about four o'clock,' he said into it.

I saw what he meant. In time, I grew used to this quite contained bilinguality. Gibraltarians speak English with a decided (or, rather, an undecided) accent – a slightly staccato English altogether free of the characteristic Spanish *s*-stumblings – yet at the same time their Spanish is not the famously lazy, lisping Andalusian spoken across the frontier but a casual, slurred Spanish of their own, incorporating many English words, like *'tipol'* and *'sospán'* for 'teapot' and 'saucepan'. They suffer no ambiguity of mind, however, and straddle both traditions quite jauntily, following the bullfights and filling in their English football-pool coupons. The ambiguity exists mostly in the eye of the beholder. I was told of an Englishwoman who, arriving in Gibraltar, stopped suddenly and remarked, 'Oh, I say – your policemen dress just like *our* policemen!' The Gibraltarian who told me the story said he had spent a long time trying to think of a way to clarify her mind, but had finally given up, deciding that it would be simpler to work wholeheartedly for Gibraltar's independence.

★

Present-day Gibraltarians have a bizarre racial background. When the British took the Rock, in 1704, the resident Spaniards were allowed to evacuate it peaceably, and they settled in the nearby Spanish village of San Roque, where they continued to regard themselves as the rightful inhabitants of Gibraltar. A small settlement of Genoese, however, elected to remain in Gibraltar under British rule, and later they were joined by other Italians and by some of the Sephardim – the descendants of the Jews of Spain, who had taken refuge in various parts of the world – who came to trade and settle in Gibraltar by way of Portugal and Leghorn. Since Queen Anne, in 1705, had declared Gibraltar a free port, the local population carried on a lively trade with North Africa and with Spain, and new strains gradually insinuated themselves into the native population; Portuguese settled in large numbers, members of the shifting British garrison often elected to stay in Gibraltar, and eventually Spaniards and Maltese and more Italians came and took root. The present population is a thorough fusion of these mainly Mediterranean elements, and is predominantly Roman Catholic; the Jews, however, have adhered to their faith, and have had a profoundly important influence on the well-being of the colony.

Gibraltar really has two quite separate histories: the small, private history of its native inhabitants (the noun 'native' is frowned on, probably because it has always been used rather indiscriminately by the British), and its long, more spectacular history as a fortress that has never lost any of its importance through a succession of European wars – an importance that even now, for all the shift in strategic emphasis, has not in the least diminished in the eyes of any of the bristling military types I spoke to. I spent a good part of my time in the Garrison Library – a graceful, well-kept building with a notice board cluttered with small, diffident announcements of phonograph recitals, country-dance-group teas, and committee meetings – looking through its impressive collection of works on Gibraltar. Eventually, I settled down with the 1777 edition of *A Journey from Gibraltar to Malaga, with a View of That Garrison and Its Environs*, by Francis Carter, Esq., F.S.A. His preface put me firmly in my place:

> There have been hitherto no other accounts of this coast published in our language but the cursory remarks and vague descriptions of English gentlemen, who, making but a few days' residence at its capital towns, often only as many hours, could not be expected (how much merit soever they might otherwise possess) to give any regular history of a people with whose language they were wholly unacquainted: I have known Spain from my very childhood, since the year 1753, to 1773; all my time (except for five years spent in France) was passed in Andalusia and the kingdom of Granada; during so long an absence from my native country, I sought consolation through the study of that in which it was my lot to reside.

I decided to go respectfully on with Mr Carter:

> The Moors under Tarif-Abenzarca, in the year of Our Lord 714, were the first who noticed the natural strength of the place; they built, peopled, and fortified both the castle and town . . . The hill lost its ancient name of Calpe on the arrival of Tarif, who called it after himself Gibel-Tarif, or Tarif's mountain; Abdulmalic, historian of the kings of Morocco, deduces its present name from Gibel-tath, or the Mountain of the Entrance, being the key that led them into Spain; but Leo Africanus says expressly its truest derivation is from Gibel-fetoh, which in Arabick signifies the Mountain of Victory, [and] Abulcacim Tarif Abentarique calls it by a similar name, Jabal-fath. Hence Gibraltar by the Spaniards.

Gibraltar was occupied and reoccupied several times in the wars between Moors and Spaniards before Spain settled down in possession of it, in 1462, and set about restoring its fortifications. When Queen Isabella of Spain died, in 1504, she commanded in her will that her heirs undertake the sacred charge of holding Gibraltar. It was she who awarded Gibraltar its coat of arms – a castle with a key pendent and an inscription that reads, 'Seal of the Noble City of Gibraltar, the Key of Spain'. In spite of her injunction, Gibraltar fell to a combined British and Dutch fleet in 1704, during the War of the Spanish Succession, and, over Dutch protests, the British dug themselves in, fending off a few abortive Spanish attempts to regain it until the Treaty of Utrecht, in 1713, left them in ratified possession. In a Gibraltar bar one night, I over-heard an intricate argument over what was precisely implied in the wording of the treaty, which made it clear to me that loose prose, particularly in treaties, is not a thing to leave lying about.

Treaty or no treaty, the Spaniards seem never quite to have given up hope of recovering the Peñón, as they call the Rock. Through-out most of the eighteenth century they besieged it with waspish repetition, but it was in 1779, during the Maritime Wars, in which Spain allied herself to France for the single purpose of recovering Gibraltar and Minorca, that the four-year-long Great Siege – the most dramatic single episode in Gibraltar's knobbled past – was launched. An enormous and excited Franco-Spanish Army en-trenched itself on the isthmus facing the Rock, little more than a cannon shot away. As every American schoolboy knows, the British were greatly extended elsewhere at the time, and could not reliably be expected to sustain the garrison (which amounted to about five and a half thousand men) from the sea. Gibraltar's number appeared to be up.

I read several accounts of the Great Siege in the Library – even one in the faded handwritten original – and it was not difficult for me to imagine myself back to the circumstances of it, particularly since I had only to glance out of the window to verify places and distances. In the same way, both sides must have noted each other's every activity throughout the four years. The garrison had the good fortune to be commanded by General George Augustus

Eliott, in every sense the right man to have on one's side. (In the Alameda Gardens there is a greening bust of him – beetle-browed, with a great hook nose – and a copy of a portrait of him by Reynolds hangs in the Gibraltar Museum.) All during the cruel deprivations of the siege – at one point, ammunition was so low that the batteries had to restrict themselves to firing three shots a day, which they referred to as the Father, the Son, and the Holy Ghost – Eliott maintained a roistering, good-humoured discipline, and, beyond that, was able to show remarkable military ingenuity. In November, 1781, he had the audacity to launch a secret night attack, using a third of his men, on the forward Spanish batteries, and completely destroyed them. (Sortie Day is still observed by the Army in Gibraltar.) Eliott also encouraged his men to think up schemes that might break the stalemate, and eventually gave his permission to one, Sergeant-Major Ince, to tunnel long galleries close to the surface of the Rock, at a height of six hundred feet, from which to fire down on the Spaniards. The galleries still exist, with some of the guns in position, pointing dizzily down at the present airstrip. It was an astonishing piece of engineering, considering the times and circumstances, and one that made a good deal more practical sense than the detailed plan with which a Spanish engineer approached the Due de Crillon, the French commander, for building a vast mountain, higher than Gibraltar, a short way inland, 'thus depriving the fortress of its chief advantage.' Crillon declined to build the mountain, but he did put all his eggs into building ten floating batteries – huge, heavily armed hulls filled with damp sand and cork to prevent their catching fire. The British could watch them being readied across the bay, and as the climax of the siege drew near, thousands of spectators gathered on the surrounding hills to see Gibraltar fall. On the morning of September 13, 1782, the ten batteries lumbered to their stations, about a thousand yards from the shore. At his home in Sussex, prior to coming out to assume the Governorship, Eliott had with quiet aplomb practised using heated cannon balls, and he now proceeded to rain red-hot fire on the batteries until, by afternoon, wispy flames began to show from the *Pastora*, the flagship of the attacking fleet. Crillon's supporting craft arrived too late, and by midnight most of the anchored ships were ablaze or had blown up. Spanish and French casualties numbered about two thousand, and Gibraltar was still intact. Crillon withdrew, and in the next month Lord Howe brilliantly manoeuvred a relieving fleet into the bay. The siege petered out the following February, and although the Peace of Versailles clipped back the British Empire and let Spain keep Minorca and Florida, Britain sat on Gibraltar, and Spain lost its last chance to negotiate for its restoration. On the Spanish and French side, the Great Siege was mismanaged, but this in no way dims the doggedness and audacity of the garrison. By the time I had read two or three accounts of the siege, and had noted General Eliott's elevation to the peerage, as Lord Heathfield, I might have cheered aloud had it not been for the presence of two formidable-looking ladies in the Library.

'If Jimmy gets a horse, he'll be absolutely all right,' said the first.

'Yes, and since it *is* an English company . . . ' said the other.

I replaced the heroic documents and left.

★

All British schoolboys, at some stage or other, are given a toy fort and a miscellany of tin soldiers, often handed down by a graduating generation, with which they acquire a tidy sense of nursery strategy, and something of this addiction has gone into Gibraltar's evolution as a fortress. It is so neatly ingenious. Burrowing in the wake of Sergeant-Major Ince, engineers ran rabbit-wild inside the Rock itself, and now there is an estimated thirty miles of tunnelling, concealing who knows what. (Characteristically, the loose excavated rock was used as the foundations for the reclaimed dock areas and for the seaward extension of the airstrip.) Since the place depends for its water supply mainly on rainfall, great catchments cover the higher and steeper slopes, the rain running into enormous reservoirs inside the Rock. Roads have been masterfully imagined, to give unlikely access to even the upper Rock – tidy little roads, with a goodly lining of green shade. Bare though the Rock may look from the sea, its semi-tropical vegetation is surprisingly profuse and varied – pines, cypresses, and wild olives abound – and throughout the town there are, of course, multitudes of those small, parade-ground garden patches that British service-men manage to conjure out of whatever wilderness they find themselves in.

The First World War and, more dramatically, the Second under-lined the stupendous importance of Gibraltar as a military, naval, and air base; it virtually kept Britain afloat in the Mediterranean, especially during the period when the Axis controlled practically the entire Mediterranean coastline. I recall putting in to the Rock a few times during the war, when the immediate vicinity was aboil, and finding it a brisk beehive of military efficiency – so much so that in the end we scarcely bothered to go ashore, for life in the fortress was even tenser and more controlled than it was on shipboard. Gibraltar's very existence at that point was like a blow struck. Whenever we spotted the great doubled fist of the Rock from seaward, it always cheered us up. On this occasion, the second morning I was there I watched three destroyers slip from the harbour, with much booping of sirens, and turn in line into the bay. I must say they looked stirring to me. It is the efficient com-pactness of everything – dockyard, harbour, airfield, fortifications, roads, barracks, hospitals – that gives the place its air of intense, concentrated importance, like a clockwork microcosm. Since, as my friend Francis Carter remarks, 'the English being a nation that, in all their colonies spread over the face of the globe, study more the useful than the grand,' and since Gibraltar still has its thumb on the approaches to the Mediterranean and its eye cocked toward Spain and Africa, there seems little likelihood that Britain will ever seriously consider giving it back to anyone. Even to the small grey pillow of cloud that, by repute, hangs perpetually over the fore-head of the Rock, Gibraltar is stiff with Englishness, with that ripe, determined cheer and relentless go that the English emanate. When something has to be done or solved, however unpleasant, the English take a rare, secret pleasure in getting on with it; it is when there is no particular task or hardship in sight that they falter. Unlike the Spaniards, they have little natural talent for being alone, although they suffer their boredom dauntlessly. On Main Street, I noticed Spaniards eyeing pretty women with their habitual delighted Mediterranean wonder; the British servicemen, on the other hand, looked at them with quiet, furtive desperation, as they might have eyed forbidden candy. In the Alameda Gardens, I played on a fiendishly contrived miniature golf course, full of traps and obstacles, which seemed to represent, *in parvo*, the ferocious ingenuity of the whole place, and as I came away I passed a sign that read:

These gardens are cultivated for your pleasure.
Please co-operate by observing these rules:
1   Do not touch the plants or walk on the flower beds.
2   Keep dogs on a leash while in the garden.
3   Do not leave litter in the garden.

Below, the same text followed in Spanish, but the Spanish read as if it had been unwillingly dragged there, like a child forcibly dressed up for an occasion. All through the town, there is a tyranny of well-groomed signs. Every eventuality has been provided for in advance, every small aspect of the place accounted for. I read my way through no less than five volumes of statistics on the colony, and could not help marvelling at their minuteness. Perhaps this is why Gibraltar has no *mystique*; it has all been patiently organised down to the last detail. Even the resident ape population has an officer in charge of it. The colony has an impressive array of social services, and pays scrupulous attention to itself.

Relations between Gibraltarians and British, however, have not always been quite as amiable as they now appear to be. In the past, Gibraltar suffered from what is officially called a 'fortress mentality'; Gibraltarians complained that military considerations were apt to take precedence over the well-being of the community, and the pointed aloofness of the British tended to put the local inhabitants on edge. It is not difficult to understand this ruffling of feelings. The British govern their colonies gently but firmly, as a nanny might ('Yes, dear, but Britain knows best'), with a kind of instinctive gamesmanship – a tacit underlying assumption of superiority that provokes a slow, shuffling resentment, although on the surface their rule is so cool, so efficient, so fair and just that one must always seriously admire it on paper and in retrospect. Now, however, the edginess has all but gone. In 1950, by Royal Instructions, a

Legislative Council was created, presided over by the Governor
and consisting of twelve members – three civil-service officials,
two members nominated by the Governor, and seven elected
members (a majority), all seven of whom are Gibraltarians. This
naturally gave Gibraltarians a substantial measure of control over
their own affairs, and has been taken extremely seriously by the
local population; the British colonial officials, too, have been forced
to concern themselves more minutely and less blandly with
Gibraltar's internal affairs. Two or three times during my stay, I
found myself in the midst of colony-shaking arguments –
arguments that seemed to be a part of a regular, running
conversation. They generally arose over some small local matter
currently preoccupying the Legislative Council and almost always
led into large speculations on the future of the colony, since the
Gibraltarians, having now got a grip on their own destiny, feel the
day to be at hand when they will have to choose – or at least
approach Nanny with the question – whether they will have
complete self-determination. Even though they have fought
energetically for their present representation, they remain sharply
divided over what they want next. From all the argument, I
gathered that Gibraltarians are very proud of the steps they have
taken toward governing themselves, and that their speculations on
the future are a kind of muscle-flexing – a rather abrupt extension
of their new-found sense of responsibility. The chances are that
they will gain almost complete control over internal affairs in the
colony, at the same time leaving the British pretty much in charge
of the place *qua* fortress. Local happenings are national issues –
Gibraltar has all the problems of being a full colony with no more
resources than those of a small town.

★

Gibraltarians are serious people, and they are also awesomely
industrious. Several times I met the mayor of Gibraltar, Mr J. A.
Hassan, C.B.E., M.V.O., J.P., as he darted in and out of other
people's offices, but I was never able to corner him until one
sunny afternoon when he picked me up on the road and drove me
into the town. A small, high-voiced man with a wiry, intense

intelligence, he talked eagerly and excitedly to me as we sat in his car outside the freshly painted Town Hall.

'You've probably been trying to puzzle us out and put us in pigeonholes,' he said, with a sudden, charming smile. 'Well, I'm glad to tell you that we won't fit, either as Spaniards or as Englishmen. We have learned enormously from the British in that we follow the rules – we respect punctuality and efficiency, we keep our word, and we believe in fair play, the law, and an ordered way of life. Spaniards find us puzzling. For instance, I was talking recently to a Spanish officer, and he said to me, "Look, Hassan, you've been mayor now for the last twelve years – you must be doing well for yourself." The truth is that I have been so absorbed in civic affairs and in constitutional reform, which is my pre-occupation, that I have had scarcely any time for my law practice, and, as you know, we receive only a token salary for our administrative duties. The officer was horrified when I told him. We like to think that we embody the best elements of our dual temperament. Our elections are orderly and fair, and we would not think of corrupting them. At the same time, we do feel ourselves to be Latin in the sense that the positions we take are never purely theoretical ones – we shift and adjust them until they fit our particular situations, bearing individuals in mind. Gibraltar politics are *human* politics, not in the least theoretical. I would call myself a Socialist in economics and a liberal in politics, yet you may hear me occasionally referred to as a right-wing capitalist. Actually, the definitions need scarcely ever arise here; the place is small enough to allow us to act *particularly*, in terms of what we immediately want to achieve, for the general good. I have lost count of the number of committees I sit on, but we get our business done because we are all so continuously in touch with one another.' So saying, he darted quickly out of the car.

Later, I spoke to him in his office overlooking John Mackintosh Square, and again I got the impression that even if plans and decisions on the future of the colony did not yet exist on paper, they were already humming about in the mayor's head. 'We have all had to learn the art of compromise from the British,' he told me. 'But I think that we have also taught them many things, and have made them grow a little more human in their application of principle. As you probably realise, we have been trying our wings for the last ten years, and we fly, on the whole, pretty well.'

*

Gibraltar's Main Street has a surprising habit of filling up and emptying quite suddenly; cruise ships arrive and land their passengers for a two-hour jaunt through the bulging shops, and as quickly spirit them away. (It is quite astonishing how many people turn out to have either landed at or touched at Gibraltar. In 1878, General U. S. Grant was given a banquet in St. George's Hall, the chamber that Sergeant-Major Ince hollowed out of the rock, and in 1919 the Abbé Henri Breuil discovered, in the course of a walk, the site of a shelter of the Mousterian period, about 40,000 BC, at the base of the Rock on the north front.) Tourists are so important to Gibraltar's economy that shopkeepers enjoy a special dispensation to open on Sundays should a ship dock. The limited duty that, thanks to Queen Anne, makes almost everything cheaper in Gibraltar keeps its streets well trodden and its cash registers ringing, but Gibraltarians seem thoroughly bored with their own plenty. You cannot, after all, buy a watch or a high-power telescope all that often, nor can you go on gazing like a hungry sailor into windows draped with satin cushion covers and brimming over with papier-mâché models of the Rock that play 'Annie Laurie'. Nevertheless, tourism looms large in Gibraltar's future, and the foundations are already laid for two vast new hotels, even for a casino. It is, however, difficult to imagine how the Rock can, like some genial Gulliver, bear any more human traffic. The prosperity of the place has already caused every local inhabitant who can afford one to get himself a gleaming new car, with the comic result that there are more cars in ratio to the population in Gibraltar than practically anywhere else in the world. The consequences, though, are far from comic, since it is constantly necessary to press oneself flat against the walls of the already narrow streets to avoid being run down. Moreover, there is scarcely anywhere for cars to go except into the Rock itself. 'Yesterday, I drove my car the quarter of a mile from my house to the office,' one official told me, 'and then, after I had crawled about for half an hour looking for a parking place, I had to drive back home, only to find that the space outside my house had been filled. I was an hour late for work.' The steps to be taken are so obvious that it is only a matter of time until cars are eliminated from the town, yet the people have grown so to look forward to their weekend jaunts into Spain that their cars have become for them symbols not only of prosperity but of escape from the cramped confinement of the place.

Relations between Spain and Gibraltar, like those between Britain and Gibraltar, have not always been as temperate as they now are; in fact, it is only in the past two years that they have returned to being at all easy. As recently as 1956, General Franco, drawing himself up to his full height of five feet four inches, declared in a rare press interview that the return of Gibraltar to Spain was a matter of honour for every Spaniard, adding that 'the present state of Gibraltar is contrary to the whole spirit of postwar Europe' − a typically bizarre statement, considering the present state of Spain. In 1954, the year marking the two-hundred-and-fiftieth anniversary of the British seizure of the Rock, Franco gave vent to a savage burst of propaganda and invective against the proposed visit of the Queen in that year to Gibraltar, and he managed to whip up a great deal of agitation at the time, perhaps because he felt then that he had the United States on his side, but more likely because he has always smarted under the slighting treatment he has had at the hands of the British. At any rate, the British Embassy in Madrid was stoned and mobbed, and the Queen's life was actually threatened by letter. Franco also referred obliquely to a secret agreement allegedly made by Churchill during the Second World War, by which Spain would receive Gibraltar in return for staying neutral. But the British did not budge, and the Queen made her visit in peace. Franco's rampage subsided in the following year, but not before he had closed the Spanish consulate in Gibraltar, barred Spanish tourists from visiting the Rock, and provoked a flurry of measures and countermeasures that made the crossing of the frontier, for both Spaniards and Gibraltar residents, corrosively difficult. Most of my Spanish friends conceded that 'the

Gibraltar question' was nothing more than a convenient escape valve for the General, through which he expressed his more sinister irritations; in any case, not one of the Spanish workers with whom I spoke in cafés on both sides of the frontier considered the return of Gibraltar anything short of a disastrous prospect. 'It's not a matter of honour in *my* soul,' said one cheerful little waiter. 'It's a matter of daily bread – or, let's say, daily cigarettes. I'd like to see Franco feed us just once the way we eat off Gibraltar.' Since Franco has subsequently become much more of a beggar than a chooser, the animosity has subsided, and Gibraltarians are again able to take their pleasure in Spain. 'Lot of fuss about nothing,' growled one Army major when we discussed it. 'There's only one thing that Franco can do about Gibraltar, and that's to saw it off.'

★

When the time came to leave Gibraltar, I decided to walk to La Línea and take a bus along the coast of Málaga, more or less following the route of my mentor Mr Carter. The morning was sunny, and so still that the sound of hammering, and even of voices, floated up from the dockyard. In front of the Governor's Residence, the guard was changing itself again, with a crunch of boots and a tight punctuation of commands. I stopped to read one last notice, which in itself was a monument to the place:

> The public are warned that under the provisions of paragraph (35) of section 3 of the summary conviction ordinance it is an offence to encourage the rock apes to come down from the upper rock or to feed them at any place other than the Queen's Gate Road, between the aerial standard and the Queen's Gate, or at Queen's Gate, and any person convicted of such an offence shall be liable to a penalty not exceeding £10.

In Gibraltar town, shops were beginning to open up, and barrow-loads of flowers stood in the main square. As one walks toward Spain, the town actually grows more Spanish – the cafés are dingier and smaller, and a crowd of women buzzes about the open fish market. I began to meet the steady stream of workers tramping in for their day's work, lunch in hand and brown, creased faces squinting in the sun. As I left the town and started to cross the width of the airstrip, I already felt Gibraltar beginning to recede and loom. Looking up at the rock face, I could just distinguish the small dotted line of Ince's gunports across it, and I felt that, from some small lookout on its woody forehead, an ape might possibly be watching me go. To reach the Spanish frontier, one has to cross the Neutral Ground, a windswept expanse of scrub, smelling of the sea, with occasional concrete pillboxes dotted about. At the gate on the British side, two blue-uniformed policemen saluted briskly, glanced at my passport, and, addressing me by name, wished me a good morning and passed me through to the Spanish policemen on the other side. These leafed their way slowly through the passport, peering at it page by page. It was all very formal. How long was I to be in Spain? I replied that I lived in Spain. Oh? Then what was I doing in Gibraltar? I had been visiting Gibraltar. Oh. The faces of the Spanish policemen had not mastered the impassivity of their British counterparts. They changed quickly from suspicion to puzzlement to curiosity to wonder. I could go now.

At the other end of the Neutral Ground, I walked through an arch, past an indifferent customs official who was picking his nails, and came into the main plaza of La Línea. The transition was comically sudden. Rickety café tables and chairs sprawled across the sidewalks and into the road. The white walls were blinding in the sun. Dogs lay snoring in the gutters. Children were splashing water over one another from a fountain, spraying it into the air in great, glistening arcs. Men lounged about in twos and threes, talking and gesticulating. Women with bulging vegetable baskets called out, laughed, and scolded. It was hard even to think myself back across the odd half-mile into Gibraltar. There everything had been so polite and brisk and private; here the life of the place was spilling out of the houses into the street – old clothes and slippers replaced the neatness of uniforms. I pushed my way past two donkeys into the cool dark interior of a café on the heels of a fat little Spaniard who had waddled across the frontier in front of me and who was greeted jovially by the two or three men sitting over dominoes at a zinc table close to the bar. They had begun to talk excitedly when one of the men jerked his head in my direction, and they all stopped and looked at me. The waiter came forward. What did I want? I replied that I wanted a glass of beer, and could he tell me where I could catch the bus for Málaga? The bus would be outside in the plaza in about twenty minutes' time, he told me, but I would not be able to get back to Gibraltar tonight. It did not matter, I said, since I had only been visiting the place. Officially? No, I was only curious to see what it was like, and what went on there. The men began to laugh, and the small, fat one came up to me. 'The Señor has come at a good moment,' he said, and winked. 'We can show him what goes on, all right, and how amiable we feel toward the Peñón. Although Spain is our mother, Gibraltar, you must understand, is our aunt, and, as it happens in human life, aunts are always kinder to us children than mothers are.'

As he spoke, he was undoing his belt, and, pulling on a string that was fastened to it, he reverently drew a bottle of whisky from the recesses of his trouser leg. 'A gift from the Queen of England to the disloyal subjects of General Franco!' he shouted, thumping it proudly on the bar.

The others cackled, and he wormed a bottle of English gin from his other trouser-leg. 'A gift from the Governor of Gibraltar to Lucho Montesinos! May he keep on his profitable fat feet these many years!'

While I drank my beer, he unpinned two cartons of cigarettes and a variety of small articles from the lining of his jacket and piled them up beside the bottles. 'Now, Señor,' he said to me, 'I am going to uncork this glorious whisky, and, early in the day though it is, we will drink a toast together to Aunt Gibraltar, who is so kind to us, and whom may God reward with many years of life. If ever it should be ours again, we will tidy it up and present it once more to the great Queen Isabel, who is so gracious. Is she not?'

The others nodded and smiled. We drank.

In Spain during the fifties, I would often visit friends who had retreated to a small mountain village, well off the beaten track. The silence was towering, absolute. I got to know the place and its inhabitants, and when I heard of a remote house for sale, well beyond the village, I bought it, and I spent a part of each year there. The village had once been self-sufficient, but it was changing, as all Spain was changing. The village became my Spanish microcosm, and I wrote a number of pieces from there, chronicling both the quickening pulse of Spain and the village's slow dying. I have pruned the pieces of dated material. From the beginning, I took care not to name or identify the place; and I see no reason to do so now.

A. R.

Notes from a Spanish Village
1974

You cannot stumble on the village. For one thing, the road ends there, and, for another, you cannot see it from below – not until the church looms above you, and houses begin to show on the carefully groomed terraces, dotted haphazardly here and there, with no apparent access. Around the last, climbing corner, more of the village appears, as though the houses had suddenly shown themselves in order to see who was coming. It is a perplexing place, in that it has no real centre except a quiet paved square beside the church. It has grown up among the terraces that line two bowls in the steep side of the valley. Each house appears to have been conceived separately. There are no streets. The paved road becomes a dust road, then a track winding up and up. Above the top rim, the sky is fiercely blue. My son and I have often tried to make a map of the place, but it defeats us; only an aerial photograph would show the curious contours of the ground. We are used to being surprised by the place – by the way each house looks out on a different village, a different-shaped mountain. The mountains set the atmosphere – grey rocky crests hazy in the heat, with a fringe of pines on the tree line and, on the lower slopes, olive groves and long rows of darker-green almond trees. We climb steadily up, with the slow, bent-kneed plod that the villagers use, turning to look down over the village, a patchwork of ochre roofs and green terraces, and then we walk over the crest onto a small, fertile plateau, on the far corner of which stand our house and, beside it, a little ilex forest, which falls steeply away to the next valley, far below. From the house, there is no trace of the village, and no sound other than the jangle of goat bells, or the bark of the dog on the adjoining farm. Sitting on the stone terrace, I can hear insects rustling in the wheat, the whirr of birds' wings, the stirring of leaves. Sounds of our well – the rattling chain, the thud and plunge of the bucket, the creak of the wheel – loom loud in the attention. Over the village hangs the same towering silence. The hollows form acoustical traps, so conversations across the valley will float into hearing, the words just indistinguishable but the tune clear. The sound of an occasional car does not break the silence so much as puncture it slightly, thus underlining it. On still afternoons, we can hear the children singing in the forest, shepherded by the nuns. The silence is such that we are careful about breaking it.

★

I first went to Spain in the early fifties, almost by accident – certainly without forethought, for I knew and felt little about the country beyond a strong antipathy for the Franco regime. I had not been there very long, however, before it dawned on me that Spain was going to matter a great deal to me, and become a part of my life; I found it recognisable at once, in the way that something one has been looking for subconsciously is recognisable. What caught me so quickly was an energetic sense of immediacy, a relish for the living moment: when Spaniards sat down at a table, they instinctively shed any preoccupation other than that with the food in front of them and with the immediate company. Their past was too brutal to bear remembering, their future out of their hands, so they chose to live in a vivid, existential present, which made conversation easy and open in spite of the pervasiveness of the regime. At that time, too, they were delighted by the appearance of foreigners among them, being curious, hungry for some notion of a way of life other than their own, because they had been cut off from other countries from 1936 until 1948 and longed for anything to break the stalemate of their isolation. The shame of the Civil War still hung over everything, a brutal ghost, from whose shadow the people were tentatively emerging. Doubts remained, however, and the few scattered foreigners who showed up provided some hope, some positive distraction. The country was poor and without luxury of any kind, but a simple dignity abounded, a graceful rhythm that soon had me converted. I set out to learn and explore as much of Spain as I could – the language, the terrain, the history, the character. To enter another culture from choice is always invigorating: we do not have any habits, so everything catches the attention and becomes grist to our minds. Not to know the word for, say, soap can be exasperating, but learning it is a small adventure in which the soap glows momentarily, as though seen for the first time. Even street names start up trails of discovery. Who was General Goded? Finding out unravels the whole complex knitting of the Civil War. We discover a new past, wholly different from our own.

★

Communications in the village depend on word of mouth, and are at the mercy of memory. In the store, Doña Anna tells me that Don Anselmo wishes to see me, though she cannot remember when she got the message. At my convenience, she says. But I walk down the spiralling path right away, respectful of the summons. Don Anselmo occupies an extraordinary position in the village – virtually that of headman. Although he has given up being mayor after almost forty years, he is deferred to and consulted regularly, and everywhere he is shown the same reverent respect. Stories about him abound, for from time immemorial he has been called in to arbitrate every kind of dispute, quarrel, or disagreement in the village and its surrounds, and locally his judgments ring as famously as those of Sancho Panza – even among the foreigners, who have often come to him for counsel. A broad, bulky man, he is profoundly ugly, massively ugly, except that his ugliness is easily trounced by the tangible kindness of his look and manner. He owns and runs a small *pensión*, which has the village's only bar and terrace. He bought it, he told me once, so that those who wanted to see him would always know where to find him. Don Anselmo has never bothered much about the *pensión*, except that he likes to do the cooking, and I often talk to him in the kitchen while he is preparing soup or skinning rabbits. The bar is sparse and bare, with family photographs on the walls and a huge stuffed armchair that serves as Don Anselmo's rostrum. I owe to him almost everything I know about the village; he has both a prodigious memory and a voluminous journal and can reach back not only through his own lifetime but practically to the village's coming into being, for his father was mayor before he was, and he claims the ancestral memory as his own. He is not only well informed but endlessly curious; he questions me often about the foreigners – where they come from, what they do, what they feel about the village. Some of them he likes, others he treats with a grave formality.

On the day I got his message from Doña Anna, I found him deep in his chair, gazing into thought, the newspaper unopened on his lap, his face furrowed like a ploughed field. 'How goes it?' I asked him. 'Well enough,' he replied. 'But my wife has given me all these illustrious articles to read, and it has propelled me to think very much and to wish to consult with you.' He waved at a pile of magazines beside the chair, and, picking them up one after another, I found that they were all opened to articles on automobile pollution. I realised what had been happening. Don Anselmo's wife, a bright, birdlike woman, is a great devourer of magazines and serves as a kind of information bank for her husband. Don Anselmo was wearing his prophetic look. 'I'm thinking of talking with Guillermo about banning cars from the village.' He eyed me speculatively.

'But, Don Anselmo, there are hardly twenty cars in the place!'

'Twenty-two,' he corrected me. 'And I realise that they affect neither our air nor our chests in any serious way. The only nuisance they do is to come back late and wake up Nicolás in the house by the road. He is old and needs his sleep. No, it is only that I have been reading these learned articles, and I am astonished that in the face of this terrible knowledge not a single town has taken any step to confront the matter. For that reason, I am of the opinion that we must take the step, although we are not in immediate danger. It might lead other places to follow our example. First, I thought I would consult with you over what the foreigners might think. Would they understand? They must certainly be more conscious of this pollution than we are. I intend to talk to them, in any case.

Don Anselmo's plan never quite came to pass, although it pre-occupied the village for some time. Were the number of cars to increase, Guillermo announced, they would all have to be left on the level ground below the church. But it is an unlikely prospect.

Next year, in accordance with Spanish educational policy, the village school will be closed down and the children taken by bus to a central regional school some thirty kilometres away, in the market town. Those families with children may very well move closer to the school, closer to civilisation; some have already made the decision. Don Anselmo, in despair, proposed a voluntary school in the village, for both foreign and local children. 'We could have the first multilingual village in all Spain,' he announced dramatically, throwing his arms wide. I wish that every one of his plans had come into being.

★

Eugenio, who comes to turn over the terraces and cut back the almond trees, tells me the wistful history of the village every year. From its beginnings, the village's main sustenance came from making charcoal and cutting wood to burn, thus fuelling the surrounding countryside. The men would go out from Monday to Friday onto the long wooded slope behind the village, extending halfway up the mountain, to build the careful piles of small wood and twig, which were sealed over except for a small escape at the top. The wood smouldered away, eventually turning into charcoal. For their cooking, the villagers always started the charcoal outside, in a three-legged stove, over a fire of twigs, and then transferred it, red-hot, with tongs, to iron burners set in tile in the kitchen, fanning it with woven-straw fans that the women of the village made in their houses. The women were also very skilful at drying and preserving food for the men to take out with them during the week. The men slept out, and Eugenio showed me a sumptuous sleeping bag he had sewn for himself out of sheepskins, which he never uses now. Around 1958, butane gas in cylindrical containers made its appearance, and in no time *butagas* had transformed the countryside. It was, of course, easier to use than charcoal, but, more than that, it seemed to show that Spain was creeping forward after being stagnant for so long. For the charcoal burners, however, gas meant that their work stopped dead. Most of them were able to find jobs in construction, because the building boom had begun by then; for that, though, they had to leave the village – sometimes for good. It felt as if the place had surrendered all its energy and slumped into disuse. Don Anselmo did his best to animate the place, with schemes to buy looms and to found a pottery, but the villagers had fallen victims to a disheartened listlessness. Besides, by then a handful of foreigners had settled in the place, and work on their houses, or in their houses, kept the village ticking over, in a semiretired kind of way. I still get charcoal from Eugenio, who prepares a pair of burnings every year, but the straw fans have disappeared forever. Don Anselmo remains hopeful. 'I can see a time coming when they will be pleading with us to make charcoal again,' he says. 'Oil and gas will give out, and we shall become an important source, I know it. I have longings to see our village come back to life. That it may still be possible sustains me as I decline.' What Don Anselmo never mentions is that the men of the village supplemented their money from making charcoal by picking up and distributing contraband cigarettes, until the contraband traffic dwindled, roughly when the charcoal did. He refuses to hear any mention of contraband. Even his optimism about charcoal he keeps for public occasions; when he talks in private, I can see how thoroughly he has identified the dying of the village with his own dying.

★

After Franco became head of state, his photographic likeness was displayed prominently in all town halls throughout Spain. Every few years, a new photograph was sent around, so that the Spanish people might be suitably attuned to the growth in stature of their little Generalissimo. As mayor, Don Anselmo received these photographs over the years and duly hung the current likeness in the small office that serves as town hall. He did not, however, destroy the old photographs but kept them carefully. One day, he motioned to me and told me he had something to show me. He led the way along a back corridor, up a few steps, to a locked door, which he opened with a key he produced from his wallet. The room was stale and dusty, entirely empty except for a single straight wooden chair, but around the walls hung, in sequence, a whole row of official photographs of Franco. As my eyes moved slowly along the walls, Franco aged steadily, almost imperceptibly. Don Anselmo put his hand on my shoulder. 'I would appreciate that you do not mention this in the village,' he said solemnly. 'I come here from time to time to meditate on mortality, on the mortality of all of us. I find it curiously comforting. A new picture is due next year, and Guillermo has promised it to me. I have the feeling it may end the series. But I have said that before. Now, let us leave. I feel that at this stage a glass of wine might be appropriate.' He locked the door carefully, but the photographs have remained in my head.

★

Tourism washed over the village, leaving it unperturbed, if not untouched. At one time, busloads of tourists used to labour up the road and spill out into the small square, perhaps lured by the prospect of seeing Spain as it once was, but there was nowhere for them to go and nothing for them to do. As often as not, they would find Don Anselmo asleep in his armchair, the priest asleep on his porch, and a pervasive, yawning indifference to their presence – and to their custom, for Don Anselmo runs his *pensión* as an amplification of his house, without thought of profit. A small handful of foreigners live permanently in the village, but either they have chosen the place for its staunch sense of privacy or they are fiercely eccentric – like the Brigadier, who day after day pores over his campaign maps, waiting for the Second World War to resume. Every now and again, someone from the outside world decides that the village is a private Eden, crying out to be shared with an imported elite. We watch with some alarm as the building begins, the mason and the carpenter pitching in with faintly un-comfortable pleasure over having work to hand. But not all ideas of Eden coincide. Prospective buyers come and go, dithering over their decisions. To some, the silence looks alarmingly like total suspension. Refrigerators and swimming-pool filters, moreover, lie far beyond the technological resources of the village, and more than one foreigner has fled the place in despair, the idyll lost for want of a stop valve. The most threatening settler to date was a Swiss woman who envisioned the village as a setting for her own private arts festival, and who whipped up a cluster of small chalets, with pool and performing space, to house her captive celebrities. She goaded and bullied her workmen to the point where she had hired and fired every available hand in the place, earning herself a staggering collection of unrepeatable nicknames. The artists she managed to lure there left after a few days, discovering that they were expected to serve as lapdogs – that their main function was to relieve the boredom of their patroness. Judging by the gleam I notice in local eyes whenever she is mentioned, I would not be surprised to see her houses begin to crumble in the course of the coming year.

★

To come to rest in the village from somewhere in the outside world is not the easiest of transitions, and those who try it occasionally find themselves the victims of 'village paranoia'. They abuse or assault the mailman, or complain that the phone in the *estanco* is tapped. The victims gradually begin to suffer from their chosen isolation and often conjure up a conspiracy that winds in the whole village, down to its animals and machines. The postman is accused of burning letters or throwing them away, but since he is quite prone to do this, the accusation serves nothing but the paranoia. The villagers treat such an outbreak with uncommon indulgence. They have seen it before and look on it as an unfortunate but inevitable consequence of civilisation. But then they are indulgent of any eccentricity, among themselves as well, looking on it as no more than the expression of extreme differentiation. A bald Venezuelan violinist who once lived there, in a solitary house on the crest, had such delusions of social superiority that he insisted that his house be known as the Castle. The villagers not only complied but addressed him in the bar, in the store, in the *estanco*, on the road, as 'Your Excellency'. Sebastián, who drives the bus to town, stops sometimes at a spot where his grandfather went over the edge and gets out to pray. And when Javier, the shepherd, comes down in the afternoon to sit on the wall outside the *pensión* and carries on a long conversation with his dog, those who pass are careful to greet the dog as well as Javier, whether the dog is there or not. I often get the notion that the villagers look on the foreigners among them as a species of household pet, for I have overheard them on the bus comparing the antics of various foreign households, as excited as if the presence of these strange people were a running comedy, an endless television serial. Only drunkenness turns them cold; any willing surrender of dignity reduces them to a tight silence.

★

At one time the only telephone in the village was in the *estanco*, the store that sells tobacco and stamps in a wooden kiosk set back in one corner, surrounded by wine barrels and sacks of beans. Consuelo, who runs the store, came in from her kitchen drying her hands, put on her spectacles wearily, and cranked the apparatus before asking for a number in Frankfurt or New York, while the caller fidgeted on the sacks. Most of the foreigners have learned the inside of that store by heart at some time or other, because a call either came through with disturbing speed or took the best part of two days. Waiting does different things to callers: some of them rushed from the store in rage or tears; others fell asleep or drank themselves into silence; and one Dutch girl, under Consuelo's tuition, learned the Spanish word for every object in the place. In private, Consuelo complains bitterly about the telephone, for she has to suffer a bleak series of uncomprehending and incomprehensible rages. One year, she was so beset by foreign hysteria in the *estanco* that she pleaded with Don Anselmo to have the telephone removed altogether, and he managed to placate her only by praising her forbearance (she is infuriatingly taciturn) and pointing out that without the unfortunate machine no one would be able to summon the doctor, who lives in the next village (another cause of foreigners' hysteria). Myself, I suspect that Consuelo revels in these long delays – not so much because she wants company in the store as because she has that most Spanish distrust of mechanisms and any dependence on mechanisms. Not without justification do the villagers associate the coming of machines with the coming of foreigners, who did bring in a whole host of pumps, generators, filters, sprinklers, tractors, and assorted vehicles, without which the village had existed quite happily, and all of which made noise. (Spaniards, of course, want all of them or want none of them.) Julián, the nearest we have to a mechanic, does his job with brilliant eccentricity. One day, he fitted an ingenious ratchet stop of his own devising to our well wheel, to take the weight of the bucket; yet he has never made another. He has kept the postman's prewar motorbike running by making spare parts in his shop, but he dislikes new cars and repairs them warily and bizarrely: the Brigadier's car would start only with the glove compartment open after Julián had been at it. 'I like to be boss of the machine, even to make it,' he once told me. 'Machines should be single things. Something is needed? Something is solved. But when the machines all come at me, ready-made and perfect, there is no place for me.' I know what he means. Our house remained for years a place of perfect silence, for although we had electricity, we scarcely used it, following the sun instead. Ultimately, however, I bought a refrigerator, which starts up through the night with a thunderous purr. I am waiting for it to break down, so that I can give it to Julián, in the interests of research.

★

The attraction of Spain in the nineteen-fifties lay in its apparent permanence. It was well out of the technological stream, and it had the kind of climate that simplifies physical existence, besides being cheap to live in. Most of all, it had an immemorial look and feel, the landscape bleached and whittled down, the rhythm stark and clear, the style frugal. (Ironic now to realise that those who settled there became, unwittingly, the impulse behind the destruction of that rhythm – but since the dignified frugality of the Spaniards stemmed from poverty and lack, such retrospections are self-indulgent. Only a minority of Spaniards feel, as Don Anselmo does, the loss of that equilibrium as a tragedy.) People strayed to Spain from mixed motives. It served as a mecca for alcoholics, with liquor cheap and available always, just as it attracted would-be bullfighters and flamenco dancers, moths round that antique lamp. Writers and painters dug themselves in quite happily, since they were looking, above all, for time, and Spain seemed as close as anyone could come to a continuum. Yet living there became something of a test, for the simple life, as anyone who has embarked on it must know, can turn out to be insurmountably complicated in its mechanics, and quite often sends would-be villagers screaming back to civilisation. To set up a small, self-contained world, ignoring the surrounding currents, proves too much for all but a few hardened eccentrics. Those who settled in Spain in small, elitist groups suffered the isolation of castaways: the silence drummed on the roof like rain, and news from home became the only reality. A clear distinction has to be made between tourists, expatriates, and foreigners. Tourists descend on a place in obedient droves, like migrant birds, either following well-beaten tracks or creating them for other tourists. For them, to be in a foreign country is a change, a difference, a chosen astonishment. Above all, their stay is, by definition, temporary and pleasure-bent. Spaniards regarded tourists as a badge of well-being and economic health until they began arriving on a seemingly endless belt, forcing the country to feed, fuel, and amuse them at a thoroughly un-Spanish rate. For once, the fatalism of the Spaniards served them badly: their hospitality lost them their house. Expatriates behave quite differently. They have left their own countries on a long lead, never quite severing the link with home, never quite adapting themselves to their exile, clinging to one another for company, haunting post offices, magazine stands, and banks, waiting expectantly for money from home, anything at all from home. Expatriates are generally getting their own countries into perspective, to the point where they feel strong enough, or desperate enough, to return to them. Foreigners, conversely, live where they are, leaving their pasts and countries behind them for the place they take root in. In one sense, they are lucky: they are free to enter a new context unencumbered, with clear eyes, and are often able to savour a place in a way that escapes the inhabitants, for whom it has become habit. But however well a foreigner adapts himself to a place and its inhabitants, however agile he becomes in the lore and language, there is a line he can never cross, a line of belonging. He will always lack a past and a childhood, which are really what is meant by roots.

★

The real frontier to cross is that of the language. The Spaniards themselves are not famous with other languages – not as linguistically accommodating as, say, the Dutch, who can shift languages imperturbably. They do, however, have great linguistic kindness, in that anyone with a minimal supply of Spanish discovers conversations being put together for him, being turned into small language lessons for his benefit. At first, Spanish is an easy language to enter – regular, uncomplicated, straightforward to pronounce – and most foreigners who settle in Spain quickly acquire a form of 'kitchen' Spanish, which allows them to shop, ask directions, go to banks and offices, and order in restaurants. However, that stage may well become a plateau on which they stay, enacting formal conversations, the language technically accurate but without much emotion. Germans probably speak the most wooden Spanish of all, striding through sentences and subduing them one by one, while the English wield it with a mixture of distaste and disbelief, as though not sure it will work. But so kind are Spaniards that their talk will often limp along in sympathy with any stranger making heavy weather. In the village, this comes to be something of a problem; Joaquín, the mason, for instance, has done so much building for newcomers to the language that when he is explaining anything he cannot help breaking into a kind of baby talk, which his workers now all imitate. Don Anselmo's wife is often pressed to give language lessons, but she is so energetic that she has acquired three extra languages over the years while her pupils floundered about in chapter I of *Don Quixote*. Not that language is insurmountable. Little Doña Anna, who in her store has to confront shopping lists in Finnish as a matter of course, has evolved a series of elaborate mimes for recipes and foodstuffs, which bring extra-linguistic results – prodigious performances from hungry aliens, who circle balletically round plump Doña Anna, waving arms and drawing animals and vegetables in the air. The greater hazards arise with those who cannot bear to undergo the embarrassment of learning a new language, and pretend to know it or, at least, to subdue it. We have one such eccentric settler, who after some years believed that Spanish had descended on him by osmosis. Whenever Spanish was directed at him, he would nod vigorously and say, '*Si, sí, sí!*' It served him well enough until one day Joaquín came to replace a tile on his roof. When the mason had finished, he gesticulated at the roof and made a small emphatic speech in Spanish, to which our neighbour replied with his usual '*Si, sí, sí!*' A couple of days later, he came back from the town to find his house being completely reroofed and Joaquín and his men beaming at him enthusiastically.

★

In the course of summer, friends come to visit, and once they have got over their first awe of air and silence, tried their hand at drawing water, wielded hoe and spade, made their own solitary forays to Doña Anna's store to bone up on her vast and complex lexicon of gestures (returning on occasion with unlikely purchases but delighted nevertheless with the exchange of extra-linguistic good will), they find their own crowded worlds receding and get used to drowsing away the afternoons in a hammock in the ilex forest, attempting to sketch the asymmetrical bulk of the mountain that looms behind us, reading the books I surely now know by heart, and in general reducing their lives to a rhythm that other modes of civilisation have made impossible. Some of them come with a firm intention of mastering Spanish, step by step, hour by hour, but the rhythm of our village is not one that makes for the pursuit of firm intentions, and over the years I have inherited an impressive collection of Spanish grammars. With time, the outside world does subside and diminish, and the visitors fall in with the rhythm of the sun, waking and sleeping in accordance with a natural order, not with their own. It comes more easily to some than to others – than to those, say, who have turned the ringing of the telephone into a natural sound and grow anxious in its absence. To settle down in the village is a conversion of a kind, and although I am practised at it by now, it still takes time, because one is rooted forever in two worlds, and for some people the simplification that village existence requires may be – however desirable – forever impossible.

★

Below the house, thickly overgrown and by now scarcely distinguishable from the undergrowth, stand the walls of seven houses, their roofs long gone. We often walk among the ruins, for they exude silence like a message and give an odd aura to everything – the mountains hazy through the window sockets, the toolmarks on the stone, the rusted iron rings in the walls. The goats eye us indignantly, their bells clanking as they withdraw to the end of their tethers. We have used some of the tumbled stones from the ruins in laying a stone terrace, embedding them in the ground with their flattest surfaces uppermost – a caveman's jigsaw puzzle. We have been given the history of the houses many times. At the turn of the century, they, along with our house and the adjoining farm, formed a separate, self-sustaining *aldea*, a small village of close to two hundred people; indeed, I have seen it marked on survey maps of the time – a round, emphatic dot. The story of its decline is a recurring one in Spain: the young people moved to the larger village below; there were not enough hands to attend to crops and animals and maintenance; the old people were left alone with the children; the place faltered, failed, and was abandoned. The house we occupy would have been one of the ruins by now if we had not shored it up, but, with the ruins below, it is not hard to feel like a castaway or a survivor. Once, I came back to the house after a hiatus of two years to find that the vegetation had marched tall across the terrace and was fingering the front door. I felt I was just in time. Sitting beside the well on an evening of silk dark, with stars crowding the sky, I find it easy to imagine the village without any human presence whatever – all signs soon consumed by inexorable vegetal muscles, the fruit thudding to the ground unheard. We are the most strident and extravagant species on the whole planet, but not the most durable, as the ruins keep saying. The house feels more and more like an outpost; the insects and the plants have designs on it. I hope sooner or later to make peace with them.

★

Through the glass door of the café I catch sight of Gonzalo, the mailman, and I go in pursuit of him, for he is famously elusive and,

I suspect, secretly disapproves of mail. He is not only the mailman but an itinerant gardener, and in the village they will tell you with great mirth how, while he works, he is prone to park a bundle of letters in the fork of a tree, where they will be found years later, wound round with growing ivy. Scratching himself gloomily, he leads me to his office and produces a handful of letters and two telegrams, all long out of date. He is a hoarder of unopened letters, a renowned inducer of paranoia. This time, he is more disgruntled than usual. 'Nine newspapers a day used to come to this village,' he tells me, 'and nobody minded when they got them. Now I have to deliver thirty every day, and magazines besides, and everybody pursues me. Why can't they listen to the radio?' I walk back to the café in the glinting sun and find Don Anselmo in his armchair, newspapers all around him. For years, he has worried about the fate of the village, having seen it dwindle from a healthy, settled community that thrived on agriculture and charcoal-making for fuel (not to mention contraband) to a skeletal place populated mainly by the old, its terraces uncultivated, its trees uncared for, and some of its houses sold to foreigners or to Spaniards from the city. At Christmas, most of these houses are shuttered and dark, their scattered swimming pools filled with green slime. Only a few hardened settlers stay the year round – people who have burned their bridges, painters obsessed with the light, hopeful novelists, refugees from their old lives, waiting for the mail and dreaming of cities. For the local people, they form a captive layer in the village, cared for like communal village pets, nicknamed, talked about. But they adapt in different ways, to different degrees. For some, the village remains a setting into which they fit themselves with all the trappings of their former lives, brushing aside the language and becoming sturdy custodians of their own habits, like the few resolute English, who walk their dogs, fetch their out-of-date newspapers, and have supplies of tea sent out to them. Others adapt with zeal, learning local lore and dialect, to create for themselves what they are missing; namely, a past in the place. I used often to brood on the possibility of living there all the year round, but I decided I could do so only if I were to plunge into the business of working the land and living by an agrarian calendar. Eugenio always encourages me, for he tells me that on most days he finds himself the only person moving in the vast landscape – a mournful experience; but he clearly expects me to turn up with half a dozen able-bodied helpers, for nothing less would rouse the stony terraces from their present sloth. No matter how close we foreigners come to the village and the villagers, however, life there can never take on for us the inevitability it has for them. There is always for us the choice of going somewhere else – a choice they have never entertained.

★

Eugenio's wife, Josefa, was born in the house and has looked after it for years as though it were a shrine, appearing after storms to see if perhaps a tile on the roof has loosened. Lately, she has taken to eking out Eugenio's seasonally variable profits by looking after the empty houses of the more affluent (and consequently more absent) foreigners, and this activity makes her the most difficult person in the place to track down. I recall Easter two years ago, when I went to my house by chance, and had to recover the keys from Josefa. She was on her care-taking rounds, but the first two swimming-pooled houses I called at were most un-Spanishly chained shut. I ran her to ground in the house of an absentee Irish tycoon, and she insisted on settling me in his most expansive armchair, pressing on me his best brandy in a balloon glass and a cigar from his humidor, while she filled me in on village happenings. She is powerfully hospitable, but she prefers the houses in her charge to their owners, absences to presences. She scrutinises visitors to our house, for she feels that they ought to suit it rather than it them. She always questions me anxiously about the house, afraid I may sell it or somehow transform it. But I can always reassure her, for over the years I have become as possessed by the sturdy quiet of the place as she is. Was I going to make a road for cars to reach the house, since I had the right to, she once asked me. I told her that I had decided instead to build a drawbridge. I think she still wonders when I am going to begin.

★

To stop at Doña Anna's store is an imperative, and its contents are as familiar to me as a working bookshelf – I can reach instinctively for what I need. She emerges from the gloom at the back, a bantam librarian, at any hour of the waking day. Summer, with its abundant custom, lends her benevolence; in winter she is testier, knitting away the time. We have reached an arrangement over the years whereby she tots up my purchases on strips of newspaper, saving them in a drawer until just before I leave, when she sets aside an evening to add them all up, again and again, touching her thumb to her fingers. A pocket calculator would change her life, in every sense; but the luxury of not carrying money is worth the stumbling of her fingers and thumb, however much it may cost me – or her.

★

Although I know only a few of the foreigners who live in the place – there are supposed to be twenty-seven, but no one seems in a position to make an accurate count, since one or two have apparently not been seen for years – I know the nicknames of a good many of them. The villagers never attempt to pronounce foreign names but have a collective genius for fastening identifying nicknames to the strangers in their midst – and, indeed, they do it to one another, too. The nicknames have a knack of settling on the most distinguishing characteristics: a Dutchman who remains here to nurse his alcoholism is known as Señor Sacacorchos, Mr Corkscrew, and actually has a corkscrew look; a finicky Englishman with the habit of checking all his pencilled bills for errors is called El Matemático, the Mathematician; a German who is wont to talk to imaginary animals is known as El Ventrilocuo; a Venezuelan violinist and his blonde, parrot-tempered wife are always referred to together as Los Demoledores, the Wreckers, so often does the sound of breaking glass and furniture resound from their enraged house. But who is the one they call La Sudadora, She Who Sweats? And will I be able to recognise La Manoteadora, She Who Waves Her Hands, in a place where everyone does? I'm sure I will. Not many know their own nicknames, for the system is so arranged as to give the impression to everyone that he is the nicknameless exception. I know mine through the accident of coming down behind Gonzalo's house one afternoon while he was trying to identify the recipient of an overseas letter as his wife ran through the whole cast of nicknames before my ears. But, for luck's sake, I would no more reveal it than I would leave nail clippings or hair trimmings lying about.

★

One day, the sound of the bell floats up from the church. We stop talking. It goes on tolling. We stand still and listen to it. In a small place of around a hundred souls, which is what we number in summer, a death reverberates. Who has died? Antonio, the retired baker, who reads only old newspapers and so is always full of strange news? Consuelo, who used to sell us chickens, all of which she knew by name? The old people inhabit a continuum in the village. They are its most permanent fixtures, they are honoured and listened to, and their absence remains tangible. When we go down later in the day, people are standing about in twos and threes, talking. Consuelo, on her terrace, is wearing a black shawl. It is Doña Esperanza, of the high orchard, who has died, after being ill for more than a year. I remember her as someone wrapped in sadness. Doña Anna has closed her store. The whole village has stopped. Joaquín the mason, Doña Esperanza's nephew, is sitting on the wall outside the café, strange and grave in suit and tie. Inside, Don Anselmo silently hands a glass of brandy to everyone who enters. There is not much conversation. The whole village will attend the funeral; and until it is over we will all think about death. There will be much headshaking and much spoiling of the children.

★

I do not own a watch and pass the summer without ever knowing the time. There is nothing to know it for, except the morning bus. Doña Anna's store is her house, and so is always open except for periods of sleep. Now and then, if the air is still enough, I can hear the chimes from the church clock wavering up to us, but never distinctly enough to count them. We have a crude measure of our own, however. As the sun rises, it projects through the top window and onto the white back wall a rectangle of orange light, which yellows and descends in the course of the morning. Thanks to a visiting watch, we have marked a crude scale on the wall – the first touch of light is approaching six o'clock, the top of the picture is nine, its bottom edge ten. It serves for the summer. I think I have twice missed the bus, but that may not have been the sun's fault, for Sebastán, unless he is forewarned, is apt to leave on whim, as long as there is at least one passenger for conversation. He, too, is watchless. And the church clock, bought by subscription six years ago, often veers ten minutes in either direction from the correct time, they tell me. But how do they know?

★

To live in the village, even temporarily, is to translate existence into a pure particularity. The silence is primordial, and the only sounds that violate it are those that I make myself. I grow more respectful of the natural world, and feel my presence as something of an intrusion. But I think of being there less as an escape than as a corrective; it gives me time to put my priorities in order. Although Spain has loomed large in my life, my specific attachment is to the village – to the children I have seen grow up and to the villagers I have watched grow old. However much one learns about and understands a country in terms of events, it is the lived experience that matters most, and I looked forward keenly to picking up the long, unfinished conversations, the view from the inside.

★

There is a sense in which all Spanish villages are interchangeable: they have in common a manner of being, a vantage point, and, in this present Spain, a plight. Having lived in four separate villages, I think I would feel at ease in any – in its rituals and hierarchies, in its dingy, loquacious café, in its human rhythm. Spanish villages bear to each other family likenesses. It is only when one gets to know a village by name – landscape, houses, people – that it becomes a quite separate drama, a web of connections and commitments, even of argument. Not that our village is ever rent by civic strife – it has waned considerably from its self-sustaining, self-regulating days, and is now administered bureaucratically from the anonymous outside as part of the region. Still, it generated its own garbage collection ahead of other villages, and the forces of law and order have had no cause to visit since local traffic in contraband stopped, except for one occasion, when a drink-crazed Norwegian ecologist let the air out of the tyres on the twenty-odd cars in the place, walking about four mountainous miles to do it.

★

To a village as small as ours, rituals are essential, and I go down the path in late morning to enact the rituals of arrival – the gnarled handshakes, the embraces, and the formal exchanges that might be scripted in stone. There is much headshaking and hand-wringing, accompanied by the gnomic sentences that seem so indigenous to the Spanish language, the natural proverbs that crop up in village conversations. Later on, I gather; bit by bit, all that has gone on in my absence, in many differing versions, variously edited by the tellers, and I put together the missing time, which is difficult, for the people here do not talk in years but in seasons, enumeration by weather and fruits and harvests. I listen a lot at first, and the happenings emerge – a forest fire, a death, a family feud – to fill in the gap in my time. It has been a winter of wind; but without much rain – alas, for the *cisternas* in the village are filled from the guttered roofs, and the supply of summer water depends on the ferocity of the winter rains. From May on, however, we do not talk of the weather, for it is steadily blue and hot and dry, with only infinitesimal variations. In summer, village life shifts down to half speed. Time stretches, people walk more slowly, everything moves in a sunstruck drift. May, however, has its surprises. I woke one morning early, to seemingly less light, and went out on the terrace to find myself in an eerie cold greyness. A cloud had settled on our small mountain, and I was standing in the middle of it, barely able to see the nearest almond tree. In under an hour, the sun had burned it away, but even in that short time I felt that I had been in and out of a separate season.

★

In the world of the village, death is a reduction, and among the old ones its inevitability sits like an attendant bird, like imminent nightfall. I feel the reduction more on this occasion, for during my absence Don Anselmo has died. His absence is almost as tangible as his presence, for it was he, more than anyone else, who gave the place a direction and a human shape. He had been mayor, as had his father, and he carried the annals of the place in his head, its past as vivid to him as its present. From his huge, worn armchair in the little *pensión* that he ran and where he was always to be found, he dispensed advice, stories, help, and unflagging kindness – something like a tribal headman, with a patient ear and an inexhaustible generosity of spirit. He had become so identified with the place that its well-being mattered more to him than his own, and I could not help feeling that with his death the spirit had gone out of it. I would often call on him in the late afternoon, and on this occasion, when that time of day came around, I felt at loose ends, I felt the deprivation of his death. One afternoon, I went down and collected the key to the small cemetery from the priest's house. I sat under a cypress tree, remembering an afternoon with Don Anselmo in that same spot, where he had told me about the other occupants of the sandstone niches, bringing them to life one by one. His own niche bears only his name and the legend '*Primera Y Última Morada*', first and last resting place. For Spaniards, death is neither a surprise nor a puzzle, since they invoke it so often in their daily conversation. As they approach it, they make of it a familiar, a silent companion to whom they look more and more. I find it easy, sitting here, to imagine Don Anselmo back into being, to play back a conversation with him, to hear his solemn voice recounting some part of the long narrative of the village. Now that he is dead, it is as though the place had suddenly lost its memory, as though all its annals lie there encased in stone, unreadable now, fading, buried.

★

It was during the sixties that I saw most of Don Anselmo. His wife knew both French and English and was an inveterate reader of magazines, which she summarised for Don Anselmo. It was thus that he became passionately interested in ecology, for he discovered that he had been its unwitting champion all his life. I once gave him a copy of *The Whole Earth Catalog*, and it was never far from his armchair. What excited him was the discovery that agricultural self-sufficiency and village-size communities were constantly invoked as ecological ideals, and he began more than ever to feel that the village of yesteryear had been something of an ecological Eden, if a threadbare one. Gravely, he began to advance schemes by which the village might give a further lead to the rest of the world. He tried to ban cars from the place, but since the old people depended on the bus, he relented. Our air, besides, is milk and honey. He proposed advertising for hippies to come and make fertile lately abandoned land, but he was dissuaded by some horrified foreign inhabitants. He considered bringing back the bartering of crops and goods, a ritual over which he had once presided, but since the only commodity that certain inhabitants could produce was money, he was again defeated by circumstance. He was always trying to think up small, productive enterprises for people in the village, but he could not prevent the drift toward the town, where the pickings were more immediate. In his later years, when the village ceased to be a working place and instead lived well enough off the leisure of others, a sadness grew about him, for his ideal had almost existed and, ironically, had been eroded by progress. Almost the last time I saw him, his conversation caused me to feel that he had given up and had equated the death of the village with his own. I remember well what he said. 'I have decided that what those learned people tell us about how we are using up the world, how we must live in harmony with what we have, has come too late for us. Perhaps it *could* have happened if we had heeded, but I do not think that it will happen now. Yet here we once lived just like that, although we no longer do. That pains me – I find myself thinking more and more of those days, and wishing them back.' Some eight months later, I had a letter from my son, who was there at the time, telling me of Don Anselmo's death, and of his funeral, which brought out the whole population, and many from the region, in mourning for his huge lost presence and for the past he took with him. We do not stop at the *pensión* now, as we once did. As Eugenio once said, out of the air, 'I cannot bear to look at that empty armchair. It is too big for any of us.'

*

I have spent many days, in different years and seasons, alone in the house, as I am now, the silence huge and unbroken except by my own noises, by occasional birds and sheep bells, and sometimes by the fluting sound of children singing from the pinewoods across from the house, children from the summer retreat, out walking with an accompanying nun. Nobody comes, except by intention. Eugenio appears at odd times, to attend to the trees or to do the accounts. The almond crop is poor, he says – it was a winter of wind, not enough rain. I help him carry fertiliser down to the lower terrace, and then spend an hour or two clearing brush in the ilex forest behind the house. A cuckoo makes its slow way up the valley, loudmouthed against the quiet. I sit on the terrace and gaze. The edge of roof shadow is suddenly a foot closer to my chair. It is something I have always noticed about Spaniards – how so many of them sit in their own silence as though it were a bubble enclosing them, oblivious, wholly absorbed. Gerald Brenan writes about them, 'As they sit at their tables outside the cafés, their eyes record as on a photographic plate the people who are passing, but on a deeper level they are listening to themselves living.' It is something I absorb from the house, which seems to impose a silence of its own. I often think of it when I am far away from it: standing stony and empty, its eyes shuttered. I read, cook, draw water, write, gather wood, not according to plan but as these things occur to me, and from time to time I wander up through the forest, to lose myself, or to watch the late sun on the mountain across from it, changing the colours on its face, etching its shadows sharply. Music tinkles away below me in the neighbouring village, for they have there the beginnings of a rural disco. I walk slowly back through the ruins of the seven houses below ours, all that is left of the working hamlet it once was. Don Anselmo remembers it – remembered it. Now summer vegetation claws at the stones, and only our presence keeps it from taking over our house and similarly levelling it. It is natural, at the house, to think like a castaway, and it makes for stark thought.

★

Some of the foreigners who have come to rest in the village tell elaborate stories, carefully edited and well rubbed in the telling, of how they first stumbled on the place and forgot to leave. As my time here runs out, I think that they are not so farfetched, for the urgencies I have created for myself elsewhere seem trivial by now, and the timelessness I have grown into is something too rich to leave cursorily. But the day comes closer, inexorable as the shadow on the terrace, and I find myself looking at stones and trees as though for the last time, trying to fix the atmosphere of an after- noon like a print on my memory. Yet it is already imprinted there, from countless seasons and occasions, so completely that I can return to it in my head, in piercing detail. I know the stones marking the path as distinctly as faces, and a good number of the trees. I can summon up any time of day – the haze of early morning, the limpid, brilliant blue of noon, the ochre light following sunset that honeys the white wall. I can turn on the seasons – the drumming of the great rains, the white astonishment of the almond blossom in February, the pacific drowse of summer. I prowl through the house at will, fingering the talismans on the shelves and playing back sounds, footsteps on the path, the thud of fruit falling, the rattle of the bucket in the well. Most of all, I can in time induce the silence of the place, as an easement of mind. I suppose it has become for me what Gerard Manley Hopkins called an inscape, for although I can recall in like detail other places I have lived in, none have the same brilliance in my memory. I have the house and the forest in my head, out of time, and now to go back to it is only to confirm its existence. It and the village have been left behind, in a fold of time, and the new Spain might almost be another country. While it presses eagerly forward, the village looks wistfully back.

I take a last walk through the ilex forest, I pile up the newspapers in the niche by the fireplace, to yellow in their good time, I seal jars against the ants, I return to Eugenio the tools he has lent me, I prepare to close the house, as though it were a time capsule that will wait, sealed and safe, until I can open it up again. Except that, this time, I feel there is something of a difference. The house has stone walls at least two feet thick, and I have always felt that, short of a cataclysmic disaster, it would wait there, in its silence, for me to open it up again. This time, however, the hazards do not emanate from the ants, the termites, the clawing vegetation, the earthquakes, or the thunderbolts. The human world has become more precarious than the natural world, and I feel that I will owe my next return less to the obdurate, stony permanence of the house than to the restraint of our own wilful humanity, which has let us survive, however precariously, until now.

Remembering Robert Graves
1995

Had he lived, Robert Graves would have been a hundred years old in July of 1985; as it happened, he died at ninety, in November of 1985, in the village of Deyá, on the rocky northwestern coast of Majorca, where he had made his home for half of his long life, and where I first met him, in the summer of 1953. We enjoyed a close friendship, in the form of an endless conversation, until it was abruptly and irretrievably severed in 1961. Very seldom do I think of those years, but I was considerably formed and changed by them. With the centenary, Graves's name was very much in the air, with three biographies, a documentary film, an endearing memoir of him by his son William, symposia on his work, and an act of homage by the Majorcan government. Carcanet Press, in Britain, is to reprint most of his work – an eight-year project, since he published more than a hundred and thirty books in his lifetime. His life and his writings so interact that they cannot be unravelled: writing was how he lived.

The English have always kept Graves at a distance, as if he were an offshore island, out of the mainstream – something they quite often do with English writers who choose to live elsewhere and are still successful. Even so, he is now firmly lodged in literary history, and critics may write of him without incurring one of his famously withering broadsides. Those who know his work well probably think first of his poetry; many people, however, know his name only from the television version of *I, Claudius*. Generally, the book of his that first springs to mind is *Good-bye to All that*, the autobiography he produced in 1929, out of a time of great personal stress.

Never was a title more fervently meant: as he put it, the book dealt with 'what I was, not what I am'. Its tone is one of blunt irreverence; by writing it, he was shedding his past, and turning his back on England and what he saw as the hypocrisy of its values and public institutions. He wrote it as one who had survived the tyrannies of conventional schooling and the dehumanising horrors of the trenches, and no book of his did more to imprint his name on the attention of the public. He fled England just before it was published, leaving behind him a past he had chosen to renounce, even though he had already been irrevocably formed by it.

Graves had an Irish father, a German mother, a Scottish grandmother, a patrician English upbringing, a Welsh predilection, and a classical education. His whole personality formed itself from a mass of oppositions, of contraries. His father, a minor poet and a celebrated writer of Irish songs, worked as a school inspector in London. A widower left with five children to look after, he remarried, in 1891, a grandniece of the German historian Leopold von Ranke, and this genetic connection was one that Graves often invoked. Narrow-minded and pious both, his mother imposed a stern morality on her husband and children, and saddled Robert with a moral scrupulousness that left him socially inept and ill-prepared for the rigours of an English public school. In 1909, Graves was sent to Charterhouse, where his middle name, von Ranke, occasioned general derision, even outright persecution, as did his piety and his priggishness about sex. Although studies were not fashionable at Charterhouse, he took refuge in them. He left school just as the First World War was breaking out, and some ten days later he enlisted with a commission in the Royal Welsh Fusiliers. Not yet twenty, he was in France, and at the front, amid the running horror of death and decay every fearful day. In July, 1916, at the beginning of the Somme offensive, Graves was wounded by shrapnel, four days before he turned twenty-one; shortly afterward, the notice of his death from wounds appeared in the London *Times*.

He talked to me often about the war. My father had been wounded in the same battle: my mother kept in a small box the bullet that had been taken from his lung; I could scarcely hold it. Graves told me once that he considered himself exceptionally lucky in knowing that nothing that happened to him afterward could ever match the horror that he had gone through in the trenches.

The war left Graves in a precarious state, shell-shocked and suffering from severe war neurosis. It was during this time that Graves, accompanying his close friend Siegfried Sassoon to neurasthenic treatment, met the presiding physician, Dr W. H. R. Rivers, who had once been an anthropologist and was now a neurologist. After the war, Graves continued to visit him in Cambridge, where Rivers was a professor. Rivers planted in Graves's mind an interest in matriarchal societies and woman rule, which would later find fuller expression in his controversial work *The White Goddess*. More immediately, Rivers made Graves see that his cure was in writing: that the unconscious was the source not only of his nightmares but also of his creativity. He urged Graves to use his poetry to explore his pain. I think Rivers did more than anyone to show Graves just how his life and art were essentially connected. From that time on, Graves wrote whenever he could, wherever he was, convinced that in poetry lay a hope of sanity but at the same time suspecting that his 'insanity' made his poetry possible: were he to be entirely sane, his creativity might dry up. He needed his madness, his nerve. The poetry was in the pain.

While Graves was still in the Army, he abruptly proposed marriage, after short acquaintance, to Nancy Nicholson, then eighteen, sister of Ben Nicholson, the painter. She had strong feminist opinions for her day and refused to assume the married name of Graves (her two girls bore the Nicholson surname, her two boys that of Graves). Now a civilian and without qualifications or money, Graves elected to go to Oxford and eventually read for a degree in literature in the hope that it might lead to a teaching post. Money remained a recurring problem, although he and Nancy were full of plans as to how to earn it.

They were mired in domesticity; he shopped, cooked, washed, attended to the children, and wrote furiously all the time. By now he and Nancy had become more comrades than lovers, joined in a constant money worry. Enthralled by some poems of a young American poet he had read in *The Fugitive*, Graves had begun to correspond with their author, Laura Riding. They exchanged literary opinions, and Graves, impressed by her intelligence and her near-belligerent confidence, invited her to join Nancy and him to work with them. She arrived in England in early 1926, and for the next thirteen years she was to dominate Graves's existence, to prove his nemesis.

★

Laura Riding's influence on those who knew her owes more to her emphatic presence than to her writings, although it would have meant death to say it to her. I have known seven people who were close to her during her time with Graves, and something of the same dazed and faraway look came into their eyes whenever they spoke of her. Certain of her own supreme worth and intelligence, certain that her poetry was bringing a new clarity to language, Riding felt her work had been too sparsely appreciated at home, and she accepted Graves's invitation, hoping to find in Europe some like-minded souls. Graves had accepted a post lecturing on English literature in Cairo, and a week after her arrival in England Laura embarked for Egypt with the entire family, who already regarded her as an essential presence. The stay in Egypt proved less than fruitful, and after four months Graves resigned, and sailed, with the family, back to England. He was entranced by Laura. Where Graves wrestled with dualities, Laura was single-mindedly certain. The ferocity of her judgments occasionally verged on cruelty. To Graves, she was at once a demanding mentor, a clarifier, and a stimulating collaborator, utterly without doubts. He was also deeply in love with her. At first, he and Laura and Nancy declared themselves The Trinity and lived together. Soon, however, he moved to London to work there with Laura. Graves saw Laura's coming into his life, through poetry, as a magical event; he could do nothing but accept it.

The continuing story of Robert and Laura is a turbulent one, often painful, sometimes touching the edge of madness. Graves bore it stoically: the break with Nancy and the children, a rival for Laura's affections, her suicide leap from an upper window and her convalescence. In October of 1929, he and Laura left England behind, and made their way eventually to Majorca. The success of

Good-bye to All That had shown Graves a way to survive as a poet. He said often that he bred show dogs in order to be able to afford a cat. The dogs were prose; the cat was poetry. Thanks to his show dogs, he was able to buy land and build a house, and to start up with Laura a small colony of clarity and literary industry in Deyá, which she ruled by will and whim. Graves now gave way to her entirely, declaring her work far above his. In 1933, he wrote the two Claudius novels, and they came out to great acclaim the following year. Laura disparaged them, although they were the source of all funds; he begged his friends never to mention any of his work in front of her, and in new publishing contracts he insisted that a work of hers be published along with his. He discussed endlessly with Laura his growing interest in goddess worship. To it she added the vehemence of her own ideas, and soon she became to Graves not simply critic and mentor and lover and poet but muse. Later, she claimed to have been the source of all Graves's notions of poetry as goddess worship. She was not. She was much more: she was their incarnation.

By 1936, the Spanish Civil War was looming and, as foreign residents, Robert and Laura were given the choice of leaving immediately on a British destroyer from Palma, the capital of Majorca, or remaining to take their chances on an island that had shown itself to be predominantly pro-Franco. They left, and the Spanish frontier closed behind them. Although Graves went back to England, it was no longer his country. Any return to Spain seemed unlikely, war in Europe being nearly inevitable. The couple felt themselves fugitives, refugees; relations between them had grown more distant, although Graves remained unswervingly loyal to Laura. A sign came in the form of an adulatory mention of her poems in *Time* by one Schuyler Jackson, a friend of a friend of Graves. Intrigued, Laura abruptly decided to return to America; arrangements were made, and Graves found himself in early 1939 accompanying her to Bucks County, Pennsylvania, where the Jacksons had a farm. Again, events took several savage turns. Laura assumed what she considered her rightful place at the centre of the magic circle, and took upon herself the rearranging of the lives around her. Jackson's wife was declared a witch and driven to breakdown. Graves was given his notice as collaborator and champion. She and Jackson were eventually to marry and move to Florida. Broken in spirit, Graves returned to England just as war was breaking out in Europe.

Graves never saw Laura again, yet he remained forever mesmerised by her: if her name came up in conversation, he would frequently go silent, slipping into a trance of memory. His rejection by Laura had wounded him deeply, but he refused to speak ill of her. In any case, he had found refuge in a new love. Alan Hodge, then a young poet and later Graves's valued collaborator, had brought his young wife, Beryl, into the circle, and they followed Laura and Robert to America. As the dramas unfolded, Robert found in Beryl's company a quiet, cool sanity that he badly needed, and a devotion to which he was not slow to respond. With Alan Hodge's eventual blessing, Beryl joined Robert in England, and she never left him. War had broken out, uncertainties loomed, but Graves settled down with Beryl in the Devon countryside, and for the next six years he poured out work – writing poems, producing historical novels for which he did prodigious reading, and collaborating with Alan Hodge on a crisp, eminently sensible, and often humorous study of English prose style, called *The Reader Over Your Shoulder*, the most useful of all his books, as he said. His life with Beryl was calm and sustaining; it was also spiced by her humour – something Graves had not enjoyed for some time.

*

Graves has described how, at his desk in early 1944, he felt a sudden surge of illumination, and began feverishly writing the manuscript that was to be published as *The White Goddess*. Subtitled *A Historical Grammar of Poetic Myth*, it was to become a sacred book to a fair number of poets, and to enjoy a great vogue in the sixties, though more as a 'magic' book than as a brilliantly argued synthesis of all Graves's most fundamental preoccupations: his reading in the classics, his conversations with Rivers, his immersion in both Celtic and classical myth and history, and his own firm sense of what was required of a dedicated poet.

Since the Bronze Age, the figure of an all-embracing female deity

– a Moon Goddess, an Earth Mother, controlling seasons, fertility, and the cycle of birth and death – had been worshipped throughout Europe until challenged by the male gods of the Graeco-Roman world. With Christianity, goddess worship disappeared, preserved, according to Graves, by poets alone as a divine secret – or through the worship of a muse. From his vast reading, Graves created a monomyth that gave order to his deepest convictions and restored to poetry some of the sanctity he felt it had lost by neglecting myth for reason.

Graves was a deicide; he had made from the great tangle of his existence a religion that he could feel true to, and which could resolve the contradictions and oppositions in his thinking. As a devotee, he was privy to the Goddess's will. He always bowed solemnly nine times at his first sight of the new moon. To the supplanting of the Goddess by a Father God he attributed all the ills of the modern world.

It is, of course, possible to read *The White Goddess* as pure wish fulfilment, as a projection into human history of precisely what Graves needed to believe in, ingeniously disguised as investigative scholarship, which would justify the succession of young, beautiful muses whom Graves lit on in his later years. In it merged his fears and his ecstasies – his exacting mother, his war-horror, his trials with Laura, his sexual terrors and longings, the state of inspiration he equated with being in love, the coming together of dualities in a poem.

At the time, T. S. Eliot worked for Faber & Faber, and although he was somewhat overawed by the manuscript of *The White Goddess*, he was certain of its importance and agreed to publish the book. The war ground to an end, and Graves began to raise his hopes of returning to Spain. He and Beryl now had three children, William, Lucia, and Juan; a fourth, Tomas, was born later, in Deyá. In 1946, Graves pulled strings and received permission to return. In the spring of 1946, a small plane landed them in Palma – Graves, Beryl, and the children. They found that Robert's house, Canelluñ, and its garden had been tended and maintained, books and papers in place. The villagers were delighted at the return of Don Roberto, as an omen of sorts. He had come back, to begin Deyá again.

★

A mountain chain runs along that coast of Majorca, and from its lower slopes the land falls away steeply to the Mediterranean. The coastline is broken by protruding rocky headlands, enclosing long, fertile valleys and small, secret beaches. Deyá comes as a surprise, perched halfway between mountain and sea. The upper part of the village is cone-shaped, with the houses on each other's shoulders, winding down from the church at the crest. Nothing is flat except for the terraces that descend like a series of steps from the base of the overhanging mountain, the Teix, which dominates and dwarfs the village, making it feel small. The terraces are planted with olive trees – puffs of silver-green – and with gnarled almond trees. At sunset, the great wall of the Teix goes through a constant shifting of colour and shadow: light gold, ochre, amber, deep grey, dark. A short main street is lined with the village's essential outposts – butcher, baker, grocer, telegraphist, garage, café. The folds in the landscape form acoustical traps, so that miscellaneous sounds – the crack of an axe, a mule braying, conversation, the thud of a boat's motor, a girl somewhere singing – float in, breaking the mesmerising silence. In the hot summer sun, the village seems suspended, half asleep. The land is so up-and-down that every window frames a different view, the air so clear that around the full moon the whole face of the Teix is drenched in bright silver, towering above the sleeping houses, the moonlight almost bright enough to read by.

Spain in the early fifties seemed to be still waking up, coming back to life, docile under Franco. Its frontiers had been sealed off from the rest of Europe since the beginning of the Spanish Civil War, in 1936, and had remained so throughout the Second World War. The country felt worn out, threadbare. Travelling was unpredictable, traffic sparse, food hardly plentiful. Agricultural communities like Deyá, however, had fared better through these lean years, for they could feed themselves, working the land by hand and mule. To local people, shuttered up for so long, foreigners were something of a novelty – a situation that in ten years changed beyond anyone's imagining. Deyá's population in the fifties must have been about five hundred. For the villagers, the foreigners' antics fulfilled the function that television does today.

One evening in the summer of 1953, I was sitting on the terrace of a small *pensión* in Deyá, watching the sunset play itself out on the face of the Teix. I had gone there, with quiet in mind, on the advice of a travel agent – I had no idea that Graves lived there. Suddenly, through the beaded fly-curtain, Robert erupted. He cut a formidable figure – tall, bearlike, with a large torso and head, a straw hat, a straw basket shouldered, and a look set on the edge of truculence. He sat himself down and started asking me a series of questions, as though mapping me. Then he reached for the book I was reading – Samuel Butler's *Notebooks*. He crowed with pleasure and began looking for his favourite passages, telling Butler anecdotes with zest. Abruptly he got up, thanked me for the conversation, and left. After I came to know Robert well, I found that he often assessed people suddenly by some sign – a mannerism, a stray remark, a misplaced enthusiasm. I imagine that if I had been reading Ezra Pound's *Cantos* my memory of Graves might fill no more than this paragraph.

At the time, I was teaching at Sarah Lawrence, which left me long free summers. I had published some poems in *The New Yorker* and also a book of poems, slim in every respect, but I had begun to feel that writing and teaching went uneasily together; I had no idea how to live as a writer, though. What I wanted, emphatically, was to own my own time. It was this that drew me to Robert's existence – how he was able to live in the slow rhythms of Deyá and yet keep up a vigorous writing life. Robert was fifty-eight at the time, a veteran; I was twenty-seven, and an aspirant, no more. It was his lived example that led me to cut loose, to decide to live by writing.

I ran into Robert at odd moments during that summer – at the beach, in the café for the mail delivery, in the village store – and each time he would launch straight into conversation: what he had been writing that day, how to cope with ants. One afternoon, he took me back with him to Canelluñ, his house beyond the village. There, sitting in his workroom, narrow, high-ceilinged, and walled with his essential books, we talked about poetry. At that time, I was immersed in poetry, and read it voraciously; I also knew a whole host of poems by heart. Robert's prodigious memory was even more crammed, and this meant that sometimes, on a walk, one of us would produce a poem from the air which we would then explore with a fine editorial point, questioning it, sometimes rewriting it, or even parodying it. It was a conversational mode we often returned to, as a kind of game.

A few foreigners lived in Deyá the year round – a sculptor, a clutch of painters, a writer or two – for houses were easily available and cheap to rent. It had regular visitors, who returned faithfully each summer, and a few families from Palma summered there with their children. Life was frugal, somewhat bare-boned – water drawn from the well, cooking done on charcoal, electricity supplied by a local turbine that came on at dark and ran until eleven-thirty, when it winked three times and, ten minutes later, candles lit, went out. So simplified, the days seemed slowed. Robert and I exchanged letters over the winter, I returned the following summer, and eventually I resigned from Sarah Lawrence and moved to Spain.

From 1953 on, I spent part of each year in Deyá, usually renting a different village house, whitewashed, sparsely furnished, stony, and cool. I came to know the Graves household very well. Its centre of concern was always Robert, but Beryl, who knew his changes better than anyone else, kept him attached to daily realities – the garden's needs, who was coming when – and she had a way of bringing him back to earth with an oblique humour, which the children caught and copied: they would tease Robert by asking improbable questions, and he would answer in kind, teasing them back.

Robert's children knew his moods well. In quick succession, he could be stern and mischief-bent, angry and benevolent, greedy and fastidious, arrogant and gentle. He was also an inveterate maker of rules, and would blurt them out defiantly at table. He usually forgot them at once, as did his children. I always thought that it was Robert who first pronounced the rule that 'poets shouldn't drive', for he said it to me often enough. When I reminded him of a poet he liked who had once driven a school bus for a living, he only smiled wryly.

Canelluñ sat in a considerable garden, which had to be watered morning and night, and secured against sheep that might stray in. The house looked out to sea, and from a wide hall it gave onto the living room and kitchen on one side and Robert's workroom on the other. I grew used to having him suddenly rise, unplug himself from the conversation, and cross the hall. He would sit at his work-table, dip a steel-nibbed pen into an inkwell, and go on from where he had left off, without forethought or hesitation. When he reached a stopping point, he might wander into the garden, taking his thinking with him; pass through the kitchen absent-mindedly; and return to the text. Quite soon, I realised that, apart from days of emergency or obligation, he wrote every day of his life, not on any strict schedule but whenever a piece of time opened to him. When he wrote, he was detaching himself, composing himself, putting himself in order.

Graves kept away from machinery of any description; I never saw him touch a typewriter. In the thirties, he and Riding had come across a young German Jew whom they immediately took to. They taught him English, then offered him a job as secretary. He left Majorca with them, served in the Royal Navy in the Second World War, and afterward returned, with his family, to work again for Graves, living in a cottage by the entrance to the Canelluñ garden. His name was Karl Goldschmidt, but he had changed it in the Navy to Kenneth Gay. He had become, through many books, Graves's conscience: he was a meticulous copy-reader. Where Robert's time was concerned, he acted as watchdog, suspicious of strangers. After a morning's work, Robert would leave his handwritten pages for Karl, and they would be on his desk, immaculately typed, by late afternoon. He would then subject the text to another severe mauling. Eventually, the finished manuscript would be given to Castor, the mailman, when he came to work in the Canelluñ garden. To Robert, the mails were sacred. His mail would be left for him in the village café, and he would appear religiously at the same hour, open his letters, and, very often, share their contents with any friend who was there. He was also a prodigious letter writer, it was nothing for him to fill his inkwell and write some thirty letters in a day – to friends, to editors, to critics, to newspapers. He wrote me once, 'Find a place where things are done by hand, and the mails are trustworthy.' It may have been as well that he antedated the fax machine.

★

Deyá often seemed to me like the stage of an enormous natural amphitheatre, demanding from its new settlers some sacrifice, some drastic behaviour – and, indeed, many dramas took place among those who alighted there, in some of which Robert played a part, inevitably, for he considered Deyá *his* village. It is the setting of many of his poems; it served as his vocabulary – the landscape his thought moved in. He approached new arrivals with curiosity and diffidence. If he took to someone, he would often create, out of a few essential facts, a whole identity, holding it out to the new-comer as though it were a coat that had only to be slipped on to fit. Those who proved unwilling to have their essential selves thus reconstructed would have 'let him down', and the coat would not be proffered again. These identities were fictions of his, fashioned to accommodate strangers into his orbit. In Deyá, he was an insistent Prospero.

During the fifties, the demands of school fees and other expenses kept Robert at his worktable. Late in 1954, he found that he had taken on more work than he could cope with, and he asked me if I would help him by doing a rough first translation of Suetonius's *The Twelve Caesars*, for Penguin, while he himself translated Lucan's *Pharsalia*. I went to work, and every so often Robert would appear, to talk and to check my progress. Ignoring the Latin, he would go over my latest pages, glasses cocked, pencil at the ready, humphing from time to time, leaving behind him an undergrowth of correction. I had done what I considered a finished version, so when he had gone I would pore over his corrections, for they were all improvements. Over that winter, I learned about writing English prose. The severity with which he corrected his own work he would apply equally to the writing of others – a habit that made him an impatient reader of his contemporaries. He became for me then the reader over my shoulder.

I also learned about the mysterious alchemy of translation.

Robert was a first-rate classicist, and in the course of writing the two Claudius novels he had immersed himself in Roman history, but, much more than that, he would talk about life in Rome in the first century AD as easily as he would about life in, say, present-day London. In a sense, he had been there.

He decided that Suetonius was part gossip columnist, part obit-uarist, and had to be rendered in an appropriate English. Some-times he took questionable liberties with an original text, as he did in his version of the *Iliad*. He could not always keep a rein on his impulse to improve and tidy up a text, even if it was not originally his. The one translation of his that he made into a true English masterpiece, however, is his version of Lucius Apuleius's *The Golden Ass*. It was a text he deeply loved, and he so put on the original the spare clarity and cadence of his own prose that *The Golden Ass* more properly belongs among his own books – he made free with the text, for the sake of its English coherence. A good translator, he insisted, must have *nerve*. Nerve he had, in abundance. I had no idea then that I would turn to translation later in my life, but when I did I began to appreciate that brief apprenticeship, that gift of nerve.

★

Deyá remained quiet throughout the fifties, except for surges of summer visitors. Between books, Robert accepted invitations to write on a variety of subjects, and he took great pride in the swiftness and sureness with which he dispatched these tasks. Writing prose was a precise craft, he maintained, and a writer should be able to give matter of any kind the language it asked for. Robert also left his books behind him, quite literally. In 1956, he undertook to write a novel around the trial of Dr William Palmer, a likable Victorian racegoer and rogue, on a charge of poisoning, for which he was hanged – unjustly, Graves thought. He brought from London all the books he would need as background to the period and set to work. It was as though William Palmer had come to stay in Canelluñ, in Robert's workroom, for Palmer usurped his conversation whenever he emerged. Robert worked on the book strenuously over a two-month period, and when it was finished, immaculately typed by

Karl, the books were posted back to his London bookdealer, and William Palmer was never mentioned again.

Poetry, however, was an altogether different matter. Whenever he felt the nudge of a poem, he would put aside all else to make way for it. For him, poems were not just sudden pieces of writing: they were events. He subjected his poems to the same fierce scrutiny to which Laura had subjected them. He had a remarkable ear for the movement of a poem; even his lesser poems are beautifully fashioned. He went through many poetic manners, and was adept in all of them, but latterly he took to suppressing in each new edition of his *Collected Poems* his earlier, crankier poems, in favour of his later muse-poems. Muse-poems were either poems he felt had come to him magically, written from inspiration rather than intent, or poems addressed to a muse – love poems, but love poems that recast love conflicts in the language and manner of myth, and in which the lovers themselves act out mythical patterns.

Madness and fear of madness loom often in his poems, at the opposite pole from his sturdy common sense. Yet the poems he considered inspired rather than contrived came from the beauty and terror of madness, of the irrational; some of his images he claimed he fully understood only years after writing them. The onset of such madness was what he always feared and longed for: it moved between dream and nightmare, between desire and revulsion: and it came infallibly from falling in love. In writing, however, common sense often had the last word:

> For human nature, honest human nature
> Knows its own miracle: not to go mad.

At that point, into his sixties, Graves occupied a singular and increasingly admired ground among his contemporaries. He had redefined the obligations of the poet, which he sustained by a body of mythological connection, a whole cosmography, and a poetic creed that was coherent and rooted in the past. Few other poets had fulfilled the poet's function with such grave dedication or had cast it in such a visionary light. Only Yeats, whom Graves chose to despise, had sustained poetry with a mythology of his own devising, though one far less well informed and thorough than Graves's.

In workaday Deyá, I saw much of Robert, quite often with the children and Beryl, on Sunday picnics to the beach, and sometimes alone, in his workroom or at the café. I would question him about the past, about writers like Hardy, whom he had met, whom he could even imitate. He would try out on me the arguments in his current writing, inviting criticism and disagreement, which he usually resisted stoutly, sometimes crossly. He was tigerish over matters of language: his dictionaries were thumbed and ink-stained. He could be infuriating, in his pigheadedness, his often wild misjudgments. His utter disregard for privacy caused trouble between us more than once: he would broadcast matter from close conversations, sometimes recklessly. Robert and I were, however, used to each other. It was difficult to register disagreement with Robert; he was used to sweeping people along with him. With close friends, he would concede differences of opinion, although he clearly viewed them as temporary aberrations. I was often an aberrant friend. In those years, he was writing steadily, even jauntily, enjoying in Deyá a kind of equilibrium that seemed as if it might go on and on, like the agrarian round.

Every so often, word came his way that would give rise to what Beryl always referred to as 'golden dreams'. These stemmed from the time when Alexander Korda contracted to film I, Claudius, in 1934, with Charles Laughton as Claudius. Bad luck dogged the film, and it was never finished; but Graves lived from then on in hope of another such windfall. What did come was an invitation in 1956 to lecture in the United States. Graves had waved off such offers before, but money was now an important consideration, and we held a summit meeting, Robert, Beryl, and I, to talk it over. I had an apartment in New York which he could use as a base, and I promised Beryl that I would travel with him. The arrangements were made, and he set to work preparing three lectures. I went to New York ahead of him, and met him at Idlewild. He arrived somewhat warily; but, startled by the crowds that attended his first lecture, by the discovery that he had unsuspected legions of readers, he expanded, and decided to enjoy himself. Dealing with publishers and editors by mail, Graves generally struck his boxer stance. Meeting them at dinners in his honour, however, he turned benign, and answered questions with his oblique, teasing humour. He visited the *New Yorker* offices and agreed to write stories as well as poems for the magazine. At the Poetry Center of the YMHA, he lectured on *The White Goddess* – by far the most lucid summation he ever made of that 'mad book', as he used to refer to it. He looked the very icon of a poet: magnificent head, crowned with grey curls; stoutly in his own skin; in full command of his flights of argument. In the introduction to one lecture, he explained that on his last visit to America he had lost twenty pounds in weight and two thousand dollars, and that now, having regained the weight, he had come to make good his other loss. He teased his audiences with erudition; they went away spellbound, and bought his books. His visit made it clear to him that he need not worry about money, about the children's school fees: a number of his previous books were to appear in new editions; he had firm commitments for those in the works or in his sights; and there was enough talk of screenplays and movie rights to revive his 'golden dreams'. I had never seen Robert in front of an audience – it seemed to me that he thought only of readers, not of listeners – and was astonished, not just by his utter domination of his listeners but by his extraordinary lucidity. He sounded remarkably sane, but when he read his poems I realised that his mad self was merely lying in wait somewhere for him, and that he expected it and needed it.

Travelling, we replayed his lectures, sorting out the people he had met, paging through books he had been given, bountifully inscribed, and we continued to talk about poetry. Once, on the train from Boston to New Haven, he nudged me. About three rows away was a book face down on the arm of a seat, its owner asleep. It was *The Reader Over Your Shoulder*. I had heard him tell, many times, a possibly apocryphal story about Arnold Bennett, who had carried in his wallet a five-pound note to give to the first person he found reading one of his books: on his death, the note was found, still folded, in his wallet. Graves waited until his reader awoke, and then he moved to an adjoining seat, introduced himself, told his Arnold Bennett story, signed the book, and gave his startled reader ten dollars, swearing he would claim it from his publisher.

We took long walks, in the Village, on the West Side piers. One night, he wanted to see the moon, which we found only after walking a few blocks; at that moment, Deyá was on his mind. Once, in the West Village, he stopped me and pointed: out of a sixth-floor window a horse's head was protruding. The building housed a police livery stable. One evening, returning home, he stopped, silent. After a while he said, gruffly, 'Don't much like that chap.' 'That chap' was Robert himself, at his previous night's lecture. He flew back to Europe, Beryl's shopping list ticked and executed, on a Pan American plane that carried Toscanini's coffin in the back of the cabin. He wrote me a letter from the plane, which arrived in an envelope bearing the legend 'Fly with the stars the Pan American way.' Robert had crossed out 'stars' and written above it 'dead'.

That first trip was something of a coming out for Robert. Where he had previously been reluctant to leave Deyá except for obligatory holidays in England, he now accepted invitations to travel, to give lectures and readings, to write magazine articles, to be featured in a *Playboy* interview. On his travels, he made new friends, some of them in movie circles; Alec Guinness and Ava Gardner both visited him in Deyá. Later, in the sixties, he became something of a cult figure: *The White Goddess* was a source book for readers of *The Whole Earth Catalog*. The BBC came to Deyá to make a television film about him. The State University of New York at Buffalo was preparing to pay him handsomely for the scratched manuscripts he had saved in the attic of Canelluñ. His mail had become voluminous.

As I think of it, that first foray made Robert suddenly aware that he had not only a literary reputation but a public self – he could enthral an intelligent audience by his wit, the easy way he displayed his great learning, his humour, his downrightness, his poetic intensity, and, of course, the elegance of his language. Clusters of people, many of them young, waited after his lectures to ask him questions or murmur some fervent homage to him. He had more than enough money, and could count on a handsome advance for any new book. He met celebrities who wanted to meet him, and, talking with students, he breathed in some of the early fervour of the sixties. His letters, which were usually full of the family, the garden, and the work in hand, now talked of famous visitors, movie options. His royalties could now make Canelluñ more comfortable, and buy Beryl a new Land Rover. Yet, on that first visit, he had been perfectly conscious that he was playing himself, reinforcing his eccentric image. I think that as he began to travel more he steadily lost that consciousness. Never exactly modest, he became increasingly arrogant, increasingly defiant in his views. The golden dreams, he was certain now, were real.

Change was coming precipitously to Spain at the same time, even to villages as far-flung as Deyá. Mass tourism changed the face of Spain, and was to sustain the Spanish economy into the eighties. Bottled gas replaced charcoal in the kitchen, cars and buses began to multiply on the roads, foreign newspapers appeared in the kiosks. The equilibrium that the village – and Robert – had enjoyed throughout the fifties was suddenly over forever.

*

In late 1958, I left Deyá, first to sail the Atlantic with some friends in a Nova Scotia schooner, then to settle in Madrid. I saw much less of Robert after that, but we still exchanged letters. Since I first came across Spain, I had become immersed in it, quite apart from Robert, for Robert's interest in Spain was distant; only his locality, Deyá, concerned him. I learned Spanish through those years, and I travelled all over Spain, looking and listening and reading. In 1960, *The New Yorker* published the first of a series of chronicles I wrote from Spain – anti-Franco, as were all but a few of the Spaniards I knew. Robert scolded me for writing it: it was impolite, he maintained, to criticise one's host. I found this attitude ridiculous, and said so. We stopped short of a serious falling out, but I came to realise that, inevitably, I was withdrawing from Robert's orbit.

Robert had always been ready to laugh at himself; now I felt he was losing his irony. He had grown deeply serious about the Goddess, and, more and more, he laid down her law. I had always viewed the Goddess as a vast, embracing metaphor, and I thought Robert did, too, somewhere in his mind. I never believed in the

Goddess, any more than I believed in a Christian God. I realised, however, that Robert did believe, insistently so, and that the belief sustained and justified him.

In late 1959, Robert underwent a prostate operation, in London, which had serious complications. He was found to have a rare blood condition and had to be given massive transfusions, which left him weak for months. To a number of people, his son William included, that trauma had much to do with increasingly irrational behaviour on his part throughout the sixties. The allowances his friends made for him were exceeded by his growing insistence that he was somehow a spokesman for his times, that his long-held views were becoming generally accepted as the truth. It seemed to me when I met him later that year that he was losing all sense of the 'otherness' of other people: now they had only to fit into his script.

★

In *The White Goddess*, addressing the question of why so few poets continued to write throughout their life, Graves explains:

> The reason is that something dies in the poet. Perhaps he has compromised his poetic integrity by valuing some range of experience or other – literary, religious, philosophical, dramatic, political or social – above the poetic. But perhaps also he has lost his sense of the White Goddess: the woman he took to be a Muse, or who was a Muse, turns into a domestic woman and would have him turn similarly into a domesticated man. Loyalty prevents him from parting company with her, especially if she is the mother of his children and is proud to be reckoned a good housewife; and as the Muse fades out, so does the poet . . . The White Goddess is anti-domestic; she is the perpetual 'other woman', and her part is difficult indeed for a woman of sensibility to play for more than a few years, because the temptation to commit suicide in simple domesticity lurks in every maenad's and muse's heart.

In 1961, he began a poem, 'Ruby and Amethyst', thus:

Two women: one as good as bread,
Bound to a sturdy husband.
Two women: one as rare as myrrh,
Bound only to herself.

In July of 1960, I went to visit him in Deyá briefly, for his birthday, with my wife and son. Robert as a baby had been touched on the head by Swinburne while being wheeled in his pram on Wimbledon Common; I had Robert touch Jasper on the head, for continuity's sake. Robert was newly consumed by a letter from the agent William Morris, who had suggested that *The White Goddess* might make a singular film, and he had been asked to provide an outline, for which he had made notes. Would I take them and see what I could make of them? The notes were indeed fertile, even daring in places. Then he wrote me, once I was back in Madrid, that he had found the person who must play the White Goddess. He had also found a new muse.

She was Canadian by nationality, with a Greek father and an Irish mother, and she was called Margot Callas. Graves met her in Deyá during that summer of 1960, and was instantly entranced by her. She was intelligent, witty, highly intuitive, certainly beautiful, and it was not long before Robert was discovering a clutch of other qualities in her. It was not long, either, before new poems began to flow from him, and Margot occupied his whole mind. Once more, the Goddess had sent him a sign.

Not for the first time, or the last, Graves was captivated by what he pronounced firmly to be a manifestation of the Goddess. On each occasion, he became possessed, partly mad; on each occasion, he wrote, furiously, poems, only poems. He would shower his muse with them, and with letters and tokens of faith. Beryl, who knew him best, accepted these muses with a calm that others found inexplicable: she had learned how necessary they were to him. As in his years with Laura, he would refuse to hear a word against his muse. Now, as high priest, as voice, he spoke for the Goddess: only he could interpret her wishes, her commands.

Toward the end of 1960, I had to go to New York briefly, and I went by way of London, where the Graves family had gone for a

Christmas visit. Robert spoke only of Margot, obsessively, and gave me some letters and tokens to take to her in New York. I did not know then what that would mean.

I remember that snow was lying in the city when I arrived, and that I went first thing to *The New Yorker*, to turn in a piece. I spent ten days busily, made plans to sail back to Spain on the Leonardo da Vinci, and delivered Robert's tokens to Margot. She, too, was returning to Spain, and took a cabin on the same ship.

Inevitably, we talked during the voyage about Robert. She, too, was taken aback by the insistence in his redefinition of her. She had been given no say in the matter; in Robert's eyes, her muse status required only her acquiescence, and her nature was anything but acquiescent. We talked of many things besides Robert, and during the voyage realities intervened: Margot and I fell precipitously in love. By the time we reached Spain, we were lost in each other, and had decided to leave behind our present lives. She made her way to Majorca, I to Madrid. A month later, we met up in France, and came to rest in a water mill in the French Basque country. Robert was not on my mind.

I had not thought what his reaction might be, but I could not have imagined its ferocity. Margot came in for no criticism: the Goddess had swung her axe, as predicted. I came in for all his rage. She was no longer muse, I no longer poet. The poems that followed our desertion claimed the next section of the *Collected Poems*. It was not until later that I saw this as a pattern that had arisen several times before. In the mythic pattern of *The White Goddess* the poet succumbs to the rival as the inevitable death-in-love that he must undergo; in reality, however, the rival became the arch-betrayer. Robert, in those slowly declining years, came to see his reality wholly in terms of mythic inevitability; and the myth was his alone.

We never spoke again, Robert and I. Over the years, Margot and I had many meetings and partings. I would hear of Robert occasionally, for I still saw friends we had in common. New settlers had flocked to Deyá, and land was being snapped up, houses were being built. It had grown too busy to be any longer Robert's village. The Goddess proved ever more insistent: a new muse had manifested herself, and Robert was once more writing poems – muse-poems.

When his *Complete Poems* are published, I think they will reveal that in his strongest poems Robert is less a love poet than a poet of opposition and contradiction, of two-mindedness, much more questioner than worshipper. His muse-poems, finely wrought and tense as they are, all follow the same single-minded plot. Some read like imitations of him – perhaps because the muses he chose latterly were more and more his own creations. The stance he struck became ever more adamant, even shrill. I think he had stopped listening – to those close to him, to his own common-sense self, even to his own misgivings.

Of the thousand-odd poems that Robert wrote, I can think of a considerable handful that are sufficiently strong and singular as to belong unquestionably to the canon of English poetry. That may seem meagre; but what most distinguishes him as a poet, I think, is how he chose to live, his dedication to the office of poet. In the first chapter of *The White Goddess* he wrote:

> Since the age of fifteen poetry has been my ruling passion and I have never intentionally undertaken any task or formed any relationship that seemed inconsistent with poetic principles; which has sometimes won me the reputation of an eccentric.

That remained his measure, all his long life.

Robert's vindictiveness toward me did not reach me except by rumour, and there I was hurt mostly by its untruths. I felt for Beryl, but she was wisest in Robert's ways, and, giving him the room he needed, she allowed him his follies, whether wishful or actual. I had my own work to do, and I continued to do it, just as Robert would have. I realised then, as I do now, that many of my writing habits I absorbed from him, like the sanctity of the writing table, which I set up wherever I am. I remain attached to village life and to the agricultural round. When Margot and I first parted, I bought a small house on the edge of a Spanish mountain village, and spent every summer there with my son Jasper. For the last ten years, I have gone every winter to the Dominican Republic, where I have a house above the sea, and where, honed to essentials, the days simplify and slow down, as they did in Deyá. I revise what I write, scrupulously. I still bow nine times to the new moon; and I still read his poems, or listen to them in my head.

In the spring of 1985, I made a brief visit to Spain, with Margot, to visit Deyá, to see Beryl and some of the children, and to take farewell of Robert. His mind and memory had been failing steadily, and now he lay on a cot in the room adjoining his workroom, dozing, silent, beyond communication. It was as though he had gone into one of his trances and had not returned from it. At one moment, however, his eyes opened and widened; and it seemed to me that in them still lay all the wisdom and mischief in the world.

Waiting for Columbus
1992

For some time, I viewed the coming of 1992 with a certain dread. It could hardly have escaped anyone's attention then that on October 12 five hundred years had passed since Christopher Columbus first stepped ashore on what was for him a new world, however ancient its inhabitants. From the vantage point of Europe, he began to make a vast unknown into a known, and the date has been nailed down in history as that of the discovery of America. Not surprisingly, 1992 lay steadily in the sights of many quickening interests, public and private, and countless plans were laid to turn the year into a circus of near-global celebration. It is understandable that governments should seize on such occasions for a bit of national brio, the satisfaction of having come a long way. It puts some kind of affirmative stamp on a doubtful present; and, besides that, it gives a year a 'theme', which can be echoed inexhaustibly in exploitable form. The year 1992 was a prospective gold mine: the books, bumper issues of magazines, television specials, documentaries, simulations, and reenactments, and the coins, medallions, ship models, maps, museum exhibits, and other icons. One Spanish sculptor, Antoni Miralda, set in motion plans for a symbolic marriage between the Statue of Liberty and the statue of Columbus that stands on a cast-iron column overlooking the harbour of Barcelona. Outsized wedding garments and jewellery were put on display in various capital cities, and the symbolic ceremony was held on St Valentine's Day in Las Vegas. It occurred to me that if only Columbus had had the foresight to acquire the fifteenth-century equivalent of an agent his descendants would have raked in much more gold than even the Admiral dreamed of amassing, abundant though these dreams were, during his various sallies westward.

Of the thirty-odd countries that pledged themselves to official quincentenary fervour, Spain outdid all the others in extravagance, spending hundreds of millions of dollars on the event. Spain, after all, made the initial investment in the Admiral's enterprise, and clearly looked to 1992 as a way of reaping even more than it already had from that first outlay. That year, Spain was the setting for a World's Fair (in Seville) and for the Olympic Games (in Barcelona), and Madrid was named Europe's City of Culture for the year. All these events attracted intrusions of tourists – tourism being an industry that Spain has been turning to great advantage since the sixties. Spain was ripe for a year of self-congratulation: since the death of Francisco Franco, in 1975, it has made itself into a responsible and sophisticated modern democracy, an active and energetic member of the European Community, with a new and zippy life style and an aggressive self-confidence. Spain trumpeted the quincentenary: in 1988, the Spanish government established a foundation in Washington, DC – SPAIN '92 – 'to engage Americans in a thoughtful exploration of the impact of Christopher Columbus's voyages and to strengthen the cultural traditions which unite Americans and Spaniards', in the words of its brochure. Spain also had built meticulous replicas of the three ships that made the first voyage – the Santa Maria, of a design the Spanish called a *nao*, slower and statelier than the caravels Niña and Pinta. They were launched by members of the Spanish Royal Family in the fall of 1989, and set sail in a reenactment of the voyage. Later they showed themselves around the Caribbean before turning up to lead the tall ships into New York Harbour on the Fourth of July. They were not, however, the only replicas of that little fleet; several were built – enough to stage a round-the-world caravel race if they all remained afloat after their strenuous year of simulation. One replica of the Santa Maria was built in Barcelona by a Japanese publisher, who intended to sail it all the way from Barcelona to Kobe, Japan, thus fulfilling Columbus's original plan, which was to find the trade route from Spain to the lucrative East.

Ever since the quincentenary loomed, however, there arose a countercry, close to an outcry, over the global fiesta, and it mostly came, understandably, from the countries of Spanish America – the discoverees, as it were, which were of course given no choice about being discovered. What came to these countries with the conquest was nothing good – violent invasion, massacre, enslavement, exploitation – and a number of voices strongly suggested that 1992 be observed as a year of mourning in Spanish America and the Caribbean. Cuba was scathing in its denunciations of the celebrations. I was sent a copy of the *Declaration of Mexico*, circulated by a group for the 'Emancipation and Identity of Latin America'. To give the declaration's gist, I quote its first and last articles:

> Whereas October 12, 1492, which according to a Eurocentric version of history was the 'discovery' and/or 'encounter between two worlds', marked the beginning of one of the greatest acts of genocide, pillage, and plunder in human history, and whereas the intention to celebrate its 500th Anniversary constitutes an act of arrogance and disdain for the peoples of the Third World . . .
>
> . . . we have resolved not to participate in any activity related to the official celebrations of the 500th Anniversary, since such participation would legitimise the historical system of injustice and dependence initiated on October 12, 1492, and the spurious character of its celebration.

Rumblings from Latin America notwithstanding, the country that dressed the quincentenary in the most official pomp and gravity was the Dominican Republic, which, with Haiti, occupies the island Columbus christened Hispaniola – the first whole territory subdued and settled by the fortune hunters from Spain. Santo Domingo, the present-day capital, was the first outpost, the first colonial city in the New World, and its cathedral contains at least some of the Admiral's remains. (Havana and Seville claim to have the other parts in their keeping.) For the country's President, Dr Joaquin Balaguer, then eighty-four, the quincentenary had been an obsession from an early age, and his long life seemed to have been single-mindedly aimed at October 12, 1992. As far back as 1986, Balaguer instituted the Permanent Dominican Commission for the Fifth Centenary of the Discovery and Evangelisation of America – the longest and most pompous banner flown in the name of the event. He appointed as head of the commission his close friend and ecclesiastical henchman the Archbishop of Santo Domingo, Nicolás López Rodríguez, who viewed the landing of Columbus as the most momentous event in Christendom since the Resurrection. Balaguer clearly expected the quincentenary to bring to his country an attention and a sense of importance until now earned only by a rich crop of exceptional baseball players. Columbus, in his *Journal of the First Voyage*, speaks of the island as 'the fairest ever looked on by human eyes' – an endorsement that is still used liberally by the Dominican Tourist Office.

The country certainly seemed so to me when I first went there, over ten years ago. Outside its capital and two or three lesser cities, it is rural and agricultural, dotted sparsely with small villages, outposts of subsistence, so that its beautiful and immensely varying landscapes always dominate. Dominicans are among the most cheerful people in the world, and I found myself going back to explore further. I eventually settled on the Samaná Peninsula, in the extreme northeast of the country, a narrow arm of land, thirty-two miles in length, that protrudes from the bulk of the mainland like a lobster claw into the Atlantic and forms a very long and narrow bay on its south side – a natural harbour that at different times has attracted the acquisitive attention of foreign powers, the United States among them. A low mountain spine runs along the peninsula, falling away on the north to a long sand coast and on the south to strings of beaches and small enclosed inlets. The whole peninsula is covered with coconut palms, whose easygoing crop has been for many years its principal source of revenue. Samaná is quite literally the end of the line: if you follow its single road to the tip of the peninsula, you find yourself facing a white beach, a reef, and beyond, the open Atlantic. It was on Samaná that Columbus made his last landfall on the first voyage of discovery, and from there he set sail for Spain with news of what he had found.

★

As a place, Samaná is one of those geographical oddities which seem to invite a correspondingly eccentric history: it feels itself only marginally connected to the rest of the country; on early maps, it is sometimes shown as an island. A broad expanse of marsh

– the estuary of the River Yuna, which flows into Samaná Bay –
joins it to the mainland. In the past, most likely, the marsh did
provide a shallow waterway across the neck of the peninsula to the
north coast, an escape route for privateers bottled up in the bay
when piracy was at its height on the Spanish Main. In those days,
Samaná afforded just the kind of retreat the buccaneers needed;
and, indeed, it has given refuge to a great variety of runaways in
its long past. It has the look and feel of an island, and it has an
islandlike history – a series of intrusions and violations, all coming
from the outside. It is one of the poorest provinces in the country,
with the leanest statistics, but the land is bountiful, and its inhabitants follow a way of life that has allowed them to survive,
however frugally, for an immemorial time.

In the sixteenth and seventeenth centuries, Samaná was often
raided by English and Spanish ships in search of buccaneers and
runaways. It was not until 1756 that a group of Spanish colonists
was shipped from the Canary Islands to found the town of Santa
Barbara de Samaná. In 1807, while the French were briefly in
possession of the entire island, General Louis Ferrand, Napoleon's
commander in Santo Domingo, published a detailed plan for a
new port, with a miniature French city neatly squared beside it, to
be built in Samaná and named Port Napoleon: Samaná was to
become a rich coffee plantation, Port Napoleon 'a cultural capital
between East and West'. General Ferrand died, and the French lost
possession of the island before the work was begun, but the plans
for Port Napoleon still exist. Between 1850 and 1874, the United
States Congress was seriously studying a plan first to rent and then
to annex the Samaná Peninsula, and establish a permanent naval
station in Samaná Bay. The idea of acquiring Samaná for the
United States was something of a fixation in the mind of William
H. Seward, who was Secretary of State under Presidents Lincoln
and Johnson, and who had previously engineered the purchase of
Alaska from the Russians. On three or four occasions, agreement
seemed close, but Congress voted against annexation, and when
further offers to lease Samaná Bay were made General Ignacio
María González, newly elected President in Santo Domingo, took
a firm and popular decision that no part of his country should be

yielded up to foreign ownership. The Germans and the English had also shown a commercial interest in Samaná. Even so, the place was hardly prosperous: the population of the peninsula when annexation was being considered was under three thousand.

Samaná had received an intrusion of settlers in 1824, when President Jean-Pierre Boyer of Haiti, who had just occupied Santo Domingo, decided to ship in immigrants from the southern United States to populate the remoter parts of his new colony. Some three hundred of them settled in Samaná, and you can still hear the sing-song English of their descendants in the market, or shake the huge hand of a man named Samuel Johnson on the dock. Don León, who keeps our local store, tells me of his childhood in Samaná, some sixty years ago, when there was no road to town and he had to row to market – a two-hour haul – sometimes twice a day. But he remembers a Samaná that was more prosperous than now, with a chocolate factory, an icehouse, a soap works, and a busy maritime trade. Samaná harbour is now mostly a landfall for small boats making an Atlantic crossing or cruising the Caribbean. In January, when the trade winds are blowing right, we see them straggle in, flying a variety of flags, sea-weary. Last winter, I found a plastic pouch of water on the beach with instructions in Norwegian. I do not know Norwegian, so I added its contents to the sea.

It was Samaná itself, and not Columbus, that drew me in. Turns in the road revealed sudden beauties, to gasp at. Everything moved at walking pace. A car looked somehow absurd there. The place felt as if it were adrift, unanchored to anything. I explored the villages and the coast, I asked questions, I listened a lot, and eventually I acquired a piece of land just inside the point where Samaná Bay opens to the Atlantic: land that rose in a broad bowl from a small enclosed beach to a ridge, and fell away to the road on the other side; land that faced south across the bay and was thickly overgrown – well staked with coconut palms, all nodding seaward. Don Justo, who sold me the land, told me that he had not seen it in years, although he lives only a few miles from it. He had sent a man four times a year to gather the coconuts, but he did not think much else could grow there. Now he comes often, amazed that I have coaxed it into fruit.

In the Dominican countryside, campesinos live mostly in clumps of houses, settlements rather than villages – *aldea* is the Spanish word – that are dotted here and there, usually close to a water source. My land fell away steeply on the west side to a small, flat clearing through which a freshwater stream flowed by way of a small lagoon into the sea. Five houses stood close to the stream, accommodating in all about twenty people – men, women, a tribe of children. After buying the land, I made arrangements to stay in a room in one of the houses, and I hired the men of the *aldea* to help me build a small house, and to clear the land for cultivation. During that time, I got to know my neighbours very well indeed. We were some nine miles beyond the last town – that is, beyond public market, post office, electricity, telephone, hospital, and hardware store – and everybody depended on the small country *colmados*, which sold the basics: rice, oil, sugar, salt, rum. What we lived in – our bounded world – was, I learned from them, our *vecindad*, or neighbourhood, which meant roughly the piece of coast you could encompass with a sweep of the arm from the ridge. Within the *vecindad*, you knew the inhabitants, down to the babies, and if you did not actually know them you had heard about them, in story form, and you inevitably shared their crises and daily dramas.

When you settle in a place, what you absorb, and to some extent take on, from those who live there is their vantage point: the way they see the rest of the world, their preoccupations, the web of their attention. Most of my neighbours are *analfabetos*, they neither read nor write. They are, however, passionate, dedicated talkers, often eloquent. Their mode, their natural wavelength, is to put themselves in story form. Their lives have no written archives, their years no numbers or dates; for that reason, a quincentenary is meaningless to them. They have saved their personal history in the form of a set of stories, well polished with telling, stored, ready. I have heard some of them recount their lives, a rosary of stories, on different occasions, and noticed how they vary with the telling. Everything that happens eventually circulates in story form, embellished by its tellers. Don León listens avidly to the radio news in his store and passes on his edited versions of it to his customers, who disperse it further on the way home. Travelling so, from teller to teller, quite ordinary happenings often turn into wonders.

In 1950, George F. Kennan made an investigatory journey through a number of Latin American countries. On his return, he wrote a report that was not circulated at the time, but that he refers to in his memoirs. I quote one passage:

> The price of diplomatic popularity, and to some extent of diplomatic success, is constant connivance at the maintenance of a staggering and ubiquitous fiction: the fiction of extraordinary human achievement, personal and collective, subjective and objective, in a society where the realities are almost precisely the opposite, and where the reasons behind these realities are too grim to be steadily entertained. Latin American society lives, by and large, by a species of make-believe: not the systematised, purposeful make-believe of Russian communism, but a highly personalised, anarchical make-believe, in which each individual spins around him, like a cocoon, his own little world of pretense, and demands its recognition by others as the condition of his participation in the social process.

I can feel the exasperation behind that passage: the exasperation of a diplomat accustomed to clarity; the same exasperation that travellers in a Western hurry will stumble over in Latin America. Yet Kennan is putting his finger on a linguistic mode that is familiar to anyone who has lived in the countries of Spanish America, that I come across every day in conversations with my neighbours, that is at the core of Borges's writings. To Borges, everything put into language is a fiction, and should not be confused with reality. The fictions we make are ways of ordering and dominating the disorders of reality, even though they in no way change it. The 'truth' of a fiction is less important than its effectiveness; and, since reality is shifting and changing, our fictions must constantly be revised. For my neighbours, their stories are a form of continuous self-creation, and a way of taming and domesticating the world outside the *vecindad*, the great, fearful unknown.

This fictive cast of mind, while it animates the *chisme* – the daily gossip that serves as our newspaper – is something of an impediment to serious discourse. I sometimes notice in the discussion I listen to on Dominican radio that what takes place is less an exchange of views on a given question than a series of restatements of the question, each distinctly personal, each with a neat resolution. It is perhaps too extreme to say of Dominicans that they are devoid of objectivity, yet that is what I often feel. It is as though they had no overall grasp of their own situation, even though they have at the ready a rich variety of explanations and personal remedies. For them, once a problem has been put right in words, it can be forgotten. The reality is another matter altogether.

Listening to the Spanish spoken in the Dominican Republic, I quite often come on words so bizarrely unfamiliar that I have to reach their meaning by scrutinous questioning, for I have never heard them anywhere else. One such word, of Afro-Hispanic origin, from the language arrived at by the Africans brought as slaves to Hispaniola, is the noun *fucú* or *fukú*. It is often spoken with a certain dropping of the voice. *Un fucú* is something ill-omened, likely to bring bad luck, something in a person or a place or a happening that has doom about it. At the materialisation of a *fucú* in any form, Dominicans cross their index fingers in the air and exclaim '*Zafa!*' – loosely translated as 'Change the subject'. At least they used to, I am told by the elders in my neighbourhood: perhaps the custom has waned because there are so many obvious public *fucús* in the country now that the day would be one long '*Zafa!*' The word has entered not just my vocabulary but my consciousness; I am able to realise that some people and elements in New York have a *fucú* about them for me. It helps me save time.

The most interesting *fucú* of all among Dominicans, however, is the superstition that has existed for centuries that bad luck would dog anyone who spoke aloud the name of Cristóbal Colón. That called for instant crossed fingers and a loud '*Zafa!*' One referred instead to the Admiral, or the Discoverer. The official propaganda surrounding the quincentenary has had to face down the *fucú*, as it were, for the name has somehow kept coming up. But the campesinos still believe in *the fucú* that C— C— brings bad luck, perhaps with more fervour now than before. One of my neighbours told me solemnly that the word *colonia* – 'colony' – came from the name of Cristóbal Colón, an error I saw no point in correcting.

In the evenings of those first days, when we had finished work and bathed and eaten, we would sit by the stream and talk as the dark came down. My neighbours were full of questions, mostly about life in the United States, which I answered with some care; and in my turn I questioned them closely about their lives and the ways of the place. We have continued so ever since. In the evenings I hear feet on the stones of my terrace, and someone will materialise, always with an offering – Sandro with fish, Felipe with an egg – and we will sit on the warm stone and talk. A kind of natural barter plays a large part in my neighbours' existence, and, indeed, they like nothing better than a 'deal', an exchange that pleases both sides. I have to remember that I am a *patrón*, a land-owner, and I have to assume the role sometimes: to settle a dispute, or to come up with money for medicine – a debt that is always paid off with a day's work. Dominican society is a curious web of family connections, of debts and favours owed, of patronage and reward – a system that, while it functions well enough in remote country settlements like ours, has turned Dominican politics into a tangle of corruption. My neigbours are natural anarchists. Pucho, who has worked with me since the beginning, and now lives, with his family, on the land above mine, insists that he has no loyalties other than to what his eye encompasses, and he leaves no ground un-planted, for that is what makes unquestionable sense to him. One evening, he found, in a catalogue that had come with my mail, a rowing machine. He was delighted, for he has a long row to the reef where he goes fishing, and hates rowing; when I explained that people in cities had rowing machines in their houses to keep healthy, he looked at me pityingly.

As I discovered by the stream, history for my neighbours is mostly hearsay, vague rumblings in a dateless clutter of past, anchored by a few facts brought home from school by the children. For most of them, the past, though it has engendered their present, is an irrelevance. So at one point, for a few evenings running, I told them a fairly simplified version, though quite a detailed one, of Cristóbal Colón and the first voyage, the first landings, the coming of the Spaniards, and the subsequent enslavement of their country. I told them what I knew about the Indians – the Tainos and the Ciguayos – who when Colón arrived had been living an unvarying rural existence. They made their settlements by fresh water, close to the sea. They fished, they bartered work and harvests, they lived communally. They were also innocent of money, as my neighbours often are, though not from choice.

Some of my neighbours became quite indignant at my version of the arrival of the Spaniards, and, indeed, I did myself. Although I had read fairly extensively about the conquest, I had always done so in the historical mass, so to speak; I had never been physically close to the scene before, and I felt myself suddenly waking up to those happenings as quite easily imaginable realities. When the house was finished and the books were unpacked, I started to read that history all over again, beginning with where I was – with Columbus's landing on Samaná – and then going mostly backward, reading what I could find about the conditions of life in Hispaniola before that catastrophic disembarkation.

★

In early January of 1493, aboard the Niña, with the Pinta in attendance, Columbus was bowling along the north coast of Hispaniola, on an easterly course. Of all his landfalls so far, Hispaniola had proved the most rewarding. Its natives were friendly and docile, its vegetation was sumptuous, and he had found enough gold to fuel expectations of more. It would be his territory, he had decided, his base for any future exploration. Fixed firmly in his sailing mind, however, was the urge to return to Spain with all dispatch, on the first good wind. He had lost the Santa María, grounded on a coral reef on Christmas Eve, but its timbers had been used to build a small fort called La Navidad, where the Admiral left behind a garrison of thirty-nine men. The standard histories have him rounding the northeast corner of the Samaná Peninsula and deciding to make one last landfall, to take on fresh water and provisions for the return crossing, and, if possible, to careen and caulk his two remaining boats, which were taking water. According to his log entry for January 12, 1493, the two ships entered 'an enormous bay three leagues wide, with a little island *una isleta pequeñuela* in the middle of it', and they anchored between the little island and a shallow sand beach. The following morning, the Admiral sent a boat ashore to treat with the Indians, as he had been doing with regularity over the past three months. These Indians, however, were quite different in appearance from the ones so far encountered. These wore their hair long, plaited with bird plumage, and they blackened their faces. Also, unlike most of those so far encountered, they carried arms – longbows and arrows. The crew persuaded one of them to return to the ship and talk with the Admiral. By this time, the Spaniards had most likely acquired a certain basic vocabulary, and, as usual, the Admiral questioned the man assiduously on the whereabouts of gold, and delivered an invitation to his cacique, his chief. The Indian was fed, given some trinkets, and returned by the boat's crew to his beach. On this occasion, some fifty-five Indians had gathered, and seven of the boat's crew bargained for bows and arrows, as they had been ordered. They had acquired two bows when something caused the Indians to go back to collect their arms. Leaving nothing to chance, the seven Spaniards attacked them, wounding one Indian with a sword slash in the buttocks and another in the breast with a crossbow arrow. This brief skirmish, most likely founded on a misunderstanding, has gone into the annals as the first shedding of indigenous blood in the New World – the first, faint inkling of the slaughter that was to follow. Three days later, the wind turned westerly, and, with four of the long-haired Indians added to the onboard evidence of the New World, the Niña and the Pinta put out well before dawn and set course for Spain. In his log the Admiral referred to his last anchorage as the Golfo de las Flechas, the Bay of the Arrows.

The Journal of the First Voyage, the written source of the discovery, is a strangely diffuse document, very far from objectivity even when it is being a ship's log, for some of its landfalls are still being argued over. (There is no original of the document. The version we read is an annotated text of a 1530s edition prepared and in many instances paraphrased by a later visitor, the diligent friar Bartolomé de Las Casas, from a less than complete copy made by an errant scribe; but not even this text was known about until 1825, when it was published, circulated, studied, and, in 1828, translated into English.) Some of the journal is first person, some third person (Las Casas's paraphrase), some in the shorthand of terse nautical observation. Columbus's own observations sometimes have the true awe of a man seeing unimagined wonders for the first time, but they are interspersed with passages of self-congratulation, lavish reassurances to Their Majesties, small sermons and other bursts of missionary zeal, inflated promises of bountiful gold, and a very eccentric geography. Columbus was in his forties by then, and for the last ten years his sole preoccupation had been to persuade some rich and powerful patron to underwrite an expedition of discovery. He had presented his arguments many times – as often as possible – first to the Portuguese court and then to Their Catholic Majesties in Spain, and he had obviously made them as alluring as he could. He was familiar with Marco Polo's chronicles, and cast his own expectations in the same high tone, conjuring up a vision of a New World that, since it was so far entirely imagined, could be wondrous in every respect. He became a practised exaggerater. He was shrewd enough to realise that he had to satisfy a multitude of interests, and his arguments were consequently many-faceted: for mercantile interests he would discover the route to the East that would open up trade with Cathay and with Cipango (Japan); for the Crown he would claim all new lands and found for Spain a colonial empire; for the Church he could promise converts, he would find the Garden of Eden; and beyond all these interests he dangled the promise of gold in abundance, at a time when Spain's treasury was exhausted. He had voiced these expectations so often that when he did find land what he looked for first was a self-justifying confirmation of them. His New World existed for him in the fiction he had made of it before he discovered it, and there was often a considerable disparity between what he found and what he said he found. After exploring the coast of Cuba, in November, he insisted, and continued to insist, that it was Cathay; yet he did not continue west. By then, from the natives he encountered he had picked up enough stories of gold for it to be fixed abidingly in the forefront of his attention. For him, the rumour of gold brought wish and reality together. Forgetting about the East, he followed the Indians' indications and turned back in the direction of Hispaniola.

Among a handful of anecdotes that Dominicans like to tell about the conquest is one that I have heard in a few variant forms. As fact it is improbable, but as essence it is peerless. It became the practice of the caciques to retreat from the arriving Spaniards, leaving placatory gifts in their path. The story has one such cacique leaving as an offering his beautiful daughter, bound to a stake, and wearing nothing but a gold ring in her nose. The Admiral, arriving at the head of his men, stops them suddenly with spread hands, gazes at the girl for a gravid minute, then points a trembling finger and asks, 'Where did you get that ring?'

I keep thinking of those first encounters, particularly from the point of view of language. The Spaniards and the Indians had no language in common, and Columbus had to communicate as tourists do nowadays in markets beyond their linguistic reach – by pointing and gesticulating. While that probably served well enough to get the ships' companies food and water, to make gestures of friendship and good intentions, and even to emphasise a particularly urgent interest in anything made of gold, it cannot have made possible the communication of anything abstract, like the claiming of all the Indians' lands in the name of Ferdinand and Isabella, or the fundamental tenets of the Holy Roman Church. Over various landfalls, the Spaniards probably began to assemble a sketchy vocabulary of native words, but there are signs in the journal that Columbus was prone to the affliction of beginners in any language – an overwillingness to understand. Hearsay for Columbus was whatever he thought he heard, and hearsay was the basis of his golden promises in a famous letter that he addressed to Their Majesties on the return crossing. Besides the gold and the Indians, Columbus was carrying back with him a great fund of information that he had sifted from the Indians' stories, some of it more imagined than real. *The Journal of the First Voyage* has a kind of speculative edge to it, an awe in its voice, a looking-at that before very long became a looking-for. The second voyage, from 1493 to 1496, was no longer looking for gold; it was going after it. With the second voyage, the conquest really began.

On the first voyage, Columbus went through an orgy of naming – christening capes, headlands, bays, points, rivers, and islands, and entering the names meticulously in his log. For him, giving them Spanish names was synonymous with claiming them for Spain, and his naming grew more diligent as the voyage progressed. No matter that everything was already named and understood by the Indians – from now on, Spain was to impose itself on Hispaniola, a God-appointed enterprise. Whatever form of life the Indians had achieved up until now was an irrelevance, since it was about to be ended, irrevocably.

The landfall in Columbus's Bay of the Arrows, of first-blood fame, is identified in the vast majority of books about Columbus as the beach called Las Flechas, on the south coast of the Samaná Peninsula. Facing that beach is a small, neat jewel of an island known as Cayo Levantado, assumed to be the 'little island' Columbus identifies in his log. Las Flechas lies along the coast from our beach, about a mile farther into the bay, and I must have passed it hundreds of times by now, for the road to town runs just above it. It has served to keep Columbus on my mind. The first time I explored it, I looked for some kind of marker, since Columbus's landfalls have been well labelled, but it was as anonymous as when he found it. Beyond a broad, untidy straggle of coconut palms, which always cast for me a kind of cathedral gloom on the beaches below them, lay its curve of sand, three small fishing boats pulled up, a litter of fishing gear, and Cayo Levantado riding at anchor about a mile offshore. I talked to an old man who was resting his back against one of the boats. I asked him about the beach and Columbus. 'Colón? Colón? Now, I've heard that name.'

*

Since about the first century, Arawak Indians had been migrating north from the South American continent through the islands, and so had settled Hispaniola a good many centuries before Columbus arrived. Those island Arawaks of Hispaniola are now generally referred to as Tainos, from the name for their upper class, for, although they had originally brought with them their own plants and methods of cultivation, they evolved a way of life distinct to the island. What we know of their mode of existence in Hispaniola has reached us mainly through the assiduousness of four chroniclers who came on subsequent voyages – Bartolomé de Las Casas, Peter Martyr, Guillermo Coma, and Gonzalo Fernández de Oviedo. Yet the more I read in the chronicles about how the Tainos lived, the more I realise that their life resembled, in most of its fundamentals, the present life of our *vecindad*. Taino artifacts are everywhere – the neighbours will bring me pieces of red pottery they come across, or an axe head, still lime-encrusted. Their life-sustaining crop was the root cassava – manioc, yucca, tapioca. It gave them bread, and they grew it in conelike mounds of earth called *conucos*. Cassava, yams, and sweet potato, along with beans, maize, peppers, and squashes, were their standard plantings, none of them at all demanding of attention or labour. They also grew cotton and tobacco and some fruit – pineapple and papaya in particular. With an abundance of fish, they were self-sufficient. A docile people, they were feudally organised under a cacique. They lived in small settlements close to fresh water, in simple houses, well roofed against the rains. Only hurricanes or droughts upset this equilibrium.

The selfsame crops are all flourishing in our *vecindad* at this moment. Pucho has a great spread of yucca growing just under the crest – a staple that feeds him year-round. Now we have additional staples – coconuts, bananas and plantains, rice, sugar, coffee, many more fruits – but the land and the fishing still provide practically all our food. Taino words are on our tongue every day – hammock, cassava, maize, tobacco, potato, canoe. Although the Taino population of Hispaniola was wiped out within thirty years of the discovery, it is as though the Tainos had left their mode of life embedded in the land, to be reenacted in a surprisingly similar form by the campesinos now. Rich soil, a benign climate, and plants of predictable yield guarantee basic survival, although today on a threadbare level. For the Tainos, however, it appears to have been an abundance, and their world was apparently both stable and peaceful. While the Tainos knew the whereabouts of gold, they made little use of it except for small ornaments. Sometimes, sitting on my terrace, I imagine what it must have been like for the Tainos, similarly perched, to see the caravels come into sight. Even today, when a boat of any size enters the bay we come out to gaze, as we do when a plane flies over.

In the letter Columbus wrote on the return crossing to Ferdinand and Isabella (it was addressed to Luis de Santangel, Crown Treasurer, for transmission to Their Catholic Majesties), he expanded on the nature of the Indians he had encountered, speaking of their timidity, their innocence, and the fact that they went unarmed and were both friendly to and fearful of the Spaniards − perfect material for conversion and for service to the Crown. He did report, however, that he had heard of an island peopled by warlike Indians, Caribs, who were known to eat human flesh, and who made sorties on the outlying islands. The details he gave of them − that they wore their hair long and carried bows and arrows − appear to have come from the confrontation and flash of force at Las Flechas. When his boat's crew told him of that encounter, he wrote of himself in the journal, on January 13, 1493, 'In one way it troubled me, and in another way it did not, i.e., in that now they might be afraid of us. Without doubt, the people here are evil, and I believe they are from the Isle of Caribe, and that they eat men . . . If these people are not Caribes, they must at least be inhabitants of lands fronting them and have the same customs, not like the others on the other islands who are without arms and cowardly beyond reason.'

When the seventeen ships of the second voyage reached their destination in Hispaniola, with a company of about fifteen hundred, some domestic animals, and a variety of seeds, plants, and provisions, the long equilibrium that the Tainos had enjoyed ended. Columbus found the fort he had left destroyed, all the men dead − they had abused the Indians and had been overcome in turn. From this point on, Columbus never hesitated to show force in all his dealings with the Indians. They were to be subdued and turned to work in finding and extracting gold, before all else. The Spaniards as yet had no substantial permanent settlement, but they set out on expeditions to the interior, to track the gold. The course of subsequent events was perhaps set from the beginning by a fatal misunderstanding. On the first voyage, Columbus read from the gesticulations of the Indians he questioned that gold existed on the island in abundant quantities, and he reported that as fact. In truth, while gold did exist in the Cibao and in other alluvial placers, it was not widespread, plentiful, or easily accessible – certainly not to any degree that would satisfy the Admiral's by now burning expectations. Yet he continued to insist that it was, and drove the Indians more and more ferociously to produce it.

It did not take long to turn the feelings of the Tainos for the Spaniards from fear to hatred: they first rose against them in early 1494, and suffered fierce retribution. When a fleet of four ships left for Spain, in February of 1495, about five hundred Indian captives were aboard; nearly half of them died on the voyage. Columbus meanwhile set about crushing Indian resistance once and for all, which he did with a formidable force of men. He eventually secured the submission of most of the caciques, established a fort in the centre of the island, and then decided on the site of the new capital, Santo Domingo – at the mouth of the Ozama River, in the south. From every Indian over fourteen the Admiral demanded a tribute of a small piece of gold every three months. The caciques begged to be released from the tribute of gold, offering instead to plant a vast stretch of land expressly for feeding the Spaniards, something to them of infinitely greater worth. But the Spaniards, fired by both greed and impatience, were unrelenting.

Failure to pay tribute resulted in increasingly brutal punishment – quite often, according to Las Casas, the cutting off of the Indians' hands – until, in 1497, orders came from Spain, in the form of Letters Patent, decreeing a *repartimiento*, a sharing out, of the colony. The plan was later modified to become one of granting the settlers *encomiendas*, tracts of land to use and cultivate, along with an Indian community to do each settler's bidding, with the understanding that the *encomendero* would in time convert his Indians to Christianity. The granting of *encomiendas*, however, was less about land than about Indians: in practice, a settler would be given a whole Indian community, under its cacique, to cultivate the land, to dig for gold, to do anything at all that the master might command. Religious instruction was not uppermost in the settlers' minds. By 1500, the enslavement of the Tainos was complete. The seven years of

Columbus's governorship of Hispaniola had been chaotic for the Spaniards and disastrous for the Tainos. His authority over the Spanish settlers had frayed and eroded, and the revenues he had promised the Crown had not been realised. Orders came from Spain that he was to be replaced as governor by Francisco de Bobadilla; and when Bobadilla arrived in Santo Domingo, in August of 1500, his first act was to arrest Columbus and his two brothers, Bartholomew and Diego, and send them back to Spain in chains.

As for the Tainos, they were by now dwindling in number. Most of the detail that remains to us of that human erosion we owe to the extraordinarily observant and intelligent chronicle of Bartolomé de Las Casas. As a young man, in Seville, he had seen Columbus return in triumph from the first voyage in 1493, and his father and uncle had both preceded him to Hispaniola. He landed in Santo Domingo in 1502, and in his ten years there he was to bear witness to the steady extermination of the Tainos; in a growing state of moral outrage, he was led eventually to join the Dominican order and to dedicate his life to arguing the rights of the Indians and denouncing the brutalities of the conquest in his writings and in public debate in Spain. He often made his case in an eloquent polemic, but it is the details he patiently recorded in his history of the Indies which make his case for him now. He had a keen sense of the fatefulness of the times he was living in, and of the dangerous precedents being set. Were it not for him, we would know far less about the Tainos and their progressive destruction.

Among Las Casas's careful records we have his transcription of a sermon that the Dominican friar Antonio de Montesinos preached in Santo Domingo on the last Sunday of Advent, 1511, castigating the cruelty of the settlers and reminding them of their Christian obligations:

> Tell me, by what right or justice do you hold these Indians in such a cruel and horrible servitude? On what authority have you waged such detestable wars against these peoples, who dwelt quietly and peacefully on their own land? Wars in which you have destroyed such infinite numbers of them by homicides and slaughters never before heard of? Why do you keep them so

oppressed and exhausted, without giving them enough to eat or curing them of the sicknesses they incur from the excessive labour you give them? And they die, or, rather, you kill them, in order to extract and acquire gold every day.

And what care do you take that they should be instructed in religion, so that they may know their God and Creator, may be baptised, may hear Mass, and may keep Sundays and feast days? Are these not men? Do they not have rational souls? Are you not bound to love them as you love yourselves? Don't you understand this? Don't you feel this? Why are you sleeping in such a profound and lethargic slumber? Be assured that in your present state you can no more be saved than the Moors or Turks, who lack the faith of Jesus Christ and do not desire it.

Witnessing the massacre of Indians, Las Casas himself wrote, 'Who of those born in future centuries will believe this? I myself who am writing this and saw it and know most about it can hardly believe that such was possible.'

It may be that from the beginning the Tainos were doomed by the disturbance of their rural way of life. Their settlements were the known world to them; to be moved left them helpless. (The Spanish word *desalojamiento*, 'to be turned out of home', is a word my neighbours always utter with a hush of horror.) Their finely balanced agricultural rhythm was broken. The domestic animals – cattle, pigs, horses – that the Spaniards had brought thrived on the vegetation and trampled free over cultivated land. The Tainos, besides, had no resistance of any kind – to European diseases, to the hard labour they were subjected to in the mines, to the demands and brutalities of the settlers, to the conditions of slavery, in Hispaniola or in Spain – and they died in vast numbers. The bitter cassava has a poisonous juice, which is squeezed out before making bread; the ubiquitousness of cassava meant that for the Tainos an easy means of suicide was at hand, and they used it liberally. A few fled – some, without doubt, to the Samaná Peninsula. An outbreak of smallpox in 1518 further reduced them. Most latter-day writers on the landings of the Spaniards concur in the opinion that what probably afflicted the Tainos more than anything else was the microbes and viruses introduced by the Spaniards. Las Casas estimated that some three million Tainos had died between 1494 and 1508, a figure now considered to be an exaggeration; but, as to the Taino population, there can be no definitive figures, only guesses. What is definitive is the fact that by the 1530s virtually no Tainos were left except a few hundred who had fled to Cuba and possibly a few who survived their slavery in Spain. As a people, they were extinct.

The letter Columbus wrote to Santangel for Their Majesties, with its glowing version of what he had discovered, was printed in Barcelona in 1493, and almost immediately translated into Latin. It sketches the Indians' way of life in a mode that carries echoes of Eden, Arcadia, and Columbus's own earlier fantasies. It caught the European imagination at once, this vision of unclothed, unarmed innocence, and it was to flower later in the writings of Montaigne, in the noble savage of Rousseau, and in other written Utopias. It also gave the newly discovered lands an aura of promise and freedom that served as a spur to the many westward migrations from Europe that followed. With conquest, however, the Spanish view of the Indians changed quickly. The shift is visible in Columbus's own writings: the docile Tainos, friendly, eager to please, later become 'Cowards'; fear of the warlike Caribs takes precedence, a show of force is paramount. The native is animal, the paradise wilderness, both to be dominated and subdued. First seen as Ariel, the Indian is soon turned into Caliban: beast, slave, less than human.

The depletion of the Taino population left succeeding governors of Hispaniola with a serious lack of labour; new labour had to be found if the colony was to be of any further use to Spain. Hence, by 1518 African slaves were being brought to the island. They were stronger than the Tainos, better fitted for work in the mines and for cane cutting. Sugar had been introduced in 1515, and Hispaniola was turning from its exhausted gold-workings to agriculture. At the same time, however, Hispaniola was receding in importance to the Spanish Crown. In 1500 Alonso de Ojeda had discovered the coastline of what is now Colombia, with evidence of gold in quantity; and as news of that and of the later subjugation of Jamaica and Cuba, the excursions of Juan Ponce de León to

Florida, in 1513, the further probing south by Vasco Núñez de Balboa, and Hernán Cortés's conquest of Mexico in 1519, filtered back steadily to Santo Domingo, many of the settlers determined to follow in these tracks and abandon the colony for more immediate reward. To survive, if not to prosper, Hispaniola needed a settled population. Instead, Santo Domingo was becoming little more than a way station on the Spanish Main. The first Spaniards came less to colonise than to return home wealthy. The surge was westward. When López de Velasco came to write the official geography of the Indies, in 1574, he reported a population in Hispaniola of a thousand Spaniards, half of them in Santo Domingo, and thirteen thousand African Negroes, with large tracts of the island abandoned. The present population of the Dominican Republic is two-thirds mulatto, one-third divided between white and black. No one claims Taino blood.

★

Although Columbus has been mythified by history as the discoverer, he cannot be made to bear the blame for the greed and the brutality of those who came after him – men of a less visionary disposition. What set the ruthless tenor of the conquest, however, was the extravagant expectations that Columbus had created in his quest for patronage. His eagerness to confirm these expectations shows in what he chose to see on the first voyage. His later life seethed with frustration, as though he could never forgive the lands he had discovered for not giving him what they had promised, or what he had made them promise. His obsession with fulfilling the expectation of abundant gold kept him from giving any thought to the territories he was meant to be governing, or maintaining any authority over the settlers. It was less the inhumanity of the settlers – although Las Casas has left us plenty of evidence of that – than the stupidity and mismanagement of the unfolding enterprise, coupled with the intrusion of disease, that made the Indians extinct in so short a time.

Living in Samaná off and on over these last years has without question made me Indian-minded in reading those chronicles. I find them horrifying. Whatever consequences the first voyage of

Columbus may have had for the planet and for our present existence, I cannot see that the ensuing thirty years were other than a human disaster for Hispaniola, a record of cruel and pointless conquest that could have been otherwise. Pucho asks me a lot about the Tainos – I once read him from Las Casas the descriptions of their common crops and agricultural practices, and he was as startled as I was that everything was all still growing within shouting distance, that we were more or less enacting the Tainos' agricultural patterns, using their words, living more or less as they did except for our clothes and our discontents. Even though the Tainos were his precursors rather than his ancestors, even though his language and his religion come from the Spaniards, it is with the Indians, the victims, that he identifies. When I told Pucho earlier this year that sometime in 1992 three caravels would sail into Samaná Bay, past our beach, to anchor off Las Flechas, and some actor would come ashore in a Columbus suit, he was all for gathering a few picked men from the *vecindad* and taking the actor hostage, as a gesture.

Legends require simplification, and by the time Columbus became legend and statue he had been enshrined as the discoverer, in some sense the founder, of the New World, although this did not really happen until the nineteenth century. Nor was it entirely a Eurocentric view that gave him the name of discoverer – it appealed as much to North Americans to fix on the image of the Admiral's first, frail landfall as a legendary beginning. The discoverees are glossed over; the fate of the Tainos is hardly common knowledge. Plans for the quincentenary made clear that in the case of Columbus the clarification of history was giving way to its Disneyfication. The image of Columbus that loomed largest was the heroic one – in television series, in two feature films, in the gloss of magazine re-creation, and in the gush of highly coloured simulation. A few years ago, an Italian film crew came to shoot part of a historical drama about Columbus on the north coast of Samaná. They used a group of villagers as extras, and left them somehow stranded in a time warp: they have never quite recovered from the experience, and talk of nothing else. In Samaná, we all felt like extras by the time the quincentenary had run its course.

By far the most imaginative suggestion I heard about an appropriate acknowledgment of the quincentenary was made on Dominican television by the Dominican economist and historian Bernardo Vega, just as President Balaguer was preparing to attend a summit meeting of Latin American and Iberian heads of state in Mexico. Vega urged him to advance the idea at the meeting that since the Club of Paris, an organisation that keeps a supervisory eye on Third World debt, was already excusing the debts of some African countries, it should make the year 1992 memorable by wiping off the slate all the European debt accumulated by the countries of Latin America, as partial compensation for the wealth that had been extracted from that region, starting in 1492.

In the decade following Columbus's first landfall, the island of Hispaniola, for the Spaniards who descended on it, *was* the New World – its earliest incarnation. The first reports and chronicles also whetted the colonising appetites of the other seafaring countries of Europe. As the conquistadores ventured farther and farther into the southern continent, establishing their maritime base at Cartagena, from which harbour the gold-bearing ships set out on the Spanish Main, a whole host of adventurers began to arrive on the scene, to take part in the general land grab in the Caribbean and to launch almost two centuries of piracy. In 1586, Sir Francis Drake occupied and sacked Santo Domingo. French buccaneers set up their harbours of operation on the island of Tortuga and on the north coast of Hispaniola, and on their sorties they also discovered the Samaná Peninsula, a natural hideout, well placed for raids on the gold lanes to the south. The remaining Spanish colonists could not muster sufficient strength to drive the French out. In 1697, they ceded the western part of the island altogether to France, and subsequently France peopled its new colony, Saint-Domingue, with bigger shipments of African slaves, to work in the increasingly lucrative sugar plantations. Spain's control of and interest in the colony waned considerably, and in 1795 it ceded the rest of the island to France. But, fired by news of the French Revolution, the slaves of Saint-Domingue began to rise in revolt, and, in 1804, succeeded, in establishing the independent black republic of Haiti. Their revolutionary zeal and their determination to stamp out slavery led them into a series of aggressions against the rest of the island, and in 1822 a Haitian army occupied Santo Domingo and took over the whole island. It was the Haitian occupation that drove the colonists to unite in sufficient force to confront the invaders, to defeat them, and to declare, on February 27, 1844, the independent existence of the Dominican Republic.

The history of Hispaniola after Columbus – a history of factionalism, of foreign intrusions, of plot and counterplot – set a pattern that has continued into the island's turbulent present, and led to the republic's having had more than forty different governments between 1844 and 1916. It is a history that implies a deep division – a division between a few individuals with the ruthlessness to aspire to power and domination, on the one hand, and a quiescent people who have learned to survive whatever calamities break over their heads, on the other.

The Tainos were victims of the conquest, and, in a sense, those who have inhabited the farther reaches of the island have continued to be victims ever since. At no time was the colony free of foreign presence, of foreign domination, even after independence had been at least nominally achieved; and in this century it is the United States, rather than France or Spain, that now casts its long shadow over the island's affairs, to the point of direct intervention on two occasions. The United States Marines occupied the Dominican Republic from 1916 until 1924, when political chaos threatened civil war; and in 1965, on the same pretext, President Lyndon Johnson sent an occupying force to the island when street fighting in Santo Domingo threatened to spread and engulf the whole country. Between these two occupations came the long dictatorship of Rafael Leónidas Trujillo, who remained firmly in power from 1930 until 1961, ruling with such harsh authority that my neighbours still tend to lower their voices when they speak of his times.

I follow this history, and the history of Samaná in particular, with a kind of despairing fascination, for it reveals a pattern that I see persisting into the present – a kind of fatalistic acceptance. The Caudillo-Presidents of Dominican history – Pedro Santana,

Buenaventura Baez, Ulises Heureaux – ruled as strongmen, like the caciques of old, and, in a way, laid the ground for Trujillo's absolute and unopposed rule over the country. They were his precursors. I quite often recount to Pucho what I have been reading, but it surprises him not at all, for he remembers the days of Trujillo, and finds none of the brutalities of Dominican history difficult to believe. Like all Dominicans who were alive at the time, he remembers exactly where he was when the rumour spread that El Chivo was dead. 'We did not dare to believe it at first, so we all went indoors and whispered,' he told me once. 'We stayed up all night, wondering. And then, the next morning, when the news was sure, we all went out, every single person in the village I lived in, and walked about and talked the whole day. Nobody thought about working. But we talked in whispers, because we were still afraid.'

Thirty years dead, Trujillo still mesmerises Dominicans. In conversations he comes up all the time. '*Cuando Trujillo*' – 'in Trujillo's day' – I hear someone say, and a story will follow, of a horror, most likely, but always recounted with an edge of awe in the teller's voice. Any impending disaster – a gasoline shortage, a dearth of cement, a national strike – will cause Trujillo to be evoked: what my neighbours most fear is chaos and breakdown, and what he stamped on the country during his long rule was an unbreakable order, an authoritarian predictability. He lasted longer than any of the tyrants who preceded him, he amassed more power, property, and personal wealth, he made the military into a personal force for control, he dispensed patronage and punishment with such remorseless cunning as to paralyse his countrymen, and yet he still is remembered by a good many Dominicans as a stern father, who would take care of every eventuality, whose whims were law, but who would save them from chaos.

The mould in which Trujillo cast Dominican society has not been broken. In many ways, the country under Trujillo resembled the Hispaniola of colonial days: a feudal society with a governing elite and a large, docile peasantry. The two-thirds of the people who lived in rural areas accepted both their poverty and their powerlessness. Crime was punished mercilessly, as was opposition in any form. Life was predictable, and accepted with a fatalism that I still encounter every day. '*Somos infelices*', the rural Dominicans say very often, meaning 'It is our destiny to be poor.' At the other extreme lies the capital – Ciudad Trujillo in the dictator's day, Santo Domingo now – where military, fiscal, and commercial power is concentrated, where fortunes, deals, and decisions are made, where favours are peddled. In his heyday, Trujillo was estimated to be one of the richest men in the world; he instituted a form of state capitalism in which he was the state. The identification of political power with self-enrichment is fixed forever in the popular mind, and, indeed, it has hardly been disproved by the elected governments of the last thirty years.

Trujillo's death left the country floundering in uncertainties. It had no institutional structure to maintain it. Pressures from the United States, which feared then that the Cuban Revolution might spread to the Dominican Republic, led to the holding of democratic elections in December of 1962. Although Dominicans had only a sketchy understanding of what democracy meant, they elected a populist President, Juan Bosch, who promised sweeping social reforms and political freedom, even to the Communists. Those promises proved too much for the elite and the military, and nine months later Bosch was overthrown and exiled in a military coup. A junta ruled uneasily for eighteen months, until the constitutionalists rose in a popular surge against the military; they seemed almost on the point of defeating it when Lyndon Johnson ordered in the Marines, to quench what was the closest to a revolution that the people of the country had ever come. Elections were held again in 1966, and have been held every four years since.

My neighbours remain distrustful of democracy as they know it. A change of party in Samaná means a change of all official posts in the town, from governor to itinerant mailman, but apart from that the campesinos see little or no improvement in their lot. Some, embittered by the lack of opportunity and of paid work, turn their eyes elsewhere, but the majority fall back on the ingrained pattern, the preoccupation with finding food every day. Only the luck of the climate and the bounty of the soil have kept them from misery.

As for democracy, their participation ends with the elections, for Dominican Presidents do not govern so much as rule by decree. In Samaná, the pattern still has not changed. We live at the end of the line, the receiving end of whatever may come from the capital – government decrees, price rises, shortages, delays – and everything makes us wary of life outside the peninsula. Although all my neighbours vote proudly on Election Day, dipping their index fingers in indelible ink to make sure they vote no more than once, they do not expect anything to change. They all tell stories of electoral frauds, vote buying, false counts, as though to insulate themselves against disappointment.

Although the Dominican Republic shares Hispaniola with Haiti, the landmass is virtually all that they do share. Dominicans harbour a deep prejudice against Haitians, an inherent racism that is seldom voiced but is pervasively present. It stems in part from the violence of their history – Dominicans never forget that it was from Haiti that they wrested their independence. And now that their country is considerably more developed than its threadbare neighbour, with a much higher per capita income, they do not welcome those Haitians who filter across the frontier, except as braceros, cane-cutters who work in conditions not far removed from slavery – a circumstance that has brought the Dominican Republic the censure of the United Nations Commission on Human Rights.

Of the many cruelties perpetrated by Trujillo, the most barbaric of all took place in October of 1937, when units of the Dominican Army, acting on a direct order from the dictator, hunted down and massacred between 15,000 and 20,000 Haitians – men, women, and children – in the Dominican provinces adjoining the frontier. The event was covered up at the time, and today Dominicans go silent when it is mentioned.

During Haiti's difficult years, when those who could fled the country, it might have seemed that the simplest solution would have been for the Dominican government to open temporary refugee camps in its territory; but, with Dominican attitudes as unyielding as they are, it's not surprising that Haitians in their despair chose to chance the open sea rather than look toward the forbidding frontier to the east.

*

Dr Joaquín Balaguer began his political career in the thirties, as a loyal servant of Trujillo, in a variety of official posts and eventually as Trujillo's puppet President – the post he occupied when Trujillo was assassinated. Balaguer's image could not be more different from that of his master – he is small, meek of manner, frail, soft-spoken, well known as a poet, scholar, and historian – yet, unscrupulous and politically astute, he has never strayed far from the exercise of power. He won the elections of 1966, which followed the American intervention, and governed steadily until 1978 – a period in which the country enjoyed a brief prosperity, thanks to a surge in sugar prices – and he returned to power in 1986, at the age of seventy-nine, and was reelected in a dubious election in 1990. He is now blind, yet his hold on power has been as tenacious as ever Trujillo's was, his mode of governing as autocratic, his use of patronage in government appointments as cunning, his command of the military as secure. He has used propaganda zealously, seeking to appear in the role of a benign grandfather who has given his entire life to his country. Yet nowadays, the length and breadth of the country, on the minibuses and in the market, you hear no good words for Balaguer – not even from those who voted for him. When I was last in the capital, you could read the same legend scrawled on corner after corner: '*Que se vaya ya!*' – 'Let him leave now!' And what brought discontent to a head was, as much as anything, the quincentenary.

When Balaguer was returned to office in 1986, he launched a vast programme of public building, mostly in the capital – construction projects that had a great deal to do with the appearance of the place and bore his name more often than not. It was as though Balaguer, in his last years in power, were set on fulfilling in new concrete Trujillo's obsession with public self-enshrinement. He also had firmly in mind a project he was determined to carry through: the building of a huge lighthouse, the Faro á Colón, to commemorate Columbia's landing in 1492.

The idea of a lighthouse as a monument to Columbus's arrival was first put forth in the middle of the last century, and it stayed alive until, at the Fifth International American Conference, held in Santiago, Chile, in 1923, a resolution was passed to build such a lighthouse monument on the edge of Santo Domingo 'with the cooperation of the governments and peoples of America'. In 1929, an international competition was announced, with a prize of $10,000, for the design of such a shrine. The entries were sifted by a special commission, and in 1931 an international jury met in Madrid to study 455 submissions, from forty-eight countries. The award went, finally, to a young English architect, J. L. Gleave, who was still a student, and artists' impressions of his design for the Faro appeared in the Dominican press of the day. Time passed; then Trujillo took up the idea of the Faro with characteristic grandiloquence, planning a complex of buildings around the light-house, including a new Presidential palace for himself, and actually breaking ground for the project in April of 1948. The money promised by the other governments of Latin America was not forthcoming, however, and the Faro remained merely a plan. For Balaguer, however, the building of the Faro remained, from the years of the competition on, a matter of deep commitment: it was his destiny to build it, to bring it to completion. He bided his time, and in 1986 work on the Faro began in earnest. The quincentenary was six years away. There was no time to lose.

Over these past few years, I watched the Columbus Lighthouse lumber into being in the Parque del Este, on the east side of the Ozama River, looking across to the Colonial Quarter of Santo Domingo, and to the cathedral, where the lead casket with Columbus's remains lay, before being transferred to the finished lighthouse. At first, a forced clearing of the area around the site dismantled the shanty-towns and drove out about fifty thousand people, many of whom were given no promise of rehousing. On the bare, muddy expanse left by the bulldozers, the Faro began to rise.

We think of lighthouses as vertical towers that project a light horizontally, for ships to see. The Columbus Lighthouse, however, is a horizontal structure, like a recumbent beast, designed to throw its light vertically, upward. It has a long base and two stubby arms – the shape of a long cross or a short sword. Since it was clearly intended as one of the new wonders of the world, its scale is immense: it is nearly half a mile long; walls slant upward from each arm to meet at a point a hundred and twenty feet high, and are crowned with a beacon that is to project on the sky a lighted cross visible as far away as Puerto Rico, some two hundred miles east. It has the look of a concrete pyramid with one long extended arm: a humped, dinosaur look; an anonymous, inert greyness. Grass has now grown over the razed barrios, along with newly planted stands of trees bordering a web of new approach roads. At first sight, it has a curious effect on the eye, puzzling rather than impressive, and seems mournful and forbidding. You could easily believe that some huge, unnameable secret weapon was being assembled deep inside it. It puts me in mind more of Dr No than of Columbus.

Since Balaguer resumed the Presidency in August of 1990, things have been going very badly in the Dominican Republic. The elections were held that May, and we listened avidly to the first returns on the radio – the neighbours excitedly, for Juan Bosch appeared to be leading Balaguer. Suddenly, however, the electoral count was suspended, incomplete – nobody understood quite why. After a tense day or two, we were all back at work, while in the capital a bitter wrangling began. It lasted weeks, and finally, in mid-June, the electoral junta announced that Balaguer had won. Even so, the combined opposition votes exceeded his by half a million, making him very much a minority President. No one doubted that there had been electoral fraud. I knew of some in Samaná. Electoral fraud is not easy to bring off in our present political climate; for having done it, Balaguer did elicit some admiration. Those who had hoped that he might abandon his construction projects and give some attention to the backward state of the country's agriculture – which is to say, to the bare livelihood of those who lived outside the capital – were soon disenchanted; one of his first acts was to set in motion plans for the rapid completion of the Faro á Colón. That year was a drastic one for the campesinos, first in soaring prices of basic foods, and then in serious shortages of fuel and, of all things, sugar. The price of gasoline rose, and rose again. Perhaps even worse was the precarious state of the country's electrical grid, which occasioned nationwide daily electricity cuts, sometimes of twenty hours – cuts that played havoc with refrigeration, and with commerce in general. If there was hunger in the countryside, there was misery in the slums on the edges of the capital. Balaguer continued in Olympian indifference, unperturbed, deaf to dissent.

The ironies surrounding Balaguer's obsession with the Faro were ever more apparent. How much had the Faro cost to build? Twenty million dollars? A hundred million? People guess, but nobody will ever know, since Balaguer does not make public such accountings. Its light was to be the brightest in all the Americas, a stunning irony in a country whose electrical system is all but bankrupt. When the Faro is switched on, the campesinos said, the lights will go out in all the rest of the country. Besides, they remind you, sailors have no need of lighthouses anymore. And, they added, when he switched on the Faro, poor Balaguer wouldn't even be able to see the light.

I eavesdrop a lot on the long bus trips to Samaná, and in 1992 the general talk always came around to the Faro, for it became, understandably, the incarnation of discontents, an object of concentrated scorn among the campesinos. At times, you heard the fervently expressed hope that when Balaguer pressed the button to switch on the Faro he would somehow be subsumed into it and projected skyward, and, with him, all politicians, to join Columbus in his Faro, because they've been doing to us the very thing that he did, haven't they, with rice now at five pesos a pound. It was not rage, however, that they directed toward the Faro – Dominicans, as they tell me often, are not good haters. They are too good-natured. Instead, they made the Faro into a national joke, a monument to absurdity – not just the absurdity of their own situation but the absurdity of all such monumentalising, at a time when the world is more bent on tearing down shrines to the past than on building them. The five hundred years that the Faro was enshrining represented for the campesinos a very different history from that promulgated in the official publications of the quincentenary commission in Santo Domingo.

As it turned out, the inauguration of the Faro did not exactly fulfil Balaguer's lifelong dream; instead, it engendered a new respect for the *fucú* throughout the country. The world leaders who had been invited to attend the ceremony sent their excuses, to a man; the Pope, who was in the Dominican Republic to attend an ecumenical congress, pointedly absented himself. More poignantly, however, Balaguer's sister, his long companion, died the day before the event, and he himself could not be present. Although the Faro sends its light skyward at appointed hours, visitors mostly ignore it, and the people take the only revenge that is in their power by never mentioning it, by effectively forgetting its existence.

*

Balaguer's other interest in his policy of Dominican glorification has been, inevitably, tourism, and in the late eighties, especially, the country has seen a rash of hotel building and resort-making along the Caribbean coast, in the south, and on the wilder, Atlantic north coast, bringing with it all the furniture of tourist occupation, and all the expectations. It appears at first a very simple and agreeable proposition to those who live there: tourists come with money, and wish to stay, and so one must offer them something that will cause them to hand over some, if not all, of their money. It appeals to the young in the *aldeas* who have other ideas than trudging back and forth from the *conucos* all their lives. And it appealed enough to the first tourists so that the Dominican Republic has been turned into a kind of modern discovery, worthy of being called unspoiled.

Not for long, however. Already, two towns on the north coast have been overtaken by mass tourism and turned quickly into over-crowded, traffic-ridden nightmares. Huge projects, some of them bearing Columbus's name, have started up, foundered, and failed, leaving monumental arched gateways leading to wilderness. Restaurants open in hope and quite often close in disappointment. There is work, of course, in construction – 'building bars we can't afford to go into', as Orlando, the mason, likes to remark. We talk about tourism a lot by the stream, most seriously whenever there is a question of selling land. For a campesino to sell his land would mean money in the hand, something never known. But would the money in the hand last as the land lasts? In reality, the coming of tourism has made very little difference to the life of our *vecindad*, except for the occasional work it has offered in construction. It has, however, brought with it a great deal of *illusión*, high hopes, great expectations.

Porfirio, who has a house above mine, by the road, a favourite meeting place in the neighbourhood, got a job as a foreman, building a small hotel in town – a good job, which gave him, after a year, enough to leave it and buy a black-and-white television set, and an automobile battery, which is recharged once a week. Every night now, the blue light flickers in Porfirio's house after sundown, and of an evening there will be thirty neighbours cross-legged in rows, transfixed but still talkative, with sleeping children among them. Sometimes I have gone up to see Porfirio and sat for a while, listening to the audience reaction. No matter what soap is sobbing its crisis on the screen, they are giving the drama only minimal attention. They point out the clothes, they crow at the food, they ogle the cars, they embrace the commercials. They are gazing through a window at a world they instantly want, and tourists are to them somehow emissaries from that world.

The inevitable discontents that are fuelled by the coming of tourists have led a lot of country people to leave behind them a life that, predictable though it is, gets harder rather than easier and holds out no hope of anything else. They may go to the capital, where they find that unemployment is chronic, prices are high, survival is much more precarious. Or they may take a more drastic course. In Samaná sometimes, on moonless nights, we will hear a boat pass, a boat of some power, but without lights. It is a *yola*, most likely – an open boat setting out with perhaps twenty people who have paid over most of their savings to the boatmaster to take them across the dangerous waters of the Mona Channel and land them, illegally, on a beach on the west shore of Puerto Rico. Some of the boats come to grief, and the sharks turn crossings into tragedies. Of those who land, some are caught at once, some later; but a good many filter in, an address in a pocket, are looked after at first by other Dominicans, then find work, hoping in time to send some money home and to save enough to make the flight to New York, untroubled by immigration, armed with more addresses, to find better work, eventually to become legal, with the dream of saving enough to set up a small *colmado* back in the *vecindad* they began in. One of the men from our neighbourhood went in a *yola*, worked in Puerto Rico for three months, was caught, and was returned by plane, his first flight. The fine he had to pay consumed all the money he had saved. We all turned out to welcome him back, however, and he has become something of a counsellor to others with *yolas* in mind. A nurse I know in town went in a *yola*, which was stopped about a mile out by the Dominican coast guard and turned back, the money confiscated (and later shared with the captain of the *yola*, she was sure). Every time I return to Samaná, there is an absence, a space: someone I know has gone in a *yola*.

In the Dominican Republic, Christmas and Easter are marked by the return, in flocks, of *Dominicanos ausentes* – those who live in the United States – on a visit to their pueblos, bearing gifts, wearing the gold chains and bright new clothes of success, and full of stories of colour and light, even if the chains, and possibly the roll of bills, have been borrowed for the occasion. The myth is perpetuated. I have spent considerable time explaining some of the complexities of that other world to my neighbours – things like paying for heat, which is incomprehensible to them. But it is a world they have come to want fiercely, even if only in the form of sneakers – simply, a better life. Over the last twenty years, there has been a Dominican diaspora that has taken almost a million out of the country.

I am by now used to the fatalism of my neighbours. It is a cheerful fatalism rather than a despairing one, mostly, although hopes and expectations are scarce. I know a good number of Dominicans, however, who are acutely aware of the situation in their country and have a clear view indeed of a possible future for it. Among them is a farmer, Gilberto, with whom I often talk, for he experiments indefatigably with new seeds that I bring him. I asked him last summer what he would like to see happen in his country.

He did not hesitate for a second. 'More than anything, I wish this country would lose its memory,' he said. 'We're still slaves of our own history – what happened to us is what we still expect to happen. I long to see the age of the *abuelos*, the grandfathers, Balaguer and Bosch, come to an end. Over thirty years, they have made it harder for those who live in the campo, never worse than now. I'd like to wipe out our present parties and politicians, all the corruption and patronage and secret deals, all the intrigue. I'd like to see an end to this weakness we have of always looking for a leader, a father – a grandfather, even – who will save us, who will make all our decisions for us, whom we can curse and grumble at. Our parties don't have programmes. All they do is parade their candidate for saviour, hoping enough of us will say, 'That's the man!' We need parties that put forward programmes, not saviours. We need young technocrats in the government who can come up with a national plan that will open up the country, give it work, and, most of all, *involve* us in our own country, give us some hope. I'd like to see all our children literate, our teachers and doctors paid decent salaries, the police, too, so that they didn't have to turn to crime. If only we modernised our agriculture, if we diversified from our sugar dependence, we could be the garden state of the Caribbean. We wouldn't need tourism to save us. Tourism is another kind of slavery for Dominicans. Spaniards call tourism *putería* – whoring – and that's what it is, pleasing foreigners. It's corrupting, it's like a pollution. Take Samaná. If the government gave Samaná a million dollars for agricultural projects, well supervised, we could be exporting fruit and vegetables year-round, to other islands, to Florida, and living well. We could have solar energy and irrigation systems and crops year-round. Instead, they talk of a golf course. Can you imagine what an insult it is to us, who have always lived from the land, to put down a golf course among us? Or to build that monstrous monument to Columbus? As far as I'm concerned, Columbus didn't so much discover America as bring into being the Third World.'

Samaná, at the end of the line, has always had a trickle of tourists, but its facilities are still frail and few. The place survives, however, on rumours of imminent prosperity; and while many of its projects have foundered, some are coming to fruition. At the moment, the place lives in a kind of limbo of possibilities, and the *chisme* this year has been a little headier than usual. The mayor of Miami made a visit, in 1991, expressed his undying love for Samaná, and promised to send a consignment of used official cars from Miami, which have so far not arrived. A group of conservationists has been taking a growing interest in Samaná for the last three years, and a plan is afoot to have the bay and the peninsula declared a Biosphere Reserve, to maintain the native species, including the manatee, to prevent pollution of the bay, and to protect the habitat of the humpback whales that spend their breeding time in the bay from late January until early March every year, before their migration north. It has not been easy for me to explain to the neighbours just what a Biosphere Reserve means, or would mean to them. They are mystified by the notion; I think they see themselves as having to dress up as Tainos.

Most of the *chisme*, however, surrounded the opening of a luxury hotel, on an outcrop of rocky coast overlooking the beach at Las Flechas and facing the little island of Cayo Levantado. The hotel took shape in fits and starts for three years, and a number of men from our neighbourhood worked on it at various times. It is built in James Bond Caribbean: red roofs, verandas, palms wild and potted, a private force of uniformed guards, and a tariff that, if the *chisme* is close, sets everyone's eyes rolling. About a quarter of a mile from the hotel sits the small town of Los Cacaos, hugging the beach and sprawling up the slope – a jaunty, easygoing, raucous community of people, who are quite fired up by the sudden transformation of their coast. If any one of the inhabitants of Los Cacaos had in hand what a guest pays to sleep a night in the hotel, he would instantly be among the richest in town. Tourists, as a rule, want to go shopping; and shopping in the town of Samaná offers the slimmest of pickings. There is the market, where goats' throats are often cut in public; there is a hardware store like an Aladdin's cave; there are vendors of hats made of varnished palm leaves; and there are three shoeshine boys who stare gloomily at tourist sandals. But there is not much more except for the roar of motorcycles, the main attainable dream of young Dominicans. I cannot think that much good can come from placing two such disparate groups, so far apart economically, in such sudden proximity. At best, they trouble each other; and certainly the hotel's presence feeds local discontents, when people at scarcely survival level live in such an opulent shadow. They fear that very soon their own beaches will be closed to them, as has begun to happen, and, worse, that they may be forced to move – to yield up their land to the needs of tourism – by government decree. The tourist enterprises that have been successful in the Dominican Republic are those in which the tourists are enclosed in vast, caged, patrolled compounds, the concentration camps of leisure, with Dominican workers shipped in during the day and out at night. The fence makes sense. The division is dire. Besides, after the first flush of construction tourism does not bring the abundance of work it initially seems to promise. The revenues do not filter down in any noticeable way to the local inhabitants. I would not be surprised to see some local merry men form a latter-day Robin Hood band, swooping down from the palm trees and turning Samaná into a tropical version of Sherwood Forest.

Simultaneously, however, another future hovers over Samaná. In October of 1990, the Dominican government signed an agreement with an American-owned company called Once Once, S.A., granting it the right to explore for oil in certain parts of the country, among them Samaná Bay. While it is difficult to see how the place might become a tourist mecca, a Biosphere Reserve, and a centre for oil exploration all at once, such considerations are of little concern to Balaguer, who will not be around to face the consequences. Nor do my neighbours show much alarm or consternation at these prospects. Whatever may come to pass, it will happen to them as it happened to the Tainos, without any regard for their preferences; it has become their nature to accept rather than want. They gaze at the cruise ships that nose into Samaná Bay with the same wary eyes, the same unease, with which the Indians watched the coming of the caravels.

*

Columbus's first voyage is by now a matter more of legend than of history; but two scholars, Dr J.L. Montalvo Guenard, in a thesis published in Puerto Rico in 1933, and the Dominican historian Bernardo Vega, in a recent paper, have, from a close reading of the text of the journal, made a strong case for Columbus's Samaná landfall taking place not on the beach of Las Flechas but at Rincón, at the far end of the peninsula. They have convinced me; but it is unlikely that the history books will be revised. I tried to explain this quibble to Pucho, but he only looked at me with a mixture of scorn and alarm that I could find nothing better to do with my time. The idea that the new hotel may be founded on a historical misplacement tickles him, however.

It seems to me salutary that some serious arguments over Columbus and the Spanish Conquest arose as they did at this precise stage in our global history, since they raise disturbing questions about the meanings and evaluations of the past – questions that matter not to historians alone. We live in a postcolonial world, and we have, in our time, grown steadily more adamant about human rights, more sensitive to their violation. It seems to me that this must inevitably affect our reading and reassessment of history. It is why we gravitate to seeing the conquest through the eyes of Las Casas rather than those of Columbus, and why we are grateful for his clarity, his humanity, and his indignation. We may argue about human rights, for they are, in a sense, abstractions, but we do not argue about human wrongs. We recognise them physically; we can point to them, in the past as in the present. Shame and indignation are our measures, as they were to Las Casas. Confronting human wrongs is our common cause at present. About the wrongs of the past we can do nothing, but we can at least look at them squarely, and see them clearly.

Misadventure
1988

I have spent a good part of my life living in remote places, and almost always they have served up adventures in the form of small happenings that suddenly raise enormous questions, happenings that still rumble in my mind.

One of the most vivid of these occurred in the Dominican Republic, when I spent a string of shoeless winters in its most remote province, beyond the reach of mail, telephone, electricity, newspapers, and running water. My neighbors lived mostly by fishing and subsistence farming, and over the years we grew to know them well. The men from a nearby settlement had helped build our small house above the beach, and they would often wander up of an evening to sit on the stone terrace and talk, always bringing some offering – an egg, a hand of bananas, some coffee beans in a leaf. Few of them could read or write, but they were no less than eloquent in conversation, and inexhaustibly curious. They would ask endless questions about life in the United States, for many of them had a relative who had made the hazardous journey there; and we in turn learned their ways. Nothing delighted them so much as making small deals, a kind of barter that we all lived by, sharing harvests and catches by way of the children, a band of small, swift messengers.

Two neighbors in particular, Pucho and Porfirio, both fishermen, often helped me on the land when the sea allowed, and with them I made a deal, to bring them fishing gear from the *gran mundo*, as they always called it, in exchange for an eatable share of their catch, an arrangement that served all of us well over the years. One morning, I had returned from my weekly visit to the nearby town to get some supplies and to pick up a batch of mail, and was sitting on the terrace slitting open envelopes from what seemed increasingly another world, when Pucho and Porfirio appeared on the path, bearing fish, among them two squat *cofre*, or boxfish, to which we always looked forward. They perched on the edge of the terrace, and we exchanged news.

Among the mail spread on the warm stone of the terrace were two or three mail order catalogues. Porfirio began to leaf through one of them, stopping here and there to point to an illustration. 'Alejandro, what is that?' I tried to wave off his questions; I sensed trouble ahead.

Sure enough, he eventually reached a double page spread advertising a rowing machine. 'Alejandro, what is that?' I could no longer put him off. '*Es una máquina de remar,*' – a rowing machine, I told him. Pucho grabbed the catalogue, and the effect on both of them was electric. They crowed with delight. 'And how much does this wondrous machine cost?' Porfirio now had the scent. I made a rapid calculation: 'Almost four thousand pesos.' They whistled, but their eyes were already gleaming.

'Do you know?' Porfirio stood up suddenly, and pointed far out, to where the waves broke. 'To get to the reef out there where we fish, Pucho and I, we row for almost an hour. And back, when we're tired. And when we fish nights across the bay, that is a two hour row for us, and the same back! But with this magnificent machine –'

'Porfirio!' I stopped him with a hand. 'Take a good look at the picture. People keep these machines in their houses.' Both pairs of eyes looked at me in disbelief. 'You mean, there is no boat?' Pucho said. I shook my head. 'And no water at all?' He could hardly contain himself. 'So people in the *gran mundo* have this expensive machine at home to make themselves do the thing we most hate doing in our miserable lives?' I could do nothing but confirm their horror.

Porfirio waved the catalogue indignantly. 'Alejandro, forgive me, but this world in here seems crazy to me. Why would sensible people, who can afford to buy fish, want this torture instrument in their houses? It is far beyond my understanding.'

There was little I could say, for I felt much as they did. Feebly, I tried to explain. 'People there sit at desks for too long, so they have these machines at home for exercise.'

They frowned in unison. 'Exercise?' Pucho had trouble with the word. 'And what is exercise?'

I gave up. From then on, I got rid of the catalogues whenever they appeared. In that place, they had come to seem increasingly subversive. I discovered later, however, that it was as well Porfirio had stopped at the pages with the rowing machine. Three pages further on, a tanning machine had been lying in wait.

Basilisk's Eggs
1976

Being an occasional translator, more by accident than by design, I feel somewhat rueful about the whole question of translating between languages. Its mysterious nature can become something of an obsession, for each act of translation is an unprecedented exercise; yet it is an obsession shared by a minority of people who live and read in more than one language, or whose work requires them to function simultaneously on different linguistic planes – spies, displaced persons, the Swiss, international soccer referees, interpreters, travel guides, anthropologists, and explorers. Translators enjoy the status, more or less, of literary mechanics, reassembling texts from one language to function in another; and even if they do more than that, their work is likely to get little more than a passing nod, if it is mentioned at all – understandably, for there can be only a very small body of readers capable of passing judgment on translations, and most of us are glad to have them at all. Translators require the self-effacing disposition of saints; and, since a good translation is one in which a work appears to have been written and conceived in the language into which it is translated, good translators grow used to going unrewarded and unnoticed, except by a sharp-nosed troop of donnish reviewers (we call them 'the translation police') who seem to spend their reading lives on the lookout for errors.

As far as translations go, the English language is well served. Its great range makes it capable of accommodating Indo-European languages quite comfortably, and in recent years our book thirst has given rise to a steady flow of translation, discovering other literatures and giving foreign classics a new lease on life. I remember once checking up in Spain to see which English-language writers were most translated into Spanish, and being astonished to find complete, leather-bound sets of Somerset Maugham and Zane Grey leading the field. The translation barrier is a chancy one, and not everything that crosses it arrives in the best of condition. Vladimir Nabokov once remarked (as few but he are in a position to remark) that while a badly written book is a blunder, a bad translation is a crime. It has occurred to me at times that the translation police might well be given statutory powers to revoke the licenses of unreliable translators, as a service to language.

It is one thing to read a book in translation; it is quite another to *read* a translation, for that requires two languages, two texts, and an attention hovering between them. Such close reading of translations has something in common with solving word puzzles, perhaps, but it can prove extraordinarily revealing about the nature of the two languages – about the nature of language itself. Just as knowing more than one language shatters the likelihood of confusing word and thing, so reading the same work in more than one language draws attention to it as a literary construct – gives the work an added dimension, which may or may not enhance it.

It also draws attention to quite another quality of literature – namely, its translatability or untranslatability. Straightforward linear prose can usually pass without much effort into other languages; but there are some works of literature whose verbal complexity appears to doom them to remain in their own language. Lyric poetry, where compression of meaning is most intense, and in which the sound pattern forms part of the total meaning, comes high on the list of untranslatables – Rilke would be a good example – and yet this does not prevent odd felicities of translation at the hands of poets, or even variant translations of the same poem. It is precisely those works that seem by their linguistic intricacy to be untranslatable that often generate real brilliance in a translator. If anyone doubts that pleasure can come from translation, let him look, for instance, at Henri Bué's 1869 version of *Alice in Wonderland* in French, in which even the puns are rendered by equivalent puns, or Barbara Wright's versions of Raymond Queneau, or the Gardner-Levine rendering, with the author's help, of Guillermo Cabrera Infante's *Tres Tristes Tigres* – works in which wordplay apparently indigenous to another language is matched in English.

For a translator, untranslatability can be as much a lure as a deterrent.

I keep pinned on my wall a remark made in an interview by Octavio Paz: 'Every translation is a metaphor of the poem translated,' he says. 'In this sense, the phrase "poetry is untranslatable" is the exact equivalent of the phrase "all poetry is translatable." The only possible translation is poetic transmutation, or metaphor. But I would also say that in writing an original poem, we are translating the world, transmuting it. Everything we do is translation, and all translations are in a way creations.'

Translation has always been more haphazard than systematic, depending on the enthusiasm of publishers and the dedication of individual translators. Andre Gide used to maintain that every writer owed it to his own language to translate at least one foreign work to which his talents and temperament were suited, and there is no question that translation has become a more serious and systematic endeavor. The most admirably concerted effort of translation into English in recent years has been the rendering by various hands of the new writing from Latin America – probably the most energetic and inventive body of literature, particularly where the novel is concerned, in present-day writing. Its reputation preceded it into English – a perfect recipe for disappointment – but by now its main works have appeared in English and continue to appear with minimal delay, so that rumor has been given fairly immediate substance, and readers are able to experience it in its impressive diversity. It is a literature with a surprisingly recent momentum. The Uruguayan critic Emir Rodríguez Monegal puts his finger on the year 1940 – the year the South American continent became culturally isolated as a result of the Spanish Civil War and, on its heels, the Second World War, and was driven into a preoccupation with its own national identities. From that time on, a reading public has been mushrooming in Latin America, and writers have been virtually summoned into being. It seems a long time since the Great American Novel has even been contemplated in the United States; but Latin American novelists seem to have their sights set on nothing less. The continent has dawned on them as unwritten history, untapped literary resource – the indigenous Indians, the

Spanish Conquest, the stirrings of independence, the subsequent tyrannies, the bizarre immigrations, the economic colonisation from Europe and the North, the racial confusions, the paradoxes of national character, the Cuban revolution and military oppressions, the great sprawl and struggle of the present. There exists in Latin America now such enthusiasm about literature that writers are attended to like rock stars. What is more, the writers all read one another, know one another, review one another, and are refreshingly pleased at one another's existence, as though they felt themselves part of a huge literary adventure, a creative rampage. They are enviously placed in time, for part of their literary experience has been to read all the diverse experiments that have taken place in other literatures in the course of this century – experiments of which they have been avid students but not imitators, for their own writing is hugely inventive and varied in its manner.

Just as it would be practically impossible to discover anything like a unified culture in as sprawling a context as Latin America, so it is unfeasible to find or create a common language, for in the hundred and fifty years since the majority of the Latin American countries gained their independence from Spain the language has been steadily diversifying – separating itself from Castilian Spanish much as American English did from English English, breeding varieties of urban slang, breaking up in many directions – so that writers in search of a new realism seemed doomed instead to an inevitable regionalism. It is to Jorge Luis Borges that Latin American writers owe one powerful and influential solution to this dilemma, for Borges wrote in a language of his own – a highly literary language, unlike language in currency, a language that draws attention to itself, mocks itself, casts suspicion on itself. From Borges came the beguiling reminder that language is a trick, a manipulation of reality rather than a reflection of it – a notion that stems, after all, from Cervantes. His economy, his playful erudition, his ironies, his treatment of rational knowledge and language as fantastic games dazzled not only Latin Americans but also, in the first translations of his work, a whole crop of American and European writers. He has been both source and challenge, especially to the younger writers, for, although repudiating his archconservatism, they have taken a cue from him in looking for the concomitantly appropriate language for their own fantastic realities.

★

The two writers who have dominated the literary scene in Latin America are Borges and the Chilean poet Pablo Neruda, who died in late 1973. What is most curious about their coexistence is how little they have to do with each other as writers, how seldom they met or even mentioned each other as men, how drastically different their work is, and yet how Latin American each is, in his separate way. Borges's collected work is as sparse and spare as Neruda's is abundant and ebullient, metaphysical as Neruda's is free-flowing, dubious as Neruda's is passionately affirmative or condemnatory. Where Neruda is open and even naïve, Borges is subtle and skeptical; where Neruda is a sensualist, Borges is an ascetic; where Neruda writes of tangible, physical experience, Borges's fund of experience is purely literary – he looks on reading as a form of time travel. Although Borges roots his stories in Buenos Aires, Latin America is for him something of a metaphor, a geographical fiction. Neruda, quite to the contrary, celebrates, in hymnic joy or rage, the inexhaustible particularity of the Latin American continent. For him, language is largesse, and his human concern made his political commitment inevitable.

The lives and careers of these two writers have diverged as widely as their work. Borges, suffering from a gradual congenital blindness, lived from his earliest years *within* books and language, fascinated by stories of his soldiering ancestors and of the celebrated knife-fighters of Buenos Aires. What probably distinguishes him most as a writer is the profoundly disquieting effect he has on his readers. However remote and literary his subject matter may appear, he makes the experience of paradox so tangible and eerie that it persists almost as a spell – if after reading Borges one were, say, to miss a train, the event would be dressed in ominous significance. What Borges helped to do for Latin American writing was to rescue it from the slough of naturalism into which it had fallen and make it once again the province of the individual imagination; but he remains a difficult master in his sheer inimitability. Neruda has proved to be an influence more to the taste of present-day Latin American writers, if a less directly technical one. His output was prodigious, a progression in which he shed poetic selves like skins, moving from an early wild surrealism in the direction of human engagement and political commitment, never losing his vision but deliberately simplifying his language. It was a lesson in turning literature to account that was not lost on the younger writers, who for the most part see themselves as similarly engaged. Neruda himself, after a long diplomatic career, served as President Salvador Allende's Ambassador to Paris from 1971 until 1973, and died in Chile twelve days after the coup of September 1973 – a death that inevitably became symbolic. It is the intensity and scale of his commitment to Latin America that keep him an important figure for the writers who have come after him.

For some years now, I have been translating poems of both Borges and Neruda, coming to know both men well and their work even better, for one never enters the being of a poem as completely as when one is translating it. It is an odd exercise of spirit, to enter another imagination in another language and then to try to make the movement of it happen in English. Untranslatability that no ingenuity can solve does arise, which is to say that some poems *are* untranslatable. (I keep a notebook of these untranslatables, for they are small mysteries, clues to the intricate nature of a language.) To a translator, Borges and Neruda are exigent in different ways. Borges learned English as a child, read voraciously in English, and has been influenced in the formal sense more by English writing – Stevenson, Kipling, Chesterton, Anglo-Saxon poetry, and the English poetic tradition – than by Spanish literature. In his stories, he tends to use English syntactical forms and prose order – making his Spanish curiously stark but easily accessible to English translation. Indeed, translating Borges into English often feels like restoring the work to its natural language, or retranslating it. In his poems, Borges leans heavily on English verse forms and on many of the formal mannerisms of English poetry, so that translating his poems calls for technical ingenuity and prosodic fluency, precision being all-important. His poems are so thoroughly objectified, however, that no great leaps of interpretation have to be made in translating them. It requires only the patience to refine and refine, closer and closer to the original. Neruda's poems present absorbingly different problems, though not just in their extravagance of language, their hugely varying themes and forms; what distinguishes them is their special tone, an intimacy with the physical world, the ability to enter and become things. (Neruda was commonly referred to in the conversation of his friends as *el vate*, the seer.) To translate his poems requires one to enter them and wear them, on the way to finding a similar tone in English. Neruda's larger poems have a vatic intensity that is difficult to contain in credible English, and has its closest affinities with Whitman, an engraving of whom always sat on his writing table. But his more personal lyrics are within closer reach of English, and, given linguistic luck, are not unre-creatable. Translation is a mysterious alchemy in the first place; but it becomes even more so in the experience of entering the language and perception of two writers who have read human experience so differently and have worded it in such distinct ways – of becoming both of them, however temporarily.

It is interesting to compare the fate of these two writers in translation. Borges has earned such attention in English, and the body of his work is so comparatively small, that translating him in his entirety is a feasible project. (This has not been entirely to Borges's advantage, for some of his earlier critical writing, which would have been better left in the decent obscurity it enjoys in Spanish, goes on being dragged into English.) The interest in Borges has one advantage, however, in that his work has been translated by many hands, giving English readers a choice of versions, and a chance to realise what every translator must: that there is no such thing as a definitive translation. Something of the same is true of Neruda's work, and it has benefited particularly from the variety of its translators, since he was so many different poets himself; but, however assiduously he is mined, his work is so vast that only a fraction of it is likely to come satisfactorily into English. He waits, in his fullness, in Spanish. For that reason, I am discouraged from continuing to translate Neruda; but every now and then a poem of his so startles and absorbs me that its equivalence begins to form in English, and I make a version, for the awe of it. Translation becomes an addiction in one special sense: one can always count on it to take one again and again to the threshold of linguistic astonishment.

It is worth noting that both Neruda and Borges put in time as translators. Neruda produced an energetic translation of *Romeo and Juliet* in 1964, and Borges was an early translator of James Joyce, of Virginia Woolf's *Orlando*, and of William Faulkner, the American writer who, with Whitman, has had the most pervasive influence on Latin American writing. As might be expected, translation has always mesmerised Borges. In an essay on versions of Homer, he has a sentence that is also destined for my wall. 'No problem is as consubstantial with the modest mystery of literature,' he writes, 'as that posed by a translation.'

★

'Anything to do with Latin America never sells' used to be a half-humorous maxim in English publishing circles; but with time the opposite has turned out to be true. There was a point in the mid-sixties when publishers began to take that continent very seriously indeed and became literary prospectors, bent on staking their claims. Such avid attention propelled Latin American writers into a period of prominence that is commonly referred to as *el Boom*, and certainly there seemed more than coincidence to the fact that so many good novelists should be producing such rich work at once, all over the continent. Is there something about the Latin American experience, apart from its labyrinthine variety and the fact that it is largely unwritten as yet, that makes it exceptionally fertile ground for inventive fiction? The clue lies, possibly, in a phrase used by the Cuban novelist Alejo Carpentier in an introduction, written in Haiti, to his own novel *El Reino de Este Mundo*. I quote the relevant passage:

> [In Haiti] I was discovering, with every step, the marvellous in the real. But it occurred to me furthermore that the energetic presence of the marvellous in the real was not a privilege peculiar

to Haiti, but the heritage of all [Latin] America, which, for example, has not finished fixing the inventory of its cosmogonies. The marvellous in the real is there to find at any moment in the lives of the men who engraved dates on the history of the continent, and left behind names which are still celebrated . . . The fact is that, in the virginity of its landscape, in its coming together, in its ontology, in the Faustian presence of Indian and Negro, in the sense of revelation arising from its recent discovery, in the fertile mixtures of race which it engendered, [Latin] America is very far from having used up its abundance of mythologies . . . For what is the story of [Latin] America if not a chronicle of the marvellous in the real?

Lo real maravilloso, the sense of Latin American reality as an amazement, not only physically but also historically, pervades Carpentier's own novels; and it is an element, an aura, that appears in the work of many Latin American writers, however else they may differ in preoccupation and vantage point. The compass of Latin American novels is less that of a total society than of its smaller, more eccentric microcosms – families, villages, tribes, cities, regions. For Latin Americans, theory is the enemy, human eccentricity the norm. *Lo real maravilloso* is a touchstone, not a fiction; and what the Latin American writers are doing, confidently and inventively, is giving it widely varying individual substance, finding for it the language it demands.

The most remarkable incarnation of *lo real maravilloso* to date – and by now almost the definition of it – is the long novel *Cien Años de Soledad*, or *One Hundred Years of Solitude*, by the Colombian writer Gabriel García Márquez, which was first published in Buenos Aires in 1967 and is still reverberating – at last count, in twenty-odd translated versions. The novel has had a legendary publishing history. García Márquez began to write it in January of 1965, and, as it was in progress, it began to take shape as a rumor. The Mexican novelist Carlos Fuentes published a tantalising intimation of the book in a Mexican review after reading the first seventy-five pages, and fragments appeared in two or three literary magazines – extraordinary parts of an unimaginable whole. When Editorial Sudamericana published the book, it sold out in days and ran through edition after edition in a continent where native best-sellers hardly ever arise. The book was immediately moved by reviewers beyond criticism into that dimension of essential literary experience occupied by *Alice in Wonderland* and *Don Quixote*. Invoked as a classic, in a year it *became* a classic, and García Márquez, to his discomfort, a literary monument. If it was not the Latin Americans' *Don Quixote*, people said, it would do to go on with. It was everybody's book, for, however intricate a construct it was on the metaphysical level, it was founded on the stark anecdotal flow of Latin American experience, and everybody who read it discovered a relative or a familiar in it. (García Márquez told me that following the appearance of the German edition he received a letter from a woman in Bavaria threatening legal action on the ground that he had plagiarised her family history.) I saw a copy of the book sticking out of a taxi-driver's glove compartment in Santiago de Chile a few years ago, and he told me he had read it five times; and a group of students I knew in Buenos Aires used to hold an elaborate running quiz on the book, even using it as the basis for a private language, as enthusiasts once did with Joyce's *Ulysses*.

I have already read two or three books, a cluster of essays and reviews, and a profusion of magazine articles on *One Hundred Years of Solitude*; and there must be an uncountable number of theses, both written and to come, unpicking it over and over. It is a difficult book to deal with critically, since it does not yield to categorisation or comparison; and there were some bewildered reviews of it, in England and France especially. García Márquez himself, who is the most generous of spirits, declared early on that, having suffered for years as an itinerant newspaperman, he would not deny interviews to his fellows. 'I decided that the best way to put an end to the avalanche of useless interviews is to give the greatest number possible, until the whole world gets bored with me and I'm worn out as a subject,' he said in one interview; but the world proved tenacious, and printed conversations with him appeared all over the place – some of them whimsical in the extreme, because he doggedly refuses to translate the book into explanation, and is addicted to playing with language and ideas, if not with his interviewers, for he often refers, cryptically and tantalisingly, to the forty-two undiscovered errors in the text.

The criticism that has accrued around *One Hundred Years of Solitude* – and I have read studies on elements as diverse as the biblical references in the text and the topography of the province of Magdalena, in Colombia, in which both the book and García Márquez are rooted – is the best testimony to his inexhaustibility, and is compulsive reading, in that a classic is a book that one cannot know too much about, a book that deepens with each reading.

The Peruvian writer Mario Vargas Llosa published, in 1971, a 667-page vade mecum entitled *García Márquez: Historia de un Deicidio* (García Márquez: The Story of a Godkiller), a biographical and critical study that painstakingly elucidates the writer's background and influences, his four early books and stories, his preoccupations (or *demonios*, as Vargas Llosa calls them), his literary ancestors, and the writing of *One Hundred Years of Solitude*. Vargas Llosa's book is unlikely to be translated into English, and that is a pity, for it is a most absorbing chronicle of a book's coming into being, of a long and complex creative unwinding. His main claim for the novel is worth quoting in full:

One Hundred Years of Solitude is a *total* novel, in the direct line of those dimensionally ambitious creations that compete with reality on an equal footing, confronting it with the image of a qualitatively equivalent vastness, vitality, and complexity. This totality shows itself first in the plural nature of the novel, in its being apparently contradictory things at once: traditional and modern, local and universal, imaginative and realistic. Another expression of its totality is its limitless accessibility, its quality of being within reach, with distinct but abundant rewards for each one, for the intelligent reader and the imbecile, for the serious person who savors the prose, admires the architecture, and unravels the symbols in a work of fiction, and for the impatient reader who is only after crude anecdote. The literary spirit of our time is most commonly hermetic, oppressed, and minority-centered. *One Hundred Years of Solitude* is one of those rare

instances, a major contemporary work of literature that everyone can understand and enjoy.

But *One Hundred Years of Solitude* is a total novel above all
because it puts into practice the Utopian design of every God-
supplanter: to bring into being a complete reality, confronting
actual reality with an image that is its expression and negation.
Not only does this notion of totality, so slippery and complex,
but so inseparable from the vocation of novelist, define the
greatness of *One Hundred Years of Solitude*; it gives the clue to it.
One Hundred Years of Solitude qualifies as a total novel both in its
subject matter, to the extent that it describes an enclosed world,
from its birth to its death, and all the orders that make it up –
individual and collective, legendary and historical, day-to-day
and mythical – and in its form, inasmuch as the writing and the
structure have, like the material that takes shape in them, an
exclusive, unrepeatable, and self-sufficient nature.

One Hundred Years of Solitude, as everyone must know by now, tells
the story of the founding of the town of Macondo by José Arcadio
Buendía and his wife, Úrsula Iguarán, and of the vagaries of the
Buendía family through six generations of plagues, civil war,
economic invasion, prosperity, and decline, up to the impending
death of the last surviving Buendía and the disintegration of
Macondo. The presiding spirit of the Buendía family is the old
gypsy magus Melquíades, who, finding the solitude of death
unbearable, returns to instruct those members of the family able to
see him, and whose coded parchments, deciphered, ultimately, by
the last Buendía, prove to be the book we are reading, since
Melquíades is able to see backward and forward in time, as the
novelist is. Melquíades's parchments 'had concentrated a century
of daily episodes in such a way that they coexisted in one instant,'
just as García Márquez has done. Throughout the torrential
progress of the book, time is both foreseen and remembered, its
natural sequence disrupted by premonition and recurrence. Magical
happenings, supernatural perceptions, miracles, and cataclysmic
disasters are so closely attendant on characters and events that
the book seems to contain all human history compressed into the

vicissitudes of a village, and yet each of the Buendías is eccentrically and memorably separate as a character. García Márquez is bewitched by the notion of fiction as a form of magic, which can make free with human time. For the novelist, 'everything is known', as Melquíades reiterates in the book. And toward the end of the novel García Márquez observes, in the persona of Aureliano Buendía, that 'literature was the best toy ever invented for making fun of people' – a conviction that would certainly be shared by an antic Borges.

The same preoccupation with literature as a secret language is apparent in the fact that García Márquez has strewn the text with personal allusions – dates correspond to the birthdays of his family and friends, his wife appears fleetingly as a character, as he does himself, family jokes are written in – adding to the book a private dimension of his own. In the same way, the book invokes the works of his fellow Latin American novelists. The names of characters from novels of Carlos Fuentes, Julio Cortázar, and Alejo Carpentier crop up in the text, a passage recalls Juan Rulfo, and there are scenes consciously in the manner of Carpentier, Asturias, and Vargas Llosa, in a kind of affectionate homage. 'Every good novel is a riddle of the world,' García Márquez remarked to Vargas Llosa; and the more one discovers about the book and its genesis – thanks largely to Vargas Llosa – the more one realises that García Márquez emptied himself into it totally. It is the coming into being of the book, in fact, that turns out to be the most revealing clue to its extraordinary nature.

To Vargas Llosa, García Márquez made a statement that would appear to be another of his whimsies except for the fact that he has emphasised the point many times. 'Everything I have written I knew or I had heard before I was eight years old,' he said. 'From that time on, nothing interesting has happened to me.' Talking to the critic Plinio Apuleyo Mendoza, he also said, 'In my books, there is not a single line that is not founded on a real happening. My family and my old friends are well aware of it. People say to me, 'Things just happen to you that happen to no one else.' I think they happen to everybody, but people don't have the sensibility to take them in or the disposition to notice them.' *One Hundred Years of Solitude* is so full of improbable happenings and apparently grotesque invention that it seems at first perverse of García Márquez to claim these as part of his boyhood experience. Yet I think that these statements have to be taken very seriously indeed, for, on examination, they throw a great deal of light on the genesis and nature of the novel.

*

García Márquez was born in 1928 in the township of Aracataca, in the Colombian province of Magdalena, in the swampy region between the Caribbean and the mountains, and for the first eight years of his life – the crucial years, by his own account – his parents left him behind in Aracataca, in the care of his maternal grandparents, Colonel Nicolás Márquez Iguarán and Doña Tranquilina Iguarán Cotes. His grandparents had settled in Aracataca when it was little more than a village, in the wake of the pulverising civil war, the War of a Thousand Days, which lasted from 1899 until 1903, and in which Colonel Márquez had fought on the Liberal side against the Conservatives, Aracataca itself being a Liberal outpost. They had lived there through the frenzied years of the 'green gold' – the banana fever that brought foreign exploiters and relative prosperity to the region and then subsided around 1920 in a wave of disaffection and economic distress. The grandparents were first cousins, and enjoyed a position of esteem in Aracataca, occupying the most prominent house in the place – a house that they peopled with stories. It was through his grandparents that the bulk of the material that later gushed out in *One Hundred Years of Solitude* entered García Márquez's awareness; they remain, he says, the dominant influence in his life, in their separate ways. Vargas Llosa's account of the novelist's childhood draws attention to circumstances and events in these early years that later found their place in the novel. One of García Márquez's earliest memories is of his grandfather's leading him by the hand through the town to see a traveling circus – a foreshadowing of the first chapter of the novel. The Colonel would read to the boy from the encyclopedia and from *The Thousand and One Nights*, the only books he remembers from these years, and would ply him with stories of the civil war, in which the Colonel had been a companion-in-arms of the

Liberal General Rafael Uribe Uribe, whose exploits became the model for Colonel Aureliano Buendía in the novel. To read the history of the War of a Thousand Days is bizarre enough; but to have it recounted and embellished by an old man who took part in it, and who must in any case have assumed mythic proportions for the boy, must have lodged all that material deep enough for it to go undented by fact or subsequent experience. Tales of the banana fever, which brought Aracataca a sudden prosperity and a foreign population, reached him in the same way – from the people who had lived through it. His grandfather waited throughout his life for a chimerical pension promised to Liberal veterans by the Conservatives but never delivered – a state of affairs that is the spine of García Márquez's earlier and most celebrated story, 'No One Writes to the Colonel', a noble invocation of the spirit of his grandfather. There are other precise precedents: as a young man, Colonel Márquez had been forced to kill a man in a dispute and, although in the right, had had to settle in a new town – the same circumstance that leads to the founding of Macondo by José Arcadio Buendía. García Márquez remembers his grandfather's saying to him repeatedly, 'You cannot imagine how much a dead man weighs.' Colonel Márquez also fathered a crop of illegitimate sons during the civil wars, as does Colonel Aureliano Buendía in the novel. Already, the two worlds are difficult to keep separate. People, events past and present, real and fabulous, the encyclopedia and *The Thousand and One Nights* – all occupy the same dimension.

García Márquez has always claimed that his literary style came from his grandmother, Doña Tranquilina; and she is certainly the source of the novel's extraordinary women, whose domestic intuitions challenge the excessive and often misguided rationality of the men. He recalls her waking him up in bed to tell him stories; and she would keep up a running conversation in the large, empty house with dead relatives, so that to him the house seemed peopled with presences. She appears to have drawn no distinction between legend and event, nor would any such distinction have made much sense to García Márquez at that time. It is to her that he attributes the blurring of the magical with the real. In an interview with Plinio Apuleyo Mendoza, he cites one example:

When I was about five, an electrician came to our house to change the meter. He came a number of times. On one of them, I found my grandmother trying to shoo a yellow butterfly from the kitchen with a cloth and muttering, 'Every time that man comes, this yellow butterfly appears in the house.'

The memory is transmogrified in the novel into the character of Mauricio Babilonia, whose appearances are always accompanied by yellow butterflies. Another of the magical happenings in the novel – when Remedios the Beauty, an unearthly creature beyond human love, whose appearance drives men wild, ascends one day into Heaven as she is folding sheets in the garden – is clarified by García Márquez in conversation with Vargas Llosa:

The explanation of that is much simpler, much more banal than it appears. There was a girl who corresponded exactly to my description of Remedios in the book. Actually, she ran away from home with a man, and the family, not wishing to face the shame of it, announced, straight-faced, that they had seen her folding sheets in the garden and that afterward she had ascended into Heaven. At the moment of writing, I preferred the family's version to the real one.

Similarly, the strike of banana workers in the novel, which ends in their being massacred, is based on the killing of striking banana workers in Ciénaga, in the province of Magdalena, in 1928. García Márquez remembers hearing stories of it as a boy, but at the same time hearing it denied by others, who accepted the official lie, that it had never happened, just as the survivors in Macondo are made to disremember it. As a boy, listening to the running fables of Aracataca, he drew no line between the fabulous and the real, the true and the false, the subjective and the objective. With the stories, a world entered whole into his imagination. The problem when he faced the writing of *One Hundred Years of Solitude* was to find a way of reproducing that wholeness.

Without further example, I think we can take García Márquez with complete seriousness when he talks of the superimportance of those first eight years. They also throw light on the 'solitude' of the title, which is the solitude he describes himself as experiencing in the vast house in Aracataca, with its ghosts and its stories, temporarily abandoned by his own parents to the care of the two eccentric grandparents, whose lives seemed so remote from his own. All the Buendías in the book are similarly enclosed in the glass bubbles of their own destinies, fulfilling separate fates, touching one another only briefly, in passing, possessed by their own secrets.

Given that his early life was a tangible experiencing of *lo real maravilloso*, this was far from a guarantee that García Márquez was to become a writer; if that were so, we should be knee-deep in extraordinary novels. More had to happen; and perhaps the decisive experience was a journey García Márquez took with his mother back to Aracataca to sell the house of his grandparents some ten years after he had left it, on their death. He describes the shock of discovering the town, and the house of his childhood, transposed by time, shrunken, empty, altered. The experience, he says, imprinted deeply in him the desire to find and preserve the Aracataca of his grandparents, the wholeness of his first world; he could not credit that it no longer existed. It did exist; or, at least, it would. On that same journey, Aracataca was metamorphosed into Macondo, the mythical Aracataca of his boyhood; for as the train came to a halt close to the town he saw out of its window the name Macondo on a sign. Macondo was the name of a run-down banana plantation; but it also had a certain currency in local legend as a kind of never-never land from which people did not return.

From that point on, García Márquez lived an itinerant life that produced four books, stories, film scripts, and a slew of newspaper articles. He began, very young, a book – which he never finished – called *La Casa*, an evocation of the legendary house of his grandparents. He threw himself into a literary apprenticeship, reading Amadís de Gaul, Defoe, Rabelais, Balzac, Hemingway, Faulkner, Virginia Woolf, Camus – all the authors who have been invoked as influences on his work. But he was after something in which they could only assist him. He became a journalist, first in Colombia, then in Europe and the United States, turning his attention to writing on his own when he could; but these were turbulent years for him, and the book inside him seemed perpetually out of reach. It was not until he was settled in Mexico in the sixties, writing film scripts after a period of barrenness, that he suddenly found what he had been seeking so long – the focus and the manner ample enough to contain the wholeness of his early vision. He describes to Vargas Llosa how, one day in January of 1965, he was driving his family from Mexico City to Acapulco when the book tugged imperatively at his sleeve. 'It was so clear that I could have dictated the first chapter there and then, word for word.' He turned the car, went back to Mexico City, closeted himself for the next eighteen months, working every day without letup, and emerged at the end with the complete manuscript of *One Hundred Years of Solitude*, which was immediately accepted by Editorial Sudamericana, in Buenos Aires, and was published, in June of 1967, with almost no emendations.

The four books García Márquez wrote on the way to *One Hundred Years of Solitude* – the novel *La Hojarasca* (*Leaf Storm*), published in 1955; the long story 'El Coronel No Tiene Quien Le Escriba' ('No One Writes to the Colonel'), published in 1958; the novel *La Mala Hora* (*The Evil Hour*), of 1961; and the collection of stories *Los Funerales de la Mamá Grande* (*Big Mama's Funeral*), of 1962 – are now, inevitably, combed by readers for any signs of and references to the huge flowering that followed; and, indeed, *Leaf Storm* is set in Macondo, which also makes a more substantial appearance in *Big Mama's Funeral*. It is easy to understand the frustration García Márquez felt on the publication of each book, for he had not yet found a way of writing adequate to contain and keep whole the intricate vision he had of his own many-layered Macondo. But the early books show him to be a considerable story writer; 'No One Writes to the Colonel' is a meticulously well-written, spare story, its character beautifully drawn. The early stories are understated and ironic, but by the time García Márquez came to write the story 'Big Mama's Funeral' the surface realism had begun to crack, and excursions of fancy intruded into the narrative. In the novels, too, he was experimenting – in *Leaf Storm* with writing of the same reality from different vantage points, and in *The Evil Hour* with the complexities of a text within a text. But a spare realism could not contain the bulging of the imagination that was showing up increasingly in his work.

Two things were still lacking to the novelist – a unifying tone and manner to contain the immense running narrative, and some device to allow him the all-seeing vantage point he required as narrator. It is worth taking another look at where García Márquez stood in relation to the material, the unwritten book, at this stage. He had clear and detailed in his head the magical Macondo narrated to him whole by his grandparents, and the boy's perception of it in its wholeness, and he had the memory of going back later and perceiving its disintegration, its death. This double perception made him into a magical being, a child with foreknowledge. The novelist also has foreknowledge. But what must have eluded García Márquez all this time was where and how to situate himself in relation to his narrative.

The solution, clearly, must have come to him in the form of Melquíades, the old gypsy magus, who is befriended by José Arcadio Buendía, the founder of Macondo, and who occasionally returns from death to attend certain of the Buendías. Melquíades knows past and future. He records the whole history of the Buendía family in code on his parchments, but they are condemned to live in time, and cannot know it. So as Melquíades the novelist could situate himself in the proper magical relation to his narrative, since for him, too, everything is known. Melquíades's parchments are to be the novel.

The first sentence of the novel shows just what use García Márquez makes of his magical persona: 'Many years later, as he faced the firing squad, Colonel Aureliano Buendía was to remember that distant afternoon when his father took him to discover ice.' In it we are projected forward from the present to a vantage point in the future from which we look backward at what is taking place. We are situated in both dimensions at once. Thus the story is told, looking backward, of a present full of premonition; and memory and dream and fable and miracle are able to intrude into the narrative without any inconsistency. The novel as story is freed from linear time, and sentences are able to refer backward and forward, although firmly rooted in the physicality of the present. 'When the pirate Sir Francis Drake attacked Riohacha in the sixteenth century, Úrsula Iguarán's great-great-grandmother became so frightened with the ringing of alarm bells and the firing of cannons that she lost control of her nerves and sat down on a lighted stove.' The accident causes her family to move to a settlement where they befriend the Buendía family, and is repeatedly invoked as the initiatory event in the eventual history of Macondo, for Úrsula eventually marries José Arcadio Buendía and, as a consequence, 'every time that Úrsula became exercised over her husband's mad ideas, she would leap back over three hundred years of fate and curse the day that Sir Francis Drake had attacked Riohacha.' The remote past crops up in the running present; the generations of the Buendías reflect one another, forward and backward. And as Aureliana Babilonia, the last surviving Buendía, is given by his imminent death the insight to decode the parchments of Melquíades, he discovers 'that Sir Francis Drake had attacked Riohacha only so that they could seek each other through the most intricate labyrinths of blood until they would engender the mythological animal that was to bring the line to an end.' The narrative continues: 'It was foreseen that the city of mirrors (or mirages) would be wiped out by the wind and exiled from the memory of men at the precise moment when Aureliano Babilonia would finish deciphering the parchments, and that everything written on them was unrepeatable since time immemorial and forever more, because races condemned to one hundred years of solitude did not have a second opportunity on earth.'

★

In a long published interview with Fernández Brasó, García Márquez spoke of his search for a style:

> I had to live twenty years and write four books of apprenticeship to discover that the solution lay at the very root of the problem: I had to tell the story, simply, as my grandparents told it, in an imperturbable tone, with a serenity in the face of evidence which did not change even though the world were falling in on them,

and without doubting at any moment what I was telling, even the most frivolous or the most truculent, as though these old people had realised that in literature there is nothing more convincing than conviction itself.

It is the word 'imperturbable' that leaps out; it is the key to the running tone of *One Hundred Years of Solitude*. Surprising events are chronicled without any expression of surprise, and comic events with a straight face; the real and the magical are juxtaposed without comment or judgment; the dead and living interact in the same unaltering prose dimension. García Márquez is an accomplished exaggerator, as was his grandfather, by repute; but his Neruda-like lists of wonders have a numerical exactness which humanises them and makes them into facts of perception. The rains that devastate Macondo last 'for four years, eleven months, and two days.' The astonishing is made matter-of-fact, and the matter-of-fact is a running astonishment: 'Colonel Aureliano Buendía organised thirty-two armed uprisings and he lost them all. He had seventeen male children by seventeen different women and they were exterminated one after the other on a single night before the oldest one had reached the age of thirty-five. He survived fourteen attempts on his life, seventy-three ambushes, and a firing squad.' The spinster Amaranta Buendía has a clear and unperturbed premonition of her own death:

> She saw it because it was a woman dressed in blue with long hair, with a sort of antiquated look, and with a certain resemblance to Pilar Ternera during the time when she had helped with the chores in the kitchen . . . Death did not tell her when she was going to die . . . but ordered her to begin sewing her own shroud on the next sixth of April. She was authorised to make it as complicated and as fine as she wanted . . . and she was told that she would die without pain, fear, or bitterness at dusk on the day that she finished it. Trying to waste the most time possible, Amaranta ordered some rough flax and spun the thread herself. She did it so carefully that the work alone took four years. Then she started the sewing . . . One week before she calculated that she would take the last stitch on the night of

February 4, and, without revealing the motives, she suggested to Meme that she move up a clavichord concert that she had arranged for the day after . . . At eight in the morning, she took the last stitch in the most beautiful piece of work that any woman had ever finished, and she announced without the least bit of dramatics that she was going to die at dusk. She not only told the family but the whole town, because Amaranta had conceived of the idea that she could make up for a life of meanness with one last favor to the world, and she thought that no one was in a better position to take letters to the dead.

The book is rooted in the domestic detail of the Buendía household; tragedy, disaster, and death are accommodated, along with magical events, as they intrude into the continuing life of the family. One of the Buendía sons is shot in another part of Macondo:

A trickle of blood came out under the door, crossed the living room, went out into the street, continued on in a straight line across the uneven terraces, went down steps and climbed over curbs, passed along the Street of the Turks, turned a corner to the right and another to the left, made a right angle at the Buendía house, went in under the closed door, crossed through the parlor, hugging the walls so as not to stain the rugs, went on to the other living room, made a wide curve to avoid the dining-room table, went along the porch with the begonias, and passed without being seen under Amaranta's chair as she gave an arithmetic lesson to Aureliano José, and went through the pantry and came out in the kitchen, where Úrsula was getting ready to crack thirty-six eggs to make bread.

In addition to maintaining its even, unsurprised tone, the narrative is reduced starkly to its physical essentials; the astonishment is left to the reader. The novel is crowded with events and characters, comic, grotesque, real and unreal (the distinction no longer has meaning), and the transitions are bland and direct. The touchstone is the running narrative of the writer's grandparents, as perceived by the innocent, unjudging, undifferentiating eye of the boy in Aracataca. When movies are first shown in Macondo, the townspeople 'became indignant over the living images that the prosperous merchant Bruno Crespi projected in the theatre with the lion-head ticket windows, for a character who had died and was buried in one film and for whose misfortune tears of affliction had been shed would reappear alive and transformed into an Arab in the next one,' and 'the audience, who paid two cents apiece to share the difficulties of the actors, would not tolerate that outlandish fraud and they broke up the seats.' In Macondo, the wheel is invented with daily regularity.

But the ruthless paring down to physical essentials and the even, matter-of-fact tone are not the only distinguishing features of the book's style; its other remarkable element is its rhythm, its flow. The sentences are constructed with a running inevitability to them. The narrative never pauses but flows on, impervious to the events, disastrous and wondrous, it relates; it is time flowing, the steady current of day-to-day detail. In that flow everything is synthesised and swept along, everything is contained. It is the rhythm that lends the book its feeling of process. Nothing stops the flow of the narrative. Conversations are gnomic exchanges in passing. The book flows on like running water to its inevitable end, which leave us holding the deciphered version of Melquíades's parchments, ready to begin them again.

Things go round again in the same cycles; progress is an illusion, change merely an attribute of time – these attitudes implicit in the book exude from the history and being not just of Aracataca\Macondo and Colombia but of the Latin American continent. Yet the manner in which this fate is accepted and come to terms with is what gives Latin Americans their distinguishing humanity; their measure is a human one. The solitude of the Buendías is their fate; but their reactions to that fate are supremely human – obsessively Promethean and absurdly courageous on the part of the men, tenacious and down-to-earth on the part of the women – and are always leavened with a humorous energy. They assume to the full the responsibility of being their idiosyncratic selves. For the inhabitants of Macondo, there is no body of outside knowledge to refer to. What they know is what they perceive; what they come to terms with is their fate, their own death. García

Márquez's twin obsessions – with the original, eccentric sense of human awe lodged in him as a child, and with the discovery of a language ample enough to contain that view in its wholeness – come together so inextricably in *One Hundred Years of Solitude* that the world becomes a book.

The degree to which *One Hundred Years of Solitude* has been acclaimed in translation is a measure of how successful García Márquez is in universalising his material. Almost monotonously, the book has been named best foreign novel as it has emerged in other languages. The Italians and the Yugoslavs turned apoplectic in their praise of it, while English reviewers almost universally referred to it as 'a fantasy' – a term one must be extremely cautious about applying to García Márquez. Obviously, the book was not being lost in translation; but then for a translator it raises no insurmountable technical problems. The language is crystal-clear and physical, the wordplay is minimal, the vocabulary exotic but containable. The challenge for a translator lies in reproducing the extraordinary running rhythm of the original – García Márquez's sentences are carefully phrased, musically, for the ear; the narrative movement is orchestrated by their rhythm, as García Márquez's own recorded reading of the first chapter makes particularly clear. I can only wonder whether the rhythm of the original is possible to maintain in languages with a sound pattern drastically different from Spanish. But where the rhythm is concerned the English translation, by Gregory Rabassa, is something of a masterpiece, for it is almost matched to the tune of the Spanish, never lengthening or shortening sentences but following them measure for measure. García Márquez insists that he prefers the English translation to the original, which is tantamount to saying they are interchangeable – the near-unattainable point of arrival for any translator.

*

The enthusiastic attention universally attracted by *One Hundred Years of Solitude* propelled García Márquez into a limelight he had not reckoned on, and for a time he became the running prey of literary interviewers and inquisitors, and the center of international curiosity. The question that preoccupied readers most – as it must have preoccupied him – was, What could he write next? *One Hundred Years of Solitude* had freed him from the obsessive pre-occupation with unloading into language the Aracataca of his grandparents as he had perceived it; yet it had put a strain of expectation on his work. In 1972, he published a collection of seven new stories, under the title *La Increíble y Triste Historia de la Cándida Eréndira y de su Abuela Desalmada* (*The Incredible and Sad Tale of Innocent Eréndira and Her Heartless Grandmother*). The title story had had two previous existences – one as a long anecdote in *One Hundred Years of Solitude*, and the other as a film script – and now it arrived in a longer and more exotic version, like a written circus. Eréndira burns down her grandmother's house by accident, and she, in revenge, prostitutes her granddaughter in carnival pro-cession through the villages of an interminable desert landscape to recoup her losses. The bare bones of the anecdote are fleshed out in the story, however, with an exuberance of detail and a mythic extension that clearly carry over from the novel; and in the other stories the realistic surface of things has all but disappeared. 'The Sea of Lost Time', 'A Very Old Man with Enormous Wings', 'The Handsomest Drowned Man in the World', 'Blacamán the Good, Vendor of Miracles', 'The Last Voyage of the Ghost Ship': the titles alone give some indication of where we are – face to face with magical events and extraordinary figures that, although they are no longer in Macondo, belong to the same dimension and wavelength, in which wonders are natural happenings. Most con-spicuously, the style continues in the vein of exotic enumeration, imperturbably precise in the face of wonders.

One of the stories, 'The Last Voyage of the Ghost Ship', is written in a manner that attempts to bring all its elements into a fusion even tighter than in the novel. Once a year a boy in a seaside village has the vision of a huge liner without lights sailing across the bay in front of the village. He is disbelieved, first by his mother and then, on a subsequent occasion, by the villagers, who beat and ridicule him, so the following year he lies in wait, in a stolen rowboat, and leads the liner aground on the shoal in front of the village church. The story, dense in physical detail, is a running narrative of six pages, a single sentence that encompasses past and dream as part of a flowing present, a stream of consciousness not confined to any one consciousness – for characters intrude in the first person, the focal point keeps shifting, the objective and the subjective are parts of a larger whole. Again, the images are threaded on the continuing string of the rhythm. It was clear from this story that García Márquez had not yet satisfied his linguistic curiosity.

Extravagant of imagination, these stories showed him more determined than ever to embrace the wondrous as part of the natural – to destroy the distinction, to insist on the marvellous as real. He also seemed to be trying to embed linear narrative episodically in a larger language; but he could not abandon it, for he is an instinctive storyteller, most probably because of his profound experience as a listener. The compulsion intrudes into his conversation; he enfables his day. On one occasion, in Barcelona, when we met after an interim, I noticed that he had given up smoking – surprisingly, for he had been a fierce smoker. 'I will tell you how to be free of smoking,' he said to me. 'First, you must decide that the cigarette, a dear friend who has been close to you for many years, is about to die. Death, as we know, is irremediable. You take a pristine packet of your favorite cigarettes – mine were those short black Celtas – and you bury it, with proper ceremony, in a grave you have prepared in the garden – I made a headstone for mine. Then, every Sunday – not oftener, for the memory is painful – you put flowers on the grave, and give thanks. Time passes. For me now, the cigarette is dead, and I have given up mourning.'

In occasional interviews, García Márquez spoke of the book he was writing: a phantasmagorical study of a dictator who has lived for two hundred years; an exploration of the solitude of power. The book was a long time in the writing, and was promised long before it arrived, but was eventually published in March of 1975 under the title of *El Otoño del Patriarca*. The first Spanish reviews were tinged with disappointment, since the reviewers obviously wanted to be back in Macondo. It took time for the book to separate itself from the powerful shadow of *One Hundred Years of Solitude*. Besides, it is a book requiring very attentive reading at first, until one grows more comfortably familiar with its extraordinary style, for it goes even further, along the lines of 'The Last Voyage of the Ghost Ship', toward fusing all its sprawling elements into one single stream of prose.

The book is set in an unspecified Caribbean country which is under the sway of a dictator who has lived longer than anyone can remember; and it is no more specific of time and place than that. Its point of departure – and the starting point for each of its six chapters – is a mob breaking into the decaying palace to find the dictator dead. As they poke wonderingly among the ruins of the palace, with 'the felt on the billiard tables cropped by cows', they begin to brood, in their collective consciousness, on incidents in the dictator's reign, and the narrative shifts to these events, then passes without pausing into the dictator's consciousness, back into events and other consciousnesses, in continuous change. Linear time is abandoned, and even deliberately confused; everyone has forgotten the sequence of events while vividly remembering and juxtaposing the events themselves. Each chapter encompasses two or three crucial episodes in the dictator's career – set pieces of the imagination, like separate García Márquez stories inserted in the flow – alongside the natural and unnatural disasters: the occasional massacres of plotting generals, the coming of a comet, the occupation of the country by marines of a foreign power, the eventual selling of the country's sea. The dictator himself is never named, and there are only a few fully rounded, fully identified characters: the dictator's mother, Benedición Alvarado, the simple woman who accompanies him anxiously into power, and in whose memory, when his attempts to canonise her have failed, he declares war against the Holy See; his crony General Rodrigo de Aguilar, who, when he is discovered to be a traitor, is served up by the dictator, roasted and garnished, at a feast of his brother officers; the novice nun Leticia Nazareno, whom he impulsively marries and is dominated by, and who, with her young son, already a general, is torn to pieces by specially trained wild dogs; Manuela Sánchez, the gypsy queen, who beguiles the dictator into transforming suburbs for her pleasure; José Ignacio Saenz de la Barra, his sleek and sinister favorite, who initiates a reign of terror the dictator can only survive, not control. The narrative keeps being picked up by other voices, other consciousnesses, always sharp in physical detail. There is a pervading domesticity to García Márquez's frame of reference; in one long passage we follow the dictator through the long and finicky ritual of going to bed, in the course of which he patrols the palace, dressing objects in asides of memory.

Technically, what García Márquez does in *The Autumn of the Patriarch* is to dispense with the sentence altogether as the unit of his prose, and substitute an intelligible flow that encompasses several shifts in vantage point. In one passage, the dictator is being besieged in his palace:

I already told you not to pay them any heed, he said, dragging his graveyard feet along the corridors of ashes and scraps of carpets and singed tapestries, but they're going to keep it up, they told him, they had sent word that the flaming balls were just a warning, that the explosions will come after general sir, but he crossed the garden without paying attention to anyone, in the last shadows he breathed in the sound of the newborn roses, the disorders of the cocks in the sea wind, what shall we do general, I already told you not to pay any attention to them, God damn it, and as on every day at that hour he went to oversee the milking, so as on every day at that hour the insurrectionists in the Conde barracks saw the mule cart with the six barrels of milk from the presidential stable appear, and in the driver's seat there was the same lifetime carter with the oral message that the general sends you this milk even though you keep on spitting in the hand that feeds you, he shouted it out with such innocence that General Bonivento Barboza gave the order to accept it on the condition that the carter taste it first so that they could be sure it wasn't poisoned, and then they opened the iron gates and the fifteen hundred rebels looking down from the inside balconies saw the cart drive in to center on the paved courtyard, they saw the orderly climb up onto the driver's seat with a pitcher and a ladle to give the carter the milk to taste, they saw him uncork the first barrel, they saw him floating in the ephemeral backwash of a dazzling explosion and they saw nothing else to the end of time in the volcanic heat of the mournful yellow mortar building in which no flower ever grew, whose ruins remained suspended for an instant in the air from the tremendous explosion of the six barrels of dynamite.

What García Márquez is after is a language that can contain individual consciousnesses but is not confined by any one, a language that can encompass a whole human condition, that can accommodate the contradictory illusions of which it is made up. Objective truth is only one illusion among a number of illusions, individual and tribal. Consciousness can be neither linear nor serial. The text, though still as sharp in physical particulars as ever, raises infinitely more problems for the translator than its predecessor did, for its sudden shifts in focus have to be handled in language in such a way as to take the reader's attention with them. Rabassa manages these beautifully. Again, his version is more than a translation: it is a matching in English of the original.

The book's preoccupation is with appearance, deception, and illusion, with lies transformed into illusions by the power of belief. Behind illusion there is only solitude – in this case, the solitude of power. The dictator, who can neither read nor write, governs 'orally and physically'. His power is beyond reason:

> you find him alive and bring him to me and if you find him dead bring him to me alive and if you don't find him bring him to me, an order so unmistakable and fearsome that before the time was up they came to him with the news general sir that they had found him.

The only person ever to tell him the truth is his double, Patricio Aragonés, as he is dying of poison meant for the dictator, but the dictator knows that truth is only his own whim, and language only another deception. Tuned in to the betrayals of others, he survives long beyond the point where his power has any meaning, a shambling old man–child trying to get a night's rest for his accompanying infirmities from his own grotesque and imperturbable image. Close to death (his second death, since he used the death of his double in order to claim rebirth), he broods:

he learned to live with those and all the miseries of glory as he discovered in the course of his uncountable years that a lie is more comfortable than doubt, more useful than love, more lasting than truth, he had arrived without surprise at the ignominious fiction of commanding without power, of being exalted without glory and of being obeyed without authority.

The illusion of his power is, however, sustained by everyone around him, so that he has no choice but to wear it. He keeps alive by his acute cunning, his nose for deception; at one point (after he has been taught to read by Leticia Nazareno), 'the final oracles that governed his fate were the anonymous graffiti on the walls of the servants' toilets, in which he would decipher the hidden truths that no one would have dared reveal to him, not even you, Leticia, he would read them at dawn on his way back from the milking. ... broadsides of hidden rancor which matured in the warm impunity of the toilets and ended up coming out onto the streets.' Fictions outlive the need for them but refuse to die. The only refuge from deceptions is in solitude, yet it is out of solitude that we create the fictions to sustain us.

In *The Autumn of the Patriarch* García Márquez moves toward a complete mythifying of experience, into a total flow that cannot be checked by any reality. Realities of Colombian history occur as fact, legend, and lie, all three; rumor, gossip, fairy tale, dream, illusion, memory all tumble over one another in the book's perception. It has to be taken whole, for wholeness, again, is what it is after. The grossness of its cruelties and lecheries is told in an even, unwavering tone, grotesque in detail; they are part of the book's condition. García Márquez is more concerned with dictatorship as myth in the popular mind (that fountain of invention to which he appears to have unlimited access). Like *One Hundred Years of Solitude*, the book ought to be given three or four readings, for it deserves them, and rewards them. It is a formidable piece of invention, and it pushes the discoveries of *One Hundred Years of Solitude* further, closer to a contained whole. García Márquez's writing has always been illuminated by the transformations his imagination is capable of making, the humanity of his perception, his accurate astonishment, even on the small scale, in a phrase or a minor incident. Patricio Aragonés upbraids the dictator for 'making me drink turpentine so I would forget how to read and write.' The dictator, waking up suddenly in fear, 'felt that the ship of the universe had reached some port while he was asleep.' And, we are told, 'on one national holiday she [the dictator's mother] had made her way through the guard of honor with a basket of empty bottles and reached the presidential limousine that was leading the parade of celebration in an uproar of ovations and martial music and storms of flowers and she shoved the basket through the window and shouted to her son that since you'll be passing right by take advantage and return these bottles to the store on the corner, poor mother.' The 'stigma of solitude' can be made bearable only by the transforming imagination, as it was in the tales told García Márquez by his grandparents, as it is in his own inexhaustible capacity for containing these transformations in language. He abundantly outdoes his origins. What García Márquez is showing us all the time is the humanising power of the imagination. In all his writing, the imagination is no mere whimsey, nor a Latin American eccentricity: it is a way of dealing with the mysteries of existence, an essential tool for survival, as we say nowadays. The people of Macondo live in a world full of mysteries, without access to any explanation. All they can count on to make these mysteries bearable is the transforming power of their own imaginations, through the anecdotes and fictions they construct to bring the world into some kind of equilibrium, to find some kind of comfort for the separate solitudes it is their fate to inhabit.

For García Márquez, the marvelous, which he equates with the human, contains the real, and can transform it at will. 'They should take the hens out of their nests when there's thunder so they don't hatch basilisks,' says Benedición Alvarado on her deathbed, and at once we know where we are. García Márquez talked to Vargas Llosa about an aunt who haunted the house of his childhood – the same aunt who sewed her own shroud. 'Once, she was embroidering in the passage when a girl arrived with a strange-looking hen's egg, an egg with a protuberance,' he said. 'I don't know why our house served as a kind of consulting room for all the mysteries of the place. Every time anything out of the ordinary cropped up, which nobody understood, they went to the house and asked, and, in the main, this woman, this aunt, always had an answer. What enchanted me was the naturalness with which she settled these questions. To go back to the girl with the egg, she said, "Look! Why does this egg have a protuberance?" Then my aunt looked at her and said, "Ah, because it is a basilisk's egg. Light a bonfire on the patio." They lit the fire and burned the egg as if it were the most natural thing in the world. I think that naturalness gave me the key to *One Hundred Years of Solitude*, where the most terrifying and extraordinary things are recounted with the same straight face this aunt wore when she said that a basilisk's egg – I didn't know what it was – should be burned on the patio.'

In Memoriam, Amada

Judas Roquín told me this story, on the veranda of his mildewed house in Cahuita. Years have passed and I may have altered some details. I cannot be sure.

In 1933, the young Brazilian poet Baltasar Melo published a book of poems, *Brasil Encarnado*, which stirred up such an outrage that Melo, forewarned by powerful friends, chose to flee the country. The poems were extravagant, unbridled even, in their manner, and applied a running sexual metaphor to Brazilian life; but it was one section, 'Perversions', in which Melo characterised three prominent public figures as sexual grotesques, that made his exile inevitable. Friends hid him until he could board a freighter from Recife, under cover of darkness and an assumed name, bound for Panama. With the ample royalties from his book, he was able to buy an *estancia* on the Caribbean coast of Costa Rica, not far from where Roquín lived. The two of them met inevitably, though they did not exactly become friends.

Already vain and arrogant by nature, Melo became insufferable with success and the additional aura of notorious exile. He used his fame mainly to entice women with literary pretensions, some of them the wives of high officials. In Brazil, however, he remained something of a luminary to the young, and his flight added a certain allure to his reputation, to such a point that two young Bahian poets who worked as reporters on the newspaper *Folha da Tarde* took a leave of absence to interview him in his chosen exile. They traveled to Costa Rica mostly by bus, taking over a month to reach San José, the capital. Melo's retreat was a further day's journey, and they had to cover the last eleven kilometers on foot. Arriving at evening, they announced themselves to the housekeeper. Melo, already half-drunk, was up-stairs, entertaining the daughter of a campesino, who countenanced the liaison for the sake of his fields. Melo, unfortunately, chose to be outraged, and shouted, in a voice loud enough for the waiting poets to hear, 'Tell those compatriots of mine that Brazil kept my poems and rejected me. Poetic justice demands that they return home and wait there for my next book.' For the two frustrated pilgrims, the journey back to Bahia was nothing short of nightmare.

★

The following autumn, a letter arrived in Cahuita for Baltasar Melo from a young Bahian girl, Amada da Bonavista, confessing shyly that her reading of *Brasil Encarnado* had altered her resolve to enter a convent, and asking for the poet's guidance. Flattered, titillated, he answered with a letter full of suggestive warmth. In response to a further letter from her, he made so bold as to ask for her likeness, and received in return the photograph of an irresistible beauty. Over the course of a whole year, their correspondence grew increasingly more erotic until, on impulse, Melo had his agent send her a steamship ticket from Bahia to Panama, where he proposed to meet her. Time passed, trying his patience; and then a letter arrived, addressed in an unfamiliar hand, from an aunt of Amada's. She had contracted meningitis and was in a critical condition. Not long after, the campesino's daughter brought another envelope with a Bahia postmark. It contained the steamship ticket, and a newspaper clipping announcing Amada's death.

We do not know if the two poets relished their intricate revenge, for they remain nameless, forgotten. But although it would be hard nowadays to track down an available copy of *Brasil Encarnado*, Baltasar Melo's name crops up in most standard anthologies of modern Brazilian poetry, represented always by the single celebrated poem, 'In Memoriam: Amada', which Brazilian schoolchildren still learn by heart. I translate, inadequately of course, the first few lines:

> Body forever in bloom,
> you are the only one
> who never did decay
> go gray, wrinkle, and die

as all warm others do.
My life, as it wears away
owes all its light to you . . .

When Judas had finished, I of course asked him the inevitable question: Did Baltasar Melo ever find out? Did someone tell him? Roquín got up suddenly from the hammock he was sprawled in, and looked out to the white edge of surf, just visible under the rising moon. 'Ask me another time,' he said. 'I haven't decided yet.'

Fictions

Many writers trudge through my attention, some of them passing fancies only, some becoming lifelong friends, and some unfailing reminders of the wonders and complexities of putting-into-words. I read other writers with an extra antenna out, taking in not just what is said, but also how, watching what the words do. Just occasionally, however, the work of a single writer will take possession of my whole awareness, bringing an unexpected light.

The writer who has most caused in me the vertigo of realisation has unquestionably been Jorge Luis Borges. I first read him in the fifties, and went on to translate him for an English edition of his most celebrated volume, *Ficciones*. I met him in 1964, in Buenos Aires, when he was already blind, and maintained a friendship with him until he died in 1986. We met in different parts of the world, and had many long conversations, about writers and writing, and very often about language itself. Over the years I have translated a fair amount of his poetry; and I have never stopped rereading him, finding that mischievous, elusive wavelength, hearing that soft, ironic voice in my head.

I found at once with Borges a coincidence of mind, not simply an enthusiasm for his writings, but more, a complete accord with the view of language implied in all his writing, a view he would often enlarge on in conversation. Borges referred to all his writings – essays, stories, poems, reviews – as fictions. He never propounded any particular theory of fictions, yet it is the key to his particular lucid, keen, and ironic view of existence. To make his thinking on the matter as clear as I can, I will put it in the form of precepts:

★

A fiction is any construct of language – a story, an explanation, a plan, a theory, a dogma – that gives a certain shape to reality.

Reality, that which is beyond language, functions by mainly indecipherable laws, which we do not understand, and over which we have limited control. To give some form to reality, we bring into being a variety of fictions.

A fiction, it is understood, can never be true, since the nature of language is utterly different from the nature of reality.

A fiction is not to be confused with a hypothesis, which poses a fiction as a truth and attempts to verify it from the reality.

A fiction is intended principally to be useful, to be serviceable, to be appropriate, to make some kind of sense of reality.

Fictions bring things to order for the time being only. Given a shifting reality, they have constantly to be remade.

We are physical beings, rooted in the physical cycle of life-and-death. Yet we are also users of language, fiction-makers, and language and fictions are not, like us, subject to natural laws. Through them, we are able to cross over into a timeless dimension, to bring into being alternate worlds, to enjoy the full freedom of the imaginable.

Language itself is an irony – while we use it to create systems and formulations that are intelligible, coherent, and permanent, the reality they purport to put in order remains shifting, changeable, and chaotic, making it necessary for us all the time to revise our fictions, to dissolve and re-form them.

We are capable of generating the fiction of immortality, yet it in no way exempts us from death.

A book is an irony, mocking the person who writes it. By making his fiction out of language, the writer moves it into a timeless dimension, while he must remain rooted in time.

Our larger fictions – social theories, political systems, the idea of a Supreme Being – are not inherently true but are sustained for a time by belief. Most of them eventually outlive their usefulness.

Works of literature are reliable fictions, our fictions of enlighten-
ment, our solace. Poetry and prose are merely different modes
of fictions, poetry attempting to move closer to experience as a
happening, prose maintaining a certain lucid distance.

The most common of all confusions is to imagine that we have
changed reality when all we have done is to alter our fiction of it.
It is crucial never to lose the sense that our fictions are in fact
fictions, even while appreciating their usefulness, and suspending
our disbelief when we choose to.

Reality is given to us: making fictions of it is in large part what we
do with it.

We are all *ficcioneros*, inveterate fiction-makers – it is through our
fictions, private and public, that we make sense of our world, and
find some equilibrium in it, it is through our fictions that we create
ourselves.

★

These words are in no sense Borges's – he did not philosophise,
considering philosophy simply another branch of the fantastic and
the fictional – but they are more or less the bones of his thinking
about language and literature. In Borges's universe, in our universe,
there is no single truth, there are only multitudes of fictions; and we
have to choose amongst them, to find those that fit us. More than
anything, we continue to make our own. Making fictions out of
what happens is an activity, a constant self-creation. We enfable
our daily existence.

I found this to be true among my neighbours in the Dominican
Republic, most of them illiterate. They lived by the stories they
made out of their days, by the imaginative explanations they
invented for things beyond their ken. They had no archives beyond
a series of polished anecdotes; and when they told the stories of their
lives, their lives varied with each telling. In their shared fictions lay
their morality, their way of surviving. In their imagination lay their
strength.

We live within an intricate web of fictions – the fictions of daily gossip, the fictions of a profession or a career, newspaper fictions, the fictions of writers and communicators, the fictions of entertainment, the fictions of politics, the fictions of nationality – out of which we fashion a quilt of chosen fictions, a set that suits us – fictions of our childhood, of pieces of our past, fictions of our loves and our losses, fictions of the whole web of our lives. We constantly tell ourselves stories, dividing the continuum of our lives into tellable segments, each with a conclusion.

Language, however, is a slippery and sometimes treacherous element, and can glibly stray from the reality it is meant to deal with. It is for that reason that we have to take great care over the act of putting-into-words, the fashioning of our fictions. At best, it is an act of creation, part astonishment, part invention, part wisdom.

Perhaps our fictions, if they find their way appropriately into words, ironically, are the most durable thing about us.

Acknowledgements

Editor's thanks to Jane Rose at the National Library of Scotland; the staff of the Scottish Poetry Library; Robin Hodge, who lent me his house; Stuart Kelly and Alan Taylor for their advice; and Michael McCreath for his timely help.